Zesty Entanglements
A Collection of Short Spicy Romance Stories
21 Short Stories
Ruan Willow

Table of Contents

Dedication:

This book is dedicated to people who explore their fantasies and sexuality and allow their partners to as well. Those who play in and out of the bedroom, those who never stop playing, never stop expanding and exploring their sexuality, and those who desire to please their partners and get off on getting their partner off, because that's how it should be. Mutual pleasure is mutual bliss. Trust is the secret sauce for delicious and satisfying romantic sexual relationships. Sexplore it together! Sexual pleasure is your birthright! Take it, baby, you own it! It's yours!

Tropes & Triggers: spicy open door, mostly HEA (a few are not), multiple partners, hookups, cheating (Wife's First Threesome and his too: An All Virgin FMM Story), a few stories have dark themes such as humiliation/depravity and paranormal/supernatural (wizards, witches, goddess's, she-Satan), married couple, dating couples, explicit language and scenes, intimacy, threesomes, orgy, FF (The Sex Wizards at a Halloween Costume Party Orgy), interracial (Work Merger), seduction, exhibitionism, voyeurism, sexual exploration/liberation/empowerment, kinks. NON HEA, CHEATING, DARK are labeled at the start of the stories.

Wife's First Threesome and his too: An All Virgin FMM Story

Aaron's Angel, and Mike's baby girl.

Part 1

Cheating Character

"You seriously asked Aaron if he'd fuck us?" My heart is pounding a million times a second as my eyes widen. My stomach falls into a mash of butterflies and nausea.

"Yeah. I mean. Why not? You want it. I want it. He flirted with you in the grocery store." He laughs. "A no-brainer, baby."

I drop the package of cheese on the counter. I want this but, honestly, I'm terrified. I might vomit. "Oh my, fuck me. You mean this is really going to happen?" I chastise myself. Breathe Amanda, breathe.

I gasp as Mike grabs my butt and then whirls me around to face him. My hands land on his thick shoulders. His eyes show he's very aroused, which ticks my desire for this higher.

He pushes me against the counter. The round drawer knob hits me right between my upper ass cheeks like a butt plug, but too high. I'm pinned immobile by his hard cock pressed to my belly. My breath hitches as my clit twitches.

"Yes. So, we were sitting by the bonfire last night and everyone left, so it was just him and me, so I asked him." He grins at me before he lands a peck on my lips. "Aren't I a good husband who cares about fulfilling your biggest sexual fantasies?" His grin shows he's gloating, but he's not wrong.

"Oh, fuck. Fuck. Fuck. Fuck." My hands start to shake, and my clit sends another electric jolt through my vagina. "Oh, fuck." Can I do this for real? Fantasy is one thing, but two dicks in reality is another thing altogether.

He smiles. Presses his lips to my neck, causing me to quiver. He sucks my skin into his mouth, takes little nibbles of me that feel like they may leave a mark.

I push him away and look into his smoky grey eyes. "Has he ever cheated before? Does she know what he's doing? Do they have an open marriage? Would she swing too?" My brain swirled with even more questions, but I tried to quell the crazy in my brain.

He chuckles. "Slow down, babe. No. He said he's never done this before. But he also said Melissa hasn't fucked him in over a year, so I'm guessing swinging with us would be a no."

"No way. A year? How could she not fuck him? He's hot as fuck!" My pussy juices slither out my lips as I shift my legs back and forth. I'm reminded again of how lucky I am to have a man like Mike.

"See, I'm an enlightened man because that comment doesn't bother me in the least. I want you satisfied sexually, I just want to be a part of it too," he says with a chuckle as he presses his puckered lips to mine.

It's like he had read my mind.

"You are amazing, no doubt. I'm lucky you aren't a jealous man. But guess I'd also do a female/female/male with you and love it, so we are on the same page."

He grins. "Next on the bucket list." He ticks his finger in the air.

My nipples harden at the thought. "I'm in." I giggle. "Oh, my gosh. We're going to do this?"

"We are going to do this. We will need rules, though. Only my cock goes up your ass." Mike raises his left eyebrow, and his eyes turn stern.

"Okay, that's fine. I'm sure he won't care. He probably just wants to get fucked, not caring about the hole."

"No doubt." He shudders. "Please don't ever do that to me. A year. Fuck. I'm sorry. I think our marriage would be over."

I snort. "Fuck no. I want to fuck, you know that. I agree. I think people who aren't fucking and are in a relationship should just end it. It's not a real relationship. Or go to therapy. It's sad."

He grabs both my hips hard. "Speaking of...my cock wants to invade your pussy."

"Wait, when are we doing this threesome?" I ask as he's already stripping my shirt off over my head.

He undoes my bra. His mouth goes right to consuming my right nipple, his favorite one, even though my left is a touch bigger. I smirk as he sucks my nipple hard to the back of his throat. I moan, arching my back against the counter, barely clearing the cupboards when I lean. His free hand is grabbing at my other breast. He slowly lets my nipple pop out of his mouth while seductively holding my gaze. It's slippery with his saliva under the bright kitchen lights.

"I'm gonna spank you and fuck you right here at this kitchen counter," he murmurs. "Mmmm. Bend you over right." He growls and it explodes my passion.

Thoughts of him attacking me to paddle me and fuck me sends jolts through my clit. Dang, she's a hyper bitch today! My breathing increases as he sucks my other nipple. With no sign of intent, he spins me around and pushes my chest onto the counter. He pulls my pants down to bare my ass in a quick movement.

I gasp loudly. His aggressive mode is in full display, and the fast exposure of my ass sets my pussy drooling. I brace myself against the counter, expecting an ass slap.

His phone buzzes on the counter next to my face as his first spanking slap lands on my right butt cheek. He spanks my left ass cheek, then both. After my flinch, I read the text.

"Stop, it's him," My ass cheeks sting already. "Melissa is leaving with the kids, so he wants to do it in like fifteen minutes."

He laughs evilly before taking another slap of my ass. He snatches the phone from me.

"You naughty bastard, you had to get that last spank in, didn't you?" I snicker as I straighten up.

"Yes, baby. It gives me a giant packed hard-on, plus I love the slap sound, love your ass jiggles, love how it makes your pussy wet." He leers at me with pursed lips that slip into a grin. "What's not to love?"

I try to stifle my grin, but I fail. "Oh, stop. I know all the reasons. But if he's coming in fifteen, I need to shower. I haven't showered yet today, and I don't want to be stinky for my first threesome." I glance down at my bare tits and excitement grows in me as I realize I'm going to get to show Aaron my bare tits.

He looks at me with a confused look. "Exactly why have we waited this long to do a threesome?" He shakes his head. "Fuck. I have no clue."

"I think you thought I wouldn't, and I thought you wouldn't. So ... it just never happened." I pull up my pants and grab my bra.

"Sounds like we need to talk more because ... yeah ... this really has me hot, thinking about you as pounded-out sandwich meat between Aaron and me."

"You going to let him fuck your ass?" I giggle and start to run because I know he will spank me for that comment.

He starts after me and I run away, squealing. I make it up the stairs, zipping up faster than him because, luckily for me, he'd grabbed a can of soda.

"Your ass is mine later for that comment, baby girl." His voice is full of absolution.

I have no doubts of him making good on that threat.

I zoom into the bathroom and slam the door shut. I lock it. My heart pounds heavily and I inhale deeply to try to calm down. I turn on the water to get it hot. I bet he'd let Aaron suck his cock, though, especially if he were drunk. I bet he would. I bite my lip, hoping someday I can see that.

I get a text from Mike: Extra spanking for that comment, little miss. I'll get you, my little one.

I chuckle and look at my already red ass in the mirror.

I text back: Leave me alone. I'm showering. And it's already red.

I get another text, only this time it's from Aaron. Oh, fuck! I gasp.

Aaron: Loved flirting with you in the grocery store the other day. I'm going to come and pleasure you. I can't wait. I talked with Mike btw.

Damn, is he sweet or what? I smile at my phone. He's so sexy. I can't wait for him to suck and fuck me. I'll give him a blow job. Poor dude probably hasn't had one in over a year either, if no sex for that long. I think I'd cry my eyes out if I wasn't eaten out for over a year. What a weird bitch that Melissa. I'd fuck him every damn day. She's stupid nuts.

I stick my hand in the water and it's warm, so I step into the shower stall. The hint of bleach hits my nostrils. It's a welcome smell as I draw more of it into my lungs. The water streams down my body, the heat adding to the burn emanating from the reddened skin of my ass.

"Whew!" I'm definitely not going to be able to sit after this if they spank me more. I grin. Fuck. That's kinda hot. Spanked by two men. The stuff of my secret fantasies. Well, not so secret, since I told Mike recently.

I scrub my skin with the lavender soap and take in a deep breath. The aroma calms my muscles. I lather up my hair with clove mint shampoo, the suds slipping down my naked body in sheaths of white frothy foam. The conditioner comes out in my palm and it's white and thick. It basically looks like a wad of cum. I snicker as I splat it into my hair and work it into the strands. I rinse and lather up my anus and my pussy again so I'm deliciously lavender-scented for our threesome. I'm so excited I could pop!

I dry off as I notice I've gotten another text from Mike: I suggest you keep the hot water off your ass so it can cool down before I tan it a brighter shade of red.

I stick out my tongue and take a picture. I send it to him with a laughing emoji and the word 'Brat.'

I dry off with the thick towel as I watch the three dots dance across my phone. I chuckle before saying, "I love pissing you off, so you go ballistic on my ass. Fuck, I love to tease you."

He texts me back: Sure. Go ahead. Laugh now, you won't be when you are across my knee suffering the slaps I deliver, little girl.

I bite my lower lip as my lips spread into a smile. I text back: I'd like to see you make me.

It's not a lie.

He texts back immediately: Oh, you know I can. You've been my little girl long enough to know the punishments I can deliver. And I always catch you. Keep dreaming.

I nod at my phone. "Don't I know it." I shudder as I stare, remembering how he went all savage beast on me the first time we had sex and pelted my ass like a wild man while playing with my pussy. It had made me so wet, I was so utterly shocked that it turned me on. "Who knew daddy issues would lead to that shit?" The memory sends a big shudder through me and arouses me further.

I take a picture of my reddened butt and send it to both men with a shocked emoji face. Whoever said hints ruined sex? Certainly not me!

I open my drawer and take out my spanky butt balm. "Thank you for this, Trish," I mutter to myself as I inhale the delicious scent of the lotion. My butt calls for coconut oil, beeswax, timber, and orange essential oils. Mmmm. It soothes my irritated skin so much. "I need a bit of soothing going into this feisty tryst." I scoop out a generous dollop and smear it across my butt cheeks. I cringe slightly from my own touch. It makes my ass shine like the sun.

He texts me an emoji of a raised hand.

I finish drying off and open the door slowly in case he's there, hand raised, ready to pummel my ass. I walk along, tiptoeing to the closet as my breath comes in rapid gasps and I peer around. I'm safe. I rummage in my drawer for something sexy. Do I dress in clothes or lingerie? Never thought I'd be facing this kind of dilemma and I love it.

I tap my temple. Hmmm. Not sure what I will pick. It would be fun to get undressed by them, but it would also be titillating to just shock Aaron with something sexy and see-through right off the bat. Or I could put some sexy lingerie on under my clothes and get a bit of the best of both worlds.

I shake my fists as another text buzz comes in on my phone. "He won't quit!"

I drop my towel and dash over to the phone naked.

Aaron has texted: Wow. I've never done that before. May I spank you too?

I squeeze both my lips together in a bite. Oh, dear fuck. Love the ask! But I'm in big trouble. Two men want to spank me? I'm certainly entering a devastation zone soon. They will demolish me physically, sexually, and mentally, and I can't wait to revel in the exhaustion. It will be so luscious!

I text back: You'll have to catch me first!

The thought of two men dashing after me with passion, lust, and aggression gets my blood seething hot! "Fuck me! This is going to just slay me." I clap my hands and squeal.

"I hear you, little girl," he yells up from the main floor. "Very excited, are we?"

"Fuck yes I am," I holler down. I dance, shifting my hips back and forth. "Threesome party. Threesome party. Threesome party," I sing as I shake my booty.

"Put on something delicious for us," he commands from below.

"I will," I say. Okay. That helps. I'll put on my black laced-up thong bodice and put my black dress over the top. The bodice of the bodysuit has snaps to open it at the bottom for easy access to my holes.

I'm jittery I'm so excited. "Fuck!" I mutter.

I spray on some perfume and slather some foundation across my face. Powder up the freckles on my cheeks and forehead, and smear some glittery eye shadow across my eyelids. I apply red lipstick and head downstairs, feeling like a goddess of sex.

He whistles as I walk into the room. "Damn. You look hot as fuck. You are giving me a raging boner with that, babe. Good call on the lipstick. I want that smeared on my cock. You'd better go get it and bring it down here. I'm guessing Aaron is in deep need of getting some head, and with a smear of lipstick, too. If you are willing, that is."

"Oh, I already planned on giving his cock some mouth hugs." I bite my lower lip, then stick out my tongue, biting it as I pause my stride across the living room.

"I owe you something." He reaches for my ass and I shake my finger.

"My ass needs a momentary break, lover." I raise an eyebrow as he pouts with his lower lip out, then crosses his arms across his chest.

He grunts, rolls his eyes, then sighs. "Oh, I suppose I can wait."

I hustle up the stairs to retrieve the lipstick. As I turn to leave the room, I get a fun idea. I grab our box of sex toys, because who knows what Aaron might like to try. He may have never even tried some of these toys if Melissa is such a giant vanilla prude. We need to sex him up right.

I carry the box down the stairs and meet Mike's chuckling face.

"Ambitious, aren't you? A threesome *and* sex toys?" he asks in a voice full of doubt.

"Well, I was just thinking that maybe Aaron hasn't tried some of these and might like the chance, since his wife is a celibate vanilla ice queen who doesn't share her fun cherries or her pussy cat."

He cracks up. "Wow. You do hate her. You aren't generous at all."

"Oh, I can't even imagine how sad his sex life is. Well, lack of sex life, I guess makes more sense." I shake my head. "Have sex with your partner now because, from what my pastor used to say, we don't want sex when we're dead, so fuck now."

He laughs. "Your pastor used to say that? Laugh my ass off. I want to go to his church."

"Well, no, not exactly. I added the last part." I give him a giant smirk with my tongue sticking out.

"You saucy kitten, you. I love you." His eyes twinkle with joy and lust. He snorts. "And if that's true, I don't ever want to die."

I wrinkle my nose, which makes my eyes scrunch closed a bit. "I know. I have naughty brain syndrome."

"And you keep delightfully surprising me. You are like a deep well of never-ending fun, sexy gifts." He licks his upper lip in a slow swipe.

"You have no idea." I whistle. "I'm just getting started." Oh, I'm savoring this. Entering a new era of deeper sharing has brought the yummy kinkiness to the surface in our marriage. My eyes twinkle with excitement for our future.

"Hmmm. Well, I do hope you keep sharing, because I love experimenting with you." He strokes his significant crotch lump. "He'll be here soon. Wanna suck me before he comes?"

"No. I need to get all set up." I run my hands over all the toys.

"Tally for another spank." He shakes his head and swats the air with his hand.

I giggle. "Oh, shut up."

"Another." He licks his finger and makes an imaginary dash in the air. "You sure don't want to sit down later today, do you?"

My clit tingles into a lurch and a wave of excitement follows. I wiggle my butt at him and stick it out. "Have at it, clucker fucker."

"Oh, nice one." He pauses his walk across the living room. "Hell yeah, I'm a chick fucker. Indeed, that I am. But I know Aaron is, too. No sausage parties for us." He smirks at me as there is a knock at the door.

My clit zings with a jolt and my nipples harden as I turn and see Aaron smiling through the long glass window beside the door. I smirk because his boner is already pushing out his pants. Mmm. Fuck, this is going to be a hot rendezvous. "Nothing better than a boner delivery," I say in a singsong voice.

Mike turns to give me an amused look while pointing at his own swollen meat. "Who needs delivery?"

My pussy drools and my mouth drops open. This is a dream come true for me. This will be perfectly naughty, evil sexy yummy exhilarating, and scary as fuck... the words jumble about in my head like pebbles in a jar. And a very memorable encounter.

Mike opens the door and Aaron enters. They shake hands.

"Hey, Aaron. My man. Come in," Mike says.

"Thanks," Aaron says with the biggest grin on his face.

"We appreciate your interest." Mike closes the door behind him.

"I appreciate you guys asking me. I'm beyond thrilled. I have to be very careful about this, though." He looks behind him out the window, moving his head all about. "I'm already wondering if a neighbor saw me come in here."

"Gotcha covered. You are helping me move a dresser right now. Maybe even tell Melissa that, so it's not an awkward secret. And I'll need help again in the future too, if you are interested." He chuckles and slaps his hand on Aaron's shoulder. "I have lots of furniture to move around the house. Plus, I need help holding some boards on my deck." He chuckles. "I see you being very useful to me in the future."

"Oh, I'm interested alright. And Perfect." Aaron nods to me. "Hi, Amanda. How are you?"

"Hi, Aaron. I'm really good. Thanks for coming. You're making a sexual fantasy come true for me, for us."

"Oh, don't I know it. This is one of my fantasies, too. I figure Melissa will never do it, so I do it with you two now or die without ever having done it, and that sucks. I won't hurt her. I'm not leaving her. At this point, anyway." Aaron tilts his head with an eye flick. "Can't say I'll stay a celibate married man forever, though. Maybe when kids get older, I'll go find myself a nice wife who will fuck me every day." His expression goes from wistful to a deep shade of bliss.

"Yes. You totally need that. It's a need. Not a want." I smile at him.

"You've got that right." Aaron's eyes pierce me with want and I shiver like nails bouncing on the tile floor.

Both of their eyes are on me, direct and fierce like they want to hump the shit out of me, thoughts of which send shudders of excitement through me. I bite my lip. "How about we start with a day drink?" My skin tingles all over and butterflies jackknife in my gut.

"I could use one to loosen up. It was tense while I was waiting for her and the kids to leave. I'm a bit wound up." Aaron looks lost as he rakes his hands through his dark hair.

"Done. Beer? Whiskey? Scotch? Wine?" I take a step towards the kitchen.

"Oh, I'd love a beer," Aaron says.

"Mike?" I ask.

Mike nods and says, "Yeah, I'll take a beer too. Thank you, babe, my wonderful beautiful lover."

"Welcome." I tap my heels across the floor, making sure my hip sway happens. With sugary words like that, he's likely fixing to ask for something big. But, regardless, I love to hear it.

My hands shake as I pull two beers out of the fridge. Geez, I need a glass of wine too to smooth myself out. I pull out my open bottle of Sauvignon Blanc from last night, which has about one glass left. "Perfect," I mutter as the bottle empties right at the rim of the wine glass.

I stick a can of beer under each armpit and pick up my wine glass with my right hand, cradling the bulb of the glass in my palm, the stem between my middle and forefinger. Feeling like made in the sixties porn, I carry the drinks, teetering on a spill, to the men like a good housewife. I smile away the cringe when I see their faces.

Aaron's eyes soften as I carefully walk in my heels across the carpet towards them. He stands up and takes the cans of beer from my armpits, his fingers brushing the sides of my breasts as he does. The effect is sensual and desire flares in me. Damn, I want this man.

He keeps constant eye contact with me as he says, "Thank you so much, Amanda. You're a lifesaver." His eyes show his appreciation is genuine.

"You're welcome, Aaron." I resist winking at him because that's just too cheesy.

Mike pats the couch between him and Aaron, and I take a seat. Aaron hands Mike the can of beer across me.

My heart is beating like a train speeding down a hill, my blood surging around my body so fast, my clit is literally throbbing. This is uncharted waters, but it's been a fantasy for so long that I can't quell my excitement enough to have a poker face. I squeeze my thighs together to squish my clit and sigh.

"Mmm. Yummy sigh, Amanda," Aaron says with clear enjoyment.

"She does the thigh squeeze all the time. One of the things I love about her. She's basically a nympho." Mike's grin is lusty.

Aaron looks at me with alarm on his face.

I almost spit out my mouthful of wine but manage to get it down my throat in time before that happened. "Oh, he's not wrong."

"My wife would be pissed at me if I ever said that, but then again, I wouldn't ever say it because she's not even remotely a nympho." He releases a curt laugh before he takes a sip of his beer. Then another. And another. "Whew. That tastes really good. Day drinking at my house is a big no-no, too."

"Damn. She has a lot of rules. Does she let you have any fun at all?" I give him sad puppy dog eyes. I'd go ballistic with those kind of extensive restrictions from a partner. Thankfully, Mike is nothing like that. Perhaps I'd have left him by now, though, if he had been. I know my worth.

"Every once in a while she does, but not often. I jerk off every day in the shower, though. I did it twice already today so I can actually last." He snorts. "If I didn't, I haven't had sex in so long I think I'd cum in like thirty seconds of entering you."

"A two-shower day. Did that raise an alarm with her?" I rub his thigh. I shudder inside, thinking of living life with such a hypervigilant critical spouse. I glance at Mike again with appreciation in my eyes.

He gives me a look of wonder, but then just rubs my knee with a grin.

"No, because I worked out."

"And hey. It'd be okay if you did come that fast. I wouldn't blame you. Who could ever blame you? I just feel bad you don't get pussy at all. She at least sucks your cock from time to time?"

He shakes his head, bites his lip. "Nope. Haven't had that in probably ten years."

"Fuck no!" Mike says aghast.

"Unfortunately … I'm serious." He shakes his head as his eyes fill with humility. "Nada."

"Alright, that's it. It's happening now. I'm giving you a blowjob." I take a giant gulp of my wine and hand my wine glass to Mike. He places it on the TV tray next to the couch with a proud expression.

"You game?" I ask Aaron, standing in front of him.

"Yes, but I'm going to tap you on the head when I need you to stop. This might make me explode a bit quickly and I don't want that to happen." He sounds too apologetic for something he hasn't even done.

"Me neither. But this is just about having fun together. So, no pressure or worries for what happens. K?" I lean over and smooth both my palms up his thighs. "Just let me know and I'll come right off you really quick." I rise to a stand again and push the bodice of my dress and the bodysuit off my breasts to expose them for him. "I adore giving head topless," I confess. Maybe he'll play with them while I suck him, and even if he doesn't, I'll get his eyes roaming them, which is a giant turn-on. This is the first time I've given a blow job to a man other than Mike since we started our relationship and it's so exciting, I might burst. My large breasts bounce as I move into position.

His eyes go big and round, his mouth spreads into the biggest grin. "Whew! Wow. Nice. Very nice. Just. Beautiful." He licks his lips and raises his left eyebrow. "Unbelievable nipples." He glances at Mike and smirks as he returns the look.

I love the collaboration in their gaze and thoughts of Mike watching me give him head rage my lust even more. My breath hitches as thoughts of unveiling his cock flood my brain.

"Thank you." My heart pounds as my nipples harden. "I'm actually really excited to blow you since you haven't had it in so long."

I kneel between his parted legs and he blows out a giant sigh when I haven't even touched him yet. Ah, poor man!

I reach for his zipper with a gleam in my eyes and unzip his pants. He leans his head back against the couch after taking another swig of the beer. "A beer and a blowjob. Now I think I'm in heaven."

"Nope. Not possible. Amanda's pastor said we don't want sex when we're in heaven." Mike guffaws, still savoring that joke.

I giggle.

"Well, this is heaven on Earth then." Aaron touches my cheek so gently, I almost cry. "Because you *are* an angel."

I cover his hand with mine and stroke it. I lean down towards his cock, the head of which is peeking out the waistband of his underwear, and a bulb of precum has birthed itself on top, just like a baby cherry.

I lick it off and he gasps. "Oh, fuck," he says. His chest curves in a recoil into the back of the couch as I lick his cock head again. "Fuck. Even that feels amazing." He touches my hair and gently strokes my scalp.

I smile up at him, making full eye contact, and push the waistband of his underwear down to expose his full swollen cockhead and shaft. I take him into my mouth, fully surrounding the very blood-packed head of his penis with the complete seal of my mouth. I push down his underwear to expose the rest of his veiny hard shaft. I glance over at Mike with Aaron's cock stuffed in my mouth and the grin on his face shows me he is enjoying watching me giving Aaron this sexual gift. It makes me feel good and so free to do a good job and enjoy myself at the same time. I soften my face and try to smile with dick in my mouth, not an easy thing to do, and then return my gaze back to Aaron's eyes.

Aaron holds my sheath of long blond curls back behind my head in a ponytail hold as I slide my mouth up and down the fat swollen head of his cock. I run my hand up and down his shaft as I suck him. My nipples harden further as they rub against the couch. The skin of his cock is firm and taut against my tongue as I slip my mouth over him. His thighs squeeze my shoulders as I work on his boner.

He's moaning so much it's making my pussy drip down my thighs. He taps my head after about a minute. I let his cock slip out and smile up at him.

"Whoa," he says. "I'm about to lose it and our fun will be over, so we'd better move on. Fuck. That was so hot, though. Oh, my fucking God." He shakes his head. "Damn. That was ... amazing." His chest is heaving which sends thrills through my body.

"Oh, yeah. She's really good at giving head. She can make me cum really fast too."

"Yeah, plus I haven't had it in forever. Fuck. Thank you. Damn. Not going to forget that any time soon." His breathing is still rapid as he cups my chin and looks me in the eyes. "You really are a damn angel, you know that, Amanda?"

"Aww. You are really the sweetest, Aaron. That was nothing, but I'm sure happy I was able to give you some pleasure orally. Geez. Ten years. That's just wrong."

"Can I ... can I ask for something? I mean, we need to talk about rules, but I love eating pussy and my wife hates the feeling of it. Could I ... could I eat you out before we move on?"

I gasp and my hand goes to my chest as confusion spreads across my face. "She *hates* it? What the absolute fuck is that about? Being eaten out makes me come. What the hell, hello, has your wife ever cum before?"

"Honestly, Amanda, I had thought so, but thinking back, I'm not sure she ever has." He shakes his head, making his dark curls wiggle a little bit, and I have the urge to run my fingers through them. "I try, but, she's just so, I don't know. Frigid, I guess is the word."

"Wow. She needs to come to see what she's missing, if that's the case. Buy her a sex toy." I point to our sex toy box. "I have recommendations."

"Oh. She'd never use it. Guarantee it. She just says she has no interest in sex." He peers over at the box with interest in his eyes.

"How about an illness? She should go to the doctor. There are illnesses that kill libido." I widen my eyes at him and nod.

"Oh, I've tried that approach. She refuses to go." He sucks his lower lip into his mouth. "So, could I? And ... I mean ... I'd love to sixty-nine too, but my hard-on won't last if we do that, and I've cum twice already today, so this will be over if I were to go again."

"I'm totally fine with that. I love watching her climax and come. So, go for it. Then, when I can't stand it anymore, I'll usher us into the next phase." Mike grins at me. He looks as if he's really enjoying directing all this.

I slip the bodice of my dress and bodysuit down to my feet and step out of it. Leaving my heels on, I scramble onto the couch and spread my legs wide for Aaron, while maintaining eye contact.

"Shaved. Nice." Aaron nods. "Naked with heels. I like it." He grins.

I slick my hand down my smooth pussy mound with a naughty grin. "All yours."

He downs the rest of his beer and sets the empty can on the coffee table, letting his pants fall to the ground as he moves. He glances back at Mike and says, "Sorry for the view of my ass." He chuckles. "Hope it doesn't kill your hard-on."

Mike guffaws. "I'm fine. Seen guy-ass a million times in the locker room at the gym. It's all good. Besides, I'm going to be looking at her, so no worries."

I giggle. "Love a good man butt discussion." I wiggle to get comfy on the couch.

Mike pulls his cock out. "I guess since we are showing parts. Can't have a threesome without us seeing each other. And really, my only rule is only I fuck her up the ass. You can put toys in her ass, but I want her asshole for me only."

"Perfectly understandable. I'm pretty much more into pussy myself anyhow." He kneels and brings his mouth close to my cunt. "You are absolutely stunning, Amanda. I love your pussy so much. Love your lips. They are just gorgeous. Really, a beautiful pussy."

He's so genuine, I almost blush. "Thank you, Aaron."

He gets a very naughty grin as he closes in on my pussy. "Gawd, I've missed eating pussy. My old girlfriend before I got married would let me eat her out for as long as I wanted. I was even known to eat her out for an entire hour. I made her cum so many times. I fucking loved it."

"Um. I might be in love here," I say with a giggle.

"I think the three of us are going to be a very good match-up." Mike's voice is low and thick with lust.

Aaron's breath lands on my pussy, making me squirm. He scoops my thighs from underneath with his hands and pulls me closer to him. His face is lit up, full of deep luscious want and joy.

Seriously, he's just precious.

He opens his mouth wide and lands square on my clit, causing me to gasp, and my torso to lurch forward.

"Mmm," he murmurs as he sucks my clit out of her hood.

I gasp and tangle my hands into his lush hair, ruffling his curls as he sucks on me. He moves to take each of my labia lips in his mouth, then licks my vaginal opening like a lollipop as he moans and groans. I writhe my legs about as he sucks. His fingers dig into the skin of my thighs as he begins to tongue fuck my pussy, his nose stabbing deliciously at my clit.

I'm moaning loudly as he migrates his mouth up to suck my clit again. He shoves two fingers into my pussy as he sucks, licks, flicks. Then he full-on sucks my clit with full strong suction so vigorously I'm thrashing my legs about. He rubs his face all over my pussy, wetting himself fully with my juices as he deeply groans. I'm loving how this man really gets into eating pussy. And I'm getting close to coming already.

"Mmm. Yes," he murmurs.

Mike moves swiftly to join us and comes alongside me to kiss my mouth. It's heavily luscious to feel his familiar mouth on mine while Aaron's is on my clit. The sensation of both their mouths on me at once sets me on fire. Mike travels kisses down to my nipples as I undulate against both their sucking of me. Mike sucks my right nipple hard and nibbles it as he fondles my left. My whole body sizzles like a lit firecracker.

I'm riding up that yummy climaxing hill fast as lightning. I whimper-moan in short bursts, then let out a long groan as Aaron nibbles at my clit. It sends twitches out three times in rapid-fire. My body jerks as he uses his teeth on me. I grab at both their scalps and press my fingers in.

"Oh, fuck, yes," I whisper. Then I moan louder and say, "Yes, yes, yes, yes, oh fuck yes, oh my Gawd I'm going to come, oh, fuck, mmmmmm." My clit thickens and I enter that zone where I know I can't stop it all from happening. I round the curve. It's coming for me. And hard.

My body bursts into the start of my climax like sun flares into the day at first daylight. I attempt but fail to collect myself before letting go, and I completely lose control as I drift into that delicious automatic response of convulsions. It grips me. My body twitches multiple times, my arms bending, my chest gyrating up in jerks as my husband suckles my tit, his mouth slipping and sliding about my wet nipple as my body moves through the orgasm. My body curls as I round the full corner of the climax into the descent of the delicious high. Aaron sucks at my pussy to slurp out my cum as I grunt out.

I moan as the contractions slow into aftershocks, my body still rocking.

I relax fully, slightly in awe. I'm frozen for a minute or so, my jaw slack. Finally, I can say, "Oh ... my Gawd." I fall silent again as they continue to caress me. "That was fucking awesome amazing to have you both on me like that." My chest is out of control heaving as I try to slow my lungs down by taking deeper slow breaths. "I mean ... wow!"

"Oh, you just wait, baby girl. Just wait." Mike stands up and says, "That was just the beginning. Now it's my turn to make you come." He's got the in-charge face on and I love it. "Aaron, would you like to spank baby girl's ass too? She's been naughty and needs punishment delivered." His grin is a rival to his lust, no doubt. He's loving ushering us to this next stage, and I love him all the more for it.

Aaron's eyes light up. "Well, I haven't done much spanking of a woman, but hell yes." He chuckles. "I'm in. I could get into that." He stands up and rubs his hands together, sporting a dangerous gleam.

My heart rate ramps up as I imagine them both going hog wild on me. Wow. That naughty grin of Aaron's ... holy fuck. It sends tingles to my body from my clit twitching yet again. "You guys are making my clit twitch."

"Good. Mission accomplished." Mike pulls me up as his face turns aggressively lecherous. "Shall we chase and attack you, or just bend you over this couch to administer your required spanks? How should we team take you, baby girl?"

I raise an eyebrow at him as I full-on shift my brain to the impending role-play. "Like I have a choice?" My heart begins to pound. I don't care how, I just want them to take me and ravage me like a ragdoll until I am drained of cum.

"Oh, you always have a choice. It's what you want. I mean, what I want, what we want, but ultimately what you want prevails. As always." He gives me a single nod. I nod back, knowing that was mostly for Aaron to understand that I've fully consented to it all. "Oh. And Aaron, her safe word is crazy. If she says that, stop immediately, as she's had too much. We don't ever want her to feel traumatized or we fuck it all up."

"Right. Got it. Crazy." Aaron nods. "No crazy needed."

"Yes, no crazy please," I say. "Maybe Let Aaron pick how I get spanked, I guess. Since we're spoiling him with new experiences." Well, truth be told, this is a new experience for us all. My clit is literally throbbing, heaving, sending out pounding throbs uncontrollably, like shards of glass flung out from dropping a jar on concrete. "I can't wait until you both get your hands on me." I can't hide my excitement. I feel my heartbeat even in my lips.

Mike widens his eyes, his eyebrows lifted. "Okay, right. Aaron, we should have a quick huddle chat here anyway to mesh out what we will do to her."

Part 2

I'm giddy. The butterflies are having a major party in my gut as I watch them talk, chuckle, nod, and fully conspire in their game plan to fully devour me. I suppress the urge to jump and clap.

I'm watching them, squirming from my comfy spot on the couch, so fucking aroused, grabbing at my tits, tweaking my nipples, rolling on the cushions back and forth as they talk. I slip off my heels in preparation to run because I think Aaron will pick to chase me.

"Hurry," I screech. "My pussy is so wet; I feel sloshy." I touch it and it's so slick, it's as if I slathered it with gobs of lube.

Mike gives me a direct look. "Okay, babe. We have a plan. We're going to sit on the couch and close our eyes. You go and hide. Your choice if you want to run and we take you down like lions on a gazelle or if you lay down like a puppy on your back and spread your legs for us. Either way, all of you is ours and we are going to spank, lick, suck, and fuck the shit out of you."

I spring off the couch, jump up, and actually clap. I squeal and take off searching for a place to hide as they chuckle at me.

"Oh, my Gawd, oh my Gawd, I can't wait!" I mutter as I scramble around looking for a good place to hide. Thoughts of being sexually ravaged in the context of feeling safe with two horny men is the most seductive thing ever. I'm so ready to have my long-time fantasy realized, my elation is off the charts.

I need a hidden place where I can sit curled up and just let my pussy drool. I can't decide. Being chased down and taken to heights of passion would make me feel the most alive I've ever felt in my life, like getting to eat the feeling an orgasm gives while it's also rocking my clit and my whole body all at once, squeezing my cream out of me like pounding on a rolled tube of toothpaste with the cap off.

"I can't wait to get fucked messy!" I call out as I slip behind the laundry room door. It always sticks out a bit from the wall, so it won't be obvious I'm here. I'm realizing my voice probably just told them where I am, but then again, I want to be found.

My heart thumps so loud I'm afraid it alone will give me away to the men. I'm just shaking, shivering with electric want.

I hear footsteps. I hold my breath.

Mike says, "I can often find her by smell alone. I'm so in tune with her scent and when she's been coming like she has just now, she gives it off pretty strong."

"Wow. Fuck. That is hot as fuck. You two are so primal. I take it hide and seek is a common fuck game here?" He clears his throat. "Fucking incredible. Man. And Geez. Fuck. You guys are showing me what I've been missing." He sounds wistful and grateful at once. "And, thanks again for sharing yourselves with me. This is an experience I'll draw on for years for jerking off."

Mike scoffs. "At least once a week I hunt her down like this. She loves it. And you're welcome. Or, you know, hey, you can just join us for years, dude. So far all is going good in my book." The footfalls stop and my body quivers. "I think she's this way. I just got a whiff."

I freeze in place. Damn. He's like a legit wolf tracking my pussy. My heart is beating so hard. I want to run away, but I also want to point my ass at them and let them pound me to another massive orgasm. Or twenty. Whoever said duality isn't seductive is a fool.

"This way," Mike says with confidence.

I peek out to watch him lead Aaron towards me.

They both walk into the laundry room, but they pass me by and go all the way into the room and peek into the exercise room that is just beyond. I react without thought, tear out of the laundry room, almost tripping over a laundry basket, dumping it sideways. I take off running across the main floor. They will get me, this I know, but the chase is what's exquisite. And being caught is even better.

My thumping heart is pounding up in my face as I run and pant in a wild panic, a scrumptious blend of delight and fear.

I glance back and both men are rushing at me. I squeal and hurl myself into the living room just as Mike catches hold of my arm. He turns me and wildly spanks my ass as I scream and try to get away, Aaron gets in a few slaps too as they both tag team spank me. My clit twitches and my pussy wets further as the smacks of their hands on my flesh fill the room. I'm ready to explode as they pull me to the couch. Mike flops me belly down on his lap and lays spanks across both my ass cheeks expertly with an open palm as I holler out. Aaron's hand migrates to my pussy and fondles my juicy womanhood. Mike keeps spanking me with aggressive slaps that make me gasp, and that send jolts right straight to my clitoris. It flings me closer to an orgasm, but then he stops.

I pout for my ruined orgasm. "Hey," I whisper.

"Mmmm, fuck I needed that. You got what you had coming." He sighs. "Fuck. My cock is rock hard. Give me a little kiss, baby girl. That was so hot." He leans back against the couch cushion with a pucker of his lips and a series of twinkles in his eyes.

I nod and plant a kiss on his lips, then I shift to suckle the head of his cock as my ass cheeks burn from the slaps. My want for their cocks inside me grows as I suck, imagining, and relishing the look Aaron likely has on his face as I give Mike a blow job. My pussy flares open. My heart tangles me into burgeoning knots as I relinquish my hold over my calm and let loose. Feeling sexually free, I bob my mouth on his cock fast and hard.

He moans and his body jerks as I suck and rub his frenulum with the tip of my tongue.

Aaron grabs my arm and my husband's cock slips out of my mouth. My jaw falls open as he bends me over the couch and lays five hard slaps across my ass. Then he rides his cock along my ass crack in a quick butt job while grunting.

"Mmm. Fuck I'm hard too. Gonna fuck your pussy with that bright red ass, baby girl," Aaron says with a deep lusty voice. He lets out a low deep man growl as he rubs his cock along my crack.

Loving him getting into this fully, my insides melt to mush.

Mike joins us. Grabbing my arm, he pulls me to a standing position and deeply French kisses me as Aaron continues to jerk himself vertically between my ass cheeks. Aaron's cock is slipping and sliding all over my ass, his hands firmly holding my hips. Mike trails kisses down my neck voraciously while manhandling my boobs. I drop my head back and Aaron's hands grab at my throat and slide up my cheeks pressing my head back further until I'm arched backwards to the max. He kisses my forehead all while rubbing his cock on my buttocks.

It's all a whirl of pleasure, lush with grabs and rubs. Their manhandling of me sends me to the brink of elation.

My mind blanks to everything but the moment as Mike mingles his fingers into my pussy—first riding them on the outside, then into me in an ever-increasing pumping, before spreading all my juices towards my clit. Mike gifts me kisses down my cleavage, slipping down my belly to fully lip massage my pussy mound. His tongue snakes into the skin cleft above my clit. With one firm hand on my hip as my body jiggles from Aaron's backside rubbing, he slips his tongue along my slit to sip at my pussy lips loudly. The sucking sounds combined with the overwhelming bodily sensations are intoxicating.

I'm sinking into the plump desire of these two men like I'm merely fog, yet being molded by both their hands and bodies into my own heavenly sensual bliss. It moves into surreal as Aaron runs his hands down my sides, then rides them back up to cup my breasts, grabbing and pinching at my erect nipples.

I moan as I'm barely needing to stand on my own as both men are holding me up as they love on me. I let myself fall limp, my want rolling me about as they both maul me, consume me, maneuver my body, hold me, rub me as I fall into an unfamiliar high. It's welcomed, and beyond luscious.

Mike flips me around, so my ass is squarely in front of him.

Aaron immediately takes my face in his hands and pushes his tongue into my mouth in a deep kiss. I kiss him back, rubbing my tongue along his, hungrily sucking at his lips and tongue. He presses his hard cock to my soft gut and my hands reach up to caress his biceps, shoulders, and firm chest. I want all of him at once.

Mike is caressing me, messing with my asshole, sticking a lubed finger in and out, riding my butthole. It's his familiar move, prepping me for his engorged cock. He slathers coconut oil all over my ass cheeks and anus. Wet sounds mean also he's rubbing it on his cock.

We fall into a tiny lull in their ravaging of me ... which only means one thing.

In a blur of skin and movement, they sandwich me. Aaron slips his hands under my thighs and holds me up. I wrap my right leg around him and Mike presses me to him, so I'm snugly wedged between the two of them. The strength of both of them is hypnotic, daunting, magnificent, propelling me to promised sexual heights I've never yet enjoyed. Aaron leans back slightly so I fall forward a bit. They both line up their cocks at my holes and Mike grunts.

"Three, two, one," he utters as my heart rages, then both enter me at once. Mike presses himself into my anus and Aaron penetrates my pussy.

I yell out as I'm sliding down on both hard cocks.

Having only been DP'd by Mike and a toy in the past, my world is split in two as they both pump into me at once. I scream out and grab at Aaron's chest, my arms flailing as my nails rake at his skin. My body is going in two directions at once, but then they begin to thrust in sync. They cock maul me as my body goes increasingly limp. I freefall into the dual submission of their hungry thrusts, launching me on a ride up my orgasmic climax at a frightening speed. It's all so deliciously dizzying, like the best sensual dream I can imagine. It's like a deep massage and a hard yummy fuck all at once. I'm gasping; they are grunting. We are three in ecstasy.

"Mmmm fuck me, yes, yes, yes, yes, yes. I'm your whore," I whisper as my body is flopped about between both of them. "Mmm. Fuck. Fuck my holes." It's barely audible, but I'm sure they've heard me as they shove themselves into me, pounding me harder. The rich, repetitive sound of the skin slapping is what I imagine must be lust in heaven.

"Mmm you fucking cumslut," Mike says in a growl. "You whore. Gonna make you cum like a faucet."

The dirty talk melts me and pushes me, along with the hard slams on my clit, and I'm gone into the oblivious high of another wonderful ejaculation.

"Fuck your pussy," Aaron mutters. "Mmm. Fuck you hard, Angel."

I'm awestruck. I love his name for me, instantly savoring being his '*Angel*'.

'Aaron's Angel, and Mike's baby girl,' rings in my head as they fuck me.

I can't even speak out to tell them that I'm climaxing, but my body jerks against them, and they both grunt and groan and pump into me harder yet as I whimper out my pleasure. The familiar pressure happens near my belly button. I have no control over my body as I twitch between them, and they ride me as I dive crash into intense vaginal contractions ...four, five ... it's too hard to count. I hum and whimper almost to the rhythm of a sob. I gasp as both still fuck me, my clit too sensitive, but I'm too spent to speak it. The pleasure may have slipped me into a sex coma as I can't even form a facial expression, but inside I'm screaming.

Aaron loses it first and he spurts his seed to paint my warm insides with his hot cum. "Mmmm fuck," he grunts.

He continues to pump as he empties his cock into me. He slows down his thrusts, but Mike is still ramming himself into my ass, and Aaron's body becomes the brace for his leverage so he can keep fucking me.

I sigh as Aaron keeps me upright, thankful that he is, because I couldn't do it. I'm still pinned between them and their cradling of me skin-to-skin is very soothing. Mike grunts and squeezes my hips, his breathing rapid, ramping up to a high pumping speed as he likely nears his climax. After a few more deep grunts he comes inside my ass.

We collapse as a unit onto the couch, all of us breathing heavily. Their skin feels sweaty, damp, as does mine.

No one speaks for several minutes, like we are sharing a moment of silence in reverence for the amazing sex we just shared.

Finally, I say, "Oh my fucking Gawd, that was utterly amazing, I mean ...wow...like beyond my wildest imagination, stellar. Holy shit. You guys were savage. And I loved it."

"Wow," Aaron says. "I mean wow, agreed. What a way to break a dry spell."

Mike belly laughs. "Umm. Yeah. I want to do that again. That fucking rocked. Blew my mind to have you thrusting into her at the same time as me. Like I could feel it." He shakes his head. "Just fucking unreal."

"Mind-blowing," Aaron says in amazement.

"I'm leaking all over the damn couch," I say with a chuckle laced through my voice. "You guys definitely fucked the shit out of me. And hard." DP wasn't what I expected, but I'd do it again.

Mike pulls me into a hug. "And you had a monster orgasm, didn't you?"

I nod, releasing a big sigh. "It was huge. I mean really huge! I lost count of how many times my pussy convulsed."

"That was the most amazing feeling. I almost lost it at that point. Never felt that before."

We both look at Aaron in shock.

"What? Ah, wow," I say as I reach up and touch his cheek.

He smiles slowly, and a satisfied look settles across his face.

"I'm so thrilled you got to feel that finally then."

"Yeah, that's made me come many times with her. Feels amazing as fuck. Completely unmatched by anything. And the aftershocks rock too."

"I was so floppy I couldn't even manage to add in vaginal squeezes before I came, I was so overwhelmed. But I totally loved it." I blow out a big breath as I run my hand through my curls. "I'd do it again in a heartbeat."

Aaron flips his limp cock about. "Same. Thank you, Angel. And Mike, you have a beautiful, sensual wife. Thank you so much for sharing her with me. If we never did this again, it was enough to last a lifetime. That was incredible. Unfathomable."

"Shut up. You are coming over in three days and we are repeating this," Mike insists.

Aaron smiles. "I'd love to be invited back. It will have to be the stars aligning properly for me to get away, though."

"Then we'll wait until they do. You could always text us when it works. We are open whenever." I laugh. "Fuck, it could even be in the middle of the night for all I care."

"Really?" Aaron asks with wide eyes. "You wouldn't mind?"

"Nah, I wake her up to fuck on a regular basis. She loves it."

"You are not cut from the same female cloth as my wife." Aaron shakes his head as he laughs. "She'd be pissed at me for weeks if I woke her for sex. She'd probably slap my face."

"I like it, actually," I say. "Being woken for sex, I mean. I love the urgency, the passion, the woozy feeling going right into arousal. It drives up our lust and we fuck hard during the nighttime. Plus, being sleepy and in the dark is kinda like being drunk, so it lowers the inhibitions."

"I don't think you have any inhibitions," Aaron says in a very amused tone.

"Oh, I do, they are just getting less and less as time goes on." I rub my temples. "I really need a towel. Will you get me one, hon?" I let out a raspberry. "I think I'm going to need to scrub all your cum out of this couch today, I'm seriously dribbling like a faucet."

"That's hot," Aaron says with a grin.

"It is, isn't it?" I smirk at him. "Thank you. I know this meant a lot to you, but it did to us too. We've been wanting a threesome for a while, but haven't found anyone it would work with."

"You are welcome. I mean, I do feel guilty, but she isn't giving me anything, so, not wanting to live a celibate life, I guess that's why I'm here." He frowns. "I want to fuck her, she just doesn't want to fuck me."

"Well. I'm so sorry for that. She is really missing out, you have killer thrust moves. You murdered my pussy." I soften my eyes. "And we're just so glad you're here. We appreciate you, even if she doesn't."

Mike returns with three towels, the largest for me.

I take it and rub it along my dribbling pussy, then along my ass crack. "Thanks for the big one."

He laughs. "Literally. My pleasure to give you the big one."

"I meant towel, ya goof," I say.

"I didn't." He sits on the couch and rests his head back on the cushion. "That was fucking hot."

"Indeed." I stand. "More beer? I want something."

"If the waitress is naked, that much the better," Aaron says as he reaches for his phone. "I have just enough time for one naked beer."

"Perfect." I shrug with a smile. My whole body throbs with delicious pings from being thoroughly worked over.

I open the fridge and grab two beers, set them on the counter. I open a new bottle of wine and again tuck the beers under my armpits and carry the wine glass.

"Much easier to walk with these without heels on," I mutter.

Aaron takes the beers from my armpits again, this time making extra efforts to touch my boobs with a grin on his face. I sit between them as Aaron passes Mike a beer.

"Now you're catching on." I raise my wine glass. "Cheers to friends with benefits, threesome fucking, and fucking doing it again."

They tap their beers on my wine glass, and we all take a drink.

"Because fucking makes you thirsty," I say as I bring the wine glass to my lips.

THE END

Finger Licking Good
Threesome Roommate
Rendezvous Hookup

"Lick my fingers?" Jordan asked Mariana as he presented a sauce-coated finger to her plump rosy lips.

"What?" she asked, bewildered, dropping the salad tongs.

They clanged to the floor with way too much sound.

Jordan laughed. "Well, someone has to taste it. I already did and I like it. I need another opinion." He grinned at her as she chuckled. "So, lick my fingers."

She ignored the tongs on the floor and took Jordan's fingers into her mouth. She kept eye contact with him as she did, and she knew he could see the lust in her eyes because she couldn't possibly mask it. He was so fucking sexy, and if he weren't her boyfriend's roommate, and she weren't dating her boyfriend, he'd be the next on her to-do list. He had this wave to his hair that looked styled but was natural. She'd seen it dry that way at the beach last summer. He had a body to die for and an ass she'd always wanted to grab. And this sexy man was now ordering her to lick a part of his body. Her libido couldn't take much more of this before she'd tackle him to the floor just so her thighs could encase his toned torso.

"Is it good? Or should I start over?" Jordan had been dabbling in some gourmet cooking and both Mariana and her boyfriend Sam had been benefitting from his experiments.

"It tastes good, but I need another sample." She gave him flirty eyes, which she knew she wasn't supposed to, but again, her libido had a mind of its own. She succumbed to her desire and ran her gaze down his body. He had on a dry weave, tightly fit shirt and a snug pair of jeans. He was sockless, and the aroma wafting off of him was a strong spicy one that was alluring. He'd clearly taken a shower recently, and the thought of him all wet in the shower sent a swell through her clitoris.

She had told her boyfriend recently that she'd do a threesome, but he hadn't made any moves to ask a friend. Maybe she needed to suck his cock and plead. That'd surely work.

"Okay," he said cheerfully and swiped his middle finger through the sauce.

He lifted it to her lips and held eye contact with her.

She leaned towards him, almost pressing her pelvis against his, and sucked the tip of his finger. It was time to be bold. She closed her eyes as she rode her mouth down the rest of his middle finger, taking it all the way in to the back of her throat. She attempted to rein in her gag reflex, but lost and gagged.

She fell off his finger with a raucous laugh. "Oh, my Gawd," she muttered, embarrassed.

His expression was both shocked and amused, but there was also something in his eyes that told her he liked that she'd just done that.

"Yeah," she said as she raised both hands towards the ceiling. "Gag reflex is pretty strong." She laughed at herself and shook her head. "Poor Sam, right?"

He smirked. "On the contrary." Humor filled his face as he appeared to enjoy some secret thought.

"What are you imagining?" she asked quickly, as if she had to ask.

"Something that I shouldn't say out loud."

Well, that was very intriguing indeed. She most definitely needed to know more about that thought.

Sam entered the apartment, gym bag and protein drink cup in hand. He had on a workout tank top and workout shorts. His sandy blond hair was all askew, as if he'd run his hands through it with mousse. "Whew, now that was a workout and a half."

He looked delicious to Mariana, and she instantly wanted to drag him back into his bedroom and fuck his brains out. The whole finger-sucking incident with Jordan had her randy as a swollen peach at a hungry mouth.

"Hi, Sam. Can I show you to your room?" She was not going to be subtle. He liked her aggressively coming on to him anyhow, so she never held back.

"Yes, but first, you have a bit of something on your lips." He took a step towards the two and peered into the bowl Jordan was stirring. "How's that sauce taste?" he asked with a big grin.

Her face flushed and Jordan looked amused.

She took in a deep breath, then released it. "It was ... really good." She connected her gaze with Jordan's and held it as she said, "Really good."

Sam looked back and forth between the two before catching Mariana's attention.

Mariana bit her lip, then glanced down. There was a rise of a bulge in Jordan's jeans. She was no fool. Jeans tended to mask erections, so if she could tell, it meant he had a raging boner.

"Him?" Sam asked with some surprise in his voice.

She was elated. He had paid attention. She nodded with exaggeration before she said, "Yes. Absolutely."

"Meet me back in the bedroom," he instructed with a knowing eyebrow raise. "Something red."

She skedaddled out of the kitchen with a glance back at both men. Jordan looked confused, but she simply smiled at him. She swayed her hips as she walked down the hall towards Sam's bedroom.

If he was asking Jordan to join them in a threesome, she'd gladly give him anything he wanted sexually for the next month without fuss. She'd spilled her sexual bucket list to Sam under the urge of half a bottle of wine. He had happily returned the favor and shared some new fantasies he'd conjured up recently after watching porn. She had told him she'd be willing to try them each, at least once. He hadn't seemed thrilled about a MMF threesome when she'd confided her desire for one, but now it seemed her assessment was wrong.

She searched in her drawer in Sam's dresser for something red. Her drawer contained mostly lingerie, some thongs, two tank tops, a pair of black workout shorts, and PJ pants. She needed to restock it with some items, but right now, all she needed was something sexy and red. She loved fulfilling Sam's sexual requests. She enjoyed the look of satisfaction on his face when she did as he asked. She wasn't quite sure yet if she was willing to do anything for him, but her mind was set to try most things, especially if he bought into trying her sexual whims.

She slipped into a skimpy red lace bra and panties with garters and black sheer socks that almost reached her knees. Next, she adorned her black high heels, fixed her makeup, and ate a breath mint. She laid herself out on the bed seductively. Her impatience soared as she heard the shower.

What the fuck? Sam was showering rather than racing in here to fuck her silly? That was not like him.

She considered grabbing a sex toy, because he certainly wasn't attending to her heightened arousal. She certainly didn't need him. She knew how to make herself come in about a minute and a half flat with her rose clit sucker toy.

She quickly hopped off the bed and dug in the sex toy drawer in the bedside table. Her pussy felt wet and her desire was peaking. She felt desperate and rushed as she laid back down and shimmied her panties down her thighs to expose her wanton cunt. She slopped a dollop of lube on her clit and pressed the lovely orgasm-delivering toy to her swollen bean.

Her eyes fell closed as she imagined both Sam and Jordan taking her at once on the very same bed she was writhing on. She moaned and screamed, and then squelched out a loud shriek as the toy gifted her a monstrous orgasm. Her body twitched as she rode the delicious wave.

She didn't need their actual bodies; her fantasizing about it did just the trick.

She opened her eyes and turned her head to a sound.

Both Sam and Jordan were standing in the doorway of the bedroom with boners at full mast.

"Whoa!" she exclaimed. "Holy fuck! How long have you two been there?"

"See, I told you. She's the horniest woman I've ever been with. She's an amazing sex goddess." Sam's face was full of pride and lust.

She wasn't sure she could say it yet, but she was in love with Sam. She couldn't say why she hadn't said it yet. Maybe she was waiting for him to say it, but the urge to reveal her feelings for him swelled as she took in her man. He was about to deliver her fantasy, so that pushed her button down. It was official. She was going to tell him, but not during a threesome fuck.

"Wow. She's even more yummy than I expected her to be." Jordan licked his lips and the desire in his eyes lit Mariana's passion to blazing to the sky status.

"Does this mean ... ?" She couldn't finish the question because she was panting too heavily.

"Yeah, Jordan's definitely in," Sam smirked. "As if I need to say that," he said sarcastically.

"Oh, I'm more than in. I've fantasized about this, to be honest. I've listened, and jerked, to hearing you guys fuck on a regular basis." He glanced at Sam, then at Mariana. "Sorry, not sorry. It's been kickass. You two fuck like rabbits."

Mariana guffawed as she spread her legs. "Yes, we do. Now get over here and give me those gorgeous engorged cocks. I need one in my mouth and one in my pussy."

"Yes, ma'am," Sam said.

He approached the bed first and crawled up to her, his cock bobbing as he moved forward. Jordan walked over to the bed and stood by it, pressing his pelvis towards Mariana.

"I need to feel you," Jordan said as he lay on the bed.

The two men snuggled up to her, Sam against her back and Jordan against her front.

The sandwich they made pressed her C cups firmly to Jordan and her buns wrapped around Sam's cock. He began to thrust his hardon between her ass cheeks as his hands meandered along her body. Jordan's hand slicked down her side, then cupped the side of her breast before he took her face in his hand and began deeply kissing her. His tongue spurt right into her mouth, gliding along her own tongue.

She moaned out as Jordan groaned back and she writhed between the undulating press of their bodies against hers.

"Oh, fuck, I want you both. I can't believe I get you both," she said in a breathy voice before Jordan shut her up with another deep French kiss.

They both mauled her body and she felt drunk with having four hands loving up her flesh. It was overwhelming and a rush being handled by two men at once. She twerked and thrashed against them, trying to garner as much of their touches as she could.

Sam was the first to breach her closed vulva lips. He pried them open carefully and pressed two fingers to her wet lips. He dabbed his fingers all around her vaginal opening, then dipped them in. He quickly brought his fingers to their entwined mouths and pressed his wet fingers into their kiss.

This prompted their tongues to lash against his fingers as both Mariana and Jordan tasted her juices off Sam's fingers. They both licked and suckled his fingers as he rode them around on their tongues.

"You taste amazing, Mariana," Jordan said with clear, passionate enjoyment.

Sam visited her sopping pussy again and wetted all five of his fingers with her wetness. He brought his hand back to their faces and both of them devoured Mariana's sex juice off his hand.

"I need to taste you from your pussy," Jordan declared.

He slithered down the bed as Sam pressed Mariana to lie flat. Jordan dove into her cunt like he needed it to breathe and suctioned his mouth to her fleshy womanly bits. He sucked her bean as her body thrashed while Sam took turns consuming her tits.

She writhed and moaned, quickly approaching another climax. Sam kissed her and, as Jordan took her full clit in his mouth and sucked hard, she jerked from the strength of his suck.

"Oh, fuck, I'm going to come," she said in desperation.

Sam pinched and twisted her left nipple while sucking her right.

The three-point stimulation launched Mariana into the mother of all orgasms, and she screamed. Her body fell into undulations like a puppet to her pussy contractions. A full-body orgasm descended upon her as her torso curled, her head fell back, her legs bent and rose off the bed, her toes curling.

She was a floppy rag doll soaked with sex hormones as the men positioned her into doggy position. Their grunts and growls drove her wild and raged her lust for more as they prepared to spit roast her. She wanted their cocks everywhere at once, in her pussy, her ass, her mouth, coming against her flesh, spewing spunk into her mouth. She wanted them to consume her and wring her out with so many orgasms she couldn't think straight.

Jordan pressed her cheeks and she glanced up at him.

"That's right, baby, keep looking me in the eye while I fuck your hot, tight mouth." He paused, then added, "My cunt mouthed whore."

She shuddered. He clearly had heard Sam dirty talk to her and now hearing it from him raged her lust up even more.

Sam spanked her bottom with his erection before lining it up at her throbbing slit. He penetrated her pussy while Jordan pressed his cockhead into her mouth. They both began to ride her and she thought she'd collapse to the bed. Sam's grip on her hips helped her stay up.

The skin smacks as Sam pounded his dick into her filled the room, as did his grunts and Jordan's groans.

She gagged as Jordan pushed his cock to the back of her throat and his cock twitched.

"Oh, fuck," he muttered as he sent his cum down her throat.

She gagged again, gasped and sputtered before pulling herself off his cock. She moved his cum around on her tongue.

"Quick, Jordan, get her clit. She's close, I can tell," Sam directed.

Jordan reached under her body and rubbed her clit hard, making circles around it, pressing it, mashing it as Sam railed her from behind.

She was instantly gripped by another big O as they played her G spot and clitoral head at once. She twitched and yelped as she came. As she collapsed to the bed, Sam drilled her on repeat, pounding her down into the mattress.

He came with a roar, still pumping his seed into her as he drained himself into her contracting internal walls.

The three of them fell to the bed, all three panting.

"Oh, wow," Jordan said, the first to speak. "That was the best in my life."

Mariana nodded and weakly whispered, "Same." She gasped, trying to slow her breathing down. "It was the best fuck of my whole life so far." She took in a deep breath and released it. "Thank you both. Just wow." She curled towards Sam and kissed him on the lips. She held eye contact with him and mouthed, "I love you."

He grinned big and mouthed it back.

There. They'd both said it and it felt glorious to Mariana. "You are the best boyfriend on the planet."

"I think the best on the planet applies to you, my sweet babe," he said as he caressed her face.

"I believe we need to grill up those wings. We are all famished after that." Jordan rose off the bed and made his way to the door. "Thanks for having me. And if you ever invite me again, the answer will always be yes."

He left the room and closed the door behind him.

"You really are the best boyfriend in the world for giving me that."

"Well, you've agreed to try my fantasies, so I could only return the favor."

"I'm so happy seeing Jordan naked didn't turn you off." She snuggled into his warm body.

"You are sexy enough to keep that from happening, babe." He held her close and kissed the top of her head.

"I guess we have a new fuck buddy, huh? And how convenient he happens to live in the bedroom next door!" she said with excitement.

"Oh, he was so happy when I asked him. You should have seen his face."

"Confession," she said sheepishly. "I sucked Jordan's finger." She cringed, hoping he wouldn't be mad.

"I know, he told me. We are good friends, and he didn't want to ruin our friendship, so he confessed. He said it started out innocent, but then turned hot."

"Yep, that's exactly how it happened. I didn't mean to, but it was so erotic sucking that sauce off his finger, I couldn't help it."

"Hey, I want you to have as much pleasure as possible, and I know you want that for me."

"Oh, I do!" she insisted.

"Good. Then we match."

She grinned big as she pressed her forehead to his. "We do. I love you."

He smiled back. "I love you." He sighed and caressed her cheek. "Lots of new ground covered today."

She nodded. "Yep. And good ground."

"I agree. Now let's go help our new friend with benefits make our dinner."

"I'm so ready for it all."

"You realize this now means you will be in the vicinity of two very horny men most hours of each day."

She jumped as a giddy expression overcame her face. "Yes! And I'm the luckiest woman alive!"

The End

Waking to His Alarm Cock

Zane watches as Maria and Lissa sleep. Both of them came so hard that last round before bed that Zane cheered when they both conked out. He couldn't ever get enough of his girlfriend and her friend. The sex-with-benefits had started four months ago, when they were all high. They'd been drinking and smoking all night, and then a joke turned into a dare and Zane got the women to kiss. They were plastered enough to take his suggestions and encouragement, and soon they were tribbing right on the couch.

That had been the first of many threesome trysts they'd succumbed to, and now it had become a regular thing. Zane glanced at the pile of uniforms on the floor. Maria had worked three doubles in a row at the hospital. She needed this sleeping in so bad.

Lissa had been stirring a bit, but he didn't want to jostle the bed too much for fear he'd wake Maria. The cock barrage he'd given both women not more than four hours ago should have been enough to keep his dick a noodle for a long time, but there he was, sporting a morning wood, anyway. It was like any time past 4:30 am and his cock flared like a wild bleeping beacon. Quite the alarm cock to wake up a horny hot mess every morning. He grinned. He had an alarm cock, he didn't need an alarm clock. Maria never complained because he made her come every morning, too.

Lissa opened her eyes fully and waved at Zane.

He waved back. Lissa was a kindergarten teacher at their daughter's school. If anyone spilled the beans about the three of them fucking, she'd said she'd lose her job. He had zero intention of putting her at risk because he loved their threesome arrangement. The hardest part was keeping their daughter, Morgan, from catching Ms. Hathoway in mom and dad's bedroom.

She was young, but that was just too unusual for her to dismiss, so they'd been careful to be sneaky.

Lissa pointed at Maria, closed her hands together, and put them under her cheek.

Zane nodded.

Lissa smiled. She stabbed her cheek with her tongue and closed her hand in a fist and pumped it in front of her face.

Zane nodded aggressively.

She carefully got off the bed and tip-toed around it.

Zane felt his cock thicken as she approached. She stripped her top off so her tits were bare and she laid upon Zane, readying herself to give him head.

She quickly took him into her mouth. Her nipples were solid peaks. As she bobbed on his swollen cockhead, her tits bounced. Her eyes went wide as she took his cock deep.

Zane loved that she liked to choke on his cock, and he really loved it that she had throatgasms. Maria never went there. The bonus of the situation was, what one woman didn't do, the other did, so Zane was always one happy man. Maria would do anal, but Lissa wouldn't. Maria was dominant to Lissa, and Lissa was submissive to both Maria and Zane, Zane being the most dominant of the three.

Zane's body curled as Maria gagged on him. He almost lost his gizz, but she popped off his dick and grinned up at him.

"Almost," he whispered.

"I know," Lissa said. On her knees, she pointed her big ass in the air and wrapped his cock up for a titty fuck. She rode him until he held her body tight and thrust his cock up into her cleavage.

They both were grunting, and the bed was jerking, but still Maria slept.

Zane had plans to talk with both women today about considering a full-time three-way relationship. The only way he figured they could make it work was if Lissa moved into their basement and 'rented' a room. This would not be tough to do, but the biggest challenge would then be to keep their daughter from catching them all sleeping in the same bed every night.

Zane clenched, trying hard not to come. He shook his head at Lissa as she raised an eyebrow with a teasing look in her eyes.

"Want your come," she insisted.

He shook his head. "No, I want to fuck you, and I may not stay hard after last night."

"Oh, I'll get you hard," Lissa said confidently. "I'm up for that challenge."

Maria finally stirred in the bed and opened her eyes. "Oh, my. This is quite the way to wake up. Do I get to play, too?"

"Fuck yes, you do, babe. Come here." Zane pulled his high school sweetheart to his body and kissed her on the forehead. "Get enough sleep? You were so worn out."

Zane's body crumpled as Lissa sucked him hard. "Damnit, fuck." He bucked Lissa off. "You are determined to make me come, aren't you?"

She nodded vehemently, her red curls bouncing and her pink-tipped tits shaking. "I'm hungry for your cum. Morning cum always tastes the best."

Zane hadn't ever heard that one before, but he was not complaining. "I'd love to see a muff dive first. How about you two make each other come, then you can have mine."

Maria squirmed and stretched. "Mmmm. I'd love an orgasm. Lissa, what do you say? Let's make each other shake."

Maria spread her legs and Lissa hovered above. The touchdown of their pussies was always something Zane loved to watch. Their reactions to warm pussy on warm pussy were always so damn delicious.

"I'll read you two a little snippet I wrote yesterday and you two act it out, okay?" He'd taken to writing some erotica and started publishing it on Medium. He'd been really enjoying it, and he knew this was going to be a fun hobby, and he'd go as far as he could with it. Writing had always been an interest to him, and doing construction during the day was about as far from erotica as he could get. This was helping him use other parts of his brain and sexuality, and the satisfaction level was becoming a dream come true.

"You need to get into 69 position for this, though," he instructed with relish. Watching them simultaneously eat each other out was even more arousing to him than them tribbing.

The women lined up mouth to pussy with lecherous, lusty looks.

"Mmmm, fuck yes," Zane said as he stroked his engorged cock. "Yes, more of that."

The women suctioned their mouths to each other's lips and began the mouth ride.

"Rub your chin across her moist petals, inhale her gush as you dive into her. Tongue molest her sensitive bits to make her twitch and scream as she gropes your hair, your head bobbing between her thighs." He paused as they made mouth smacks and yummy moans. "Consume her very essence as she comes with such ravishing that her body curls you up." He scrolled through the notes app on his phone for another one to read to them. "Nipples so pale pink, the color ripens to deeper hues — moist saliva-tipped nips — as they harden in between blankets and fingers. The calm barely hung on as their lust began to rage its fiery head like a flaring piston — it raged like fireworks in the night, screeching along like spilt cum in morning sunlight. Their sweaty bodies flopped together as they came. With dewy lips and gasping lungs, they laid satiated in the afterglow, her clit twitching with aftershocks."

Maria's body gyrated first, then within thirty seconds Lissa's hungry libido met her climax. Both women's bodies shuddered. He loved it when their orgasms overlapped.

They both moaned out and fell flaccid, with happy looks smeared across their beautiful faces.

Zane rose up and got on his knees. "My turn." Without a glance at the clock, he situated himself between Maria's thighs and penetrated her wet, lush cunt in a flash. He sank right in and both of them groaned.

He rode the love of his life hard, making sloshy smacking sounds as he fucked her while Lissa gobbled her nipples. Maria reached under Lissa and played with her clit. Zane harnessed his control and held off coming as Lissa came from Maria's clit spanks, then he banged Maria until she was near climax.

He pulled out and demanded in a stern voice, "Doggy."

Maria scrambled up and flipped over, quickly arranging herself on her hands and knees. Lissa knew what to do. She grabbed the big black vibrating dildo and aligned herself on her hands and knees next to Maria.

Lissa handed Zane the dildo and he penetrated her slit with it. He pumped the toy into her aggressively as he thrust himself into Maria. He fucked both women until Maria's body shook with another orgasm, then he pulled out and slid over to fuck Lissa.

Maria lay crumpled, face down in the bed, whimpering as he pounded his hard cock into Lissa. She exclaimed as she came, her contractions on his cock pushed him over the edge and he came explosively in her pussy. He knew she wanted a baby, and though no one had acknowledged it, they weren't using birth control. He let his cock slip out of her with a smile.

"Good job, baby," he said as he stroked her bottom.

She crashed down to the bed and cuddled into Maria's arms.

Zane snuggled up behind Lissa, spooning her before finally glancing at the clock. Morgan didn't have to be up for an hour, so it was time for a cum soaked morning nap.

Zane happily smiled as he dug his nose into Lissa's lush, sweet-smelling curls. Could he be a husband to two women? He sure thought he could. He settled in as his eyes fell closed.

Bliss. This was pure bliss.

The End

The Accidental Threesome,
Roommates Who Finally
Had Some Fun

"**S**how us your tits," Dan yelled from the living room.

Asheley froze in place, the piece of lettuce in her hands first quivering then descending to her sandwich. She'd been desiring such a request from Dan since they had met last year. Becoming roommates with him and Anders had brought her to believe they'd hook up, but after four months, still nothing. But now, there was this request.

"Yeah, look at that shirt, her tits are about to pop," Anders said with a voice brimming over with want.

Asheley frowned. Of course, they hadn't been talking to her. That was wishful thinking. They respected her too much. That was part of the problem. No one ever took a chance on her, and she just sat in her room masturbating with toys and porn when she had been living with two dicks for months.

Maybe she needed to make it known she was open for play, but she hadn't figured out how to say it without losing their high opinion of her. The three of them were buds. They ate together, worked out together, went to parties together, and watched sports together. In all that time, neither one of them had made a pass at her.

She knew she was sexy, glances from men daily told her she was desirable, but all the guys seemed to think of her as a friend. She'd gotten permanently friend-zoned in their group of friends, and it sucked ass.

The truth was, she'd be using Dan's comment to masturbate in her bedroom in a few minutes. She imagined herself standing in front of them as they said that sentence to her, and her clit lurched a twitch. She'd dance and tease them, then lift her shirt to show off her gorgeous boobs. And she had gorgeous boobs! Only no one ever saw them but her.

She continued to make her sandwich. A boring lunch to match her boring as fuck sex life.

Dan cheered from the living room. "Ah, fuck yes! I knew she'd have the best tits on the planet!"

That too was a line she craved to hear him say to her. She didn't feel guilty about wanting to objectify herself in front of them, she wanted them to desire her. No matter how scantily she clad herself around the apartment, loose tank tops showing side boob, tiny shorts, and even going pantless, nothing worked. No ass grabs, no titty claims, not even an accidental brush-up while cooking together in the kitchen.

She'd fantasized about walking around nude. What heterosexual man could resist that, right? With her luck, they'd probably hand her a towel and avert their eyes. She was the sister, the buddy, the 'just another guy'.

Only she wasn't any of those things.

Anders belted out, "Aw, yeah, fuck her good."

Porn watching with them had also become too agonizing. The last one she'd watched with them, she got so horny she fled to her room and fucked herself into twelve orgasms. It just wasn't fair. Living with two sexy men should mean some sex, not celibacy.

College dorm life last year had at least gotten her a few hookups, but this year had been dry as a Sahara on water pills, nothing juicy about it at all.

She glanced into the living room as she walked towards her bedroom, and the scene on the screen was a threesome. Of course it was a threesome. The woman was getting railed from behind and taking a mouth fuck. A spit-roast scene to aspire to because her face was plastered in bliss. She sighed as she attempted to view their crotches from behind the couch. That had been the other painful part of watching porn with them. They both always had raging erections.

"Ashe," Dan called while glancing back. "You gotta see this one. Eat your sandwich. Here, I'll rewind it for you. It's epic, especially when she gets a titty fuck and a butt job at once." He cackles. "Dudes were riding her crevices like fucking jockeys on steroids. Her body was flopping all over."

Asheley felt her arousal rage. She almost dropped her plate when Anders stood up because he had gray sweatpants on, and was sporting a precum wet spot.

"Fuck," she muttered under her breath. It didn't help that she hadn't had sex in eleven months, not since breaking up with Manny.

"I need a beer. Dan? Ashe?" He started to move and his cock wiggled.

Asheley's jaw dropped. It looked as if he had no underwear on with how easily his erection shifted beneath the fabric. Literally weak in the knees, she simply shook her head and ambled down the hall.

"Ashe, what's up? How come you don't watch porn with us anymore?" Dan called after her.

She froze in place, her heart pounding. This was her chance to say something, but she was terrified to. "Um. I don't know. Was just going to eat my sandwich."

"Eat it out here, for fuck's sake, Ashe. We haven't spent any time together in the past few days. You keep hiding out in your room."

"Yeah," Anders said as he sauntered across the room, two beers in hand. "Come watch with us. Or maybe you get too horny," Anders said with a snicker. "Makes you want to fuck." He burst into laughter. His face showed he was clearly just razzing her.

She'd often wondered if they heard the hum of toys coming from her room. I mean, how could they not? The other day she used her super loud one, hoping they'd bring it up, or tease her or something, anything to acknowledge it would have been hot as fuck. But she got nothing.

She froze in place with her mouth ajar. Her face reddened, and she couldn't stop her nerves from rattling her resolve. She knew she looked nervous, but it was too late to make her face blank.

"Wait, what?" Dan asked, sitting up straight.

Anders stood in front of the couch, about to take a drink from his beer, but remained motionless.

"Ashe?" Dan asked again, standing up. "Cause if you ever want to fuck, oh my God, I'd fuck you anytime you wanted me to."

Anders nodded dumbly. "Same. I guess I assumed you just saw us as friends, but truth be told, you drive me fucking crazy on a daily basis."

Dan guffawed. "Yeah, same. And when I hear your toys going, shit ..." He dropped off mid-sentence, but no other words were needed.

She wanted to cry and jump for joy at once. This meant they hadn't friend-zoned her, she'd friend-zoned herself. She stumbled over her words as she said, "I ... well ... but..." Then she smiled deeply as her inner sex kitten oozed herself to the forefront of her. "I actually fantasize with those toys, about you guys fucking me. It's why I can't stomach watching porn with you anymore. I want to fuck too much, and I can't tolerate sitting in the same room with you two."

"Get the fuck outta here. Are you being actually serious right now?" Dan's eyes widened and his expression was set in utter shock.

"It's true." She sashayed her hips as she walked down the hallway towards them. "I do want you guys to fuck me. I thought you thought of me as just another guy."

Dan and Anders both burst into laughter.

"You? Just another guy? Do you even realize how sexy you are? Come on, this is just ridiculous. We talk about you all the time." Dan ran a hand along his erection and shook his head. "You have no idea."

"Well, no one bothered to tell me!" she said, aghast. "I might be the one to tell, ya know." She knew she was coming off sassy, but it was too strong to quell.

"I'm game," Anders piped in quickly.

"Ashe, put your sandwich in the fridge and let's talk. Because, seriously, I'm in too, if that's what you want."

"I need to eat, so I'll eat while we chat." She grinned as she joined them in the living room, choosing a recliner across the room from them so she could see their faces while they discussed fucking. She couldn't wrap her head around that this was legit happening. She'd partied with these two all last year. They'd had a blast their freshman year, even played basketball and volleyball, and they often lifted together. How this had never come up before literally made zero sense to Ashe. She tried to process the fact that he had admitted they'd talked about her in a sexual sense, so how this was literally the first she was hearing of it? Her mind was blown, and they hadn't even fucked yet. How much of a mind explosion would it be to actually fuck them?

Her mind reeled as she took the first bite of her sandwich, realizing the sexual energy of the room had just skyrocketed, and she'd likely not make it through her sandwich before she had one, or both, of their cocks inside her somehow. The thought of which titillated her, making her pussy juice wet her nether lips. She shifted in her seat to test it and knew if she slipped her fingers inside her hot slit, they'd get slicked.

She started speaking before finishing chewing. The excitement of their impending hookup was too much to wait on. "Yes. I can't watch," she paused to finish chewing, "porn with you guys because it makes me too horny." She licked her lips and shook her head. Sometimes men seemed too dense to be created of the same stock as women. "Haven't you noticed me tear out of here every time we do? For fuck's sake. I thought it was obvious." She tried to temper her tantrum.

"No, I just thought you were done, or wanted to, I don't know, go fuck yourself or something," Dan said with bewilderment. "And so all this time ..."

"We could have been fucking," Anders finished.

She nodded as she chewed another bite. She smirked because stuffing her face in front of them was not exactly arousing. "I'll finish this later." She scurried to the kitchen and swiftly slipped it into the fridge, downing some water before returning to the living room.

Both of her roommates still held expressions of confusion and surprise. But she also saw lust in their eyes, so she gave a seductive look back to both of them as she nestled back in her chair. "We'd need ground rules."

They both sat very attentive to every word.

"Of course, we are still friends." Dan's face spread into a smile. "Is this going to really happen? Legit?"

Asheley couldn't stop her own grin as she nodded. "I've wanted this for a long time, but felt I couldn't ask. Plus, I didn't think you guys were interested in me that way."

"Shut the fuck up," Dan said jokingly. "Well, shit, ...all this wasted time."

Anders turned serious. "We're talking just fucking, right? Not like we will be boyfriends and girlfriend?"

"Precisely," Asheley said with absolution. "I don't want a boyfriend. That's not what I'm wanting to do now. I just want sex. If you guys are in."

Both of them stared at her in dead silence.

It lasted for too long and she stood up. "Never mind." She started out of the living room, and Dan stood up to stop her.

"Don't leave. This is like every guy's dream to hear from someone like you. And I'll fuck you as much, or as little as you want, and ask nothing more of you. If you want to stop, we stop. It changes nothing."

Asheley knew that was a load of crap. It would change everything. But she welcomed the change, and desired it.

"Deal," she said as she uncrossed her arms and unfurrowed her brow. "And I don't do anal, so double action will be tit sucking and eating me out, spit-roasting, sucking and hand jobs, or maybe double V, which I haven't done yet." She said it so matter-of-fact that it didn't even seem like she cared, but that wasn't true at all. She relaxed her stern face and added, "And, yes, I want to do this with you two very much."

They both approached her and her heart jumped, then began beating as if she were dashing off down the hallway. Her breath caught in her throat and she made a garbled sound that made her feel awkward as fuck.

"Can't wait to see your O face," Dan said as he touched her arm.

"If I say frog legs, stop whatever you are doing." She smirked as they laughed at her choice of safe words.

"You got it," Anders said as he caressed her other arm. "Living with you, seeing you as sexy as you are every day had been torture for us."

She was filled with pleasure at the sexy compliment. Her cheeks flushed and she scrunched her shoulders. It felt so good to hear him say this, she'd felt unsexy for months and months. "Really? I had no idea. And compliments get you everywhere."

"Everywhere but your ass," Dan corrected with a cackling heckle.

"Right," she said, pointing at his face. "Not into butt stuff."

"Well, no one's perfect," Anders said jokingly.

Their relationship was such that his comment wouldn't even come close to offending her. Plus, she was very confident in her wants and desires, so she didn't give a fuck if they didn't like it.

The porn ended on the screen, and another one began to load. Anders pushed the button to keep it going, then spun Asheley to face Dan. He pressed his generous hard-on to her buns as Dan caressed her arms.

Leaning in to give her a peck on the lips, he asked, "C?"

She nodded. "Yep, you guessed it."

"Knew it," Anders blurted.

"I knew it. Confession time. I've looked at your bras while they were drying in the bathroom."

She belly laughed. "Then you didn't really need to ask me, did you?"

He shook his head as he pressed his open mouth to hers and kissed her deeply.

"Mmm, ham and cheddar?"

She giggled with a nod before he kissed her again.

Anders slipped his sweatpants down and she felt him rubbing his erection between her ass cheeks. She was totally okay with that kind of butt stuff, as long as they stayed on the outside. Any poking in, and she'd say 'frog legs'.

As if he had read her mind, he asked, "This okay for you? You have the best bubble butt on campus, you know."

She snickered before Dan cupped her breast and kissed her neck.

"I'm good. If you don't hear me say it, you're in the clear." She paused. "And ribbit means you'd better slow the fuck down before I smack you."

"Got it," Dan said as he fondled her breasts. "I'd expect nothing less from you. And I can't wait to see your nipples."

Having both her roommates groping her and thrusting their cocks against her torso sent her into a rage of desire. She felt her crazy side rise to her surface. She knew she was going to blow their minds because all of her exes had told her she was an animal in bed. Not that she'd needed them to tell her.

"Remember her nipples at the pool party when she forgot a swimsuit?" Anders asked suggestively. "You kind of already know."

She remembered that pool party from last summer. She'd forgotten a suit and was going braless because the tank top was supportive. She'd just swam in the shorts and tank top. But she didn't recall either Dan or Anders ogling her that day, but she also remembers getting plastered. She laughed inside. Of course, she hadn't noticed. They were likely so expertly covert at ogling her that she had completely missed it altogether. So, they were even, and all damned oblivious. She hadn't picked up on their interest, and they hadn't on hers. It was an even starting ground for friends with benefits.

Dan pulled her tank top straps down and slipped the fabric off her breasts. Anders quickly came around the front just in time as her breasts popped out.

"Oiy, fuck me," Dan said. "Fucking perfect tits, Ashe. Fucking perfect."

She smiled with pleasure. She'd imagined him saying that so many times, but nothing beat actually hearing him say it to her face.

"Thank you," she said as her insides melted. Confirmation that she was sexy after all was very satisfying. She wasn't about to admit low confidence to them, though, that wasn't sexy at all.

"Hot as fuck tits, Ashe. Fucking spectacular."

She beamed a smile at him as both men grappled her breasts.

"Wow," she muttered as they both molested her tits.

Anders was the first to take a nipple in his mouth.

She moaned without thought. As she writhed between both men, giving ample attention to her breasts, she realized an interesting phenomenon. The arousing effect of having her nipples suckled and played with was rivaling the excitement she was enjoying that it was Anders and Dan who were doing it. She was used to having boyfriends do this to her, even strangers in her few spontaneous stranger hookup fucks, but it was somehow an entirely different thing to have her two best friends enjoying her boobies. And it was taboo, which made it even more delicious.

"Oh, don't stop, please," she pleaded.

This made both of them go even harder at her body. She gasped and felt weak. She'd snuck peeks at both of their erections, but to have them pressed to her now, and them thrusting them against her, was satiating all by itself, and no one had even broached her clit yet.

She sighed and allowed them to manipulate her body into undulations caused by them each sucking, pinching, twisting, and squeezing her breasts and nips. It was an all-out foreplay feast of tit play. She hadn't even come close to realizing how much they'd been enjoying looking at her tits all this time, but the way they were devouring and playing with them proved it.

As Anders went back to thrusting his cock in her ass crack, Dan was the first to slip his fingers into her waistband. He hooked his fingers under it and gently slid her workout shorts down. Anders took a step back and helped the shorts slide down her buttocks. He knelt down and delivered a small bite to her right ass cheek.

She squealed in delight.

Dan nuzzled her ear as he whispered, "Seeing you commando all the time has also driven us crazy."

She smiled, thrilled they had noticed. She had done it for herself, but she wasn't going to lie, she loved that they had observed her going frequently without panties.

"You noticed," she cooed.

"How could we not? It's sexy as fuck." Dan caressed down her tummy, then crested her bald pussy mound. "We're gonna have so much fucking fun."

She tittered a laugh in agreement. "Yes. Yes, we are." It was also gratifying to know they'd talked about her going commando. That thought ramped up her desire for them even higher.

"Morning sex or night sex?" Anders asked.

"Yes," she retorted in a sassy voice.

"You may not ever return to your own bed." Dan cupped her hips as he pressed his fingers into her flesh.

Having a bare pussy and ass in front of them felt naughty and yummy at once.

"You won't hear me complaining, as long as your mattresses don't suck." She released a long appreciative sigh as Dan parted her pussy lips to slip a finger into her hot slit.

"Only sucking there will be on us or on you. My mattress is new this year." Dan kissed her mouth as he began to finger-fuck her.

She slouched, almost crumpling from how their touch was stimulating her. Four hands and two cocks on her was much more overwhelming and brilliantly exciting than she had expected. She felt woozy as they played with her body, pushing all the buttons, even ones she hadn't been aware of before being with two horny men.

Anders kissed her shoulders and back, then licked down her spine, which caused her to squirm in astonishment. He rounded out his tongue ride by licking her buns all over. He pressed his fingers to the back end of her slit and started to press his fingers in. A double finger-fuck was filling her up quickly and sending her desire for a cock to inferno level.

She knew why they'd arranged themselves this way. Dan was a boob man, and Anders was an ass man. She'd watched so much porn with these two that she had elucidated info about their sexuality from their reactions, as likely they had of her as well.

"We're going to fuck you into so many orgasms you scream, Ashe," Dan said while maintaining eye contact with her.

"Please," she said in a meek, humble voice. It was already getting difficult to converse with how hard she was panting, and how much the ecstasy was filling up her brain.

Anders gripped her shoulders and spun her around, and his mouth was on hers so fast she had barely taken another breath. Dan kissed down her neck and mashed her fleshy butt between his large palms. Ashe had watched him palm a basketball so many times, and had yearned for his big mitts grinding on her big bottom. And now that it was happening, she loved his touch so much. She almost slithered to the floor like she was a boneless puddle of hormones. And then there was Anders, sucking on her erect nipples again and playing with her clit.

"Spit-roast?" Anders asked when he had released her tit from the tight suck.

Dan was finger-fucking her so hard she couldn't think. Each thrust into her, his thumb would smack against her swollen bean, and she'd cry out in pleasure.

Anders grabbed both tips of her tits and twisted them while chanting, "Tune in, Ashe. Tune in, Ashe. Can you hear me?"

She buckled with laughter and nodded aggressively. "Yes," she whispered.

"Good." He nodded to Dan, who pressed Ashe to a bent-over position.

This was it. She could now die happy having been taken in a spit-roast by her two friends. She was getting so aroused, she knew it wouldn't be much longer before she'd come.

Dan ran his cock along her labia lips, then penetrated her cunt slowly. She groaned, as did he, and his thrusts into her began slow, but sped up quickly.

Anders held her face with one hand, and fed his cock into her mouth with his other. He began light thrusts as her gag reflex reared its head. She'd never been spit-roasted and the dual pounding of both their hard cocks into her sent her into a flight of hormones zipping around her body the likes of which she'd never enjoyed.

She gagged, but Anders kept going.

First Dan growled, then he began to rail her relentlessly, beating her generous butt cheeks into constant gyrations. She had a pretty big butt for an athlete, or so she'd been told.

Anders grunted next and skated her higher towards a climax.

She slipped off Anders's fat dick and muttered, "Clit."

Dan immediately responded and rode her clit hard with his fingers, while still pumping himself inside her.

Her ecstatic realm swirled up from her gut and exploded across her body as she peaked in an orgasmic climax. Her body jerked. She gagged and fell off Anders's cock as her body twitched its way through the delicious and intense climax. The contractions bounced out of her female center and squeezed Dan's dick on repeat.

He shouted out as he pulled his fingers from her clit to grip her hips and rail himself into her. He came with a roaring yell.

Quivering and almost falling, Anders swiveled her body so her ass was pointing his way, and he shoved his cock up her so fast she gasped and sputtered. With the taste of Anders's precum on her tongue, he rode her hard and fast into his own orgasm.

She knew her friends were clean, and she had birth control covered, so there was nothing but the pleasure to savor as the three of them landed on the couch. With Ashe in the middle, she placed her hands on both their thighs.

She drew in a breath and released a big sigh. "Now, that's more like it. Watching porn together now needs to be done while fucking."

Anders laughed and Dan snorted.

"Good plan," Dan said with relish.

"I'm always in."

"Do we get to use all those toys on you?" Dan asked with hope.

"Absolutely. I'd be bummed if you didn't."

"Fuck, I can't tell you how many times I've masturbated to hearing you use those things." Dan rose from the couch, his cock half-flaccid.

"Same. And Ashe, we used to talk about it. And when you'd make sound, oh fuck, I'd spurt my cum like a fountain." Anders held her chin. "I'm not kidding, babe. It's true."

"Wow, and here I thought I was just another guy to you guys."

"Not possible," Dan said as he returned with three beers and Ashe's sandwich.

"We are going to have so much fucking fun going forward, and I finally got to see your naked tits," he declared with glee.

Ashe laughed. "And I got to see your cocks. We might not get any more schoolwork done 'cause we'll be fucking."

They tipped their beers together.

"Cheers to fucking," Ashe stated.

"Cheers to all the fucking," Anders agreed.

"Cheers to tasting each other's cum." He paused. "But not yours Anders, I'll leave that to Ashe."

"I'm in!" Ashe said with exuberance.

They enjoyed each other's company and made a date for the evening to meet in Dan's bed, and Ashe was to bring every toy she owned.

The End

On the Farm, The Farm Hand, the Pastor, and the Baker

Gastone heaved the forty pounds of compost from the back of his truck to the little shelter where patrons could purchase the rich soil for their gardens. He was worn out after a full morning of unloading the bags from the big semi to his truck. This was one of the products they sold that they didn't actually produce themselves on the farm. The compost soil, the eggs from the Amish farm, and the canned goodies like salsa and spaghetti sauce that the old woman Martha cooked down the street. She'd give them canned goods to sell, and she'd make a profit, which was much needed for her. The small organic farm had been in Gastone's family for several generations, and he was the youngest one involved with it. The only reason they made money was because they sold to the public and their produce was a novelty, being a small farm in the world of big grocery stores and big mass production farms. It was a flash of the past that many glommed onto, and they profited as a result. Local people liked buying from them because they were family run, the food was organic and fresh, and they loved the atmosphere because they also had a petting zoo of sorts with goats, sheep, chickens, and a few cows.

There weren't many farms like them around, so the local neighborhoods would flock to them and buy produce they grew that was way overpriced, but no one cared. Everyone loved coming to the farm for fun with their families, then taking home fresh, beautiful fruits and veggies. They kept expanding and hired a woman named Olga to help them cook food and freeze it. Olga worked in the farmhouse every day, cooking foods and freezing them to fill the deep freeze inside the small store at the center of the farm. No one lived in the farmhouse anymore; it served as headquarters for the farm, and housed the offices for his aunts, uncles, and parents. He was the workhorse of the farm, along with all of his cousins.

Olga was Gastone's dream of a woman. Big juicy tits that bounced when she laughed, the laughter always reaching her eyes, and sparks of delight that would radiate out of her, making her even more appealing to Gastone than just her appearance alone. How a woman could be so jovial, kind, and sexy at once flabbergasted Gastone. Olga was one of those women that men instantly liked, and many women instantly disliked. Perhaps she was too pretty and kind, and they compared themselves to her, knowing they'd never come as close to amazing as Olga Sventgarten did. She was like a fantasy Gastone had dreamt up in bed late at night when his hormones told him the only existence that mattered other than breathing was to masturbate. Sleep was not a thing, but he always knew he'd conk out after he rubbed one out to thoughts of Olga.

Olga also had cock sucking lips, which drove Gastone wild every time he talked to her. She might as well of been sucking his cock while she was talking to him for how much joy he got out of watching the woman speak. She could say anything to him, and he was transfixed, as if caught in a magic spell. He'd surely happily endure listening to her tell stories for an entire morning, which was pretty long to Gastone, who didn't like to sit still. He was a mover and doer, always working on something.

Today on the farm he had to stock the compost bags, which no one else ever wanted to do, so he always volunteered because hefting forty-pound bags was as good as lifting at the gym any day, so it meant his evening would be free because he'd be getting his workout done in the workday. Once he was done with that, he would need to tend to the animals, and then he was to help his girl cousins pick the ripe strawberries. Picking the berries at peak ripeness was always a challenge because they all came ripe at the same time and needed to be picked quickly before they rotted on the vines. The strawberries were one of the biggest money makers of the farm, however, so no one ever complained much.

Gastone hoped he'd get to bring in the batches of berries that were to go to Olga, so he could ogle her body as she'd most likely try to talk his ear off in the five minutes he'd be in the kitchen with her. He needed to ask her out, and today seemed like the perfect day to do it.

As Gastone reached the section of the farm with the strawberry fields, he spied the local teen boys hiding in the woods. He totally understood why they did, because if his dad or uncles caught the young boys watching his cousins pick strawberries, they'd yell at them and shoo them away. Gastone knew his cousins were spank meat for many. They were all very sexy, buxom women, but it was also known across the younger generation that if any of these horny dudes pestered his cousins, Gastone would beat them to an unrecognizable pulp. No one messed with Gastone. He was the most built guy locally, and yet he still couldn't hold on to a girlfriend. He had high hopes for Olga, though.

The main roadblock had been that Olga was twenty, and now that he was eighteen, he felt he could actually consider dating her. Before that, his years her junior had him holding back from coming on to her. But he'd turned eighteen a month ago, and since then he'd been building himself up, getting ready to ask her on a date. The big man wasn't afraid of women, but Olga was so special that he'd get tongue-tied around her and turn into a stupid orc right under her gaze. One time, he even fell silent and simply stared at her. She was so kind and made up for his muteness in the conversation by talking about all the pies and sauces she was making for the day.

Gastone snagged a box and chose a row of strawberries far away from his cousins. He needed to be alone with his thoughts so he could think about how to ask Olga to go out to dinner with him. He figured he wouldn't be able to even eat as he watched her beautiful face reacting to the good food, but that was reminiscent of perhaps what she'd look like when she orgasmed, so he was already obsessed with thoughts of watching her eat.

It wasn't long before his box was full and when he reached the wagon, the women were filling up. He saw it was full already.

"I'll take this load to the house," he hollered towards them with a wave.

"Say 'hi' to Olga," his cousin Macy snickered in a teasing voice.

They all knew Gastone was infatuated with Olga, and they'd tease him relentlessly. But little did they know he was going to win Olga and they'd be boyfriend and girlfriend before the month was out, if Gastone had anything to say about it.

"Have fun with Olga," his cousin Sara shouted in a sassy tone. Then all his cousins giggled.

Gastone ignored them as he pulled the wagon full of strawberries, which was heavier than one would expect, so even if he hadn't wanted to bring the berries to Olga, his cousins would have insisted he do it, anyway. So their teasing was unfounded, and just a way for them to goad him. He didn't care what they said because seeing Olga, even if only for a short time, was exactly what he wanted. He knew even a minor glimpse of the goddess would be fabulous jerking material later tonight in his room.

He approached the house, rehearsing his lines to ask her out in his head. His heart was pounding like thunder, and he writhed in his wet shirt. The extra sweat from being nervous joined his work sweat and he was worried he might stink. That would not help his chances with Olga. But with her kind heart, he figured she'd be polite, and he'd never even know if his stench turned her off.

He rounded the corner of the house, and before he even took the first step up the porch stairs, Olga bounded out of the front door. Her tits looked extra full in her tank top, and her tummy looked perfect for grabbing onto and ramming her doggy from behind. He felt his cock fill and wanted to glance down to see if his erection was visible. He shifted uncomfortably as she strode closer. It was too late. She'd likely already seen the bulge form in his work shorts. All he could do was smile and suffer through the throbbing of his cock.

"Hi," she squealed as she bounced down the steps. Her blue eyes were lit with passion and excitement. "Yay yay! You've brought me the berries! I can't wait to get started. I have so many plans!"

He loved her enthusiasm to create something she herself wasn't even going to eat. She was a culinary genius as far as he was concerned, which also made her the most appealing woman in the world to him. Sexy, kind, she could cook, and she was full of zest. But he couldn't stop imagining her O face and all he wanted to do was make her feel the most pleasure possible on the planet. Did he want to fuck her? Oh, hell yes, he did, but more so, he wanted to make her come.

"Hi, Olga. I have a load of berries for you. It's a bumper crop this year, and the girls haven't even picked a quarter of the field yet."

She didn't stand back and let him do all the work. She snatched up a box of strawberries and her eyes went big. "These are beautiful! I've never seen such gorgeous berries in my life!"

Her excitement was contagious, and he felt his heart sliding into her exuberance. "Yeah, whatever you make will sell like fire in winter."

His grandma had always said that. In a few ways, Olga reminded him of her. But he shoved that out of his brain quickly. He wanted to think about Olga, and Olga only.

"Let me carry them in for you," Gastone insisted as he ran a hand through his hair. He cringed when he felt how sweaty his scalp was. He secured two boxes of berries in his arms and hiked them into the house.

Olga had everything laid out, ready to make pies, cakes, and strawberry rhubarb sauce. She had the mixer set up: pans, bowls, utensils, and a rolling pin. She had flour, sugar, brown sugar, and the brown eggs he'd help collect yesterday when his little sister Sally had been at the farm to help collect eggs.

"Wow, you are all set up."

Olga nodded and her ponytail bobbed, her curls rising and falling swiftly. "Oh, yes. It will be a full day of baking and I'm so ready." She placed her box of berries on the table. "I'm going to use your grandma's recipes, plus my grandma's recipe for strawberry pie."

She seemed to really love her work, and this made Gastone smile. She'd grown up in a poor family across town, and college hadn't been in her cards, so to get hired by Gastone's family business had been a huge win for her. They paid her well, and her continual smiles told him that she was happy. He wanted to add to that happiness as much as humanly possible.

"I'll get the rest; you can get started. I don't want to hinder your workload then." He nodded as she scanned the room.

"Yup, it will be a day!"

Gastone left the house for another load and pastor Jeff got out of his car. He was a recently widowed man who had been coming to the farm to buy Olga's food regularly, almost daily. The man was in his early fifties with grayed temples, clear direct eyes, and a pleasant enough demeanor to not offend Gastone by his presence. But when Jeff started for the stairs of the house rather than for the store, his eyes narrowed. He was coming to see Olga?

Immediately, the hairs prickled on the back of his neck. Jeff coming this way threatened his ability to ask Olga out and he regretted not speaking up to the beauty already.

Jeff nodded at Gastone, an easygoing grin plastered across his face as he approached. "Gastone, good morning to you."

Gastone nodded and gave a curt, "Good morning." It was practically lunch, but Gastone wasn't splitting hairs over that.

"Olga around? I wanted to see what she's baking up today so I can plan my dessert for after dinner."

Gastone found it odd that Jeff would approach the house. Most patrons followed the unspoken rules and stayed away from it, but Jeff boldly walked past and started up the porch steps.

"She's here, yes," he said coolly as he quickly snatched up three boxes of strawberries.

As Jeff entered the house, Gastone fumbled with the three boxes and one fell, the berries all tumbling out. He quickly scrambled to set the other two boxes down and gently scooped up the delicate fruit. He decided two boxes a trip was the way to go with how fragile the berries were. Some had already gotten bruised from the fall, so he'd have to tell her to use them for some sort of pie or something where their perfection wasn't needed. The next batch of berries would go to the farm store to be sold fresh, so this might be his only legitimate chance to be around Olga, and now Jeff was there ruining his plan.

He entered the house and found it was empty. Olga was gone, and so was Jeff. He set down the fruit and looked around the main floor for them. They weren't anywhere to be seen. Shaking his head and fuming at his lost chance, he passed by the stairway that went up to the bedrooms. He heard a loud moan that was most definitely female. She sounded distraught, so he ran up the stairs, worried it might be Olga having some trouble.

The sounds got louder as he walked down the hallway of bedrooms. The doors were all open, but the one further down the hall, which had been his grandparents' master bedroom when they'd lived in the house. He dashed quickly, his heart beating like a freight train and his anger boosting to red alarm status over his worry for Olga's safety. How dare Jeff be doing this to Olga? And was he this stupid to be doing it, knowing that Gastone had just been at the door of the house? What kind of idiot attacked a poor defenseless woman when a big, strong man like Gastone was within yelling distance?

His anger seethed as he flung the door open, his hands at the ready to grab pastor Jeff by the neck and hurl his assaulting ass right out the second-floor window. He'd do it too. Olga didn't deserve this!

Once the door moved enough for him to see inside, he stopped cold. His heart crashed to the floor and a gasp stole his ability to speak. There was Olga, fully naked, her tits hanging like bulbs of succulent fruit, Jeff had a hold of her ponytail, so her head was upturned, her pretty mouth open wide as moans pelted out. Jeff was smacking his pelvis against her ass, making her buttocks jiggle and her whole body launch off his thrust, then get corralled back by his hair tug. His face was beast-like as he growled, slamming himself into her on repeat.

The scene was jarring. He stared as Jeff aggressively fucked the woman Gastone was about to ask out to an innocent dinner and a movie date. The pair kept moaning and releasing their pleasures into the air with moans, grunts, and sighs.

Jeff turned his head and exclaimed, "Oh, shit! Olga, you didn't lock the door!"

Gastone stood there, astounded, as his previously considered reserved pastor had his fat dick inside his woman's pussy. He wanted to pummel Jeff. Rip his cock out of Olga and carry her out of the room.

"Oh, Gastone!" Olga shouted as Jeff pounded himself into her once more.

The dude didn't even have the decency to stop thrusting into her with Gastone in the room.

"Holy fuck," Gastone muttered, finally able to speak. His thick muscles still flexed at the ready to rescue Olga from this lust-filled beast at a moment's notice.

However, Jeff was making Olga do the pleasure-filled expressions he longed to give her. Dumbfounded, he stood there in full horror as they just kept having sex as if Gastone weren't even there.

Olga's pretty face melted into what Gastone imagined must be a big O face as her body began to curl, her eyelids fluttered, and her sounds exalted to the ceiling sublime. Her body shuddered and Jeff began to crumple against her backside, his head falling back as a giant groan pelted out of his mouth.

"Hurry over, Gastone," Olga pleaded, her eyes looking sane again. "Give me your cock, I want to suck it. Please, Gastone. Please," she begged.

The look in her eyes was so wanton, all he desired to do was please her. He rushed into the room, his anger transforming to lust at finding out she wanted his cock too. He quickly unzipped his pants and slid his cock out. It was fully packed and straight as a steel rod, bobbing slightly up and down as he rushed towards Olga and Jeff.

"Yesssss," Olga slurred. "Hurry, I'm about to come again and I want your cock in my mouth when I do."

Who was he to resist this? The very thing he dreamt about daily was being requested by his ultimate woman. Granted, his fantasies never included his pastor fucking her at the same time, but his lust overpowered his gauge of righteousness, and he welcomed the feelings of not giving a fuck.

He neared her eager face, her gaze salacious and determined.

"Give it to me," she demanded.

He made himself available to her by pressing his thighs to the edge of the bed, which was still pretty pristinely made despite their action on top of it.

She reached for him, and the top half of her body crashed down onto the mattress. Now in head down, ass up formation, she snatched his cock and popped her mouth on his meaty head. She began to ride his cock with her mouth as Jeff continued to pummel her body.

Gastone was amazed a man of his age could fuck like this. Not that he was a senior citizen, but he was middle-aged and not in the shape of Gastone by any means. But he was steadily ramming himself into her, his fingers deeply depressed into her generous hips.

Gastone felt his climax rise and he knew he'd come imminently when watching Olga suck his cock, seeing her face blossom in ecstasy, and her generous tits rocking back and forth from the poundings. The skin-smack sounds filled the room in addition to all their moans. This was better than any porn video Gastone had seen and not at all the way he expected his first time with Olga would go. But he had to admit he was unexpectedly enjoying himself.

Olga hummed with his cock in her mouth and Gastone lost control. Hot cum erupted from his cock tip, filling her mouth. She gagged and then swallowed, her body jerking in a series of twitches. Her sounds went silent, then she shrieked, "Oh fuck."

Jeff released a big grunt, then his torso gyrated above Olga's backside.

Her breathing was quite labored as her face rested down on the bedspread his grandmother had made. She looked so lovely and spent, all he wanted to do was cradle her until she recovered, then fuck her into that delicious expression once again.

"Oh, my Gawd," she whispered between gasps. "That was the most intense of my life."

Gastone felt a surge of pride that he'd been a part of what she'd call that.

Jeff caught Gastone in an eye lock. "Let's switch. If she's fucked in this state, she'll keep coming. We can give her so much pleasure."

Gastone hesitated as he assessed this middle-aged man from whom he'd listened to so many messages at church. He knew the man was single, but to be fucking a woman half his age? Instead of figuring all this shit out, Gastone acted. He scurried to position himself behind Olga and stared down at her appealing round ass, her tight waist, and the bulging of her tits visible from beneath her biceps.

"Please, fuck me Gastone," she said in a sweet yet insistent voice.

He desperately wanted to give her what she wanted, and she wanted his cock. So, that's what she'd get.

If pastor Jeff could do this, he sure as fuck could do it too.

Jeff nodded at him as he lined up his cock at her entrance. "She likes it strong, and make sure you play with her clit." His lips shifted into a smile.

Gastone's emotions ran from shock to apprehension. He nodded back, not sure if he should call him sir or Jeff, then opted for saying nothing. He rubbed his cock along her closed lower lips, his dreams hitting reality as he lightly pressed a finger between her swollen labia. He continued to move his cock around her, settling on tapping his firm cockhead against where he hoped her clit was located.

She moaned then spilled, "Yes, Gastone."

It was his fantasy coming to life to hear her say his name in that heavenly tone. Gastone's brain was moving slowly as he finally hit the realization that

Jeff had already climaxed, but his erection was still strong as Olga took him into her precious mouth.

Gastone slid his cock back to match up to her sweet spot and, reaching, he played his fingers along her clit. He pressed himself into her as he toyed with her bean.

Both of them moaned. Olga's sounded muffled with Jeff's cock inside her orifice.

The men connected their line of sight as they began to fully penetrate Olga at both ends. Her sounds of pleasure made Gastone want to come again already. He blissfully rode her body, his passion raging as his cock sliced in and out of her tight, slippery hole. He could no longer see her face, but her sounds were surprisingly more satiating than he'd have thought possible. They both pounded into her as she seemed to melt between them. Her body torqued again, her vaginal muscles clamped down on his cock, almost pushing him to feel as if he were going crazy. He tried desperately to not come, barely succeeding as he slowed his thrusts a little. Then he pulled himself out for a flash of a break of her ecstatic cunt.

She fell off Jeff's cock with a series of excited sounds, followed by a silence. She looked overwhelmed, as undone as Gastone felt he was about to be himself as he pressed his hard shaft back into her.

She bemoaned with pleasure, her sighs as perfect as he'd ever hoped to hear from the mouth of a female. He felt instantly lucky, though the shock still left him feeling a bit slow mentally. But he was in the moment as much as they were.

Cum spurted from Jeff's cock, landing in splatters on Olga's face and hair.

She cooed softly as Gastone ramped up his fucking of her. He wanted to fuck her into another orgasm before this amazing reverie came to an end.

He kept riding her to the wonderful music of her joyful sounds, and Jeff positioned himself beside her. He reached under her and smacked at her clit.

Her body recoiled at each smack, and she screamed as Gastone chased his orgasm by slamming into her. Her walls began to clench on him as she climaxed with a howl.

Gastone felt his peak consume him and before he spewed, he pulled his cock out just in time as his hot seed was shot across her hair, back, and ass.

The three of them remained still as if in shock as their heavy breathing sounds filled the air.

As the action settled, the full reality of what they'd just done hit Gastone like a ton of bricks. Olga settled her body on the bed next to Jeff, and Gastone folded onto the mattress next to Olga.

"Wow," she whispered in happy disbelief. "That was the most incredible sex of my life."

Gastone wondered how much sex she'd had to make such a comment, but he didn't care. He was just so happy to have been flung into this scenario that he felt like singing and dancing like a damned fool.

"No kidding. That was like my fantasies come to life." Gastone grinned with humility. "And to think I was just going to ask you out on a date." He laughed at himself, both in shock at having the guts to say it and for being in this ridiculous situation. It was both shocking and magnificent at once.

She turned her face towards him and smiled. "Yes," she said with a happy twinkle blazing in her eyes. "I'd love to."

Gastone immediately wondered what that meant. Would Jeff come too? Were they a thing? Or just fuck buddies? But since neither Jeff nor Olga addressed it, Gastone left it alone. He'd gotten a 'yes' to his request, and that's all that mattered.

"Well, I'd love to lay here and bask in all this sexy air, but I'd better get baking. I have loads to do." She popped up as if the short rest had totally revitalized her. "How about 6 p.m.?"

Gastone nodded eagerly and stood up, slipping his still-hard cock back into his pants.

"Maybe we can use that again later," she said with a wink before she grabbed her clothes and slipped out of the room.

Jeff began to dress without a word. But he too looked very happy. "Nice to see you, Gastone." He gave him a knowing grin and a nod, and he too left the room.

Gastone glanced around his grandparents' room and imagined its walls had never seen such action, but he also wondered what else Olga and Jeff had done together. And all he wanted was to be a part of it each time going forward.

After a few numb moments where he relived what had just happened with a stupid grin on his face, he made his way down the stairs.

As he passed by the kitchen, Olga looked the same as she always did. She was cheerful and upbeat as always, fresh-faced and pleasant. "See you tonight," she said as she went back to cutting up strawberries.

"Yes, I can't wait," he said with a giddy expression.

He carried the rest of the berries in and made his way back to the strawberry fields with plans to bring the next freshly picked load to the store. His life had changed in mere minutes, but nothing could top the fact that she'd said 'yes' to a date.

The End

Backroom Three

Jenna pulled her black leggings up and threw on an old grey t-shirt over her skimpy tank top. She had to work and didn't feel like moving. Instead, she wanted to sleep and get caught up a little on lost sleep. She'd been up studying late into the night the past three nights, and it was hitting her. Going back to college at thirty-one wasn't nearly as easy as many made it out to be. She splashed water on her face, skipped makeup, except for a dusting of powder, and dashed out the door.

Her car needed a bath, she needed a shower, and the sun was beating down on her hot which meant the kitchen was going to be an inferno. She used to love cooking until she became a cook. Now, at work she did home cooking, and at home, she did microwave cooking. The job had choked the love of cooking out of her. At one point, she'd considered culinary school, that's why she got the job at the diner where home cooking was the norm and everything was made from scratch. But slaving away making homemade meals for others fifty hours a week had strangled the life out of that desire. Her current focus was nursing. She'd be done in a year and half and find a job easily because there was a shortage of nurses.

Life wasn't supposed to turn out this way. She was supposed to be done with college, settled into her career, married, and with one baby. That had been her plan, but life had a funny way of directing her different ways. Her path was surely different than her friends, whom she'd been in five of their weddings over the past few years.

She pulled into the parking lot and saw Mike's car. He'd taken the front spot which meant he was the first of the crew to arrive. Starting work at 6 a.m. over a hot stove and oily steaming frying pans always made her nauseous. Perhaps if she'd eaten that wouldn't have been the case, but she wasn't one to break with her traditions, no matter how inadequately they served her. She needed to change that.

She strode into the back door of the restaurant and waved at Manny, who was already peeling potatoes. That man could peel a potato faster than anyone she'd ever met. He always gave her looks like he wanted to flip her around, bend her over the sink, and fuck her until he came up her sweet hot pussy. He'd actually grabbed her butt a few times, to which she politely had said 'no thank you'. He was in his mid-fifties, but that wasn't the turnoff, it was more that he had a mouthful of teeth that looked as if someone had punched him in the face a hundred times and left them all askew. He had kind brown eyes though and almost always was sporting an erection. Mike said it was because he was constantly eyeing her up so his boner would pop. He'd confirmed that when Jenna wasn't at work, Manny had not had an erection. Jenna guessed that nailed it. He just wanted to fuck her. But she had gotten the same impression from Mike.

She threw an apron on over her head and tied it behind her back, securing it tightly across her double D's. She'd wished as a teen she'd grow big boobs, and by the time she'd hit eighteen, it was like her wishes had gone overboard. She'd wished her tits into existence. No one else in her family was as busty as she was so she figured she was either a mutant in the family line, or she had special powers and all her thinking on it translated into blossoming boobs. Either way, she figured they were exactly why Manny always had a hardon for her. He was a known boob man. He'd talk about tits nonstop. Anything and everything from nursing on them to fucking them. He was a true boob perv. Jenna didn't mind hearing the men commiserate about customers tits. They'd rate them and talk about them, peeking out the little circle window into the restaurant. Each waitress had a rating too. Jenna was the only one with a ten though.

She pulled out the ingredients to whip up the pancake batter and had it all but done by the time Mike appeared.

"Where have you been?" she asked only mildly curious.

"I just got head from Jessica," he said proudly.

He certainly looked like a man who had just gotten off.

"Good for you," she said, trying not to roll her eyes. Jessica gave head to everyone, so it wasn't like some special thing.

"It was really good this time, plus, I was watching Sally bent over picking up the spilled napkins, so I came hard and fast." His eyes did this weird googly eyed thing where they seemed like they might spin right out of his head. He thrust his pelvis in the air and hooted. "Good fucking way to start the day. Spewing cum down a throat."

She scoffed and began to pour circles of batter in the frying pan.

"Just would love to do your tits," he whispered in her ear as he pressed his erection to her bottom.

"Didn't you just come?" she accused as she elbowed him off her.

"Yes, but I'm still hard, wanna?" He was the worst at coming on to her, but she never gave in.

"No, now get to work on that new order, I've got number 23 covered." She continued her duty by flipping the large pancakes, then turned to preparing the bacon.

She wondered how she'd landed in a kitchen with two openly perverted dudes. The management would be livid if they knew how much sex talk went on. They never stopped in though, but the staff knew if they came back into the kitchen, more often than not they'd hear about fucking, tits, ass, or some other sexual innuendo. It was like they worked, ate, slept, and breathed sex. Sex horn dogs who never seemed to let up. If they could do two hours without any mention of sex, a sexy customer, or wanting to fuck someone, Jenna would be shocked. And all this didn't help Jenna when she hadn't had sex in six months. But she was not about to stoop down to fucking either of those two. No way. She'd wait for a date, if she ever had time to date.

How was she supposed to find an awesome man when she spent all her time either working with these nymphos or studying. She literally had no time, or money, to spend on finding a decent man.

She blew out an exasperated puff of air as she scanned the skinny window out into the main dining room. She placed the finished plate on the shelf and hit the bell. Misty appeared with a grin and swiped the plate away without a single word. She was sexy, but Jenna knew she was dating someone. If there was anyone in the diner she wanted to fuck, it was Misty. She had long red hair and a tight little butt, and perky small breasts.

Jenna went back to the grind and got started on the next order. Mike grabbed her hips from behind and humped her.

"Mike, get outta here," she spat angrily, though him doing it had aroused her to the point she was almost ready to take him up on his cheesy come ons. She just needed to fuck and any ol' dick would do. She had her dildos and clit suckers at home, which she used every day before bed, but there was something hot about being thrust into where she wasn't doing the thrusting. She sent him a look she instantly regretted.

"Oh, what was that look I just saw?" he teased. "That looked kinda randy. Do it again?" he taunted as he gyrated his pelvis. "My moves get you going? You want some cocky cock up you, do you?"

He danced around the kitchen humping the air and hooting obnoxiously. "I can get Manny and we can spit roast you."

Over her dead body. She deadpanned at him, and he skedaddled off to the walk-in pantry with a series of snickers.

The sad truth was she was getting desperate, but she certainly didn't think she was that desperate.

The rest of the day wore on and she got hotter and hotter by the minute. By 1 p.m., it was so hot in the kitchen she figured either the air conditioning was broken, or the heat outside had hit the 105 degrees that had been forecasted. She stripped off her grey shirt and twisted her face into a painful grimace. She'd forgotten she was wearing the tank top that was so loose on the arms that her bra showed for half the cup over each breast. She shrugged and decided she'd rather be cool than modest.

She compiled a BLT and slipped it into the window. Misty came again and whisked it away with a grin. It was always much cooler in the dining room than the kitchen and Jenna once again wondered why she hadn't applied to be a waitress rather than the cook.

"You forgot the rest of your tank top," Mike teased.

At that, Manny bounded out of the back room of the kitchen and ogled her.

"Nice shirt, Jenna. I like it very much." His messed up toothy grin was as vulgar as his gaze upon her. He stared at her with a gaping mouth and she expected to see drool trickling out of his mouth, but instead he kept licking his lips. Once he'd asked to suck her tits and she'd beaned him over the head with a big flour filled spoon, which had dusted his dark hair in white, making it even more salt and pepper than his natural. He'd brushed his hair but it remained whitish the rest of the day.

Bad memories were her go to and she wanted it to stop. Her mood was shit and she couldn't break free.

"You look like you ate a shit sandwich," Misty said the next time she came to pick up a plate. "You doing okay, love?"

Jenna nodded but she knew her eyes were telling Misty otherwise. "Rough week. I need a break," she muttered and added a pickle to the plate.

"I think what you need is an orgasm," she said with a wink.

"Oh, I make sure I get that daily." This made her smile. Hearing sexy talk from a sexy woman was much hotter than from the two pervs she was stuck with in the kitchen.

"No, I mean from a dick," she said smartly. Her eyes twinkled. "Always helps me."

And then she was gone.

Jenna gritted her teeth and started on the next order. The heat was making the diner busy, apparently no one wanted to cook in the heat so they'd been busy all day. Which was good because the day was flying by.

A song came on that she liked, and she danced a bit to it, making her big tits chug up and down her chest. The song helped to lighten her mood as she flipped a couple of burgers. Misty's words rang around in her head. Maybe she did just need a cock in her making her come. This would be nice not to be the one making it happen for once. But if she ever gave in to Manny and Mike and let them fuck her, she'd never be safe. They'd pester her to fuck every day going forward, and she wasn't sure she wanted to escalate their advances. She'd never snitch on them. They weren't bad people, and she doubted they'd ever do anything without full consent. She didn't want to get them fired, despite their incessant sex talk. It hadn't bothered her enough to ever turn them in. She understood horniness, it was her norm too.

Mike flitted by with several bags of rice. He was restocking the shelves from a delivery that had just arrived. He was acting manager for the day since Lauren was still out sick. He loved these days because he liked being in charge. Jenna just wanted to get her work done and get the fuck outta there. She had two hours left and it was going by fast, thankfully.

The feeling of Mike humping her backside was haunting her though. She cringed as her arousal started to ramp up. No way in hell was she getting aroused by that creep. Well, that was a bit harsh, he was a nice guy. He'd likely gotten head this am because he'd promised Jessica she could leave early and she had known he was acting manager. She was always using her love of blow jobs to get advantages. Every man who worked there had benefited from that on more than one occasion.

She slaved away for another half hour, her arousal seething. She'd always been horniest in the afternoons and her libido was flaring like a red alert beacon. It was more intense than usual and she bit her lip as she watched Mike carrying the fifty pound bags of potatoes. He wasn't an ugly man. He was quite hot with thick muscles and full lips. If he weren't so obnoxious all the time, she'd take him up on his offers to take her out for pizza and beer. But he always inevitably ruined her tiny steps into giving in to his advances by making some stupid or crude comment.

So why was it that she couldn't get his humping her behind out of her brain? She wasn't usually such a weak ass.

"It's hot in here," she complained when Mike carried two huge bags of flour in.

His thick biceps were flexed as she hefted the big bags onto the shelf. "So take off your shirt and cook topless," he said with a snicker.

And like Manny had giant elephant ears allowing him to hear everything ever muttered in the kitchen, he said, "Do it and I'll make you a very happy woman. I can do it, you know."

She didn't need to see him, she could hear his leering grin in his tone. She shuddered imagining his crooked toothed mouth suckling her bare tits. She pressed her lips together as she tried to squash her arousal from heightening. Nope. She couldn't do it. It would create a disaster situation going forward. No matter how turned on she was, she couldn't give in and let them fuck her. They'd become even more incessant with the sex talk, she just knew it. It would be a mistake of epic proportions. She'd have to quit and find a new job it would get so bad.

But...her clit disobeyed her logic and began to thicken inside her. She shook her head and yelled inside her head, chastising herself for even entertaining the idea of fucking these two horn dog degenerates.

She made two more orders and then there was a lull in orders. She could breathe for a moment. She was hungry too, and not having gotten a lunch break, she was ready to eat two burgers and a whole plate of fries. This wasn't helping her lust. Whenever she was hungry and aroused, she got aggressive. Her ex had always tried to get her to this state because he loved how wild she got in bed. The hunger and the lust combined made her a sexual beast and she acknowledged it. She was charging into dangerous territory and she knew she'd better eat quick before she did something she'd regret forever.

She started to prep a burger for herself but needed to snag some more buns. Mike had been stocking for hours, but he hadn't restocked the kitchen with hamburger buns. She left her patty on the counter and sauntered back to the pantry to look for more buns. When she rounded the corner, she saw a figure bobbing up and down in the corner of the pantry. Upon closer inspection, it was Manny. She tilted her head at him wondering what the hell he could be doing moving that way.

He grunted and she gasped, her hand flying over her mouth. He was jerking off!

He stopped his movement and spun around quickly. His erection was at full mast and curved up towards the ceiling.

"Oh, my Gawd," she exclaimed.

He smiled at her and shrugged. "I get extra horny in the afternoons, and seeing you in that tank top all askew has been driving me wild all day long." He stroked his cock right in front of her without any trace of embarrassment or apology. "You are sexy as fuck, and I'm a weak man."

His cock bobbed as he moved slightly and her desire for cock skyrocketed. Here was this man with a hard dick masturbating to having watched her all day, and she was also horny as fuck. Despite her distaste for Manny, her nipples hardened.

"Oh, fuck. Look at those nipples," he said as he beat his meat. "Thank you. This is going to be an extra good one."

She glanced down at her chest, helpless to the evidence of her true state of arousal given away her very erect nipples.

Manny chugged away at his cock and the wet sounds of him beating off pushed her over the edge.

"Wait," she exclaimed. "Don't come yet." With shaking hands, she grasped the hem of her tank top and flung it off. She tossed it to the shelf, and it landed on the cans of stewed tomatoes.

Manny groaned. "Oh, Gawd, yes," he slurred still beating his cock.

"Stop," she said with a raised hand. She undid her bra clasp and hurled it onto the shelf with the pasta boxes, which made her very huge breasts swing in pendulous sways back and forth.

"Holy fuck," Mike said from behind her.

She swiveled, which made her big boobs jiggle. She always felt like a stripper when she was naked with how big her boobs were, anyone seeing her naked was always stunned, much the way men in such establishments always appeared, wide eyed and amazed, as if hypnotized by the sight of ginormous knockers.

"Oh, you are just as beautiful as I imagined you'd be," Mike's eyes were taking her naked top half in as a lecherous expression spread across his face.

She remained frozen in place to the sound of Manny still stroking his fat wet meat, the origin of the wet skin on skin sounds were unmistakable. He'd moved closer so she could see him and his chugging hand out of the corner of her eye.

She had two choices. Grab her clothes and run for the bathroom or tell them to fuck her already.

Her heart pounded and no one moved, the only sounds in the room were distant sounds from the dining room and juicy precum being spread over Manny's large cock.

She fell slack as she realized she'd already chosen in her heart, but her brain was the one holding out.

Mike took one step towards her, his eyes full of so much lust that it ticked her over the edge.

"Fuck me, just fuck me already. Both of you, fuck me." Her voice sounded so desperate she wondered how she was allowing them to see how depraved for sex she was. "I need cock. Please. Will you?"

Manny gasped deeply and his stroking his cock sounds halted.

Mike's eyes grew even more wild with lust. "Oh, Jenna. With extreme pleasure. You have no idea how much we talked about doing this with you. You are the sexiest one in this whole damn diner."

His words sank in and she knew they could just have sex for the sake of sex, and it would likely just be a scratching of a mutual itch. She threw caution to the wind and nodded. "Yes, I want you guys to fuck me. I need cock in me. Make me come." Her desperation was evident, and it clearly turned them both on because they both had their hands on her instantly.

Manny pressed his thick dick to her backside, his hands roughly groping her tits from behind as he pressed his face into her hair.

Mike grabbed her face and came at her with his mouth open. They fell into a deep French kiss, his tongue delving deep into her mouth. He pressed his erection to her belly and thrust it against her. She tangled her hands into his hair as Manny pinched and pulled her nipples.

She moaned a sigh that not only sounded but felt primal as she sank into the feelings of their two bodies against hers. Mike ran his hands from her head down her cleavage and to her tummy as they continued to kiss. He gripped her hips next and pushed her backwards towards the more private area at the back of the pantry.

Jenna knew this would have to be a quickie because another order was likely imminent and with an empty kitchen where all three of them were missing would prompt one of the waitresses to come looking.

"We will have to be fast," Mike said sternly.

She nodded as Manny fondled her butt then humped her ass.

Mike grabbed both her tits and shoved her right one into his mouth. He sucked and nibbled, then pulled her tit to the back of his throat to deepthroat her nipple while playing with her other breast.

Manny hooked his fingers into the waistband of her shorts and tugged them down. He ground his cock against her bare ass cheeks as Mike continued his devouring of her tits. Mike suddenly grabbed her shoulders and spun her around, her big boobies getting flung into Manny's face.

His eyes lit up like the sun and he slammed his face into her breast and motorboated her. She'd have laughed at his enthusiasm if Mike hadn't been stimulating her clit, but she was halfway to an orgasm with his rubbing when Manny took her left nipple into his crazy toothed mouth. He clamped down and moaned louder than any man she'd ever had on her tits. His face looked as if he were in heaven as he loved them up.

Mike grunted. "Harder?"

She nodded, too overwhelmed to speak.

Mike bent her over while Manny still struggled to keep her tits in his mouth. Mike spanked her clit from behind, the slaps filling the pantry along with Manny's suckling sounds. Despite all her misgivings, they were giving her so much pleasure, she felt herself climbing up her arousal hill quickly. She was going to come, and it was going to take her.

Mike inserted his fingers into her wet pussy and finger fucked her more aggressively than any man had ever in her life.

She yelled out as Mike clamped his hand over her mouth. He smacked her clit in a series of fast slaps with Manny still sucking and biting her nipples, she burst into her climax. Her body curled around Manny and her tit slipped out of his mouth, but the other one remained between his fingers, and he tugged her tit hard.

She gasped and sputtered as the orgasm traveled out of her pussy and caused her body to shake. Mike quickly brushed his cock head along her slit and penetrated her while she was still riding her orgasm.

Manny stood up, held her by her ears and swung his cock in her face by swiveling his hips. She snatched his dick and slid her mouth over his cock head. She began to suck as his moans grew louder than hers.

Mike began to pound himself into her warm wet hole, the skin smacking sounds of their bodies colliding filled the little pantry. Despite not having more clit stimulation, she rounded the corner of another orgasm, being that she'd not even come fully down off the last one.

Manny manipulated both her nips with his fingers as she sucked his cock. She forced herself to slide down his shaft and she gagged. His body lurched against her and his cum exploded inside her mouth. She gagged again as she tried to swallow, but most of it seemed to leak out the sides of her mouth.

Her orgasm launched and the contractions started. She fell off Manny's cock and her face fell against his pelvis. He held her head gently to him. Her pussy walls clamped down on Mike's cock as she came again. Mike released a deep groan. He pumped two more times, then pulled out, spewing cum in splatters across her bare back.

The three of them remained still, as if stunned. All three of them were panting. It felt surreal to Jenna. The very thing she never wanted to do, she'd just done out of extreme horniness. Would anything ever be the same again?

She seriously doubted it. She'd given in and it would be forever across their faces.

But ... it had also been good. Really good. Good, better than good. It had been great! Spectacular! She'd gotten cock and she'd come twice.

"Holy shit," she whispered. "We just did that."

Manny gripped her shoulders and raised her body, a huge grin plastered across his face. "Yes. Yes, we did. And it was incredible, Jenna."

Mike sighed again and she heard him zip up his pants. "That was the best sex ever."

She turned to look Mike in the eyes. "How will I ever look at you guys again." Her voice sounded a bit sad.

Mike shook his head in a single nod as a smile crept across his face. "You won't, but don't worry, we won't expect that. But anytime you want to indulge again, just ask. We are both ready. Right, Manny?"

He nodded aggressively and his eyes were so kind. "Anytime. And thank you. But next time, I get your pussy." He chuckled.

Mike laughed. "That was crazy good. My dick is yours anyway, anyhow you want it. Any time."

Jenna tried to hide her smile, but she couldn't. "Well, it might be easier to do now that we've done it once." There was something irresistibly wicked about actually doing something raunchy she'd always said she'd never do. All the repulsive thoughts she'd had about these two still occupied space in her brain, but now so did these good feelings they'd gifted her. She smiled loving how they'd made her climax first before they even chased their own orgasms. That to her was the mark of real men. Her heart softened towards them further. "I'm sure I'd be up for more of that sometime."

Both Manny and Mike's eyes filled with joy at hearing that.

"Music to my ears," Mike said. "I'm always at your service."

"Same," said Manny. "And your tits are off the charts, Jenna. Like better than I've ever seen. I just knew they'd be killer." He couldn't take his eyes off her chest. He looked like he wanted to consume them again.

"I'd better check if there's an order up before someone catches us." Jenna grabbed her bra and Mike snagged the tank top. Once she had the bra on, Mike held it out for her.

"And anytime you want to cook naked ..." he said with a chuckle that grew into a belly laugh.

"Oh, you want me to get fired, do you?" she said, giving him the evil eye above her grin.

"No, hell no," he said. "Just saying anytime."

She secured her tank top over her chest and down her sides before following the men out of the pantry.

She finished her last half hour of work with the biggest grin on her face. She felt exhilarated and energized, even Misty noticed her change in mood.

She sauntered out into the sunshine, her keys in hand. She laughed at herself. She just needed to live a little sometimes. Life might be tough, but an impromptu threesome fuck in the backroom was now Jenna's idea of a fix that was worth doing.

The End

Work Merger, An Interracial: The Doctor, the Nurse, and the Janitor Makes Three

Just What the Doctor Ordered

I glanced at Mitch through the little window that looked out into the hallway. I had the urge to wave, but he wouldn't see me anyhow. I'd been searching for my man all day, but he'd had a busy day with a lot of office visits. Never seeing him all day made me ache all the more for him. We were set for a date this evening, and I couldn't wait. Moreover, I couldn't wait for the sex we had planned. We were going to try some new things we'd bought so I'd laid them out on the dresser before we left for work, though he'd been out to the car already, so he never saw. That's why I'd texted that all the new toys were laid out, ready and waiting for us, and he'd sent me a boner pic from his office between appointments. I loved this man, but we'd only started saying that to each other last month when we moved in together.

He loved my obsession with sex, but that had only come to me in the past few years, pre-Mitch. I'd always loved sex, but the hardcore love of it was relatively new. Mitch had helped with further development of it though, because he'd been open from the get-go. I smiled. Mitch, being five years younger than me, had ended up being a match. I'd never have been so bold as to pursue him, but I was so happy he came after me. We'd worked together for six months before he asked me out. I'd thought all his flirting had been just a way to pass a boring night shift, that is until he had stared me right in the eyes and said, 'I'm fucking serious, Amanda', and that had ticked the box for me. He fucking meant it, and he'd been showing me that was true for the past ten months.

It was cliché. The young doctor dating the slightly older nurse. But it was oh so damn good. There were no words for what our sex was like, other than orgasmic flights to the moon. I was no sap, but he literally took me there. He was a sex nerd himself, which likely was also stemming from his urge to be a doctor. He was arrogant, but in the right way, showing up as being in charge in the bedroom, and having both the skills and the enormous desire to make me cum. I'd come to gladly submit to his strong leadership in the bedroom because it was hot as fuck, and we were having the best sex of my entire life.

I gathered the supplies I needed for the dressing change and hurried to the patient's room. I had only fifteen minutes to get this done before lunch. Right before I slipped into the room, I caught sight of Mitch and waved, our smiles matching as secret naughty spies. The hospital discouraged dating other employees, but what the fuck did they expect? When people were single and around each other, fellow employees are who they meet. It was a ridiculous rule that we ignored. It kind of worked as a taboo kink for us as well, which was quite particularly delicious when we'd sneak in a quickie at the hospital somewhere. I kissed the air towards him, and he caught it and swiped it across his crotch. A daring move, but so like Mitch after all.

I finished with my patient and headed to lunch. I got a text from Mitch: I'm needed tonight. We will have to reschedule our date and the sex. He added a crying emoji.

"Damn," I muttered before grabbing a salad. I paused as I considered my options. Go home alone and masturbate, or pick up a shift and we fuck in Mitch's office during the night when things had quieted down. I grinned as I called staffing to see if they had any open shifts. I took the shift on the spot before grabbing breadsticks and a Coke.

As I sat down alone at the window in the cafeteria, I texted Mitch back: We don't have to reschedule the sex, I just picked up a night shift on 4B. We can fuck in your office again!

He texted back immediately: Genius! Excited! And I love you!

The emotions were real, but us saying them was so new it made me giddy each time I heard him say it.

I texted back: I love you too and I can't wait to fuck your brains out, doctor!

The rest of the shift flew by, and ushering myself right into the next shift was always a painful process. Hopefully, I'd get patients I could easily handle, since I'd not worked the mental health floor much, but I figured these patients would be easy and sleep through the night, so it would be an easy shift with easy money, plus time for a quick fuck. It was ideal! The question was, would Mitch have time?

I settled into my shift. The nurse manager had assigned me the easy, more stable patients, which I was so very grateful for. I hadn't worked in mental health in ages. Their charts showed they were stable, one on the verge of being discharged, but with it being late, it was not going to happen until morning. It would be a cakewalk, easy money, and basically, I was just there babysitting sleeping adults.

I was impatiently waiting for the text from Mitch. The plan was I'd meet him at his office, or a spot he happened to find, which was much harder to do, but we'd done it a few times. I smiled, recalling giving him head in the men's bathroom. Kind of crass and gross, but also hot and legitimately taboo in a hospital. We'd both get fired for sure if we got caught. But the urgency and the need to sneak around had heightened the experience even further for us.

I finished the updates on my patient's charts and then stared at my phone, willing Mitch to text me. "Shit," I muttered. I was horny and I wanted his cock in me. Orgasming at work had been hard at first, but Mitch was so persistent and his drive to make me climax ushered me into a new phase of open sexuality.

Samual, the biggest black man I'd ever seen in my life, and also the friendliest janitor on staff at the hospital, sauntered by.

"Hey Samual, what's up?" I smiled at him, noticing once again how he had the 'ual' underlined on his nametag.

"Hey Amanda, how you doing? This isn't the usual spot I find you."

"Nope, I picked up an extra shift." I swiveled in my chair to face him. His eyes went straight to my chest, as usual. He never hid his appreciation of my tits; it was there like a blatant beacon, unspoken in his difficulty in keeping his eyes on mine. It always made me smile because he never hid his attraction for me. We'd flirted a bit here and there, but we never had progressed to a date. I'd never dated a black man but once when I was a teen, but that had been so short it barely counted. He was extremely sexy, and his easygoing demeanor made him so easy to talk to.

"This is usually a quiet floor at night, unless someone ain't in the right place in their mind. I've seen it."

I wasn't any better than him as my eyes fell down his lanky, muscular body. I jumped, startled, as I noticed the significant lump at his groin. I didn't hide my lewd smile fast enough, and he returned it to me with a chuckle.

"Nighttime gets me going, it's hard to be here," he said in a suave smooth voice with a sexually suggestive loaded gaze aimed right back at me.

"I can imagine that being the case," I said in an equally seductive voice.

He eyed me up. "You ever going to let me take you out on a date? Damn shame you still single." He raised his eyebrows as he cocked his head.

This was a conundrum. I didn't want to insult him, because I'd surely date him in a quick heartbeat, but Mitch and I'd decided we'd keep our relationship a secret from everyone at the hospital. But, I also didn't want Samual to think I wouldn't date him. I was slow to answer as I watched his face.

"Aw, I get it baby, you don't need to say it. It's all good." He smiled a brilliant smile and gave me a wave. "I'll let you be."

"Wait, no, Samual, it's not that." My heart pounded as I fought the urge to tell him I was fucking a doctor already. I sighed. "That's why I'm here tonight; my man got tagged to stay."

"Oh," he said as his eyes widened. "I got you. You fucking a doctor, good for you." His face shifted into a happy place, and I was glad I had let him know it wasn't that I was not attracted to him.

I took a deep breath and decided it was time to make it clear to him. "Cause if I weren't, I'd definitely be interested in a date."

"That so. Huh. I wish I knew which doc, because I know some of them motherfuckers are kinky as fuck, and we could make it a bigger date."

A bigger date? What the fuck did that mean?

He pulled out his phone and tapped into it. He showed me a quick peek at his screen, and I saw the familiar blue icon of Pwitter, which I refused to call X because it was too lame to change an icon like that, it would forever be Pwitter to me. He turned it back around and shoved the screen in my face.

"That's me," he said proudly. The picture was of a headless black man and his @ was bigbullforyou.

I dropped my jaw as my mind started down that dirty path before I took another breath. "You're a bull?"

He nodded with a salacious grin. "And happy to be the cliché. It's true about us." He guffawed aggressively, his laughter making his body gyrate. "I take pride in that cliché, if you know what I mean."

I gasped. He had to mean BBC and instantly I was intrigued. "You are?" I knew I didn't need to spell it out for this man.

"Yup, ten, baby. All ten." He nodded with a libidinous grin that made me want him riding me doggy, commanding me with a ponytail hold and a few spanks, telling me he was in charge and taking on the business of ramming himself against my bouncing ass.

"You guys ever want a third, you DM me. You on Pwitter?"

My jaw dropped as my conversation with Mitch last week flooded my brain. We'd talked about a threesome and he'd said he'd do it, man or woman. He wasn't bi-curious, but he was into pushing me to the next pleasure plateau with two cocks if I wanted it. I'd agreed, but never had thought we'd be at the forefront of such a thing so swiftly.

"If you're speechless now, you'd be even more so if I stepped into your bedroom," he said with a confident chuckle. "I'm almost pro."

I widened my eyes and asked in a whisper, "Porn?"

He nodded. "I'm considering an offer right now. Just need myself an agent, but I'm looking."

The charge of fucking a black man about to go into the adult film business was one of the hottest scenarios I could think of. The only question was, would Mitch be into it and not be intimated by a man with such a magnificent man appendage? The fact that Mitch had brought up a threesome showed he wasn't a bit jealous, but rather confident, which was a total turn-on. I'd had boyfriends in the past who were way too threatened by any kind of swinging because they feared I'd leave them, which meant they just weren't doing what it took to keep me anyway, so they were the fools.

I eyed up Samual as my mind began to creep into the idea of a threesome legit happening. "You'd do it? But you don't even know the doctor."

"Oh, the man don't matter, baby, it's the woman that matters," he grinned, so full of sexy confidence that it melted me and made my clit do a little mini dance in her hood.

"Wow," was all I could mutter out.

"You'd be on the top of my list," he said as he fingered his lips and stared at my breasts. "I've always been dying to see those beauties."

I knew many women who'd report Samual, but his interest just fed my libido. I grinned back. "Well, I could see if he's up for it. We have a tentative date for just that type of thing in his office when we are both free this shift."

He perked up in excitement. "Oh, that so? Well, in that case, put my number in your phone and if you two are down, I'll make it a priority."

My heart pounded and my eyes told Samual 'yes' as I then glanced down at my phone to ensure I had his number right.

"Text me anytime," he said as he strolled down the hallway, looking back once to gift me another interested look.

My breathing quickened as I wondered if I should text this to Mitch. I'd rather talk about it in person with Mitch, if he was available, but I wasn't so sure that was possible.

I texted Mitch: I have an interesting proposition for your office later, but I'd like to talk to you in person about it. You free?

Fifteen agonizing minutes went by before Mitch responded: not possible. Just text me. Love you.

I smiled. He never failed to add in some affection.

I took a deep breath and with shaking hands, I typed: You know Samual the janitor? Well, he's a bull and about to become a porn actor, and he'd be into meeting up. Is this too much too soon? I totally get it if it is. Love you.

My heart thumped like a hunted beast as I waited for his response. I didn't want Mitch to think he didn't turn me on; he turned me on immensely.

A text came back quickly: Think he can be discreet?

I texted back: Yes. And if he's doing that with us, he wouldn't turn us in because he'd be in trouble just the same as us.

Mitch responded: Good point. Let's do it. I'd really love to be a part of that with you. Only problem is we will have to be quiet, and I don't like you holding back sounds.

I texted back: I could do it or you could do it for me.

I laughed when he sent back a shocked face GIF.

He texted again: I get a break in 47 minutes. Tell Samual. Don't be late.

I was filled with excited anticipation as I texted Samual the plan.

Samual texted back with an eggplant and a series of ten black hearts, with the message: All of us will be there. Which room?

I was terrified to give him the room number, so instead I texted: Meet me at the elevators on floor two in the west building and we will walk there together.

He agreed, and my pulse sent explosions of adrenaline all throughout my body. I couldn't believe I was going to get two men, and one who was on the track of gracing the screens with his legendary man meat. I mean, he had to be all that after what he'd said, and I couldn't wait to lay eyes on his monster.

The next half hour felt like I was wading in drying concrete. I checked on all my patients, did all the necessary things, then I just sat waiting, my clit already a semi.

After literally watching the clock forever, I started to make my way to meet up with Samual. I was so elated; I felt a little lightheaded as I strolled the vacant hospital halls. The usual machine bleeps sounded, the sound of a child fussing, and the sound of a call button bleating met my ears as I tread along. It was quiet, but on some floors, it was still a busy quiet at night.

I made my way towards the skyway to the attached building that housed the clinics and the doctor's offices. I spotted Samual before he saw me, and my heartbeat pummeled my chest as I realized this man's cock would soon be inside me. My nipples hardened as I approached him.

"Hi," I said nervously.

"There she is," he said in his usual sexy slur.

"You ready?" I asked, but figured he might very well have the same question for me.

He leaned down to my ear without touching me, and he said, "Oh, I'm so ready to rail you from behind, beating your nice booty with my pelvis until you coat my big black dick with that luscious white cunt juice of yours."

I grinned at him with a wicked gaze. His words traveled inside me like hot white bullets ricocheting off all my internal walls.

When I didn't respond, he said, "It's a promise."

It was too hard to speak, so I just bit my lip and let my eyes do my talking.

He ushered me into the elevator, his first touch of my body ever sending bolts of heat through me. If just a touch of his hand did that, what would his cock do to me? I shivered with joy that soon I'd get to know. Sure, these two were going to get to fuck me, but I'd get doubly pleasured, so the way I saw our union, I was making out the best.

"You don't need to be nervous, sweets, I'm a dominant, but I'll do it how you want." His tone was genuine, and his desire to make me happy thickened my lust for this threesome to happen.

"I'm nervous, but I'm also super excited," I said in a shaky and joyous voice.

"I'm going to make you come so hard you'll remember me and my big black cock for life," he said, oozing so much fearless boldness that I had zero doubts.

I visibly shuddered. "I can't wait," I said.

He chuckled and swept his hand towards the opening elevator door. "After you, my sexy sweetness." He hummed, then said, "Mmmm, can't wait to see that ass bared and getting smacked by me."

His words again raged my lust higher, and I wanted to scream I was so turned on. I tried not to run down the hall and calmly held it together, though I felt I'd lose my cool once we were in the privacy of Mitch's office.

I knocked on his office door and he called through it, "Come in, it's open."

I pushed the door open to find Mitch smiling and seated behind his desk. He nodded toward Samual. "Samual, so nice to connect with you in this way."

Samual shut the door behind him. "Likewise, Dr. Sloane."

"Mind sliding that lock across?" Mitch pointed towards the door at the slide lock he'd installed four months ago. "I added some extra protection."

Samual laughed. "Extra protection for such things is most needed."

I giggled. "Right?"

"Have a seat. Let's have a quick chat," Mitch said, taking the lead as usual.

"Well, yes sir. I respect that this is your office, and this is your woman. And I am a guest here," he declared as he settled his large frame into the chair in front of the desk that was really too small for him.

Mitch motioned for me to join him, and he pulled me to sit on his thigh. I straddled it and pressed my hot, wanton pussy to his leg.

"Thank you for that. Amanda tells me you are a bull by trade on the side, outside of the hospital." Mitch rested his hand on my upper thigh. All I wanted was for him to do a finger swipe across my mound, maybe a tickle down my slit.

"Yep, and considering film, but I'm very happy to offer my services to your sexy woman, if you deem it so," he said in a respect-filled way.

"Yes, I desire that, as Amanda does as well. This is just mutual pleasure at the most primal level," Mitch confirmed. "We agree to keep all of this between us?"

Samual nodded vehemently. "Absolutely. It would cost me my job as much as it would each of yours."

Mitch's nodding head made his body jiggle against my back. He snuck his other arm around me, encircling my waist. "And nothing happens outside of my presence, because I happen to be in love with this woman."

Samual again nodded in agreement. "I'm not about stealing any women. They must be free agents or with consenting partners like you to get the ride of this meat." He grabbed his big erection through his pants and jostled it. "If we weren't in a hospital, she'd be screaming 'til she's spent as she comes on me, 'cause I live up to the reputation." His assurance was beyond sexy, which only added to the hotness of his appearance.

It was titillating to be in the presence of two dominant men collaborating to pleasure me until I was a rag doll.

"Okay. Rules," Mitch said, leaning forward. "No anal. You can ride her buns, just not in. We can spit roast her, titty fuck her, single or doubly vaginally fuck her, and blow jobs she's good with, but no face fucking. She doesn't get off on gagging."

"Duly noted," Samual said with a flick of his fingers. "Condoms on, but I have no lube with me," he said with a spirited brightening of his face. "Always got spit, though," he said with grit.

"I've got lube," Mitch said as he leaned forward, which pushed my tits onto the desk as he reached into the drawer. Mitch raised the yellow tube of gel lube and tick-tocked it in the air. "Shall we fuck? I only have twenty minutes.

Samual stood, an intense hungry gleam in his stare. "Oh, I'm more than ready. Watching Amanda walk gets me horny all by itself, but knowing I get to put my big throbbing cock up her succulent pussy has me hard as a steel rod."

I leaned back against Mitch's hard-on and felt ready to burst. "I wish I could make as much noise as I want, but I'd better keep it contained. If I get too loud, make sure you guys shut me up somehow," I said in a teasing voice, except that I was serious.

"I'd like a few minutes after alone with her, so let's be mindful of time." He started to stand, and I hopped off his lap. "In fact, I'm going to set my phone for fifteen minutes, so we have warning."

"I can make that happen, no problem. I have good control." He grinned. "She will experience maximum pleasure at the beating of my cock."

I giggled as I squirmed.

"You can start, I'll hop in," Mitch said, sitting back down in his chair.

Samual motioned me over and I swiftly moved to his body, pressing myself to his front as his arm snatched me to him. "I think this is about the best surprise I've had in many years." He held my face between his large hands and looked directly into my eyes. "I'm going to make you come hard. What do you like? Hard clitoral pressure? Soft? Spanks? Do you like to be eaten out, because I'd start with that to get you to come before we move to dick riding. You like dirty talk?"

I nodded, transfixed by the magical sexual tale he was spinning for me. "Yes," it was all I needed to say.

"Good," he said with a wide, super-white, toothy grin.

He pulled my face to him as he bent down, and we fell into a kiss. He caressed my lips with his before inserting his tongue into my mouth. He caressed my tongue with his as he began to fondle my body while pressing my tits flush to his torso.

My hands went straight up to his biceps, and I began to explore his body, feeling up his toned muscles. His cock was an absolute monster at my tummy, his erection practically at the cusp of my cleavage. I scoffed internally, wondering that this man could practically titty fuck me while we stood sandwiched together. He was so tall compared to me.

He gripped my ass cheeks and squeezed hard, slightly lifting my feet off the carpet. I squealed when he clenched his hands harder around my fleshy bum.

He released my ass and slid his hands up my shirt as we kissed. I moaned into his mouth; his kisses were so hungry.

"Oh, baby, you taste so good. Like a cream puff." He grunted as he massaged my body with his hands while thrusting his cock gently between us. His large palms held my skull as we kissed even deeper. This man kissed like he wanted to be inside of me, deep inside.

Mitch joined on the back side of me and began to run his hands along my back, over my hips, and to cup my breasts from behind.

Mitch pulled my hair to the side and kissed the back of my neck in a series of wet, sucking kisses. "You are so sexy, baby, we're going to make you feel so amazing."

I felt fluid already as they both mauled and caressed me, lulling me into an even more wanton wench.

"Gonna be our whore tonight?" Mitch asked in a devilishly seductive voice.

"Yes, sir," I complied, noting Samual's acknowledgment of how I addressed my man. It was only during sex that I used that word, the rest of my life he was 'Mitch' or 'Doc'.

"Good, like a well-seasoned slut," Mitch said as he snaked his hand down the waistband of my scrub pants.

Samual unwrapped his condom and slid down his pants. My eyes popped wide when he unveiled his enormous cock.

"Holy fuck, that's not going to fit," I joked, completely astounded by his size. He was definitely porn star material with that big of a dick.

"Whew," Mitch agreed.

Samual laughed. "Oh, it will fit, trust me. You get aroused, and you'll be surprised what can fit up you."

I'd take his word for it, but I definitely had my doubts, but I also was excited to try to take him in me.

When we realigned back into our spaces, Mitch wasted no time but went straight away for my lips and fingered them, moistening them further with his touch. He pulled his hand out and slid my panties and pants to the floor. I stepped out of them, leaving my slip-ons off when I stepped back down. I kicked it all toward Mitch's desk. Samual pulled my top off and Mitch undid my bra. They had me naked so fast that I gave a short, muted laugh.

"You aren't wasting any time," I attested.

"Nope, now lie back on the soft chair. I want to watch him eat you out," Mitch instructed as he dropped his scrub pants to the floor.

I loved that I was fully naked, and they only had their pants off, which made it hotter. I spread out on the soft armchair and spread my legs as Samual leaned into my pussy. I had assumed bulls just fucked, but him wanting to eat me out first was getting me so hot I felt I'd burst into flames. I'd never turn down a bull who wanted to eat my pussy, no way.

He leaned and licked my slit several times, then went for my nipples, pinching, twisting, then taking a few moments to suckle each. "Fantastic nipples," he said before devouring my right one again.

"Oh, yeah, aren't they just stellar," Mitch agreed.

I glanced at him and was relieved to see only lust smoldering in his eyes.

Samual licked down my belly, visiting my belly button for a tip-of-the-tongue swipe, then swiftly licked his way down to the cleft in my lips. He pressed his tongue in there as he pressed two of his large fingers inside me. I groaned out and gripped the soft chair as he began to finger fuck me. He slid his other hand under my butt as he descended on my womanhood. He sucked each labia lip, then fully consumed my swollen clit.

I moaned, writhing against his strong sucking as Mitch appeared by my side and played with my nipples. Their tag teaming collaboration had me on the verge of climax within a minute.

"That's right, come on Amanda, come for me," Mitch urged his command as Samual mouth-molested by throbbing bean.

I neared the peak of my climax, and it gripped me, then like going over a hill I plunged into a big climax that made me yell louder than I probably should have, my body twitching in tune to the contractions belting out my pussy walls. He kept finger fucking me so hard and fast that another peak of the orgasm swept me up and I climaxed hard again.

Samual worked quickly, standing, then grabbing my body to flip me into doggy position. I wondered where Mitch would go until Samual said, "Let's flip this chair so you can get your cock in her mouth."

They both picked up the chair and rotated it with ease, as if it were a small rock.

Their strength astounded me as they lined themselves up, Mitch settling in at my mouth by kneeling on another chair he placed behind the soft one, and Samual at my ass.

He smacked his large cock against my butt, and it felt like a log. My need for him grew stronger.

He squirted lube and the squishing sounds of his jerking it across his shaft filled the room. "I'm big, and I don't want to rough you up too much, baby doll."

He was a gentle bull, which made sense with his personality, but I had wondered if he'd be more brutish.

"Dial it back for now, but if you ever want more, I've got it in me," he said as he pressed the tip of his cock at my cummy hole.

Mitch held my face in his hand and dropped his jaw while putting pressure on mine, so I'd copy him. He let go of my face and grasped his hard cock with the other, then smiled down at me while feeding it into my mouth.

I uttered a shocked cry as Samual's large dick entered me further. "Oh, shit, you are big," I said through my gasps.

"Nice and slow until you accept me," he cooed in a tender but deeply masculine voice. Listening to his low tones was seductive all by itself. He began to speed up his thrusts and his largeness went from alarming to making my eyes roll in pleasure.

As I sucked the tip of Mitch's cock, he held my cheeks. Having the familiarity of Mitch's cock in my mouth and the newness of Samual's inside me was mind-blowingly arousing.

Samual snatched my hair as he began to pillage my cunt with hard ramming stabs, man-growling just like I'd expect a bull to do, making my ass flop as if he were wildly spanking me. He pulled back harder on my hair, and I struggled to keep Mitch in my mouth. My hanging tits flopped with each pound of his long dick into me.

Mitch repositioned to stand on his chair, then knelt on the soft cushion straddling my face so he was slightly above me as Samual's rough tugging arched my back further. This move immobilized me more securely between them so he could get himself inside my orifice once more. He gently face-fucked me, since I could no longer bob on the head of his cock.

My body bounced between the two men as our sounds filled the air. I'd never been fucked by such a big cock before, and his girth hit my G-spot just right. I felt the rise of another climax, but I needed a boost, so I reached back and fingered my clit as Samual tightened his grip on my hips to all-out obliterate my swollen hole.

The timer of the phone went off, signaling five minutes were left, prompting Samual to piston himself into me so hard that Mitch backed off. My body was jerked back and forth from his forceful fucking of me, and I came hard, my internal feminine muscles clenching down on his massive dick inside me. He was so big that the contractions moved my walls, but it was as if they couldn't move much with how full I was with him. He grunted loudly and with his movements, I knew he was climaxing.

He pumped into me for a few more pumps, then pulled himself out. Next time, I'd want him to get tested and he creampie me, but that was a discussion for another time.

"Thank you, baby, that was out of the park," Samual said as he caressed my bottom.

I panted on the chair, my body all askew. I couldn't move, I was speechless, and so satiated that I wanted more.

Mitch caressed my head and thanked Samual, told him we'd be in touch. That made me smile inside because I still felt too frozen to move.

"You okay?" Mitch asked as he locked the door behind Samual.

I nodded but remained silent. It was too tough to speak.

"I'm going to fuck you now," Mitch said as he lined himself up where Samual had just been.

He entered me fast and rough and rode me, so my face rubbed the soft upholstery, my mouth hanging open wide, my eyes half closed. He reached around for a titty grab, visited my clit for a rub, then gripped my hips in a death grip as he shoved himself in me so hard and fast, I gasped and sputtered.

"Get it, babe," he said in desperation, and I knew he wanted me to climax first.

I obeyed and rubbed my clit and loss of control gripped me as I blazoned into another orgasmic high, my pussy closed in on his cock, encircling it in those mystifying cunt hugs for too many contractions to count.

He grunted and his jizz filled me, making his lessening thrusts sound more wet as his cum joined mine.

He breathed heavily as he laid upon my back, my labored breathing controlling me as well.

"Holy fuck," he said as he stood up. "That was unbelievable."

I slumped into the chair and wanted so badly to just go to sleep. "Wow," was all I said.

"You can stay as long as you need to recover, babe, but I have to get back. I'm so sorry, but that was so great. I'm a bit in shock."

I nodded in agreement. "Yes, it was incredible."

"I'll text you soon, but I gotta go. I got another call, so I have to go now." He pulled his scrubs up over his spent cock and kissed me on the forehead. "I really needed that, though. Thank you."

"Thank you," I managed as he zoomed out the door.

I laid there naked for several minutes before I got dressed, my body feeling like a twisted wet rag, but way floatier and loftier. I smiled as I put myself back together, replaying the whole delicious scene back in my head. I scribbled an 'I love you' note to Mitch and left his office, feeling way more like a woman than I ever had in my life.

The End

Servicing the Maid

Alex shoved his hands into his hair, which was all puffed up from him doing that very same thing all morning long. Things weren't going well, and he was at his wit's end. He'd crunched the numbers ten times and he'd not made a math error. He was screwed. He was going to lose his biggest money-making client because of an idiotic mix-up. His divorce had him in dumb brain mode and this was one of the dumbest things he'd done since Maggie served him his papers. Well, actually, maybe the stupidest ever in his life.

He stared at his coffee, considering drinking it, but his stomach was churning, and he knew he'd likely vomit it back up. He stared out the window at John, who was mowing the lawn. The firm was just one of John's clients. Alex and John had become friends over the years, and although John made less money, he was his own boss and, overall seemed much happier than Alex. He normally went out to chat with John, but today he was feeling so low that he literally couldn't move. He was hoping for a magic bullet to strike his brain to save him, so he didn't have to tell his best client how much of his money had poofed away overnight. Poof. Gone. Just like that. Like a fart in the wind.

That made Alex smile. He chuckled like a kid as Macy poked her head into his office.

"Mr. Crenshaw, is now a good time to clean your office?" she asked sweetly, her pretty face framing her twinkly eyes.

Seeing Macy always cheered Alex up. She was uber sexy, with curvy hips, a nice juicy ass, and boobs that looked to be at least C cups, if not D. She had intense green eyes and lush dark chocolate hair that she always had up in a ponytail, likely because of all the manual labor she did as their office maid. Alex had so often fantasized about bending her over his desk, grabbing that ponytail of hers, and railing her hard into orgasms for them both. They'd flirted quite a bit, too, but it had never gone any further than that. But he'd been married then.

He smiled hugely. Watching her body move as she cleaned his office would surely cheer him up.

"Yes, please come in, Macy. And thank you." He gave her his kindest eyes, which legit helped his mood too. "I'm not doing anything important, so feel free to make any sounds you need to."

Sounds. Oh, fuck. What he wouldn't give to hear her sounds as he fucked her. He desired to make her moan and writhe beneath his touch and from his cock. His dick was already at a semi, just from interacting with her from across the room.

She smiled and nodded. "Okay, sir. That's great. It will help me out if I can vacuum your room now, too. I have to leave early, so that's really helping, thank you." She dipped her body slightly, as if to curtsy.

She had on her usual work clothing of loose gray pants and a gray shirt. Even in drab clothing, she was the sexiest woman in the whole damn building, by far. She had two braids on either side of her temples that ran most of the course of her ponytail. He imagined how fabulous they would be for winding around his hands as he yanked her head back, making her chin jut out as he rammed her doggy.

His cock fully filled as he watched her bend over and pick up the dust rag she had dropped. He held in his sigh as he kept his eyes on her every move.

She dusted all the surfaces that likely didn't even need dusting, but she had her checklist of things to get done and she never seemed to shirk them. She was a hard worker and Alex had learned recently that she was in night school at the local community college trying to get her nursing degree. Being twenty-six and back in college had to be a challenge. He was happy for her, but it had saddened him because it meant she'd not be working as their maid for much longer.

His eyes drifted to his armoire. Inside was his impulse purchase he'd bought online late at night before masturbating to thoughts of fucking Macy in his office. His cheeks flushed with excitement. He wanted so badly to give it to Macy and beg her to put it on. A French Maid costume hung in pristine shape inside the massive piece of furniture. It was untouched, and he desired to get his cum splattered across it, dribbles of his spunk decorating the fluffy lace underskirt like baby pearls.

Alex had always had a thing for the whole French Maid costume theme, and his wife had only indulged him once in such a getup before they had kids. Then it sat unused in their big master closet for fifteen years. Just like his cock. She'd hung up sex after having kids and had never revisited her sexuality. He'd not understood her until the day she said she was leaving him for another man. Then he knew she hadn't given up sex at all, but only with him.

Macy kept glancing at him, catching his continual staring. He never once looked away. He was too mesmerized by all her movements. She was lithe and efficient, but always with a happy little bounce in her step. She was a positive ray of sunshine in his life, and he'd never been able to say it because married men don't do that. He kept his gaze upon her as she dusted the wood on each of his easy chairs and sprayed the air freshener across the upholstery. The scent was a nice, light floral that filled his nostrils.

She playfully turned and sprayed it his way. "Want some more cheer?" She sprayed it again and the mist appeared, then quickly dissipated.

"It really does help the mood to smell something nice," he agreed.

"Oh, are you down today, Mr. Crenshaw?" Her sweet eyes filled with concern and worry. She was so sweet to care.

"Yeah, I am. Lost a bunch of money for a client for a stupid choice and now I'm ..." His voice trailed off. He didn't want to say anymore out loud.

"Oh, I'm so sorry to hear that. But everyone makes mistakes," she said cheerily.

"Not this big," he said in a hopeless tone. "I've done a bad thing."

She sat in the chair, her ass cheeks barely on the seat cushion. "Maybe you can make it back quickly for them."

Alex nodded. "Not likely, but thanks for the support." He was able to smile back at her, which was never an effort to do.

"I wish I could help, but I'm sure there's nothing I can do." She wrung the dustcloth between her fingers as a little smile regrew on her face. "I could give you a shoulder massage, that might help you relax."

He sat up quickly, making his spine straighten as he widened his eyes. She'd just offered to touch him. His breath quickened as he nodded. "Oh, wow, that would be incredible." He couldn't believe this was happening. It was like a dream come true.

"Oh good. I took a massage class last year, so I've got some skills." She hopped up and made her way around the big wooden desk.

He pushed his chair back, wondering how this was going to work, because his chair back was too tall for a massage.

"Hmmm. This isn't going to work in this chair," she said while patting the soft headrest with her small hands. She looked around the room. "Do you have any other chairs? Like a folding chair or something?"

"Oh yeah, there's one in the armoire." The second he said it, he cringed. "Shit," he muttered.

"I'll get it," she offered and was more than halfway to the armoire before he even tried to think about a legit reason to get her to stop from opening the armoire's doors.

He was in trouble. She'd see the costume and think he was a freak. She'd leave his office and never grace his walls again. He'd ruined the last great thing in his life.

She flung open the heavy wooden doors and gasped, a hand over her full lips. She remained frozen, staring at the only garment hanging inside. The black and white of the costume stood out against the dark mahogany wood.

If he hadn't already been filled with dread, that was nothing compared to when she picked it up and scanned it, her direct gaze moving up and down the saucy little costume. It was agonizing watching the back of her head as she looked, yet remained speechless. He wanted to slap himself upside the head. He wanted to curl up and die. He was an evil man with a freakish desire. Who buys a costume like that for a woman he works with? It's not like they were dating or anything; it had only been shallow, casual flirting, and nothing more.

She spun around quickly, and he jumped back as saw her eyes were filled with sass and fire. "Mr. Crenshaw, is this for me?"

He froze in place, his mind desperately evaluating how to proceed to salvage his relationship with Macy.

"Because I'm the only maid in this office." Her eyes were amused rather than offended. "I think it's really hot if you bought this for me."

His entire body filled with relief that she didn't hate him. It was a very bold move and he'd envisioned her screaming at him and stomping out, swearing to never touch a single thing in his office ever again.

But, instead, she was smiling at him salaciously.

A fire scalded in her eyes as she slowly took steps towards him. His dick was fully packed with blood and felt harder than it had in literally years.

She tossed her ponytail as she sashayed her hips like a sex goddess had suddenly invaded her luscious body.

He swore he could smell her pussy, or perhaps it was just her sex appeal, but she'd blossomed into nothing short of a wonderful miracle right in front of his eyes.

"Cause if you did, I'd like to put it on for you, Mr. Crenshaw." Her face was dripping with a magically promiscuous aura. The intense gaze she held him with made his cock twitch. She dropped her eyes to his crotch and smiled even bigger.

"Because I think I've always wanted this as much as you have."

His heart pounded like he was running from a lion as she swiveled her fingers in the air.

"Macy, I ..."

"Turn around, Mr. Crenshaw, while I get this maid costume on," she said, clearly not messing around.

A single laugh involuntarily burst from his gut as he processed what she was saying.

"I'd like to give you your wish, because I'd really like to play too." Her voice was so seductive and even more enticing than he had imagined her sexy tone would be.

He stared wide-eyed at her, his dick throbbing like an overfilled water balloon. Surely even a pinky wisp of her touch would make him explode.

"Fuck," he muttered under his breath.

She spun her fingers in the air again as her smile remained just as lecherous, if not more. "Do it and I'll do it."

He obeyed, wondering if he should instead be running to lock his office door. He spun his high-backed office chair fully around and looked up. He jumped and gasped. John was at the window, and he was staring right at him.

John waved at Alex and panic seized him. He'd see Macy undressing in his office, and then he'd really be fucked. He wanted to shoo John away, but he was in the middle of washing Alex's office window.

John's eyes suddenly went wide, and he stopped moving. His jaw dropped and Alex's heart plummeted.

Shit! John would tell the other partners and they'd demand he leave the practice because of fraternizing with the maid. He shook his head helplessly as John continued to stare into the window. His day just went from tragic to devastating.

John was looking beyond him. He nodded as a grin grew across his face. Alex frowned. What the fuck?

He watched as John nodded again and then left in the direction of the small building's front door. He was doomed. John was likely coming to rat him out. He'd have to clean out his desk, and not only would he have lost his wife this month, but his job. None of his partners would want to keep him around if they knew he had Macy the maid naked in his office. He'd be a disgrace.

His heart sank further, and his dick started to deflate.

"Turn around now, Mr. Crenshaw," Macy said in a seductive coo. "I'm ready for you to see me."

He slowly turned around, figuring he might as well do the full deed of fucking Macy in his office if she was up for it. He was likely already in trouble, so why not get a climax out of it? Do the whole thing some justice and get actual sex. It had been years since his cock had tasted pussy.

As he swiveled and caught sight of her, his cock refilled instantly. "Oh, my fucking Gawd, you look incredible!" She looked better than his fantasy of her.

Her breasts barely fit inside the bodice, so her bosom was swelling out the scooped neckline with a line of cleavage that kept going like a road leading everywhere. Her petite waist gave way to her generous hips. Her shapely legs were even better than he'd imagined they'd be under those shapeless gray pants she wore. Even her arms looked feminine, and he yearned to run his hands across her firm, supple flesh. And all that was nothing compared to the absolute fire that blazed in her eyes. She was sex redefined and she was standing waiting for him.

His office door burst open, and he gasped. John sauntered in with a happy grin. "Thanks for inviting me in, Macy."

Alex's jaw fell. "Invited?" he repeated in disbelief. Never in all his wildest dreams did he imagine Macy in that costume with the groundskeeper John in his office as well. He was most certainly in a coma dreaming this, because it just wasn't possible.

"You look so sexy and hot in that outfit, honey. I wish I'd thought of it." His eyes were lit with lust, but also with something else Alex couldn't quite name.

"Thank you, John. I always appreciate your sexy compliments." Her voice was filled with glee.

"If I hadn't ever complimented you, we wouldn't be in this office altogether right now." He approached Macy and began to caress her body as if he already knew what she felt like.

They fell quickly into a French kiss as Alex filled with dread. "You two?" he asked in full disbelief.

Macy broke the kiss and bit her lip. "Yeah, we do. A girl has needs."

Alex was flabbergasted. John was even older than he was, and Macy and he'd been fucking?

"We've been here after and before hours many times together. Us caretakers take care of each other." He spun Macy around and fluffed her puffy lace skirt up, leaning down so he could peek under the skirt to peer at her ass. That was supposed to be Alex's move. Jealousy hit him like a sledgehammer as he watched his friend eat up the eye candy of Macy's ass beneath the short maid skirt.

"I have no words," Alex said, feeling like a total imbecile. He'd spent good money on a sexy costume for another man to enjoy, apparently. What kind of fool was he anyway to go buying a sexy costume for a woman he wasn't even dating? He'd taken wishful thinking to a whole other level, and he was sitting in his office chair with a dick full of fun with nowhere to put it. John was going to get to fuck Macy and he'd likely only get to watch. He felt so cheated. His face began to heat, and he felt ready to burst into beast mode like the Hulk. He'd be damned if John was going to steal his fantasy right before his eyes.

"You want to play with us too, Mr. Crenshaw? Because I'd really like it if you did." Her eyes were eager, and she seemed genuine.

His anger melted and his lust erupted. He watched with growing arousal as John bent Macy over slightly and paddled her bottom with several rapid little smacks.

"Did you get all your cleaning done before your fun, little maid girl? I think not." He spanked her bare butt, making skin smacks fill the room.

She giggled and wiggled her bottom at him as he kept spanking.

"Wanna?" she asked with her eyes glued to Alex.

He rose quickly and made his way past them to his office door, which he locked. When he turned with a passionate glaze upon his eyes, Macy smiled and clapped.

"Yay. Come punish me too, Mr. Crenshaw, for not finishing cleaning your office," she said in a flirty, haughty tone, all out daring him to take action.

John stepped aside as Alex approached. "Take a turn, my good friend. Plenty for us to share. Macy's a tigress, and tireless."

Macy bent over just a bit further and more of her bare flesh appeared from beneath the stiff little skirt. Alex's cock throbbed with his first glance at her rotund, perfect buttocks. He touched her bottom immediately, unable to keep his hands off her bubble butt. He massaged her ass as she giggled. Then he gave her a spank, then another as she squirmed and squealed.

"Oh no! Now I'm in big trouble." She shimmied her shoulders and raised her head high. "I wanna play this role play to full potential," she instructed. When he slapped her ass again, she stared at the ground while he continued to swat her bottom. "You two pretend you are having a meeting and I'll be cleaning. Then you guys start ordering me around, then touching me, and my wish is an endpoint where you bend me over that big desk of yours and fuck me."

Her bluntness stating exactly what she wanted shocked Alex to his core. He wasn't used to a woman who was not only sexual, but verbally openly so, and who actually dictated precisely what she wanted to have happen. And the fact that it matched his fantasies left him stupidly silent.

"Perfect idea, babe," John said as he got comfortable in a chair.

"Is that okay, Mr. Crenshaw?" Macy asked innocently with her facial expression to match. "Sir."

The 'sir' ticked him over the edge and a lewd expression seized his face. "Oh, it's more than okay, Macy. It's perfect."

"Good. Now sit down and keep that cock hard. I want both of you inside me, fucking me to a multitude of orgasms." She was bossy and he loved it.

He watched her in amazement. Her demure yet demanding demeanor was the sexiest combo he'd ever had the pleasure of being in the presence of. She not only exuded sex, but she was also electric with the power of it.

"Now, I'll start, then I want you guys to tell me what to do. And if I don't do it right, the punishment is at your discretion," she said wickedly, accepting her submission to them already.

She began to re-dust all the areas she'd already dusted as she eyed up the men.

John said, "Nice day out there today. I'm getting extra stuff done. How's your day going, Alex?"

Alex tried to shake the bewildered look off his face as he said, "It started out as a horrible disaster of the most epic catastrophes of my entire career, but it's now becoming the best day of my life." Alex had never done a threesome, and he'd always pictured himself with two women, but he was willing to abandon that pipe dream now.

John chuckled. "Yeah, I know exactly what you mean." He nodded knowingly. "Are there things you and the partners need done for any handyman projects coming up? Because one of my big jobs just lessened its load, so if you guys want me to get started on anything, please don't hesitate to ask."

Macy continued to look busy doing very little, dusting and re-dusting the same spots as she made eye contact with Alex, then her eyes would drift to John. She looked horny and Alex blessed the impulsive moment he had hit purchase to buy the maid costume.

His fears diminished to almost nothing as both he and John watched the scantily clad woman flit about the room as they talked.

"Why don't you dust off the surface of my desk, Macy?" he asked, but it felt more like a requirement the way he said it.

She did a cute little curtsy, then made her way to his mammoth desk.

"And don't forget my laptop either," he instructed in a stern tone.

She obeyed all his instructions and rubbed the cloth all over.

John said, "How about the windowsill? I bet that gets ignored during normal dusting."

She dutifully swiped the cloth all along the windowsill, then turned her attention back to the desk again.

They watched her cleavage as she leaned over the desk, stretching so she could reach as much as she could, then moving around to the other side and bending over slightly to extend her reach as far as possible. The very lower curve of her butt cheeks showed when she bent way over.

Both men released groans, which made her sassy smile brighten further.

Alex cleared his throat when she dusted the back of his desk yet another time. "I think you've dusted that same spot five times, Macy. You aren't doing a very good job," Alex accused in a mad voice. This game was fun.

She shoved her chest out, which made her butt pop up as her hand flew over her mouth, her eyes wide and innocent. "Oh, I'm so very sorry, sir, I was trying to be extra thorough for you." The innocent girl act struck his kinky bone hard.

"I might need to teach you a lesson on making proper progress, so you aren't wasting the company dollars redoing what doesn't need to be redone." He patted his thighs. "You're wasting our money. Now get over my lap for a spanking, you naughty girl."

She feigned shock very well as a whimper flew from her mouth. Her lower lip protruded in a generous pout. "Oh, yes, sir. I need you to punish me and guide me. I'm just not very good at being efficient, I guess. I need your hand to make me learn."

John laughed lecherously as his eyes met Alex's. Their eyes spoke a primal language of fire and lust that seemed to match in masculine dominance. Rather than feel threatened by John, Alex felt aligned.

Macy skittered over to Alex, and she stood next to his chair.

He reached up and yanked down the top of the French maid costume, which made her large breasts pop out. Her pink nipples hardened immediately upon being exposed to the air.

"Holy fuck, your nipples are even better than I expected." Alex grabbed both her erect nipples and began to fondle, squeeze, and pinch them. "They are exquisite."

"Yeah, she has killer nipples, doesn't she?" John said knowingly, with deep appreciation.

Alex still couldn't get over the fact that John had even seen her nipples before, let alone fucked her.

"They are perfect," he said, tugging them. He pulled her close and suckled one while pressing on her back. Her head tipped as she moaned, tangling her hands in his hair. He twisted her other nip as he played. After a few minutes of playing and sucking, he leaned back with a very satisfied grin. "Fuck, I needed that. I could keep going."

She caressed his face. "Anytime," she said. "And you can do it even harder next time."

His urge to dominate her raged. "I said over my lap," he said aggressively as he grabbed her arm and pulled her body onto his lap.

She squealed again, and his cock throbbed harder.

She was floppy and easy to move. He lifted the fluffy lace underskirt of the maid costume with one hand and began to lay punishing smacks across her bottom with the other one.

Her squirming on his lap massaged his cock between them, and his excitement hit the max point. He needed to slow things down or he'd come right in his pants. "John, you want a turn at teaching our little Macy a lesson?"

"Oh, I'd love a turn." He chuckled. "I've given her a spanking or two, haven't I?"

Macy giggled, then rolled off Alex and crawled over to John.

Watching her reddened butt wiggle away from him as she crawled didn't help Alex's lust to settle. Watching her dangling tits jiggle made Alex want to grab her hips and hump her backside. He didn't think he'd even need his cock in her to come.

She climbed up John's legs and placed her body across his lap.

"You have a dirty lap," she said as she pressed her fingers into a grass stain.

"Oh, you have no idea," John said with a boisterous laugh. "Well, you do somewhat, but there's a lot more to it."

He laid a good spanking on her for a minute as she yelped, wiggled, and groaned.

"Now, suck my cock," John instructed. "Just as deep as last time too, Macy. No taking the easy way with this."

Alex watched in utter disbelief as Macy slipped herself off his lap and kneeled in front of him. She unzipped his pants and pulled out his hard cock.

"Mmmm, yummy," Macy said, stroking his cock before she descended upon his erection with her mouth open.

She bobbed on John's cock as he held her head. He thrust up as he pushed her head gently down. She gagged and he grunted.

"Fuckkkkk," he spat as he stopped her head from bobbing. "Shit almost lost it. Okay, now Alex," he said in a strained voice.

"Wow," Alex said in a whisper that he figured he was the only one who could hear.

When she finally popped off John's fat cock head with a mouth pop, he exclaimed, "Whew, you are too good at that, my girl. Listen right away next time or I'll paddle you again."

She snickered almost evilly and flipped herself around and crawled towards Alex with her eyes ablaze with mischief. Her hanging tits were driving Alex wild. He wanted to watch them sway and chug across her chest as he fucked her from behind.

Alex couldn't have possibly dreamt how amazing the passion was burning in her eyes; it was like nothing he'd ever witnessed in his life. She had the light of something magnificent in her he'd never been blessed with seeing ever before. She was one of a kind.

She mounted his thighs with her upper body and unzipped his trousers. She unearthed his hard-on from his underwear and consumed his dick inside her hot, wet mouth before he even took another breath.

He played with her nipples as she sucked him. It was instant heaven and he groaned and writhed beneath her powerful, skillful sucking to the point he almost came. "Whoa," he exclaimed, and she immediately released her suction. "You aren't kidding, John."

"Nope. Not," John said assuredly.

"We'd better take that red little butt of yours to the desk for more ass-up punishment," Alex said salaciously. Talking this way to a woman was astounding, and he knew he'd cherish it for the rest of his life, even if he never got to be with Macy ever again. John may have a greater claim on her than he did, but he was also very grateful that John wasn't squeezing him out.

"Yes, sir." She remained on her hands and knees, not moving. "Make me go," she pleaded. She twisted her own nipples, and it lit him up like a firecracker.

Alex swatted her bottom and she began to crawl. She stopped. John took a turn, giving her a light slap.

Alex felt a surge of aggression grip him and he plucked Macy up and threw her over his shoulder.

She guffawed. "Go big or go home, huh, Mr. Crenshaw?"

Her shrieks of delight made his cock throb. He wanted her more than ever. He carried her despite her playfully protesting wiggles making them both gyrate as he walked. Macy the tigress indeed.

He placed her on the floor and pulled her into a deep kiss, running his tongue into her mouth in repeated thrusts. She tasted like bubblegum and smelled like fresh air. Alex grasped the costume and pressed it down her body. She stepped out of it and kicked it towards the wall.

John pressed himself to her from her now bared backside, his hands running up her naked curvy body as he ground himself into her ass. His fingers roamed up Macy all over and then to her breasts. He fondled them and massaged her while Alex and Macy continued to deeply kiss.

Her moans drove him wild, as did her hungry kissing. He was on fire; she'd drive him insane and give him the best orgasms of his life all at once. He knew his life would never be the same going forward after getting to taste the brand of her magical sex. But now he also realized maybe his life wasn't over. Instead, it was just the beginning.

They both mauled her body for several minutes, her moans never ceasing. Alex didn't care if anyone heard them. This was too good, and he was never about shushing a woman expressing her sexual pleasure. His ex-wife had been stoic and mostly silent during sex, like a damn sex doll, and Macy's exuberance was intoxicating and exciting. He'd never shush such beautiful sounds from a woman. He didn't care who was in earshot. He wanted to make her make more of them.

Both men stripped naked as she watched with an unruly savoring, and a fabulous, almost wicked, grin.

When his hands were free, he attacked her, kissing down her neck as he groped her breasts. John was working his lust into a lather pretty hot and heavy by thrusting his erection between her ass cheeks. Her body was rocked in different ways as they each caressed her body, felt up her round parts, and pressed her flat parts. Alex could smell the scent of her aroused pussy as he slicked his fingers down her belly. He pressed his fingers between her lower womanly lips at the top of the cleft near her clit. He rubbed her clit, then dragged his fingers to her slit, where he pried open her lips. Her sounds packed his cock stiffer and stiffer.

"Yes, please, sir," she moaned, with her head resting back against John's chest.

Alex played with her wetness as he spread it around her labia lips, then when he pressed two fingers inside her body, she lurched forward with a deep, enjoying groan. He began to finger fuck her ever faster as John fondled her tits and stimulated her nips from behind.

"Make her come, do it fast and hard, don't stop, she'll come fast now." John was breathless, sweat wetting the gray patches of hair at his temples.

Alex rammed his fingers into her sweet hot hole, making wet sloshy sounds as he forcefully pressed her clit, rubbing it with his other hand.

John had both her nipples between his fingers, and he pinched and twisted them.

"Oh, yesssss," she cried out and her body began to curl towards Alex. She twitched and her body jerked as she came on his fingers. Her contractions clamped down on his fingers and he kept up the pace.

"Yes, keep it up, she'll come again fast now, like rapid fire if you keep going," John coached. He sucked the skin of her neck.

Alex did as John said, and her body curled once more as her sounds changed to whimpers.

Her fingers pressed Alex's biceps as she moaned and whimpered. "Big, big, big, again, again," she said helplessly, breathlessly, as she appeared to climax again.

Her ability to flourish sexually blew Alex's mind and he swore he'd never stop until he found a woman just like Macy to spend his life with. He was shedding the 'poor me' shit, and he was shooting for the stars. He deserved it, and he'd do whatever, whenever, his future woman wanted. He might be getting to fuck Macy, but she was schooling him on what he'd been missing in life.

"In me. In me. In me," she chanted between her pants.

Alex and John spun her around. Alex shoved his laptop and papers to the side, knocking over his pen jar. The multitude of pens spilled and rolled across the desk, several falling off the edge.

"Double," she said in a barely audible whisper. "Both of you in me. Alex first. Then John."

Alex was prepared to give this amazing goddess whatever the fuck she wanted, and then some.

He dragged his hand down her beautiful back and eyed up her ponytail. He dreamt again of grabbing it and yanking her head up while he pounded himself into her. Then he realized his dream was coming true and he'd better wake the fuck up and do what he wanted. He wrapped his hand around her ponytail and pulled her head up.

She gasped and whimpered as he lined up his cock at her cum-drenched cunt. He penetrated her, his cockhead sliding in so easily and perfectly. He tugged her ponytail as he began to ride her pussy with ever deeper thrusts. He fucked her alone for a minute, enjoying every fucking second of being inside her before he motioned John to join.

This would be a trick he wasn't sure how they'd accomplish.

Maybe he was a fool, but it suddenly hit him that his cock was going to ride John's hard dick as much as it was going to ride her hole. It was a jarring thought, and one he never expected himself to ever do. But he wasn't backing down now. This was happening and they were giving the woman what she wanted.

John lined himself up as Alex made room for him. He spit on, then used his wetted fingers to press into her hole alongside Alex's cock, then began to insert his wet cock into Macy's hole.

She cried out, her head snapping back as she was stretched by John entering her as well. She grasped at the desk, but the smooth wood had nothing for her to grip, so her fingers slid helplessly across the wood, giving her nothing satisfactory to grab onto. Her hands roamed wildly, searching until she tangled them into her own hair, dragging them down her head then settling on kneading her own tits.

As they both began to thrust into her, her body skated across the big desk. After a few minutes, they found a rhythm and both fucked her in unison.

Her sounds grew even more pleasurable as she accepted the double load of them.

John pressed a hand to her shoulder on his side of her and Alex claimed her ponytail again. He pulled and she arched her back as they both moved inside her.

"I'm gonna cum and give you her alone again," John said in a breathy voice. He pounded himself hard into her several times before his body twitched.

Alex blinked back the shock of feeling increased wetness as John's cum coated both his cock and the inside of Macy. John pulled out and stepped back.

"Fuck me, sir, please, fuck me," she begged as she held both her hips, as if presenting herself to Alex.

That sentence launched him, and he snapped into the moment as he began to fuck John's cum deeper inside Macy with his deepening shoves. He relentlessly slammed his body against her ass, making it jiggle violently. She smacked her palms firmly to the desk to give him some resistance to fuck against. Her tits flopped as he smacked himself against her while pulling back on her ponytail.

"Ima isapa ingo j," she chanted nonsense words as her body began another climax curl. She reached under her pelvis and molested her clit roughly. Within seconds, her body curved towards his desk, but with his grip on her ponytail, she was pinned in place. She released a yell as her body shook.

Her walls choked his cock inside her and he was overcome by the wave of pleasure. He groaned out the largest groan, one of a man who hadn't enjoyed the inside of a woman for years, spewing his big load of cum inside her pussy. He was shaking as his heart pounded. He laid upon her panting body as he became aware of how much his skin was coated with sweat.

"Thank you, that was incredible," she murmured in a soft, satiated voice. "Never ever have I had two cocks in me. That was my first."

He chuckled as relief still reverberated around his body. "Me too."

They remained bent over the desk for about a minute before Alex rose off of her. He helped her stand and couldn't resist kissing her on her forehead as he pulled her close.

He felt like crying, but that would have been weird, so he controlled his emotions to not make things awkward.

"Was incredibly hot. I've done it only one other time, but this one was way better," John confessed.

"I think everyone in this office is jealous right now," Alex said with a low deep chuckle. He didn't even care if the other partners yelled at him. The sex had been worth every bit of agony he might end up suffering. It had been the best sexual experience of his life.

"You think I should clean all the partner's offices this way," she asked with a delighted chuckle.

Alex raised his eyes in amazement that she seemed turned on by the idea.

"The office maid slut," she cooed with a libidinous grin. "We could make a porno."

"Oh, I'm sure you'd have a few takers if you're serious." Alex wasn't completely sure, but he knew a few of his partners would likely consider it.

She shrugged but looked interested. "I'd do it."

Alex doubted that would actually happen, but the idea was pretty hot, anyway.

"Whew, I think I could curl up on this desk and sleep," she said with a light laugh.

Even her light laughter made his heart sing. He was still aroused and would have fucked her again if she'd asked.

"I have a lot of cleaning to do, I'd better get started." She looked around the room.

"Your clothes are over there," Alex said pointing.

"Thanks, Mr. Crenshaw. Sir." Her eyes still twinkled.

John had pulled up his pants and was making his way towards the office door. "Great time, you two. Let's do it again sometime." He waved and left.

"For sure," Macy called after him. She turned to Alex. "I'm serious about doing the partners. I'll leave it up to you. You let me know."

He sighed and raised his hands. "Honestly, Macy, it would be better coming from you."

She screwed her face into a thoughtful expression. As she pulled her blah gray clothes back on, she released a chuckle. "I may just do that."

John watched her grab her cleaning stuff, wave, and walk out his office door as his mind started to go wild with thoughts of more of the magnificently amazing and colorful world that was Macy. She was a rainbow of sexuality in the gray clouds of his life.

The End

The Sex Wizards at a Halloween Costume Party Orgy

Paranormal, Magical Wizards

Janna donned her witch costume as thoughts of the cashier she bought it from flared her lust. He had been so hot. She fitted the satiny fabric to her curves as she checked her bod out in the big mirror. It was a bit slutty, differing from her usual Halloween attire. But once she saw it on the shelf that day, there was no turning back. She had hustled to the checkout with thoughts of turning heads at the party. She was super horny—not having had sex for six months sucked.

Last week, with her brain launching into a lusty fantasy, she had taken the bag with the costume from the cashier in the vampire costume. She had wished she could sneak behind the counter and slip between his legs and give him head while he checked people out. She didn't really choose giving head as a first want, but that day it had flooded her thoughts. She made it home in a lusty flurry, then rushed to grab toys to imagine just that scenario.

When she was done, after an explosive self-play, she called up her friend who was throwing the party to confirm when it was and all the details. She had a notion that she was going to find someone to fuck at that party or die trying.

The day of the party arrived. She put away all her clean uniforms and noted her next workday at the hospital wasn't for two days. So she'd have time to recover from an intense sexual encounter, should that happen. She took her shower, avoiding masturbating because she wanted to be ripe if she found a hookup. She painted her nails black and proceeded to give herself a Goth look with white facial makeup, dark eyes, and black lips.

She glanced down at her massive cleavage in the costume, smiled, and left her home, ready to party her ass off and then get it fucked off.

Janna knew this day was important. She couldn't not have sex. If she wished the sex into existence, especially in this witch costume, she wondered if she could manifest it. Witches did such things, right? She wasn't sure how, but she felt confident she could twist someone's arm into causing a ruckus with her in the closet. Convince him into fucking her to within an inch of her life.

She entered the party. It was a full house already. So many thirty-somethings, her head was spinning. Surely there'd be a single man who wanted to fuck. She scanned the room and immediately spied a sexy male vampire. He would do. She also saw a sexy werewolf in a red plaid shirt who looked ideal. He was burly and looked like he could hold a woman up and fuck her at the same time. Other people were talking in little groups. A few were playing a game of darts in the corner.

She shuddered. Thoughts of sex constantly flooded her brain. Raunchy scenarios, filthy scenes, thoughts of doing different illicit sex acts plagued her, occupying every second. She had to get laid, and soon. It felt urgent, but not necessarily imminent. But she felt the universe pushing her along. Maybe it was just the mystifying witch movie she had watched last night, or the mood of the world as Halloween night birthed, but there was some draw that was propelling her along.

Her friend, Bonnie, released a squeal and rushed her. "Janna! You look amazing! Look at this killer costume! You look sexy as fuck!"

Janna loved the compliment, and it set her confidence a notch higher. "Thanks, I found it in this little Halloween shop on Tenth Avenue." She paused. That was it! That vampire was the clerk at the store!

She glanced at him quickly, trying not to let on to Bonnie that she was eyeing him up as she jabbered on about her new boyfriend. The vampire was talking to a blond woman dressed as a beer wench from medieval times. He seemed interested in her and Janna's heart sank.

But what were the chances he'd be at this same party? It must have been the universe pushing her towards him. That was too big of a coincidence. But then, she wasn't that lucky either.

"And Mark is bringing his friend, Alex. Janna, maybe you two might hit it off? Wouldn't that be so cool?" Bonnie grabbed her hands. "Will you meet him?"

Janna eyed up the vampire again before she met Bonnie's eyes. "Yes, of course."

For the next ten minutes, she watched the vampire and the wench. She sensed they were flirty with each other because they'd both talk, then laugh. They were overly animated, so they were either drunk already or enticing each other into something. She made her way closer to them so she could perhaps overhear them. Her skills of observation as a nurse never failed her in other parts of her life, and within a minute of being in earshot of the couple, she had it confirmed they were negotiating a hookup.

She practically salivated as the vampire said, "Do you like to be bitten?"

Was this a vampire joke or a sexual preference question? Janna was dying to know, but Bonnie appeared with her boyfriend and friend. Her heart sank slightly because she knew now it would be hard to listen to the couple.

"Bonnie, this is Alex. He's an accountant at the same firm as Mark." Bonnie was definitely drunk. She had that sorta wild look like she had when she and her new boyfriend fucked in front of a crowd at one of her parties. She'd woken the next morning and called Janna, stating her life was forever changed now, and she hadn't been wrong to do it. The act had totally opened her up sexually to all kinds of new things. Janna jealously listened as she would tell her of the sex clubs they went to.

She scanned Alex, wondering if he was anything like Mark. She was in if he was, but an accountant might mean he's not adventurous, but boring and vanilla. She intended to enjoy finding out.

He smiled at her with a twinkle in his eyes. "Nice to meet you, Janna. I love your costume."

His eyes fell right to the large cleft in the exposed flesh of her bosom. He won more points as they lingered there, then fell down the rest of her body, then returned to meet her eyes.

Janna watched his exaggerated leer with amusement. Was this an act of him playing out his zombie costume or an obvious sign of a come-on? Halloween always made all normal observations moot.

Bonnie was babbling. Janna had no idea what she was saying until she heard the words 'sex party', which usually snatched her interest, but she was tuned into this zombie Alex before her instead. He had a toned body and suck-worthy lips.

"I'd eat you," Alex growled with a grin.

"Oh, I taste amazing, but you have to buy me a drink first," Janna joked. She fought the urge to see more in his commitment, other than him acting out his zombie.

"Be right back," he said with a snarl, dragging his left leg behind him as if lame.

Janna watched him limp off to the kitchen.

"So? Like him?" Bonnie whispered as her boyfriend ground into her backside.

"We need to dance, babe," he said, giving me a salacious look from behind her tall wig.

"Yes, just me a sec," Bonnie said as she grabbed Janna's hands. "He's hot, right?"

"Yes, he is." Janna's heart pounded. "Is he my surprise date or is he just here?"

"Oh, well, he's just here with Mark."

"He's interested," her boyfriend said loudly over her shoulder. "I know my man, and that look he had just now."

A glimmer of having sex again burst inside Janna. She didn't need a commitment; she just wanted to feel the hands of a man exploring her, savoring her, and the explosion of orgasm from actual sex again. If they were meant to be, then they'd stick, but if not, then just sex was all she needed. She'd entertained asking Bonnie if they could do a threesome, since Mark was kinky. But she also knew Bonnie had zero desire to be with a woman sexually, let alone with a friend, so she'd avoided asking.

But if Mark was kinky, maybe, just maybe, Alex was kinky too. She certainly hoped she'd know by the end of the night.

Her new zombie friend reappeared with two drinks and handed her one. "Zombie brew for you, my magical witch."

She took the cup and glanced in it. It wasn't a beer. "What is it?"

"Zombie brew," he said with a big grin. He grabbed her drink and took a big swallow. "It's safe," he blurted with a wink.

"Ah, nice." She took a swallow herself and was pleasantly surprised. "It's delicious."

"Of course it is, it has blood in it." He cackled wildly as he revealed he had a temperament not fitting for an accountant.

The vampire and the wench returned from somewhere, both looking rather satisfied. Janna was instantly envious. If she'd approached him first and reminded him that she had just been in his shop, that might have been her with that satisfied expression instead of the wench.

But still, there was Alex. He might be as horny as the vampire, and soon she would be smiling happily too. There was still a chance she could get fucked, she surmised.

The wench and the vampire continued to banter behind her as she tried to focus on Alex. With her brain split, she was sure she sounded like a dumb idiot.

"How long have you been working there?" asked Janna, trying hard to make small talk.

"Three years. It's a great job. Boring as fuck, but it pays well, so I can't complain. Just took a trip to Florida on a break from work, so I'm a happy man." He held her gaze intently. "You like the ocean?"

"Oh, yes. Very much so."

"I'd take you with."

He was rather bold, saying he'd take her on a trip after they'd just met. But she knew it was just talk, so she didn't put too much stock in it. It was harmless BS.

"Oh, yeah?" she asked charmingly. "I'd certainly love to lie in the warm sand and sunbathe right about now."

"You'd have to be nude, though," he said with a snicker, naughtiness blazing in his gaze.

She almost spit out the swallow in her mouth, but got it down in time. Her laugh sent his face into pure enjoyment. When she recovered, she said, "Are you a nudist?"

"Sometimes, but I just really like the idea of you nude on a beach."

This told Janna several things. One, he was a flirt. Two, he was fun. Three, he was not a jealous prude. Four, he might be kinky. Five, she was intrigued to know him more.

She giggled as she smiled back at him, making her flirtatious eyes match his. "You look like a dead guy, but you certainly don't seem dead to me." She glanced down at his crotch, and he clearly had a boner riding his torn-up, blood-stained pants.

The sexual energy seemed to swirl around her body, the aura of post-sexual coitus from the couple behind her, the grinding of Mark against Bonnie, and the crystal-clear sexual innuendos from Alex. Maybe it was the zombie drink mixed with her heightened libido, and the sexiness she felt she oozed with the sexy witch costume, but the universe felt right for some kind of fucking.

The wench left the vampire once more, the top of her costume slightly askew, almost showing a blush of pink hue. Curious, Janna made an excuse to go to the bathroom and followed her. She crept along the hallway, staying back far enough away from the wench.

She slipped into the master bedroom. Janna carefully peered at the mirror in the room and watched the wench enter the walk-in closet. She heard two male voices and quickly zipped into the bedroom and hid in the bathroom.

Through the crack beneath the top door hinge, she watched the two men enter the closet. Smack sounds ensued, then lots of moaning. Janna waited on pins as there was a lull. Then the whole thing repeated.

The closet door opened, and Janna slunk back. The two men were joking around, clearly happy. They shut the door behind them and left.

Another man, the one dressed as the lumberjack werewolf, appeared. Janna's heart pounded and she wondered if his senses were anything like a magical wolf because, if so, he'd hear her panting in excitement. Her brain was transfixed on enchanted thoughts tonight. More sounds of slapping came from the closet, which made Janna now wonder if the men were spanking the wench. Lots of moans spilled through the closed door. Then he left. The wench stayed inside.

Janna stole down the hallway in shock at what she'd just witnessed. She made her way back to Alex, catching an eye lock with the vampire. He was very close to Alex, as if they had been chatting.

"I knew that costume would be killer on you," said the vampire appreciatively, yet fully lecherous at once.

Janna grinned. "You do remember me. I wondered."

He grabbed her hand, the gallant gentleman, as most vampires seemed to be, and kissed her hand. "You are not easy to forget, milady."

Enjoying the ancient reference of reverence, she smiled and blushed, resisting the urge to curtsey. That felt a bit too patriarchal for her taste. "Why, thank you."

"She's stunning," parroted Alex. "And I'd like to get you some refreshments. May I make you a plate, my dear witch?"

She cackled like a proper witch, getting into her costume's role. "Yes, that would be lovely."

This left her alone with the vampire. Her heart pattered a race to nowhere as he flashed her his pearly whites. "Having fun at the party?"

"Oh, yes. It's been wonderful." She paused. "And surprising."

"Oh?" He cocked his head. "How so?"

"Well, finding you here, meeting Alex. And ..." Her voice trailed off as she glanced down the hallway she'd just come from. The wench appeared and she was positively glowing. Janna couldn't stop her jaw from dropping as the wench practically floated across the room and landed gracefully next to the vampire.

He extended his hand to Janna. "I'm Maxwell. It's nice to officially meet you ..."

Her pause before taking his hand felt like an eternity. "Janna." She pumped his hand, but her eyes darted between him and the wench. "And what's your name?"

The wench sighed like she was getting a massage and said, "I'm Gwendolyn. The freeuse butt wench."

Janna burst into laughter, but Gwendolyn didn't change her expression at all. She looked dreamy and far off, but satiated.

Maxwell rubbed her back. "Of course you are, baby."

Janna wanted to protest or joke that she was likely right, but Alex appeared with her plate. It was loaded with all kinds of yummy foods, way too much for her to eat. "Well, that's a full plate. It looks wonderful, though. Thank you."

"My pleasure." He did a partial bow.

The two men stood side by side and Janna noticed that they looked a bit similar, though she assumed she imagined it because one was a vampire and the other a zombie, both with white faces.

"You might need to help me a bit with all this food, though," Janna said sheepishly. "I won't be able to move if I eat all of this."

"I'll help," the wench said lightheartedly. "For some reason, I'm famished."

Janna extended the plate to her. She plucked off some cheese, crackers, salami, and carrots.

If sharing a plate with a stranger wasn't strange enough, the vampire gave the wench his beverage. "Take this, Gwendolyn. I'll go get myself another."

Freeuse must mean sharing cups and plates, too.

She took it and consumed the entire thing while trying to juggle all the food in her hands.

Alex chuckled at her softly. "Can I help you out, Gwendolyn?"

"No, I'm perfect. Thanks to you two."

What could that mean? Janna blinked, and her head shifted back in surprise.

Maxwell appeared with a fresh glass and handed one to Alex. "Thanks, bro," Alex said.

"No problem."

Her head a bit foggy from the alcohol, Janna scanned the room for Mark and Bonnie. They were nowhere to be seen. Likely, they had slipped off to fuck.

"Do you enjoy groups?" Alex asked her.

It was an odd question.

"Groups? Like parties?" Janna asked, confused.

"Well, yes. That and more."

Speaking in puzzles was not a fun game in Janna's book. She contemplated leaving them, because it was getting weirder by the second.

"Please don't go," he said softly. There was genuineness in his expression.

Fright gripped her by the throat. He could read her mind? She scolded herself. That's ridiculous. She was taking the mystical nature of the night too far.

She braced herself to tear off across the room when Maxwell touched her shoulder gently.

"We can smell it on you. The fear. You don't need to be afraid."

Her fear thickened. She figured she could make it to the kitchen in five seconds flat and go find Bonnie for safety.

"They helped me," the wench Gwendolyn said. "They can help you too."

That affirmation didn't help much, not after all the closet business she'd just witnessed. And freeuse butt wench? This was now a Halloween costume?

The men both gazed at Janna. There was something comforting in both of their eyes — eyes that seriously looked exactly the same shade of blue, the same shape, and with the same intensity.

"Do you two know each other?" she asked skeptically.

"Yes. We are brothers." Maxwell tilted his head towards Alex. "See, identical."

The costumes had been messing with Janna's perceptions. But she could see the resemblance clearly with their faces right next to each other. They were the same exact height and build, too.

"Seriously? Wow. No shit?"

"Actually, we have another brother, too. We are triplets. But you met him already. Your friend Bonnie's new boyfriend, Mark."

Mark, Maxwell, and Alex. That didn't sound like a set of triplet names. Mark seemed an outlier's name. Her mind mulled this around as her gaze flicked from one face to the other.

"We are sex wizards. We can grant you your wish tonight, but only tonight, as Halloween is when our power is maxed out."

Janna's brain spun. Her mind searched for some kind of sense. But she could find none. Their faces were pleasant, but set in a serious expression. Gwendolyn was now being pulled away by another man dressed as a Big Foot. She was giggling and flirty and he gave her a swat on the butt, which caused her to squeal and run down the hallway.

Janna burst into raucous laughter. "Ah, this is some big joke! You guys got me good! Fuck, that's hysterical!"

Their expressions did not change at all. An eerie feeling descended upon Janna like a clear fog. The men both looked patient, but expectant.

"If you tell us your fantasy, we will make it so for tonight." Alex ran a hand down his groin, which outlined his erection for Janna.

Janna checked herself. Okay. She'd play along. She could be sexy and flirty just like them. "What, with that big yang of a schlong of yours?"

"Oh, I have lots of yin, too. I'm in balance. All three of us are."

She would have refuted it, but there was the fact that Alex had taken care of her by getting her a drink and a plate of food. But that wasn't enough evidence. She just met these jokers. She still couldn't get her brain around the fact that they were brothers.

"Triplets?" Sexy triplets. What were the astronomical odds of that actually happening? It seemed damn near impossible. And for her to run into all three of them? Well, it wasn't so farfetched to think three brothers would go to a Halloween party together, though. But sex wizards? That was the cheesiest come-on line she'd heard yet in her thirty-six years of life.

"We can grant your wish. I sensed your heightened unmet desires when you bought the costume the other day. I talked with my brothers, and we made a pact to help you out. The universe sent you to us." Maxwell did not smirk, laugh, or give any indication that he was lying.

It was true she hadn't meant to buy the costume that day after a double shift at the hospital. But something had sparked her to pull into the parking lot. Then she'd seen the store. Knowing she needed a costume, she decided to get that errand out of the way and she sauntered into the store.

"Universe?" she asked dumbly. She needed to talk to Bonnie. "I need to go find my friend. I'll catch you guys later."

She left and scurried away from them, not looking back. She started opening doors, which she knew was risky. She might open the door on people having sex and unnecessarily expose them. She didn't want to be an intruder, but her panic led her forward. She had wanted a hookup, so why was she fleeing men who seemed like they could fulfill that?

She opened the guest room door and sure enough, Bonnie and Mark were fucking doggy style on the bed. Bonnie was tied up with a bright orange bow strapping her wrists together. Her face rubbed the bed each time he slammed into her. She was moaning obnoxiously.

She quickly retreated and shut the door a bit too loud. She took several deep breaths. She could leave the party. But that would leave her sexless again. Or she could play along with these fools and perhaps end the night in a flurry of delicious orgasms. Scary as it seemed, she wanted the latter.

She crept along the wall, wanting to melt into it, yet wanting to all-out run back to the two mysterious men. They were intriguing, and she loved the idea of sex wizards, though she had zero clue what that really meant. As if they had a string around her waist, she meandered her way through the people back to them.

"Find her?" Alex asked sweetly.

"Yes, Mark is fucking her doggy. So, I left them." She needed to talk to Bonnie. Even though her heart was racing, and she couldn't think straight, she decided to prod them for info. "What's a sex wizard?"

They both looked immediately pleased by her question. Alex reached for her hand. "May I guide you to rest on this couch?"

She nodded and his large hand encircled her own. The move felt dangerous, but exciting to be led by him anywhere.

The three of them sat on the couch in the back corner of the room. She'd sat there many times with Bonnie, watching movies, drinking wine, and eating takeout. She knew these guys were playing her, but the thought of them fucking her garnered her courage to continue. If they were safe, she'd consider this, but she needed to talk to Bonnie before getting naked.

Maxwell cleared his throat. "We are magical triplets who can sense unmet sexual desires in women and grant their wishes."

A laugh gurgled up from her gut and spewed out of her mouth. That was the most fabulous load of shit she'd ever heard in her life.

"He's serious," Alex chimed in.

They looked as if they believed themselves. Some good convincing drugs they'd taken, perhaps?

"You saw how happy Gwendolyn was, right? That was her wish. She's the happiest she'd been in years." Alex nodded, as did Maxwell.

It made sense, sort of, but honestly, she didn't need these two fakes to get her ass smacked and ass fucked by men in a closet. "I'm pretty sure she could manage what she's doing all on her own."

"That's true. Of course. But Gwendolyn has never had anal sex or been spanked before tonight." Alex grinned deeply like some lecherous pervert or spectacularly magical genius. "We gave her the gift of pleasure with this. It was her fantasy to do this, but she couldn't have progressed to freeuse anal sex like this in just one night and enjoy it without the help of our magic."

Janna wholeheartedly believed that to be true, to enjoy being buttfucked by multiple men when she'd never had anal sex in her life? Only magic or a miracle could make that happen. The sounds she'd heard from the closet were pure pleasure, not pain.

Starting to believe they may have slipped her some drugs in her food and drink, she asked, "And what about Bonnie? Does she know all this?"

Maxwell laughed, his eyes twinkling. "She knows a little. But she and Mark met and genuinely hit it off."

Janna guessed that was possible. But the rest seemed like bullshit. "You guys are a riot. Is this some Halloween spoof?" she asked, chagrined.

"Tell us your wish and we will grant it. There will be no negative repercussions, only pleasure for you and fabulous memories to masturbate to in the future," Alex assured her.

Sexy men offering her sex pleasure. It sounded too good to be true. Should she dare tell them the truth? Or would they fuck her and leave her like a used piece of meat? But isn't this what she wanted to begin with? A hookup to simply have sex?

She took a deep breath. "I just want a sex hookup. Where I have sex."

Alex and Maxwell both tittered with laughter.

Alex spoke in a sexy voice that made Janna wet. "Well, that's way too easy. We can do that any day. Why don't you dig deeper, and we will give it to you?"

Janna felt the word rolling around her insides as her lust began to swell. It was something she'd always wanted but never had the chance to try. "An orgy, with two men and a woman."

"Good girl," Maxwell exclaimed as if he were her Daddy Dom.

Janna beamed and immediately felt sheepish that the praise kink worked on her.

"I feel you blossoming," Alex said. "Maxwell, let's strike now. She's ready."

"Do you give us permission to grant this sex wish for you?" Maxwell ventured.

These two men couldn't be any sexier, but Janna instantly wondered if they'd fulfill her wish, or if it would be other men.

"It can be us, if you desire it so," Alex said with a salacious gaze. "I'd like that very much, as would Maxwell. We've already discussed how sexy we both find you to be."

Janna nodded. "Yes, I want it to be you two, and I want to feel like a sex goddess. Full enjoyment, no guilt or shame, but the best sex with the best orgasms of my life."

"It shall be." Alex raised his arm high in the air.

Janna woke in the back bedroom. Both Alex and Maxwell were undressing her. Gwendolyn was hovering above her face.

"Can I kiss you, milady?" Still in medieval mode, Gwendolyn the wench licked her lips.

"Yes," Janna said without any hesitation. This would be her first taste of a woman's lips, though she'd dreamt of it many times.

The men massaged her limbs, caressing her flesh in hungry grabs and sensual caresses as Gwendolyn pressed her lips ever so delicately to Janna's. Their delicate kiss deepened in strength, giving evidence of mutual attraction and passion.

Janna reached up and slipped Gwendolyn's top down, exposing her large, juicy breasts. She touched them gently at first, and as Gwendolyn moaned louder, she began to grope her boobs harder. She squeezed and tugged her nipples, enjoying their rise between her fingertips as they intertwined their tongues deeper into each other's mouths.

Their moans enticed the men to roam their hands about Janna with greater force. Janna cooed her acceptance of their touch, feeling glory in the fact that she indeed felt no guilt or shame at all hooking up with all three of them.

Her euphoria began its ascent up her body as Alex and Maxwell pressed their fingers first on her mound, then along her slit. Four fingers exploring her watering cunt while she kissed Gwendolyn's nipples launched her to the edge of new sexual heights. She writhed, becoming more fluid in their hungry grasps. The press of first fingertips, then tongue to her clit sent her inner sensuality rolling and her voice into a glorious moan of pleasure.

"Ride me, baby," she begged Gwendolyn as Alex descended upon her clit, his mouth sealing her bean into his lush, conforming lips.

He began to suck her clit, as Maxwell pressed his fingers into her pussy for a rapid finger fuck. The aroma of Gwendolyn's pussy was like a trance itself as she pressed herself into Janna's open mouth. The taste of her sweet pussy was exquisite, as was the smell of dried cum from multiple men that had saturated her anus.

They worked over Janna's pussy while Alex tweaked and tugged at her nipples. The world transformed into colors and waves of pleasure. Sensations floated through her and then out of her body as she entered the first inklings of climax. She erupted into an explosive orgasm that made her body twitch as contractions rocked out her vagina with such intensity that she cried out, making sounds and nonsensical words like never before.

Elation swirled in every cell of her body. The extreme sensitivity was almost too much to accept, yet she was flung into scrumptiously living every second of it. Time elongated as her orgasm went from separate contractions to one long, constant euphoric flowing ride. She could no longer separate her sounds from her pleasure. They were one song that was her full atmosphere.

As she landed back to more familiar consciousness, she tried to push the men off her. Her clit was too sensitive, and at this point, this was when she usually ripped the sex toy off herself or smacked her lover away. But Alex pressed his erection at her engorged lips and entered her body. She was not in control, and it was divine.

His groan of pleasure furthered her realization of her own ecstasy in her orgasmic reverie, and she moaned right along with him.

Maxwell pulled Gwendolyn into doggy position. She cried out with joy as her face gyrated above Janna's as he fucked her from behind. She scrambled to kiss Janna, their lips meeting, then slipping off as the men rammed into them.

Their combined moans were a more beautiful sound than Janna had ever heard. She succumbed to orgasm once again as he smacked her clit with his pelvis. Not climaxing yet himself, he pushed her into another heightened orgasm as he pounded into her relentlessly.

Janna felt empowered in their joint feminine sexual energy as Gwendolyn came twitching against her mouth, her left tit slipping out of Janna's lips.

Janna tugged on Gwendolyn. "Sweet baby, lay on me. Let them fuck us that way."

Gwendolyn grinned blissfully, clearly enjoying this idea. "Yesssss," she said with a long slur.

She laid upon Janna, and they enjoyed a deeply passionate French kiss as the men finagled their alignment out. Janna had full confidence in them. These fuckers knew what they were doing.

"We can do this. Alex, you fuck Gwendolyn's ass, tilted to the right, and I'll enter Janna's pussy, leaning to the left."

It sounded impossible, but with their legs in the right spots, and Alex's left foot on a stack of pillows, they were ready. Janna wished she could watch the contraption of their sex working together as a foursome, but she also knew, she'd much rather be integral to the middle of it.

As the men entered the women, all four groaned out. The pumping steadily increased as did the skin smacking sounds. They enjoyed juicy orgy fucking for several minutes before Janna was pushed to climax first. Her pussy hugged Maxwell's cock and he scrambled backward as his cum spewed across all three of their skins. Alex came next, pulling out and splattering his cum all across Gwendolyn's back.

Gwendolyn reached down and worked Janna's clit, and Janna reciprocated. They grunted and writhed as they stimulated each other to the peak of panting and loud moans. Both women came together.

As they lay sandwiched together, splattered in cum, fingers coated with each other's juices, they panted cheek to cheek. It was a sensual aftercare snuggle as the men fit themselves in around their union.

"The most unbelievable sex of my entire life," Janna said in a soft, breathy, and satiated voice.

"Yes," Gwendolyn repeated, still panting as well. "Same."

The men caressed both Janna and Gwendolyn.

"That was beautiful. An array of sexuality we have not been a part of for many years. Thank you for wanting to include us." Alex played Janna's hair and cradled the two of them to his flesh.

"Yes, that was amazing. You outdid yourself. I could feel you both." Maxwell's voice was low and soothing.

It was a dream fuck. Janna was grateful she'd met the sex wizards. Being supernatural, she wondered if she'd remember this tomorrow.

"Yes, you will," Alex said. "And I'd like to ask you to go on a date to get pizza with me."

The invite felt like a joke after what they'd just done, but Janna chuckled. "Yes, Alex. I'd love to." She paused as Gwendolyn rolled off of her and nestled up to her, with Maxwell molded to her body from behind. Janna patted her cheek before glancing back at Alex. "May I ask, if you are this mystical set of triplet sex wizards, how old are you guys?"

Alex laughed heartily. "Now that's funny. Well, we will be forty-one in a month."

Janna was flooded with relief. "Oh, good, I thought you were going to say you are five hundred or something."

"We live regular life spans," Maxwell commented.

After a few more minutes of snuggling and bantering back and forth reminiscing about their hookup, they dressed back in their costumes and joined the rest of the freaks at the party. Knowing the best freaks were the ones who had gotten to realize their sex dreams. And the rest were just wannabes. Janna snickered. Too bad fuckers, maybe next year...

The End

The Genie's Wish

Dark

He wasn't a sissy, but he wanted her hands on his nipples and her breasts high above him, her hips pinning him to the carpet, her fingers roaming his skin. He wanted her to force his cock to touch as deep inside her pussy as it could. He worried his length would not please her, but he knew his girth would, so he had that at least. With a nod he pressed his lips firmly together.

"Pleasure yourself right now. Use the jojoba oil. I know you're a good boy and did as I asked. Now. Coat your hard cock thoroughly with the oil. But, remember my pet, do not come yet." Her sexy buttery voice sang out of his phone making his head spin.

His lust thickened as a rush of euphoria swept his brain.

"Don't miss your hole. Poke at it. Rub that delicious-veined cock. Stroke. Stroke. Stroke."

Hanson set his phone on the bed next to him, it sank into the soft comforter making a rectangular indent. He carefully squirted the oil in his hand and kept his palm up cradling it like it was precious. His other hand shook as he pushed the triangular play button on the audio clip. Her DM's had been coming hourly today with explicit instructions. His cock was hard as a rock cutter. One of her words and his pants instantly got tighter, his swollen cock pushed out the fabric fighting its way out of the waistband of his underwear.

He shoved the elastic down to his balls to free his cock, it swung out. He groaned. He glanced down at the shiny precum threatening to spill off the top of his cockhead, more and more it oozed out and traveled down the channel in his cockhead, leaking down to wet his shaft. He would lightly smear it down the length to mix with the oil. He shuddered with anticipation.

"Oh, fuck me," he muttered, his unbuttoned shirt slipped off his right shoulder as he shifted on the bed. He panted as he fingered his appendectomy scar as his hand traveled dangerously close to his throbbing boner. "Not yet, dumbass." His body jerked involuntarily almost spilling the oil in his hand.

He froze as her voice came melodiously out of his phone and made his cock twitch, more precum seeped out like someone squeezed his balls.

He watched the swirls on the video. They were like glowing jewel-toned glittery ripples of water dancing in darker hues.

Her voice sensuously lulled him, transfixing his eyes to his phone. "Use enough oil. Like the size of a quarter in your palm. Rub it into that delicious-veined cock and stroke. Stroke. Stroke. Use that precum oozing out and spread it all over the head of your cock. I'm imagining you doing this and I'm touching myself. I'm very wet. You are very wet." She paused. "I'm so fucking hot right now. I need you to come fuck me. Soon."

Hanson eyed up the oil assessing if he had the right amount. He grinned.

He panted harder as he stopped the video and restarted it, for the fifteenth time. He was watching the clock. Two more minutes until her next audio was to drop. He rubbed his cock lovingly with the oil, then roughly as he imagined his hand was hers. His body shook as he neared climax. He withdrew his hand quickly and laid his head back on the bed with a sigh. Fuck he wanted to come, but he knew that would disappoint her. The ceiling blurred as he stared, his contacts stuck to his eyes until he blinked several times to rewet them. He'd need to add eye drops before he left.

He switched over to her Twitter feed, feeling sorry for his swollen aching cock, and scrolled down until he found her picture in the red full bodice lingerie. Her magnificent breasts filled the lace to the point of stressing it and her body swelled into a svelte figure eight down her hips. Her luscious skin was the color of a just barely toasted marshmallow, and just as soft looking. The desire to taste her flesh filled him with a rage.

He swiped the drool from the corner of his mouth as he continued to edge as she had instructed. He glanced at the time on his phone and his panting increased. Twenty seconds until the next audio. He gasped, yanked his cock once more then shoved the beef stick into his mouth.

"Eat it with your precum on it," she had said previously. "Just right before my next audio loads."

Earlier he had dabbed the beef stick on his cock tip, then he had drawn the whole stick down his shaft through his precum dribble to coat it. She had been adamant that he get as much precum on the beef stick as he could.

He gnawed the precum laced stick, his sweet salty juice has seasoned the stick quite nicely. He moaned as he scrolled through all her pics back to the image of her pussy she had sent yesterday. It reminded him of a calla lily, pink, lush, moist, practically elegant as it dived to her lush moist insides. Her cunt was creamy like the frosting of his favorite donut. He imagined his tongue slipping in to taste her and he groaned.

The square of a new video popped on the screen. His breath caught as the unchewed hunk of beef roughly blocked his esophagus. He coughed harshly and swallowed hard to get the meat to tumble to his gut.

"Now fed with the beef stick soaked in nourishment from your own body, your precum, edging still, I want you to pinch your nipples. Lick your fingers. Pinch your nipples again. Do it," she cooed.

His hands trembled as he imagined her busty chest rising and falling with each word, each breath as he shoved the rest of the beef stick in his mouth. His nipples screamed as he jerked them, his back writhing against the soft mattress. He panted and stared at his phone. That was all he was going to get?

Another video popped up and he gasped.

"In one hour, you are to come to this address. 6435 Rosegold Lane. Come alone. Come thirsty and hungry. Come commando," she said, her honey voice thickening his cock even further. "Do not allow yourself to ejaculate until you are with me in person, and I say you can. See you soon." The three little dots blinked, then disappeared.

The dots reappeared before her message splatted on the screen. "Being late = punishment of your choosing ... but of my approval."

His cock swung as he hopped to his feet. He kicked his soccer ball over to his guitar, still out of its case from last night, and dug in the pile of clothes for his blue shirt so his eyes would pop for her. Pulling his jeans delicately over his boner, he wiggled as he slowly zipped, wincing as he carefully tugged it up over the bulge. His head throbbed. He needed water.

The rubbing pressure of his tight jeans against his cock hardened his dick more. "Ah, fuck," he muttered. "Don't come. Don't come. Don't come yet, dumbass." Her images all crowded his head as he dashed towards the bathroom. He barely shed his jeans in time, sighed as the blast of cold water doused his hardon. "Whew!" He glanced at the clock on the counter. "Time to go, fucker."

The wind was brisk just like October was supposed to be. The leaves were the right colors of the season change. His cock had flared into a hardon again as he heard her voice in his head. He relaxed a bit as he slid into his car, after which he waved to his elderly neighbor, her robe tight around her as she bent over to pick up her dog's poop. He grinned. A nice ass on a GILF was never wasted on him.

He knew the way to Rosegold Lane. He had once dated a sexy tall blond woman from the same street. She had loved giving head in public places. When she dumped him, he had cried like a baby weaned from a juicy tit.

He glared at her house as he drove past, long ago emptied of her beauty.

The ornate black metal on the house sign curled into a continuous stroke as the numerals 6435. Her house was dark except for a candle flickering in the window beside some sort of spikey plant. The dancing light looked more like mini devils partying than simple flashing light. As he pulled into the driveway, the outside spotlight came on. Setting foot on her driveway inspired his cock to swell more.

The breeze rushed his body as he stood up. He scanned the Tudor style house for a glimpse of her. He gasped and froze in his tracks.

She stood in the doorway and his cock fully filled the void to the right side of his zipper. He took a deep breath before a step, not even bothering to lock his car.

His heart pounded. His cock throbbed with each beat. His breathing raged and his back sweat.

"Hanson, welcome. Please, come in." Her breasts might as well have been a Thanksgiving turkey as ripe, succulent, and juicy as they looked, he just wanted to take a bite. Her eyes danced with mischief and her lips curled into a smile. All he could think about was how they would feel pressed around his cock.

"H-hi," he stuttered, a more foreign sound had never graced past his lips. "H-how are y-y-y-you?" What was this?

"I'm wonderful now that you are here, Hanson. Please. Come in." She leaned down, spilling her deep cleavage, and tapped her long black fingernail on the bulge in his jeans. "I see you are a good boy and brought your cock full for me."

His pride swelled. His jaw dropped open as she cocked her head to the side and licked her lips. Her perfect teeth glowed white against her dark red lipstick in the candle light that emanated from behind her. He gazed around the room. She must have at least a hundred candles lit. He wondered how long it took her to light them all as she walked to front of the fireplace.

The dark wooden mantel housed about fifty some bottles of all different colored glass, all jewel toned. "Nice bottle collection."

"Hanson," she said as snatched his chin with her fingers.

He almost came right in his pants.

"Would you like a glass of wine or a cocktail?"

Even her smile made his cock twitch. The twinkle in her eyes made him feel dizzy. He couldn't think coherently worth shit. Drink, did he want a drink? Yes. No. What the fuck?

"I'll get you something. Just take a seat. I'll be right back." She deepened her smile.

The ribbons that trailed off her skirt snaked along the ground as she walked. She hummed as she sauntered, seductively swaying her hips with each step. She glanced back before disappearing into the kitchen, her eyes full of delicious lust.

On the wall was a cuckoo clock. The little miniature woman was frozen about to spank the naked bottom of the boy over her lap. He smirked. The ornate wood carving not only made it look handmade but old, probably ancient, a family heirloom passed from one woman to the next.

He shivered as a breeze wafted through from the open front door, a full-blown autumn gale wafted briskly through her house, lifting the scent of some sort of spice. The gust made its way to the patio door she also had open. Beyond the door, her backyard was glowing green with a garden boasting about ten large pumpkins and two sunflowers that must have been at least ten feet tall apiece. They swayed in the sinking sun, their massive heads bobbed like those who pray with obedience.

He jumped as she handed him a glass with brown liquid in it. "Whiskey sour. You look like a man who likes a good shot of whiskey."

He rubbed his goatee and smiled. "You got me." Relieved he didn't stutter this time, he took a slow sip. "It's good. Thank you."

She sat next to him on the couch before taking a sip from her steel goblet. She nodded. "Red wine for me." She leaned forward and her right breast fell forward, exposing the light blushed pink skin of her areola.

He couldn't take his eyes off it. Surely, she must feel the breeze on it. A drop of drool fell from his slack mouth. He ignored it.

She leaned forward to adjust a toe ring on her right middle toe, carefully holding her wine glass upright as her full tit fell completely out, exposing her hard nipple, bumps, dips, ridges and all.

He spit out the whiskey, most of it making it back into his cup, but dribbles seared down his chin.

She giggled like a little girl, yet it was so seductive he almost came in his pants once more. Her laughter turned his heart to gold. She leaned over and licked the whiskey off his chin.

His breath came so heavy now. He wanted nothing more than to ram his cock into her.

"I really want to play with you, Hanson. Do you like to play?"

He nodded like an imbecile. All he could think about was how her pussy must look under that maroon fabric, that hint of mound that surfaced when her dress moved just right. His head swam with the scent of lavender and dill that wafted off her, an odd combo that made him want to lick every speck of her taut exposed skin, and remove the rest of her clothes with his teeth.

"You are so very sexy, Hanson. I want you to join my collection. Have you thought this commitment through?"

He could not answer as she pulled her other breast free from the boddice of her dress. With both breasts exposed, he swallowed hard as his cock twitched against the rough fabric of his jeans.

Was he supposed to say something?

She took a long slow sip of her wine and as she pulled the goblet from her beguiling mouth, she bit her lip. "So, do you want to be my plaything? I give the best rewards for good behavior." She stood up and set her drink on the wooden coffee table next to a bowl of dead multi-colored flowers. "I'll show you what you will get if you say yes."

Hanson watched transfixed as she slid her dress off her shoulders and pushed it to the floor. Naked, she did a slow spin for him. "Better not come yet. I'm not ready." Even her pointed scolding finger looked sexy. His heart beat so fast it might beat itself to death exhausted.

He swallowed hard and tried to ignore his urge to grab her by the hips, spin her around, and ram his cock into that pretty wet pink pussy of hers. The urge to come raged in him as she cupped her breasts and played with her nipples. She danced in front of the fire pulling her nipples, rolling her hips, her candlelit silhouette unfolding his true fantasy right before his eyes. If he got to fuck her, he'd do anything she said.

"Will you make me come?" she whispered as she undulated her hips, the firelight licking her skin as she rolled her body. "Lots? I really need to come. My other boys are waiting, but you get me."

Hanson's jaw dropped further, and he almost spilled his whiskey. How had he gotten this lucky to find a woman like this on Twitter who lived two streets from his house? And now he'd get what the others didn't. He'd get her.

"I knew you'd be a good pet." She swirled her tongue around her lips and left it in the right corner of her luscious lips.

She knew him? He cocked his head to the side with a smirk.

"I could tell by your eyes and the way you sipped your coffee Friday in my shop." She smiled.

Her dancing clogged his brain, her gyrations made her breasts bounce, which made his cock leak precum. His pants were undone at the top. How had that happened? He furrowed his brow as she knelt in front of him, grasping his zipper with her fingers. She slowly unzipped his jeans down his hard cock. He winced as she shoved his hand away.

"Let me, baby."

His body stiffened as she dragged the zipper down his naked shaft. He held his breath, not daring even the slightest movement for fear of her snagging his skin as she fully bared his cock. He sighed a huge sigh of relief as the zipper hit bottom.

She licked his cock from his balls up to his cockhead. He almost spewed his cum all over her face as she flicked her tongue all around the ridge, devoting the most time to his frenulum.

"Mmmm, yummy," she said as she swiped her tongue snagging the latest blast of precum bubbling out the top of his cock.

"Oh, dear Gawd," he said with a shiver.

"If you fuck me, you join my collection. Do you want to be in my collection, Hanson?"

He nodded. Of course, he did.

"Be among those who have fucked me. Who get to fuck me on repeat?" She paused and gazed deeply into his eyes.

He nodded again, salivating at the thought.

She grasped his cock by the shaft and pulled him to the front of the fireplace. She bent over and grasped the two metal horns sticking out of the stone. She gripped them like they were meant to be held during a rough fuck.

"Eat me by the fire. Then fuck me. Make me come and you get to do it over and over again, your wish will be fulfilled." She hummed and swiveled her hips.

As he sank down to ready himself to lick her pussy, he saw eyes and a smile flash from inside a blue bottle on the mantel. He froze as the mist inside the bottle swirled revealing the naked chest of a man with a cock at attention.

He shook his head. "I want this. I want you," he muttered as he inhaled the musky scent of her pussy. "You smell amazing." His cock twitched as he imagined fucking her from behind with his face covered in her cum. "Your scent loads my cock."

"I know," she whispered.

"Have we met before though?" he asked, his cock swinging as he took a step back.

"Oh, my dear, you are further along than I thought." She smiled and he forgot his name. "Yes, I'm Goddess. Remember, you've been coming to my coffee shop for months between classes. We chat every day, love. I explained it all and you have taken each step perfectly."

He narrowed his eyes and tipped his head to the side. "I have? We do?"

"Yes. The Witch's Brew coffee shop on the edge of campus. Remember? You love my secret brew and said you wanted it ... The Genie's Wish." Her look was endearing yet inquisitive with the sweetest little sexy smile he'd ever seen in his life.

The Genie's Wish. It sounded a little familiar to him and there was something comforting in her eyes as she stroked his bicep. Surely, he remembers her. A flash of her handing him a ceramic turquoise coffee cup danced across his brain. "Ah, yes."

The breeze blew through the room again and lifted her hair up, her curls looked like shells of Medusa hair, without the nasty threat of biting snake mouths. "You can leave now if you want." Her smile was so charming he almost forgot to breathe. "My collection of mutual sexual satisfaction is only open to those who have consented. Fully consented."

He stared into her eyes as they changed from green to blue to greenish-blue, right before they swirled with glittered black streaks, like her DM videos. He noticed all her dried herbs hanging on the wall in the kitchen, their stems held together by twine as if hung by feet, their wide leafy heads spread out in a fan like wispy hair. A single emerald-green jar sat atop the marble countertop beneath a spotlight. It was beautiful with a tapered neck and wide circular base, and it held his gaze as she laid kisses up and down his shaft.

His body twitched as she sucked his right ball into her mouth and gently rippled her tongue along it before doing the same to his left one. She gripped his thighs as euphoria overcame him, suffocating his fear.

"I want to stay," he whispered as she took his cockhead into her mouth.

She mouth rode his cock and popped off just in time before he spewed. "Ride me now, make me cum and our deal will be made permanent."

He watched as she spun, bent over and tipped her lovely wide curvy ass toward him. He licked his lips. The emerald-green bottle was now on the mantle and rose petals, some kind of dried weeds, and burnt orange dust surrounded the base of it. He didn't fucking care.

He took a step toward her firm ass and gripped both cheeks and spread her wide open from behind. He took a deep breath as she moaned. "Fuck me, Hanson, my lover. Fuck me. Make your choice wisely. Stay and fuck me on repeat forever or leave and never fuck me. It's your choice."

His eyes watered as his grip grew firmer on her taut warm flesh. He spread her pussy lips open with the head of his cock and the scent of her pussy spread upwards intoxicating him. With a deep breath of her, he brushed the tip of his cock along her labia lips and swirled it around her clit. Her moans were unlike any he'd ever heard before and he felt deep satisfaction as the head of his cock rested on her slit.

He pushed himself into her vagina with a giant groan. Her womb felt better than any woman he'd ever been with in his life. She moaned and the sound filled his body with joy and ecstasy as he sped up his pumping into her. He leaned forward and fondled her full breasts and as she leaned back her hair tickled his nose. It smelled like the prairie of wildflowers that bloomed behind his childhood house every spring, the aroma making him feel drunk.

He began to pump himself into her, gently at first, then he fucked her wildly as she spilled nonsense words in deep lush moans, her cascading hair swishing against her toned back. The nonsense words she uttered intoxicated him further as she pushed her ass back against his cock. He continued fucking her as her moans grew louder, sweeter, intricately swelling his sexual gratification to the greatest heights of his life.

A raven cawed. He twitched and stopped moving.

"Oh, my pet," she whispered. "Don't stop. That's just my pet raven."

He nodded and continued to ram his cock into her. He wouldn't last much longer. One, two, three, four pumps and he felt himself lose his grip as his cock spewed cum inside her pussy, he gazed at the bottles on the mantle. Their insides swirled like a mist was trapped inside. In the red one, he saw the image of a naked man with a large raging boner. As the fog in the bottle lifted, he saw the man's smile.

Her body twitched, a spasm that started at her pelvis traveled all along her body, her torso curling forward, her chin tucking to her chest. The moan that escaped her lips was the most erotic and lovely sound he'd ever heard. The contractions from her vagina squeezed his cock inside of her with such a tight ferocious grip that he couldn't decipher one constriction from another, and he somehow came again.

Feeling like he was about to pass out from pleasure, he orgasmed once more. His head spun from the multiple orgasms. He felt a huge surge of release from his cock and his body. Extreme euphoria and a feeling of lightness enveloped him, as if he weighed nothing at all. He was floating.

"Best orgasms ever," he whispered as the fog he had just seen in that red bottle cloaked his face as it switched to green. It was moist and calming yet charged with an excitement he could not explain. He took a deep breath as the grin on his face grew. He felt himself fill the air.

Below him Goddess was spinning, twirling as her hair flew out in a circle like a wide halo around her body. She was chanting something, but he couldn't understand her words, but honestly, he didn't give a fuck. She was so beautiful. He'd never felt this good in his entire life and he didn't want it to end.

His soul danced as her sweet voice said more words he didn't understand. He caught a glimpse of three black cats on the couch all laying across each other. On the wall above the couch was a painting of a pond with blurry white water lilies and green leaves. The butterfly in the right corner was flying up and then he imagined he too was a butterfly as he closed his eyes. He floated as if being carried by a giant. He was the sound of a moan sailing on the air.

When he opened his eyes, the world looked even more green. He could see Goddess holding a bottle in her hands. She looked huge, like a Giantess. He imagined curling his whole body around her hard nipple and hugging it, using his tiny tongue to lick it.

Goddess rubbed the bottle in her hands and said something, but her words were too muffled for him to understand. Mist grew out of the bottle until a buff man stood before Goddess. He was a very sexy man with the kind of muscles most men could never achieve, despite massive amounts of weightlifting and running.

Goddess set the bottle on the mantle while holding the buff man's hand. He pulled her to him, and they embraced, his cock a thick shaft sandwiched between their torsos. The buff man kissed her neck and that collarbone of hers that he wanted his mouth on too. A threesome would be amazing, and he'd even consider fucking the man if Goddess wanted it.

He drooled as he watched the man scoop up Goddess and set her on the couch. He spread her legs, which gave Hanson a view of her beautiful pussy.

He began to stroke his cock as he watched the man orally pleasure Goddess, her body writhing, her mouth open in a soundless moan.

When the man pushed his cock into Goddess, movement caught his attention. He turned and saw a man through a smoky haze. He too was stroking his cock while watching Goddess and the man fucking. He jerked his cock, a spray of sperm splattered out, smacking the green glass in front of him. He leaned forward and licked it off.

The taste of his own cum woke him from the reverie as he glanced upward at the tiny circular window at the top that he knew he'd never be able to climb out on his own. He smiled as Goddess picked up his bottle and brought him to her smiling face. She kissed the bottle and unbelievably, his cock swelled once more. He hurried to kiss her back through the glass, but he was too tired to move. He sat on the glass bottom of the bottle and curled into a ball as she hugged it and rubbed it. His turn had arrived once again as his body turned into mist and he floated out the top window.

The End

Boobs and Pizza Everywhere but not a Drop to Eat, A Modern-Day Tantalus Tale

A Greek Mythology Tantalus erotic torturous fantasy in modern day.
Dark, NOT HEA, Depraved, Torturous

Charles wiped the drool from the corner of his otherwise dry mouth. His level of thirst was reaching a painful level as he trudged through the dense vegetation. If only his feet weren't sopping wet, maybe he'd be able to tolerate the hunger, but it all made him ornery as hell.

The sun was beating down on him, but that wouldn't stop his trek. He'd known the last clue was the key to finding the lake. He also intended to make it there by nightfall, even if he had to sleep in a tree. The large snakes and gators meant he'd never be able to sleep on the ground or he'd be dinner.

Speaking of dinner, he hallucinated pizzas everywhere he looked. It was a rare form of torture his brain kept hurling him into. And damn, his cock wouldn't stop announcing his daily meat choking hadn't happened yet.

He squirmed beneath the beating sun rays as he contemplated masturbating. If he couldn't meet his other needs, maybe climaxing would do the trick.

He pulled out his cock and began to stroke himself. He was amazed that his body could still make precum with how dehydrated he was. But his balls were likely misers, stealing fluid from other parts of his body to prioritize his pleasure. They were a good pair that had never faltered in their support of his gargantuan sex drive.

That very sex drive was what had him traipsing through mucky jungles and swatting bugs. He'd traded his desk job for a quest to find the Lake of Blissful Wishes. It was a myth everyone reported, but then he found out it was real. He knew it in his gut. And it was his mission to find the hidden jewel.

One of the few wonders of the world, the lake promised a person would be surrounded by their greatest wishes and wants. The lake's Goddess would read whoever stood in its waters, and it would create the ultimate fantasy for the person who was immersed.

There was a risk, though. A danger that the lake would consume the body in torturous never-ending swells for one whose heart was not pure.

But he was pure and perfect.

He grinned as he searched the far-off landscape as he chugged his hand across his fat, hard cock. It was at full-packed mast and the build was proving delicious. He imagined a harem of women in a tent before him and fell quickly into a fantasy of fucking them all, and them all sucking his cock. He'd come fifty times in one day. Then they'd feed him grapes while he rested on the many generous bosoms of the women.

He chuckled at himself, then his expression curdled into his orgasm face. Hot cum spewed out of his cock and splatted on the earthen floor. A white puddle of jizz stood out on the black dirt like a star in the night sky. The breeze caressed his body as he shuddered.

He left the mark of his seed, and he was pleased. He summoned up a meager stream of spit to get the bad taste out of his mouth as he walked on. Coming had made him feel better. Now he must carry on, so he'd find the lake by dark.

He had read one warning that bothered him, though. The crusty, brown-paged book had said a man deserving of punishment would be relentlessly aroused but never satiated.

But that had to be foolish talk. That kind of thing never happened in real life. Besides, Charles had always been lucky in getting what he wanted. He'd made sure of it.

However, he'd done nothing to deserve punishment, either. On the contrary, he was a good man. He'd donated lots of money and toothpaste to the local shelters. Well, at least once. He'd given candy to kids trick-or-treating every year but ten. He had even taken his boss out to eat that time he passed him by for a promotion. That was going over the top. So, he was safe.

Charles knew the lake was real. It wasn't a myth. No way. It couldn't be. He'd seen pictures on the internet.

In the distance, he saw water and he started to get excited. This was going to be it, and he'd get his wish soon enough.

He plowed forward, pushing the brush aside, snapping twigs and dried grass beneath his step. The land was drying up the further he hiked towards the lake.

He gasped when he spotted a lake in the shape of a pear. It had trees around it just like the pictures. The murky waters of the lake were dark, and a light steam rose off the surface. It looked more like a nasty soup in a witch's cauldron than a refreshing lake to take a dip in.

But no matter, it didn't need to be pleasant, it just needed to give him his wishes.

Boobs. He'd decided his wish would be boobs as far as his eyes could see. He'd get to suck them all, pinch and twist and tug them, make the women moan and cry out. Then he'd titty fuck them. Every last pair of breasts, he'd come on all of them. It would be heaven.

He approached the lake and removed his shoes and then all his clothes. He'd read that whoever entered the lake must not be tarnished by clothing, but purely naked. This would please the Goddess Zeffah and she'd grant the nude swimmer his wish.

He waded into the dark waters with a giant grin on his face. His cock was hard as he imagined all the boobs he'd soon be surrounded by. He reached the center of the lake and raised his hands high in the air. The top of the water crested his armpits as he took one final step.

"Goddess Zeffah, I am here. I've come from far away. Grant my wish of a sea of large-breasted women for my pleasure."

He snickered as the wind seemed to moan, and the gurgling water swirling about his body meant something was happening.

Fear gripped him when the water rose to his chin. He tried to walk, but he couldn't move. It was as if his feet had been cemented in place.

"Please," he pleaded, his eyes round as they'd go.

The water fell to his chest level again. He breathed a sigh of relief. His stomach rumbled and his cock stirred. He had needs, and this Goddess would meet them. Thirst gripped his throat and he wanted to take a drink of the water, but the water looked too gross. He figured it was contaminated and undrinkable.

Confidence swelled in him when the water dipped down to his waist. "And give me pizza too," he demanded.

Loads of big breasts and pizza would be perfect, as far as his eyes could see.

He stared at the water and cleared his dry throat. "And a bottle of water, too."

The clouds furrowed together above his head like an angry brow, darkening the sky. A rumble birthed all around him and the wind picked up.

His excitement began to thicken, as did his cock.

Nothing happened for way too long, and Charles still couldn't move. Panic started to percolate in his gut, and the feeling of needing to vomit seethed vile into his throat.

The women began to appear on the shoreline. Brunettes, redheads, blonds, and white-haired women. Gray-hair dotted the growing sea of women. All of them had very large breasts, and all of them were fully naked, so he could see bushy mounds, shaved mounds, flat pussies, and plump ones. All the women were beautiful, and his dick engorged to a hardened fuck stick despite the cool water.

He drew in a deep breath as more and more women appeared. He cheered as they filled the shorelines. Then, to his delight, they began to enter the water and waded in near him.

One with the biggest breasts he'd ever seen, pale pink nipples with ornate gatherings of nipple flesh around the hardened nub, approached him. She held up her breast and pointed at Charles. She smiled and jiggled both breasts at him.

As far as Charles could see, there were thousands of bare-chested women, and all of them were making their way towards him.

He'd done it! He was getting his wish. He'd tweak their hardened boobie nibblets, he'd twist and torque them until they squealed, then he'd suckle every last one of them, pulling the hardened tips to the back of his throat.

He'd hold the erect nipple peaks between his fingers like a cigarette, and rub them with his thumb while the women squirmed in pleasure, then he'd get rough and make them squeak and scream.

Then he'd fuck every set of titties in the water and on the shore, spreading his spunk to coat and mark every breast.

His lust raged as a dark-skinned woman with big nipples that were almost black as night approached him. She danced towards him with the most seductive grin he'd ever seen, but when he reached for her, she jerked back with an evil snicker.

He'd reached for every woman who neared him, his cock throbbing with wild desire. He couldn't wait to slide his manhood between the orbs and screw every woman he could see.

One woman had a piece of pizza and she began to eat it, licking her lips and moaning in delight, her eyes ablaze with satiation as she chewed. She extended the pizza to Charles, but another woman grabbed her arm and she took a bite instead.

Charles's heart began to beat fast and his stomach did a flip-flop like he might have diarrhea or perhaps vomit.

The women danced near him, one coming so close that his fingers were only a millimeter away from grazing her skin before she jumped back. The shore continued to fill with naked, buxom women as they moved into the water in droves.

Boobs as far as Charles could see, and it was a glorious sight. His stomach growled as he watched more women enjoying gooey cheesy pizza, pizza with tomatoes, green peppers, onions, and lumpy succulent sausage. They fed each other greasy pepperonis laden with white, oozing cheese.

The women began to point at him and laugh.

"Yummy," said a red-haired woman with big juicy tits as she licked pizza off her neighboring woman who had small nipples on her big fat breasts.

The aroma of the pizza made Charles even hungrier. He imagined how good it would be to bite into the thick pizza. Tears welled up inside him, but he wouldn't let them spill. Not like this, he wouldn't, no way. He'd find a way to get to the women and the pizza.

"Look how weak he is," said a woman with piercing blue eyes. "He can't even move." She cackled and pointed at him, then began to kiss the woman next to her.

They all began to suckle each other's boobs and the eruption of an orgy of tit sucking sank Charles's heart. They moaned and writhed together, all getting to enjoy the wish he'd created.

"Loser," said one woman with an evil grin.

"Unworthy fucker," said a bald woman of about sixty-five, but her breasts were the most beautiful Charles had ever seen, and he wanted them so badly.

"Bastard who deserves nothing," said another.

"Slime ball, asshole, vile heartless monster."

The insults made Charles want to run, but his feet were still rooted in the muck at the bottom of the lake.

A cough attack gripped him and he leaned down to slurp the dark disgusting water for relief, but it receded as he neared.

Tears burst from his eyes as he yelled to the sky, "Why? Oh, why?"

He'd found the treasured lake only to get trapped in it.

He spied a flat-chested man appear in the mass of women on the shore. He squinted his eyes to make out the face.

He couldn't take his eyes off the man as he advanced through all the women.

His heart leapt and he shouted, "Max! Max! Is that you? Please help me! I can't move. My feet are stuck in the mud." He was saved! Max would help him.

"Charles! I will help you," Max said as he maneuvered quickly through the women. But then he stopped as a woman began to caress his face.

She pulled him to her breasts and offered him to suck. Max began to suck on her nipples as another woman pressed her big breasts to his back. They began to gyrate as a unit, suckling and caressing.

"No!" Charles called out as he watched Max titty fuck her. "Please, you are getting distracted. I need your help, Max. Please, I beg you."

With his face smeared in pizza sauce, Max titty fucked the next woman, then the next, his cum ever spewing from his cock. Max was fed tits and pizza, his face in a permanent state of pleasure.

Charles screams to the sky, his arms outstretched, his cock ready to burst without even having touched a single tit.

"Please, please, please," he pleaded of the women nearest to him. "Help me. I will give you so much pleasure, so many orgasms. I promise."

"Oh, now you care about a woman's pleasures? Too late," cackled a raven-haired woman to his right. She fed her big baseball-sized nipples to the woman on her left. She threw her head back in ecstasy as the blond woman sucked on her tits.

Charles sank into the water as tears streamed down his cheeks. They prompted the women to draw closer to him, but when he reached for them, she skittered back with witchy laughter.

The aroma of the pizza turned his stomach and he dry gagged, then retched up nothing substantial, the bile from his stomach burning his parched throat like sandpaper on tree bark. The fire in his throat and the lusty burning in his loins told him what he already knew.

This was never going to end.

The End

Pleasured by Satan

Dark, NOT HEA, Depraved, Torturous

He woke in a beautiful bed, complete with white linen flowing drapes strung along the top of the ornate black frame. Fluffy plush pillows supported his body at every protrusion and cranny. He was waking full of amazement, legit as if he were on a cloud with the exact, perfect, and right air temperature, the perfect amount of light, and dreamy feelings of perfection all around him.

He glanced down at his body, because it was somehow foreign. His fat was all gone and what he saw were deliciously toned perfect abs. He ran his fingers along the bumps and valleys, savoring all the firmness and promise of strength their presence surmised. He grinned deeply. He had wished for abs his entire life and now he'd been given a mysterious, but very welcome, gift. He was hot!

He fondled himself in all his new sexiness as he glanced around the room. The top was open to the beautiful blue sky and the walls were white, but more like clouds than solid structures. A light breeze caressed him and he sighed, savoring all the good feels.

A woman wearing only a black silk robe and black high heels strode into the room. Her blond curls jiggled as she walked, but her tits jiggled more. Louis liked this. A lot.

He watched as her breasts boomed, their pendulous weight chugging behind the silky fabric with each of her movements.

He couldn't take his eyes off her breasts sliding beneath that silk for very long. He needed to touch her. But then he got a quick glimpse of her lush full lips, her creamy white skin, and her light blue eyes. She was curvy in all the places Louis loved. She was a goddess.

"Where am I?" he asked this gorgeous creature.

She simply smiled and ran her hands over her full breasts as a lecherous expression consumed her face. She danced about close-lipped.

Unsettled that she didn't answer, he asked another question. "Who are you?"

She grinned deeper and pinched her nipples through the fabric. The peaks that poked out of the fabric after her manipulations made Louis's mouth water. He wanted them in his mouth, he wanted to play with them, tweak them, and he desired to clamp their tips between his fingers like cigarettes.

"You are in Hades. I am Satan."

That didn't seem possible — not even remotely a minute chance with how delectable she was. Someone who was this exquisite creature could in no way be the evil one.

She turned her back to him and flipped up her robe to show off her G string, which was nestled nice and snug, deep in the crack of her ass cheeks. She dropped the robe quickly and Louis immediately missed the view of her round, supple, bubble butt. He almost complained that he hadn't gotten a long enough look at her luscious ass, but the view of her tits erased those thoughts.

Louis was amazed at how he was not afraid. He should be scared. He was in a bad place, but it was so serene here and she was so lovely. How could this really be bad? Plus, his body was magically the kind of body he'd lusted after in men; whenever he found himself lusting after men in life it had always been about their nice abs.

"Did you like looking at my bare ass?" Satan asked seductively, with an innocent giggle slipping out.

Louis felt she needed a different name. Satan didn't suit her at all.

"Oh, yes, I really liked looking at your bare butt."

Butts were sexy, but boobs? Nothing compared.

She grinned deeply, clearly very pleased with his answer. "Good, I'm very happy that you did."

She sashayed around the room, which made her boobs shift underneath the fabric tight around her bosom. "I know you worked for him. The bad man with the bad hair." Her grin deepened, but seemed genuine. "I know everything."

This didn't bother Louis one bit. He was proud of what work he'd done in his life. He deepened his smug expression, which only served to enrage his lust more. This paradise with this incredible female was his prize.

She pressed her breasts from both sides, which made her cleavage even deeper, impossibly deeper.

Louis's cock thickened.

"I also know you are a boob man." She jiggled her humongous breasts, smashing them between her hands. "I might show you my nipples." She licked her lips. "Would you like that?"

Louis nodded. "Very much so, yes." He was becoming hornier by the second.

"Do you deserve to see my nipples?" she asked as she did a twirl in front of him.

Her hair was flowing and Louis longed to run his fingers through it as he sucked on her titties. He knew she must have amazing nipples too.

"Oh, yes. I do," he said as he nodded enthusiastically. He wanted nothing more than to see her delicious breasts and even more wonderful nipples.

"Maybe," she said as she continued to fondle her breasts. She slipped a finger inside her robe to play with her right nipple, but it was covered, so Louis had to imagine what it looked like. This disappointed him to no end.

"You can't see my nipples." She rolled her eyes as she pleasured herself by playing with her nipples. She moaned and swayed as she touched herself beneath the robe.

"Yes, oh yes, keep doing that. I like it." His arousal was filling his cock full, and he couldn't think of anything but seeing her bare tits. "Please," he pleaded as he touched his newly sculpted abs some more. He desperately longed to feel her bare boobs against his new chest and abdomen, with his mouth, his fingers. He started to drool, he wanted her boobies so badly.

She molested her tits as she undulated her curvy hips, as if dancing, but there was no music. She sauntered close to Louis and he reached out without leaving the bed. "I'm getting very wet, Louis."

She did know him. Clearly, she did, because she even knew his name. But Satan knows all, right? He thought he'd heard that once.

"I might show you my nipples," she taunted as she molested her breasts over the fabric. "Do you deserve to see my bare nipples?"

Louis's cock thickened as he nodded enthusiastically. "I do. Yes, I do."

"Maybe," the sexy woman replied haughtily.

Louis wanted his hands where hers were, fondling that bouncy, firm flesh of his own accord. He yearned to press and squeeze them and make them jiggle at his will. "Oh, yes. Please."

She continued to play with her giant tits, which were way too much mass for her small hands. They'd fit in his hands better, but he enjoyed that they looked like way more than a handful for his hands too.

"I'm getting very wet, Louis. From touching my erect tits. Does that turn you on?"

He wondered why she was asking this because, as she just said, Satan knew everything. He watched her tweak her nipples with his mouth slightly ajar, blood surging to erect his cock further. He must have her. He reached out to touch her and she jumped back.

"No way you can touch me," she said, as if this should be obvious to Louis.

"Why?" He resisted the urge to pout. He didn't want to look like a bratty child to this flamboyant creature, so pressed he pressed his lips together firmly instead.

She slipped her hands into her bikini top and rolled her eyes once her fingers found her erect nips. "Mmmmm," she murmured.

"Oh, yes," Louis muttered in a slow, low whisper. He needed more of this.

She moved closer to Louis again. Her presence was as tempting as a very ripe red apple in a tree above him. She hovered so low that she was within reach as he lay beneath her.

She shook her tits in his face and he was mesmerized by their pendulous swinging. They were hypnotizing him.

"You can't touch me," she persisted with a teasing expression.

Louis didn't like this tease anymore. He just wanted her bare boobs and her nipples out so he could look at them, then he wanted to grab, pinch, and pull her nipples. He asked the dumb question again. "Why?"

She stared at him like he was surely an imbecile. "You are naughty."

"What do you mean?" Louis was sure this wasn't true. He was a good man. He'd always been a decent person. "Let me kiss them," he urged.

She turned away from him, and when she turned back, she held a large bowl of grapes. "If you listen, you might get to eat from me."

Louis was in full agreement with this plan, so he nodded like a puppet. As she approached, he opened his mouth like a baby bird. She fed him a grape. Then she dropped another in his mouth. They were the sweetest, juiciest grapes he's ever had in his life.

"Mmm," he said while still chewing. The juice flooded his mouth with such goodness. "These grapes are the best grapes I've ever eaten."

Satan smiled with her perfect pearly whites. "You behave yourself and keep your hands to yourself." Her tone was commanding, and he'd never argued with a woman who was promising to show him her tits. That would be very stupid of him. Well, that wasn't exactly true. He snickered at the memory.

She pressed several grapes into her cleavage.

"Yesssss," Louis said, finally understanding what eating from her meant.

She crawled onto the bed now in just a skimpy bikini and high heels. She slowly moved around the bed on her hands and knees.

Louis enjoyed seeing her from every angle, so much so that he forgot about his need to touch her. Her movements were so alluring that he didn't even care about his own wants for a few moments. He was fully under her spell.

"Oh, yes," he whispered.

She crawled up his body and shook her breasts right in his face, slapping his cheeks with her big fleshy tits. The grapes were so wedged between her breasts that they didn't fall from her cleavage, even with her aggressive undulations.

"Mmm," Louis moaned appreciatively. "Gimme those tits."

She sat up and pulled her bikini off her pussy, tugging it to the side. She straddled him and pressed her warm, wet pussy to his firm abs.

He groaned, imagining his cock sliding in that wet, warm hole of hers.

"Oh my Gawd," he drawled out as she slid around, smearing her juices on his firm muscles.

All his life he'd admired men's sculpted abs, even lusted over them. But he wasn't gay. Never that. No way! But now washboard abs were on his own body, just like magic. He was such a lucky man. He knew it was because of all the good work he'd done in his life.

She leaned forward and pressed her grape-filled cleavage to his face.

"Oh, yes," Louis muttered, wondering if he could say anything else, but he didn't care about intelligent talk right now. Not with her big boobs in his face and her hot cunt on his skin.

She smiled a sly smile with a malicious evil eye as she laughed at him before jumping back.

"What?" Louis asked. He had been sure this was supposed to be the moment he'd get to touch her.

She snickered loudly as she threw her head back and laughed. "Just kidding, Louis." She leaned towards him and said, "Beg me."

Oh, he wasn't above doing this. "Please. Please, may I touch you?"

"More," she demanded sternly.

"Please, please, please may I?"

She molested herself with hard, aggressive grabs. She put her tits back in his face and with a smile said, "Ok. You can have them."

He sucked the grapes out one by one, enjoying each luscious orb bursting in his mouth.

She removed her top and the most gorgeous nipples he'd ever seen in his life swung out.

"Oh, wow!" he exclaimed as his dick filled at the sight of her.

He groaned, thrilled he had finally been given permission. Such yummy breasts he'd never had the pleasure of seeing ever in his entire life. They were literally perfect in shape. The roundness, and her nipples were exquisite, with little roadmaps of wrinkles framing the hard peaks. He grabbed both at once and squeezed. His dick reached a full erection with precum seeping out as he played and bounced her breasts. Once he got his mouth on her, he almost came as he toyed with each hard, erect tit. He rolled his tongue all around her hardened areola, pressing his tongue along her wrinkled, firm nuggets.

"Mmm," she moaned. "That feels so good, Louis."

He was instantly proud he had given her pleasure, and what joy it was also something he loved doing.

He licked her breasts all over.

"Motorboat my tits," she demanded.

He obliged.

She wiggled her ass as he shoved his face in her cleavage, his smile never leaving his face.

"Oh, my Gawd, yes," he slurred.

She reached for a grape from the bowl and squeezed it over her skin. The juice dribbled out and ran down. She shoved herself in his face. "Eat."

He lapped up all the juices on her skin. Between licks, he said, "I have never felt this good."

"Tongue fuck my cleavage," she said salaciously.

He obeyed and, with extreme excitement, bobbed his head rapidly up and down as his tongue rode her sweet cleavage.

She squeezed more juice on her nipples and offered one teat to Louis as she took her other one in her mouth. They both suckled her nipples, both moaning out their satisfaction.

She continued to feed him grapes and drain the juice on her skin so much that the juices ran down to his abs. She grinned as she leaned down. Her boobs smashed to his lower abs as she drank the juice from his flesh.

"Oh, yes," he said again. Other words were just too hard, and simply not right anyway. He didn't care.

"I guess working for him does have its advantages," he said with a snicker.

"Yes, it does, Louis." She gave him a knowing look. "That's the only reason you are here with this new body in this bed with me."

"I know," he said. He knew it. He'd been right all those years to do what he did.

"I know everything, but I want to hear you confess."

He'd do anything she wanted so he could keep kissing and sucking on her amazing tits.

"You must know. But I will say it." He kissed her chest and licked her skin.

"We destroyed tons of families and vulnerable people."

She stroked his hair as he told of his doings.

"We took all the advantages from those deserving of them and held them at bay, even though we knew they were suffering."

She nodded with a glorious look of triumph. "Go on."

"We mocked people. The innocent."

She fingered his hair as he sucked her nipple to the back of his throat.

"We harmed the reputations and growth of those who choose and lived different lifestyles from what we considered normal."

"Good," she said as he sucked her nipple harder. She groaned as she shoved her fingers inside her pussy.

"We led an insurrection."

"More," she said in a syrupy sweet voice. She yanked her tit from his mouth and he stared at her, aghast. "Titty fuck? Or do you want to fuck my ass?"

Oh, this was a good question. "Titty fuck," he said without hesitation. Besides, the ass could come next.

She skittered down his body and settled her chest above his groin. She smeared her wet pussy along his bare thigh.

"I made women titty fuck me at work."

"Oh, I know. I saw that."

He grinned, reliving all the harassments he had succeeded at over the years. He'd laughed at the memories of all the admins and subordinates he'd taken advantage of. He'd made them get naked down to bare butts as he had forced them to make him come with titty fucking. His boss knew and let him, and even watched the scenes. He even joined in at times, only he usually fucked them up the ass. They'd had a lot of naughty fun together.

"We've got all of eternity, right?" Louis asked.

"Yes, Louis. We do."

Louis chuckled, remembering how many butts he'd spanked over the years. To keep his secretaries – he liked that old word best – and admins in line and productive, he'd spanked them in his office. He had told them that if they wanted to keep their jobs, they'd submit to his punishments. He had gotten off so many times as he beat a woman's ass as she laid across his lap, leaned over his desk, and even stood in front of the window as he smacked her butt red. There had been a crew of window washers that had learned to come during spanking time.

They'd watched Louis humiliate the women by spanking them in front of the men on the scaffolding. Most jerked off all over the windows and then they cleaned off the window and left. Many times Louis made the women bend over so the men could see their faces as he beat their bottoms raw. It had been a glorious setup, with so many men coming each day. It became a thing.

Louis had loved the women who also got off on it. That had been the primo times, and those women had gotten special treatment. They were the ones he promoted.

She unzipped his pants and plucked his hard cock out. With a devilish grin, she pursed her lips and planted a peck on his firmness. She dragged her nipples all along his thighs and lower abdomen, and all along his hard shaft.

"Mmm, perfect, precum," she murmured, her hot moist breath blasting his skin.

She dabbed her nipple at the hole at the tip of his cock to scoop up some precum. "We need moisture." Then she spat on his cock.

"Oh, fuck yes," he said, loving every move she made.

She spit on her tits and spread it all along the inside of her breasts and down her cleavage. Then she wrapped her generous bosom around his hard dick and bounced harder with his increasing groans.

"I want you to come," she declared. "Now."

He watched her ass gyrate as she titty fucked him.

"Here I come," he said in a strained voice. He groaned out loudly as cum spewed out his cock tip. He shuddered as he came hard, his heart pounded like he'd just run. "Fuck," he yelled.

He looked at his cum splatted across her generous chest and was satisfied. But then he wanted more. Maybe he did want her ass.

"You deserve this, Louis. And you deserve more."

He nodded.

"You did the best work on Earth. And when you fucked that whore in the church parking lot and didn't pay her?" She smiled with so much lust he almost recoiled. "That was the best. So. You pick your punishment."

He was confused. "But you said I did good?"

"Yes. Pick your punishment. Spanking? Teasing? Kissing my feet? Cleaning my whole body with your tongue? Watching me masturbate and you can't touch me or yourself?"

Were these all punishments? He was sure they were not.

He cocked his head to the side as he considered his options. They weren't bad choices. "Kissing your feet can't be bad." He set his jaw in a stern line. "I choose that."

He rose from the bed as she laid back. He hovered over her feet and began to kiss and lick them. He thought it odd her flesh had no odor at all. He was winning again, this wasn't a punishment. He sucked her beautifully painted toes as she moaned.

"Where is the punishment?" He immediately wished he hadn't asked. What if she picked a real punishment for him?

She began to touch her pussy lips and clit as he suckled her big toe, then on down the line to her pinky. "You can't touch my pussy, only my toes."

He was okay with that, for now. "You wouldn't," he said.

"What's one more thing you want before I go?" she asked innocently.

"I want more of your tits." There was zero question about that.

She gave a firm single nod. "You get my tits." She laid back and her tits slid apart. "You can fuck my pussy or ass as you play with them if you want," she offered, as if she were offering him a cup of coffee.

He loved this idea. "Pussy and tits." He hungrily devoured her with his lusty eyes as he climbed on top of her. His dick was still hard as a rock even after coming from the titty fuck. This was new too, in life he'd have had to wait for his body to allow another erection, but now he was more than ready to go.

He slid his cock inside her pussy and it was heaven. And not just any heaven, but legit real heaven. He thrust into her, enjoying her vulnerable near-orgasm face. He rammed into her and savored the bliss as he rose to another epic orgasm. He released his cum with a roar into her vagina as she thrashed her head back and forth in ecstasy. She squeezed his strong, bulging biceps as she screamed.

His new abs helped him fuck her harder than he'd ever fucked a woman before, which made his release even more satisfying. As his cock pumped cum into her, she orgasmed and her vaginal muscles clamped down on his cock several times, which gloriously made him come a third time.

His body spasmed as it fed her pussy with more of his hot cum. He'd never come three times in a row like this. It was the best fuck of his entire life. He was king of the world.

He laid upon her body as they both panted. Her nipples were still hard so he sucked them and she squirmed and mewled in delight beneath him.

After he'd had his fill of sucking her nipples, he rolled off of her and lay flat on the bed as his breathing returned to normal.

"That was amazing. So amazing. The best sex of my life."

Satan smiled as she morphed into a man. He had a full set of strong bulbous abs himself. Louis's eyes drifted down as his mouth fell open. The shock choked the air out of his lungs as his eyes landed on Satan's enormous swollen cock.

Satan had long blond flowing hair, a handsome sexy face, and the most gorgeous luscious lips he'd ever seen on a man.

Satan got off the bed and gathered his robe, bikini, and high heels. Shackles appeared on Louis's wrists and ankles, but they had no chains, they only encircled him.

"You will never feel a woman again," Satan said in a voice that no longer resembled the sexy voice of the woman, but was gruff, cold, and terrifyingly monster-like.

Louis laid back in the bed as the urge to cry stole every speck of pleasure he'd just experienced. He watched Satan walk away as a door appeared like magic. It was dark on the other side. Louis noticed his perfect bottom as he strutted through the doorway.

And then he was gone. And so was the door. He felt despair like never before. And he deserved it.

The End

Forest Magic, Head in the Woods, The Strangers Hookup

Meredith adjusted her tennis skirt and shook her shoulders. It had been a great workout playing her friend Allan in a match, but she was in a rush to get home because she had a dinner date, a blind date, which her best friend had hooked her up with. The guy was supposedly a lawyer for personal injury, and her friend had said he was a major catch. Meredith knew that was to be seen, and she feared a lawyer would never be a match for her, but she'd give it a go. She wanted to find a new boyfriend, and if she didn't try things she thought wouldn't work, she knew she was limiting herself. She needed an open mind and an open heart, or she might completely miss a fabulous partner.

She was sweaty and she lamented that she was about to enter the forested area of the walk home. She crossed her fingers that her bug spray would hold out so she wouldn't get eaten by the tiny beasts. She had just enough time to shower before her date, and maybe do a little work, but her main thing was she needed a shower, and badly. The sun had beat down on them as they played, so the sweat had poured out of her. She felt like a wet mop and as stinky as a used one. No matter. She'd be fresh soon and ready to go on a date, albeit one she was kind of dreading. Blind dates sucked. She had no idea what to expect, not even the impression of meeting someone to go off of. All she had was her friend's assurance that he was a 'fantastic guy'. If he was so fantastic, why was he single?

She scoffed, realizing the same could be said of her. This helped her relax a bit. He might be feeling the exact same way about her.

She walked along, loving the feel of her moist labia lips rubbing against each other. She'd read recently that working out not only enlarged the clitoris by quite a bit temporarily, but post-workout sex was actually amazing. She'd never tried it, because she always had thought she needed a shower first before intimacy, but she really wanted to try this. Her best friend had recently told her that her partner loved sex, and oral sex especially, after she worked out. He loved her musky, sweaty scents and tastes, and she'd been shocked he even loved the sweaty area under her breasts. She'd never had a lover like that. In fact, her last partner disliked any of that. She grinned. Maybe this next guy wouldn't be so prissy and would try such things with her. Her last man hadn't even liked touching her cum. She could only hope, and she could only go upwards from that low.

She walked along briskly, mentally checking off her weekend to-do list, until she spied someone in the woods to her right, which got her to slow her pace. They were moving quickly, almost as if they were working out.

She cocked her head and stopped walking. Who works out in the middle of the forest, though? That's really quite odd.

The person's movements increased and as she peered closer, her curiosity piqued. She normally would just keep moving, the fear of the unknown and potential safety risks to her well-being occupying her brain and keeping her from taking such risks. But something propelled her forward into the woods. Perhaps it was her yearning to do something she knew was risky, or perhaps it was just her dumb brain needing to know what kind of crazy whacko would work out in the forest.

She parted the thin tree branches to allow herself to walk into the forest further. Her heart was pounding, and she chided herself for doing this. What if the person was a serial killer or ax murderer, or worse? But what could be worse than those? She didn't want to think about it, and shoving her fear out of her head, she trudged on. The bugs had started to bother her, likely because she was sweaty and was attracting them. She swung her racquet at them to get them away from her. She always had that as a weapon if whoever this was tried to attack her.

She smiled as the birds tweeted overhead. Their lovely sounds gave her a breather in her negative thoughts. She needed to stop assuming every man was out to attack her. Sure, there were men who did that, but there were so many who wouldn't.

Her adrenaline zoomed around her body as she got closer to the person. She knew she shouldn't be doing this, but she was too invested, and too curious, to stop now. This was not like her to approach a stranger in the woods, but it was also a bit exciting.

As she came upon the mysterious person, she noticed it was definitely a man. He had on a dark blue muscle tank top and shorts. He had his back to her, and he was lifting up a log.

Her mouth dropped open. Who lifts up logs? They were likely full of bugs or damp, or just covered in gross slimy stuff. She avoided touching such things, and yet here was this dude purposely touching them. How strange!

He had defined muscles, so clearly, he lifted weights. But lifting logs? She was completely aghast and quite perplexed. She crept closer and then froze. What the hell was she doing? This guy could be a bad guy, and she was surprising him by sneaking up on him. This was a bad idea, and she was filled instantly with fear, her curious nature gone as if someone had pulled the plug and drained her of it.

She needed to get out of there before he saw her and charged her. Dumb. Dumb. Dumb. She was an idiot putting herself at risk like this.

She turned and put her foot down. She cringed as her foot landed on a twig and the crunch of it filled the surrounding silence.

Shit!

That's the last thing she should have done. She should have looked down before she stepped. She remained frozen, on edge as she waited for evidence that he had heard her step on the dry twig.

"Hello?" a masculine voice called out.

Her heart rushed into flight mode, and she readied to take off at lightning speed to save her life.

"Hello?" he repeated the question. "I see you."

Panic seized her. She should run. He might be evil.

Yet she stood still. She knew she couldn't outrun him if he took off after her. He looked to be in very good shape, and although she worked out constantly, she'd never been able to beat any man in a running race. She was his for the easy plucking if he wanted, and that was her own fault.

She spun on her heels and gazed back at him. "Hi," she said in a meek voice.

"Oh, I thought I heard something," he called. He fell silent, as if it was her turn to talk.

She had no idea what to say. "I was just ... hiking." Okay, good save. That didn't seem too weird.

He had dark hair and looked very fit, even from a little distance. "Well, don't let me stop you. I'm just doing a nature workout."

A nature workout? She hadn't ever heard of such a thing. "Oh?" she questioned, feeling a little better that he hadn't rushed her with beastly intent in his eyes. Yet.

"Yeah, it's unusual, but I love nature, and it feels more primal. I get this savage surge of energy out here." He laughed. "I find I harness my inner wild man and can lift more."

Okay. That kind of made sense. There was just something primal about being in the woods. Something a bit more savage. It was a bit like having sex in the woods, which she'd done quite a bit with one of her exes. He'd been a camper and hiker, and sex with him outdoors had always raged the experience to delicious heights. She'd had some gnarly huge orgasms with him in the woods. Despite her fear, thoughts of fucking him in the woods pumped up her libido. It wouldn't take much to get her to climax now with all her workout hormones saturating her body. She had the urge to test the theory even more now facing this sexy specimen.

"Oh, I see. Well, don't mind me. Keep up with your workout." She fluttered her hands in the air, as if dismissing herself. She was nervous and it was likely all over her face.

He let out a burst of laugh, which seemed for her benefit, because nothing funny had happened. "There aren't any tennis courts in here, but if you go down the path, you'll find them."

She realized she must look off carrying a racquet in the woods. "Oh," she laughed too. "Yeah, I was just there actually, played a few games with a friend." She was the one looking suspicious now, quietly creeping up to him, basically sneaking up on him with a racquet in hand.

"Ah. Was wondering if that was your weapon of choice to ward off forest ogres," he joked.

She tittered a laugh back. "Good one. But no. Was just walking home and decided to trek a bit through the woods." That sounded like a load of crap.

He took a few steps towards her and her body jolted alert. "I'm Logan. Nice to meet you."

She nodded at him as she tried to curb her doubts. "Meredith." She smiled at him. "It's nice to meet you. I'm not used to running into burly men in the woods like this."

He rubbed his hands together. "And I'm not used to coming upon beautiful women in the woods." He grinned hugely. "So, we're even."

Rather than be offended, she felt soothed by his compliment. And a bit aroused, if she was being honest with herself.

"Ah," she said, feeling sheepish that she had nothing fabulous to say back.

"I could take a break from lifting for a bit of hike. Sounds like a great idea. Do you mind if I take your lead? I know these woods, but I haven't hiked them much, and I'd like to learn."

Well, now she was in trouble. Going further into the woods with him would be even riskier, and now her fib had her in trouble. She didn't know good hiking routes in this forest, and she might lead them to a bad spot if she took the lead.

"I'm not an ax murderer." He held up his hands. "See, no ax."

He seemed charming enough, but her hackles were raised on her back. He certainly didn't need an ax to kill her. He could likely do it with his bare hands. She was a bit terrified of walking ahead of him, too. She would be opening herself up for an attack, being vulnerable that way.

Her silence seemed to last forever.

"Okay, how about I lead then?" he asked kindly. "You can warn me if I take a wrong turn."

She supposed that would be more acceptable. "Okay," she said, though it felt against her better judgment. But the man was both cute and sexy. So, she wanted to give this a shot. He seemed eager to join her.

She took a few steps forward, as did he. Coming closer to him made this more real, scarier, but more exciting, too. The danger of it, and the spontaneousness of it, was way too alluring to pass up.

As she approached him, she saw he had kind eyes, and there was a spark of interest in them. He smiled easily and perpetually as she approached him, and he stood still, not darting or lunging for her, so she relaxed.

"I'm thrilled to meet another nature adventurer in the woods like this." His smile beamed even brighter. He had an innocent genuineness about him that she was finding very compelling.

"Same," she said, feeling more at ease near him with each second passing. He was strong looking. There was zero doubt about that, and he'd surely overpower her with very little effort. But she also knew she couldn't assume such men were all monsters. And this one seemed more like a teddy bear than any kind of brutal abusive beast.

He grabbed his water and slung his backpack over his shoulders. "I have an extra water, if you get thirsty."

Oh, what was this? He was also very observant to notice she didn't have any water and generous to offer her his extra. He was winning points without even trying. "Oh, well, that's very kind of you. Thank you." She felt taken care of already, and they'd just met. She didn't want to get her hopes up, but this was a very good sign. She cringed as her brain went there ... what if this guy could be more than just a random hike in the woods? Stop it, Meredith. Just stop it.

She followed his lead as he made his way deeper into the forest, her heart pounding way harder than the actual walking would have induced. He had a cute tight butt, a very grab-worthy man butt if she'd ever seen one. They walked in silence for a few minutes, which was bad because her mind started imagining things it shouldn't be, at least not yet, like what those hips of his would look like from behind as he thrust himself into her wanton pussy.

She gasped before she could stop it.

He froze in place and spun around. "You okay?" he asked with concern, his eyes shining with worry.

She laughed it off. "Yes, I'm good." She needed to control her wild thoughts. Or did she? She had recently made a commitment to living her life more authentically, so she shouldn't filter herself. "It's beautiful here."

He relaxed and his smile spread. His voice matched his apparent happiness. "Yes, it really is."

He turned back around, and they walked on in silence; the silence of the forest pierced only by their footsteps and bird calls. After reaching the top of a big hill, he stopped and reached into his backpack. He pulled out his water, and the extra water bottle for her. He handed it to her. "I need a water break."

She was panting lightly. "Me too. That was a brutal hill."

She noted he wasn't panting and smirked.

He returned her silly look.

"I would have never guessed I'd bump into someone like you in the woods today," he confessed.

She swallowed the big gulp of water in her mouth. "Same. But I'm really glad we did." She never believed in love at first sight, but this was undoubtedly a connection between the two of them. There were just those people she connected to right from the get-go, and he was certainly that. Not that she assumed they'd be more, but she'd go on a date with him if he asked. She'd agree without a second's hesitation. "I think if we had met on the path, we would have just nodded and kept right on jogging."

"That's likely true. So. How much time do you have? Do we need to turn back?" He glanced at his phone before pocketing it.

She glanced at her phone. Shit. She did have that blind date. She needed a shower badly. Maybe she'd just skip the shower. She didn't want to miss out on any time with this man. "I have a little more time. I'd love to keep going with you."

"Good," he said, replacing the lid on his water. "Let's go."

She could not stop imagining touching his muscles as he hiked ahead of her. Which then led to her sinking into the reverie of licking those muscles. She guessed he likely had those delectable muscles that made a V down to his groin. Her clit lurched and she gasped again. Fuck! This man had her dwelling in the no-control zone.

He stopped and swiveled to face her. "Maybe we should rest longer," he suggested kindly. He looked around. "There. Let's go sit on the big rock."

She didn't need to sit down, but she had no way of explaining her sudden outbursts, short of telling him she was obsessed with thinking about licking the muscles that lead to his dick. She couldn't stop the laugh that bubbled inside her and it spilled out.

He chuckled. "Do I get to know the joke?"

She shook her head. "Oh, it's not a joke."

He led the way to the big rock and leaned against it. "I'd love to know what brought that beautiful, glorious sound out of your beautiful lips."

Oh, well, this. Shit. If he was going to give her sexy compliments too, she was in trouble. Her libido would take over and who knows what would happen? "Aw, well, that's very sexy of you to say."

"I love your laugh," he stated plainly as his eyes danced with sparks. "Please share with me. That is, if you're comfortable, of course."

She scoffed. "You wouldn't believe me if I did." She couldn't. No way.

"Try me," he urged.

The look in his eyes had her almost convinced to tell him, but not quite.

They weren't touching, but she swore she felt his heat, even though he was three feet away from her.

"The forest gets me ..." she said, looking off deep in the woods, her voice failing as it trailed off.

"Primal?" he asked, with a hint of suggestion in his voice. He pressed his lips together and flicked his eyes upward as his eyebrow raised too.

She lost control in a monstrously big giggle. She nodded. "Umm. Yup. Yeah, you could say that." Her heart pounded. Here she was in the middle of a deserted forest with a sexy and kind man who was flirting with her. She bit her lip, but that didn't stop her thoughts from charging out of her mouth in an uncontrolled blurt as she said, "And most specifically, sex."

His body jolted as if he'd been shocked by electricity, and his face bloomed into a salacious grin. "Same," he replied with ease.

Both of them had basically just admitted to being horny. She shrugged with a saucy, flirty look. "Now what?"

He cocked his head at her. "You tell me what got you making that sound?" The suggestion in his voice was unmistakable.

Her heart raced, bouncing her nerves all about her insides. Should she tell him? Would he think she was a slut? But that turned her on anyway, if he did. However, they'd just literally met mere minutes ago. Her brain spun as her commitment to being honest and living more authentically scolded her. Life was too short to not be honest with herself and those around her. Which was why she'd made her resolve to live more in the moment in her own truth. But did that have to include sharing her thoughts of sex with a sexy stranger?

Even when those thoughts were about him? She took a deep breath, squeezed her eyes shut, and opened her mouth. But nothing came out.

She opened her eyes with a laugh to find him watching her with extreme amusement.

"That bad, huh?" He fell into a belly laugh. "Now I really want to know."

She released a big sigh and forced herself to look him in the eye. She cringed before saying, "Okay. Here goes. I was imagining licking your groin muscles."

He launched into hysterics of delighted laughter that shone out of his eyes brighter than the sun. Finally, after his laughter subsided and he took a breath, he asked, "No shit? That's phenomenal."

She touched her flushed cheeks. "Well, shit. It's the truth."

He looked so happy he should pinch himself. "And the gasp before?"

She laughed at herself and tipped her head back. As she stared up into the blue sky between the trees, she said, "I was imagining what your sexy butt would look like from above as you fucked me missionary."

He launched into another gleeful laugh. When his jovial sprint ended, he said, "You are a delight! I think I may have just hit the jackpot of the entire female gender."

She hugged herself. "Yeah, I guess I'm rather into all things sex."

"And you just keep getting better," he said in a soothing, lust-filled voice.

"I made a commitment to myself to live more in the moment and be more honest in each moment. So, there you go. You are the recipient of my new mantra in life." She swung her arms up in the air, then shoved them under her breasts. "No holds barred."

"I like no holds barred. And it's super refreshing to meet a woman who doesn't hide her wants or play games." His face still glowed with joy.

"I think I hit the jackpot meeting you." She held his gaze. She let her question percolate up her spine from her clit. "So, do you have those muscles?"

He threw his head back as raucous laughter poured out of him. "Yes."

She didn't morph her eyes to hide her excitement, instead letting it shine for him. "Could I see?"

"You really want to see?" he asked, clearly tickled to the brim with joy that she'd asked.

"Yes." She shifted so she was facing him more.

"If you want, I'll show you. But I don't want to mess this up. You're in the lead, and I'll follow whatever you want." He looked as if she'd handed him the winning lottery ticket.

"Deal," she stated boldly, her lust seething as she noted the significant rod of his erection beneath his workout shorts.

He stood up, tugged up his shirt to his armpits, and snuck his fingers under his waistband. He pressed the shorts down slowly in a prolonged reveal, stopping when his shorts lay atop of his erection.

"Holy fuck," she whispered as her eyes grew big, taking in his six-pack, his chest muscles, then falling to the most delicious defined arrow of muscles pointing to his cock. He was even more incredible than she'd imagined. "You're incredible. Oh, my Gawd. You're unbelievable."

She slid off the rock as she admired him. She looked up at him and pointed her finger at the earth, bobbing it. "More?"

He shook his head as he raised his eyebrow, his eyes growing more lecherous by the second. "You want more?"

She nodded aggressively as she sat on her knees. Her impatience at wanting to see his cock had her shaking. "I want more." Her heart pounded as she waited for his next move.

He slowly unveiled his cock. It sprung out in all its delicious length and girth, and she gasped heavily.

"Wow," she sputtered as her hands flew over her mouth. "You're fucking incredible." She'd landed in the woods and found a Greek god with the heart of a kind, and so far, quite decent man. She'd most certainly won the lottery. "I don't do this."

He chuckled with a tick of his head. "Neither do I."

Staring at him, half-naked before her, she couldn't resist her burgeoning lust at wanting to touch and suck him. "But let's?" she pleaded with her tone and her eyes. She paused as she considered for a split second if this was a bad idea or not, then impulsively charged in. "Can I give you head?" Her inner slut snapped to attention and showed herself fully in her gaze up at him. "I'd love to. It looks so magnificent." She remained still as she watched him process her request. "And just so you know, no, I've never done anything like this in my life. It's just you are so amazing. And not just in how you look."

He laughed with utter joy. "I'm good if it was! I've never been gifted anything like this before. A beautiful and athletic woman appearing out of nowhere in the woods who likes to workout, hike, and admits to liking sex, then she's asking to suck my cock? This is like my ultimate fantasy." His happiness with the situation was obvious, and it only added to hers.

She crept forward on her knees while keeping her eyes on his, but glancing down at his cock periodically. Cock worshiping a stranger in the woods was a fantasy she'd masturbated to as well, so to be doing this had her bursting with unadulterated passion. "I'm really excited, if you can't tell."

He shifted his hips. "As am I, if you can't tell," he joked as he shifted his hips, which made his rod bob.

"Oh, I can tell," she said with a laugh laced in her sentence. "I can really tell." Stating the obvious when it was sexual was quite yummy.

She rose up on her knees when she reached him and took his manhood in her hands. She started to stroke him as she stared at the hole in the head of his cock. She watched her movements as she stroked his cock, his precum already bubbling out the top. She snatched the wetness with her hands and spread it down his cock as she caught him in an eye lock. She chugged her hand up and down him as his groans began. She was no stranger to making a man come.

He threaded his fingers in her hair, pressing his fingertips into her scalp harder when his groans crescendoed.

"Oh, fuck, that feels so good," he muttered as his head fell slightly back.

She rose up and took his cockhead into her mouth. The moan he released when she clamped her mouth down on him was delicious. She rode his cockhead while stroking his shaft and rubbed her tongue extra over his frenulum. She kept mouth-riding him as his pleasure sounds filled the forest around them.

When he seemed close to his height, she popped off his cock and grinned up at him.

He grinned back as he held her head between his hands.

"Whew!" he exclaimed. "Kinda want to beat my chest right now."

A laugh bubbled out of her gut. He was funny too! She waited as they both made flirty eyes at each other.

"I can't believe I'm doing this." She leaned up and licked along the muscles leading to his groin. She groaned out as she hungrily savored his body with her mouth. She rode her tongue up and down the V several times before savoring his firm sculpted abs with her tongue, too. He tasted salty, but she wasn't turned off by knowing it was likely sweat. Geez. This forest had her at her ultimate primal feeling state with that. Or maybe she was just that horny. She visited his nipples for a tongue lashing, pressing her body against his boner. Then she licked down his body, following the lead of his muscles back down to his groin. Back to where she belonged.

She took him back in her mouth again and began to suck his cockhead aggressively. She took more of him in her mouth and gagged. Though she hated gagging, she loved how it put men at her mercy.

His body jerked in response, his torso curling towards her. "Fuck," he spat. "Ungh," he grunted.

She popped off him again and stood up. She grabbed him by his solid log of a dick and tugged him toward the big rock. "Sit," she commanded.

"With great pleasure," he stated, his eyes full of embers. "You're in charge of what happens. I'm just here for the hot ride. Wherever you decide you want to go, I'm good with it."

That declaration sat very well with her. He was giving her no pressure to continue. This man was smart. And that was a turn on too.

Once he settled against the big rock, she took him back in her mouth. She face-fucked her mouth on his cock, bobbing herself on him, bogging herself down on him to the point of another gag. Then she came off him again.

He was sagging back against the rock, leaning on his arms to support his weight. "You are driving me crazy."

She smiled wickedly. "I know." She sent him a look that surely should have told him she was loving it.

She grasped his thighs and ran her hands up and down them. "I love your thighs. I love your big cock. I love your body. I love everything about you." She thought it was funny that if she'd said all that to him in any other situation than this, he might be scared off. But saying it all while sucking his cock, he'd likely not be freaked out that she did. She reached to stroke his cock again.

"Same," he managed to get out between his labored breaths.

She released his cock and removed her shirt, then her sports bra.

"Oh, fuck yes," he said in an appreciative tone. "You have incredible breasts. Your nipples, wow!"

She nestled her body back between his legs and took him in her mouth again. She sucked him hard for twenty seconds, then popped off. She did it again. And then again.

He gasped guttural groans each time she went back on his cock. "Fuck, fuck, fuck," he chanted.

She bobbed on his cock again, her tits bouncing as she did. When his body tensed, she fell back, his cock bouncing with his bodily gyrations as she left it. She worked his cock, edging him ever closer to climax, loving every second of her cock tease.

He grasped her head between his hands, a look of desperation in his eyes. "You are really good at this," he said. A big sigh skittered out of his mouth as a light laugh. "You're driving me wild."

"Oh, that's my plan." She gave him an intense look as she took his inflated mushroom head back into her mouth again. She intended to bring out his natural sex beast, and she could sense he was close to unleashing it. And she was so ready.

She kept sucking him and popping off, edging him until his eyes revealed he was on the brink. She stood up and pulled his head down to meet hers. They fell into a kiss that flared into them, groping each other, mauling each other's flesh like two sex-deprived humans, which perhaps, for all she knew, they were. She certainly was.

When their kiss waned, she held his gaze and spoke with intense want. "Fuck me, Logan. Right here against this rock. Fuck me until my screams fill this forest as your groans just did."

He gripped her hips and turned her to face the rock. He gruffly grunted, then roughly bent her over the rock and tugged her tennis skirt up and her panties down.

Her desire swelled. She perked her ass upward at him and got her head as low as it would go, the phrase 'head down, ass up' rolling around in her head.

He pressed his full cock to her ass cheeks as he reached beneath her body to rub at the cleft between the start of her lower lips. When he graced her clit, she moaned louder, her mostly naked body writhing on the rock in response. He played her with clit hard, then spanked it with his hand. She lurched forward when he pressed his fingers inside her and pumped. With one hand finger fucking her and the other reaching around to arouse her clit, she mounted her climax and shrieked as her body gave in to her orgasm. She shuddered out of control. It was so fucking good. As the contractions traveled from her clenching pussy muscles out to her body, she rocked the wave. She moaned and mewled without dampening her natural sounds one bit.

He gripped her hips and penetrated her from behind, quickly ramming himself into her. Within a minute of thrusting, he was yanking his cock out and splattered cum across her ass and lower back.

He fell upon her panting, both their heavy breathing sounds filling the air around them. Their sweaty bodies breathed heavily as if one being.

"Holy fuck," he whispered. "That was incredible."

She twisted her head to try to look at him. "It's the primal nature of the woods," she mused.

"Well, it's definitely that." He rose off her.

She turned to face him, her face set in an expression of pure satiation. She pressed her body to him, her face upturned for a kiss. They kissed with their hands roaming all over each other again. "The forest works magic on people like us."

He grinned down at her. "I think it was magic. Forest magic." He scoffed. "And, shit, you were teasing me something fierce."

"You loved it," she cooed.

"I did. Edging is where it's at." He paused as if he wasn't sure what to say. Finally, he said, "Next time, it's my turn to edge you."

She liked the idea of a next time very much. Her date popped into her head. She became overcome with increasing terror as she realized how long they'd likely been at it. "Shit," she said releasing him and grabbing her phone off the forest floor. "I think I'm supposed to be on a date right now!" she exclaimed.

"I'm pretty sure you're on a date," he said with teasing evident in his words.

"No," she paused as guilt invaded her. "Yes, but I had a blind date set up for tonight."

He laughed again. "You're on a blind date."

"Oh, shit. He's likely just sitting at the restaurant. I feel like a total jerk." She raised her arm in the air with hopelessness. Her heart sank. She hadn't meant to stand him up, but Logan was just so incredible, she couldn't help herself.

"Ah, I see. That's why you had to go." He took a step back from her, his expression showing he sympathized.

"Damn. I'm not that woman, but I just was."

"Just apologize now. Tell him you found an amazing man in the woods and couldn't leave." His tone was joking, but he wasn't wrong.

"He won't believe that," she said sadly.

"I know, but do it anyway. Then he can go on."

She nodded. It was the right thing to do. She texted him the message, a silly look on her face. "I bet he's never gotten this excuse before."

He finished dressing and handed her clothes to her.

"Likely not. But that frees up your night. Would you like to go to dinner with me, Meredith?" His face was welcoming and pleasant.

"Yes, yes, I would. And I'm famished." She grinned. "All that cock sucking gets a girl hungry."

His face erupted into a beaming smile. "I gotta say, I love that sentence." He swatted his bicep. "And I think my repellant is wearing off. The bugs are starting to get me. Let's get going."

She dressed, then followed him back down the trail.

"I was scared of you at first, you know, then I ended up asking to suck your cock. You can't make this kind of shit up!" Her emotions were on a jubilant high as much as her body was.

"Nope, you can't. But it's a hell of a way to meet." He forged on ahead of her through the woods. He glanced back at her as he said, "I'm so glad I didn't scare you off. That scares me to think this almost didn't happen."

"Agreed." She followed him closely behind, thanking herself with every step. If she hadn't forced herself to remain steadfast, she'd have missed the best sex of her life. Now, she hoped that streak would continue, and he'd be the best dinner date of her life.

The End

Teasing Her Swollen Bean

Josie tied her silky robe and peeked out into the bedroom. Her boyfriend was still asleep, his hair all mussed up, and his right leg was out of the blankets. It was only 4 a.m., but she wasn't tired. Nope. She was horny. She was ready to grab a toy and make her body jolt with a big juicy delicious O. She'd gone to bed early the night before, so she was waking early, and she figured she'd tried long enough to fall back asleep. It wasn't happening, so she had just gotten up. It had been a long twelve-hour shift at the hospital yesterday, and she had crashed at nine. Which had been a bummer because Mason had been coming on to her pretty strongly, with promises of a massage, which of course always led to sex. She'd finally caved. She really wanted to have sex with Mason, but she was exhausted. She'd gone up first, and clearly had fallen asleep before Mason had even appeared. So, he was likely horny too—but asleep, dead as a log to the world.

She wanted to wake him. In fact, they'd just had this discussion, and both of them had said they were okay with being woken up for sex, but he looked so calm and peaceful now that Josie was reluctant to wake him. She was horny, really horny, though, but she could wait a bit to give him some more sleep. Four in the morning was way too early to wake up, even for sex.

She glanced in the mirror, and she still looked pretty damn good for having slept all night. Her hair wasn't too crazy, and she had a nice glow to her skin, probably because she'd gotten a decent sleep. Thoughts of last week popped into her head as she watched him sleeping. Mason had been on a cooking spree of homemade Asian food, and she'd watched him whipping up his culinary delights from a bar stool at their island counter. The tall chair had been the perfect perch to watch Mason work. He had just graduated from culinary school and started a job at a local restaurant called Mannie's, which had always been one of their favorites, and the first place she'd given him a blow job in public. They'd been only dating for about a month, and he had dared her to do it, so she'd slipped under the table and whipped his cock out, not wanting to be the one shying away from a dare, no way. Neither of them could have guessed that would end up being Mason's place of employment. The semi-fancy restaurant now had extra special meaning for them.

She smiled as she noticed his work clothes laid out on the dresser. He legit wore a chef hat and white chef's coat. He'd looked sexy in it the other day when she'd surprised him at work. She'd gotten a bigger surprise when she saw Zeke washing dishes. The three of them had snuck in a threesome in the bathroom one day. Zeke and Mason had been friends since tenth grade, and Josie had never thought she'd be lucky enough to wind up with a man who was open enough for a male-male-female threesome, but there they had been, and after a few drinks, with Zeke's hand up her skirt and Mason's hand on her right tit, they'd skedaddled to the bathroom for some impromptu fun. It had been beyond epic!

Now it was a thing to fuck there, but they couldn't risk sex at the restaurant anymore, not with it being his paycheck at risk. They needed to eat and had just bought a house together. It was too risky, so they had plans to invite Zeke over soon for a repeat session of their spicy tryst. She couldn't wait!

Mason stirred in the bed and groaned. He looked sexy and cute asleep. She pondered once again whether she'd moved too fast with Mason, but he seemed so wonderful so far. She couldn't imagine it going sour. He was a good man, who never said he was good. Good men didn't have to say they were good.

She bit her lip and considered snuggling up to him to wake him gently or sucking his cock to wake him with arousal. He'd clearly had a plan last night, and her tiredness had stolen their intimate time together. Maybe he'd had enough sleep and would want to come? She snickered, that most likely being the case.

She crept into the room and slowly pulled her nightstand drawer open, making the picture of them on top wiggle. The pic made her smile. It was the best one of them on the cruise trip from last year, when they were on the white sandy beach, both smiling, her in a barely-there-bikini. She slowed her pull on the drawer so the pic wouldn't rock and rattle, and peered into the drawer for her rose toy. She spied it beneath the big dildo Mason had bought her for her birthday. It was a nine incher, with a girth that made her groan more than anything she'd ever had inside her pussy before. It was legit patterned after a porn star's real cock. She had squealed and instinctively spread her legs when she'd opened it. Mason was not a jealous man, no. He was a sexy, confident man. She'd had jealous boyfriends before who were threatened by such toys, but not Mason. He just wanted her sexually satisfied. Along with all his cooking and other amazing shit, he had it together, so she felt all-in with him. He was the man of her dreams so far, and she only saw promises of that to continue. Ignoring red flags in relationships had burned her many times before, so she'd learned her lessons well.

He stirred in his sleep as she laid upon the bed, her heart throbbing for no reason other than she liked the idea of climaxing next to him while he slept. He might be mad she hadn't woken him up, but she knew he'd forgive her in a heartbeat—and then grab the toy himself. The other night flitted into her brain, when he took a video of her masturbating, then posted it to their anonymous account on Twitter. They'd started playing around with posting pics and little videos of them fucking. Headless, of course, but she had a hankering to maybe do more. Her friend Alexa and her boyfriend had started an OF, and were actually making good money off it and having a blast. Since Mason was open to it, she had been considering pushing the idea of them doing more.

She spread her thighs and smeared a dollop of fruity-smelling lube on her bean. It was a sweet smell that reminded her of the taste of it: strawberry. Her clit was already sensitive to even that simple touch, and she suppressed a moan. It wasn't supposed to be so intense, but she was so in the mood that the light touch from her own finger was skyrocketing her desire even higher.

She pushed the button on the toy to turn it on and then tapped it two more times to get it to the highest solid buzzing level. She watched as Mason shifted next to her, but he didn't open his eyes. She untied her robe and spread the fabric apart to expose her breasts and pussy mound. She sighed softly as she readied to touch the sucking toy to her more than ready clit.

She touched the toy's little circular mouth to her clit. "Fuck," she whispered before throwing her head back in a writhing motion and releasing a breathy groan. It felt incredible, so her vocalizations came out louder than she had intended. She glanced sharply at Mason to see if she'd woken him. He hadn't moved a muscle.

She pressed the toy to her swollen clit head as she launched a fantasy in her head from a porn video she'd watched recently when Mason was at work. It was one of those MILF scenes with several young men taking turns fucking her while her son was showering in the adjacent bathroom. It had tickled her taboo bone, and so she imagined herself in the scenario; not that she'd ever do it in real life, but to imagine it was harmless. She often ventured into the taboo topics when she masturbated alone.

She squirmed as her arousal began to climb, her torso twitching as the toy perfectly rode her thickened, swollen bean, just how she liked it. Her excitement was nearing her peak when Mason clamped his hand on top of hers, then he ripped the toy right off.

"I thought you were going to wake me," he said with a sly grin and playfully narrowed eyes. He swiveled the toy in the air, the buzzing hum louder now without her clit in it, muffling it.

"I thought about it, but you looked so peaceful." She gave him a demure, innocent look.

"Does this look peaceful and calm?" He shoved his pj pants down to expose his enormous erection. "I think not!" he scolded.

She sniggered and gasped. "Oh, my, that looks very awake."

"I'm hard as fuck. I must have sensed you doing this in my sleep." He rolled his hard cock against her thigh. "You know, now you'll have to wait."

"Wait? Wait for what?" She licked her lips. "For your cock? It's looking pretty ready to come inside my pussy and fuck me, that's what it looks like."

He snickered and dabbed the toy onto her wet clit, only to rip it right back off. He touched the toy down again and pulled it off, over and over in rapid succession. Each time he touched it down, her body jerked in response.

"Fuck," she muttered as she tried to grab the toy from him.

He evaded her reach and continued to tease her clit with taps, but never pressing it down for long.

"Oh, damn you!" she exclaimed with a chuckle. "Give it to me!" She was desperate to finish her orgasm. She wanted the big one where it traveled her whole body, making her want to scream before ripping it off as contractions rang through her pelvis.

"Not yet," he said. "It's in my control now." He pressed the toy down and her body lurched forward. He chuckled. "Sensitive, huh?"

"Oh, my ..." her exclamation was interrupted as he firmly secured the toy on top of her clitoral head. Her body torqued as the sensations jolted her body. "Fuck," she whispered in desperation as she clawed Mason's skin with her fingertips. "That's so fucking strong right now."

"That means you're really aroused." He propped up his head with his hand and smiled at her. "So, what were you thinking about that's got you so hot?"

She wasn't telling him! She hadn't told him half of her fantasies, for fear of him judging her. Not that he'd ever shown any signs of it, but it just felt to her like he'd judge, so she'd always kept the really taboo ones to herself.

"Something really naughty?" he asked with a devilish grin. He held the toy on her precious swollen member and she cried out again.

The sensitivity was sweet but torturous. "Oh, this is driving me crazy."

He snickered. "I know. And I'm loving it." He held her gaze. "I'm not stopping."

"Don't you want your cock in me?" she asked enticingly. "Riding me doggy, smacking into my big ass as my cunt surrounds your cock until you come?" She knew she could get him to fuck her if she started talking dirty. "Fuck my hole, Mason. Give me your cock, gimme your cum up my wet, tight cunt. Come on. You know you want to."

He screwed his face into several different expressions, starting with shock, progressing to a laugh, then to impish and lewd. "Oh, I will, but first, I'm making you pay."

"Pay for what?" she asked with exasperation as he worked the toy on her on a continuous and endless cycle, then pulled it off. "Letting you sleep?" She rolled her eyes as she released an incredulous sigh. "You gotta be kidding me."

She reached for the toy, and he pulled it from her grasp, then rose up and pounced on her, sufficiently pinning her beneath him.

"You devil," she accused as she gave him a salacious glare. "Get off me!"

He laughed. "You wanted me on you, now you've got me."

She scoffed. "Not like this, you fucker."

"Now, now, now, is that any way to talk to the man holding your favorite clit toy?" He gave her an exaggerated snotty control freak look as he slowly released her from his heavy weight. He scooted backwards and kissed her pubic mound. "Now, let's get back to the playing." He held the toy on her clit for a straight thirty seconds, her body writhing and squirming on the mattress.

She tried to muffle herself, but she was so turned on that her moans reached a crescendo peak. She neared the top height of it and he ripped the toy off.

She gasped in desperation, her anguish real and agonizing. "Oh, fuck," she said through her heavy breathing. "Oh, fuck, oh, fuck." She gave him a piercing stare that she intended as evil, as she began to relax a bit from her near-maxing peak. "Fuck, I was so close, too."

He snickered and said, "I know. That was the point."

She feigned relaxing, and then lunged for the toy.

He was too fast and yanked it away before she closed her fingers on it. "I'm not done," he mocked.

"Your cock looks angry. Let me suck it with my hot wet pussy hole." She reached for his hard dick, but he rolled away from her. She let out a disappointed shout. "You're enjoying this!"

"I am," he said as he settled between her thighs, spreading them further apart with the nudge of his free hand. "Lay still and let me, or no orgasm. I hold the key."

He was being so mean! She slid her hand over her vulva and grunted.

"I guess you don't want an orgasm anymore, huh?" he asked, clearly joking and trying to get a rise out of her. He poked his fingers at the hand that was blocking her genitals.

She pressed her lips together and slowly moved her hand, allowing him access to her womanhood once more. "Yes, I do."

"Good," he blew on her clit before readying the toy in position. "Now, let's get you writhing and almost coming again."

"Please," she pleaded as he pressed the toy to her again. Her body jumped as he forcefully secured the sucking hole over her clit. She screeched and grabbed his arm, but he didn't let up his firm press.

She rode her climax hard and was almost there. It was within reach when he tore the toy off once more. "Fucker!" she screamed as she playfully smacked the sides of his torso with her bent knees.

He smirked and pressed it down again. "Tell me what you were fantasizing about, and I'll let you come."

She fought her fear over telling him. She really wanted to come, but she didn't want him to be freaked out by her fantasy. But telling him might be hot. What if he liked it, too? Or had a similar fantasy? Mason wasn't a prude. She needed to go all in with him, despite her misgivings.

He worked her clit as she thrashed beneath him. He tweaked her left nipple, and she was ready to launch.

But she didn't, because he removed the toy again.

"Shit," she gasped, her passion burgeoning on madness at this point.

"Tell me, Josie."

"No."

"I won't be offended. You know me." He tickled the toy along her clit and slit as she tried to snatch it.

She did know him, and she didn't think he'd be a dick about this, but what if he was? She mused about the potential. But then she'd know the real him, and that was actually important to know at this stage, so she didn't lock herself into life with the wrong man.

He tantalized her clit further, blocking her every attempt to get it.

She lay flat and sighed in defeat. "Fine. It was a MILF porn video I watched. And she was fucking all her son's friends while he was in the shower."

He burst into laughter and shouted, "Yes! I love it! Finally! You're telling me this stuff!" He looked very happy and excited, and true to his word, he pressed the toy against her throbbing womanhood and held it there.

She was panting heavily, and the urge to scream throttled her throat. She released the cry as her orgasm raged higher. She released random nonsense words as the orgasm hurdled her into her full-blown climax, the ripples of the contraction traveling her body in a torrent of yummy waves. She pressed at his hand as the pleasure crept towards being too much, but he didn't budge. She screamed as she was relentlessly flung into another orgasm.

"Please," she barely was able to say.

He laid the toy to the side of her, the hum still going, and pressed his cockhead at her opening. Within seconds, he thrust himself into her, groaning in deep appreciation at fully penetrating her aching lips.

She groaned out, matching his intensity as he shoved himself into her on repeat, pounding her down into the mattress.

He grunted and growled, fucking her ever harder as she desperately grabbed at his arms and shoulders.

She dug in her fingernails as his entering her hit her G-spot perfectly, and when he adjusted his angle, his poundings smacked her clit just right. She climaxed again, her vaginal muscles clamping down repeatedly on his cock inside her.

He yelled and his body tensed, then relaxed.

The slowing of his pumping and the extra squishiness inside her pussy meant he'd come, too. He collapsed on her with a look of deep satiation.

"Mmmm, fuck, that was so good," she whispered against his shoulder as she hugged him.

"Yes, yes it was. Fucking awesome." He rolled to the side of her and pulled her into a hug. "It worked." There was evidence of a grin in his voice.

"Yes, it did. Very well." She sighed as she snuggled into his embrace. "You were mean, though," she said in a pouty voice.

"Hey, that edging sent you flying into a huge orgasm, right?" he asked with assurance.

He was right, of course.

She said in a huffy voice, "Maybe."

"MILF, huh?" He caressed her hair. "I've had that fantasy about a thousand times myself. Thank you for sharing it with me. Maybe we can role-play it and enjoy it together."

She gave a short, curt laugh. "You gave me little choice!"

"Well, maybe so, but you still shared it with me."

"Yeah, I was scared to, though."

He pulled back sharply and looked her in the eye. "Why? You can tell me anything."

"I do feel closer to you, after telling you." She couldn't deny it. She felt a stronger connection with him after sharing that secret desire. "And yes, to the role-play."

"Good, let's do more of that. The sharing. And the doing." He pulled her to his chest and kissed the top of her head. "And soon. Right after we take a nap." He yawned and hummed.

"Yeah, I might actually be able to fall asleep again. That made me sleepy." She relaxed into his body, feeling safe and loved, and damn, did he get her good with his teasing. She released a small laugh. "You got me damn good, you know that?"

"I know. I can tell when you get close now."

That made her feel good, too. She was important, and she'd never felt this way in a relationship before. Perhaps he was the one.

"Goodnight," he said in a waning voice.

"Goodnight, love you."

"Love you."

And she closed her eyes, knowing a tease was way more than just a mere tease when her lover put her pleasure first. It was everything.

The End

Around Her World

Marlayna sent Jason another saucy look. She could hardly wait for this trip, and it was finally time. She'd felt like the six months wait time from planning to evolution had felt more like six years. She squeezed his thighs, which brought his eyes from the road to meet hers.

She stared at his lips as he spoke. "I'm serious. I'm going to make you come so hard, you'll scream loud enough for the guests on both sides of our room to hear."

She seethed with excitement. "Well, I can't wait for that rush, if it happens." She screwed her face into playful doubt, her eyes blazing with skeptical mischief. She ran a hand through her long dark hair and played with the ends of a strand. "I don't scream during sex," she taunted.

He burst into laughter. "Have we been in the same bed while fucking?" He tapped the steering wheel quickly with his fingers. "Cause that's a load of crap." The smile on his face tickled her insides.

"Well, mostly I don't," she mused with an amused chuckle. She enjoyed playing with him so much.

"I'm thinking about the time that our neighbor texted me. Remember that?"

How could she forget? The neighbor had texted Jason that he heard a woman screaming and should he call the police because he thought it was coming from our house. That neighbor had spent enough nights around bonfires with Jason, and sometimes her too, to know that they had a healthy sex life. They'd gone into such discussions over multiple beers, it mostly coming up because the man was quite jealous, being in a twenty-year marriage that had landed in the sexless zone in recent ones.

"Oh, I couldn't forget that," she said, but the stain of embarrassment had only impacted her until she came that day. Then she hadn't cared at all. "That was kinda hot, actually." She bit her lip as he glanced at her.

"In the hotel room, it's going to be just like that, only better." He bobbed his head to the music.

She had accepted the reality that she was more excited about the hotel sex with her man than she was about the little weekend trip they had planned. As far as she was concerned, they could stay in the hotel all weekend and fuck themselves into hormone comas.

"I don't believe you. How will it be different?" she asked sumptuously.

His hand left the wheel, and he tapped his right temple with his finger. "Oh, I've got a plan."

She squealed with glee. He always had some sort of plan for sex, always trying new stuff or creating a narrative of dirty talk to spin for her. "I can't wait!"

He laughed. "I'm not sure which part I like better, the telling you about it or the doing." He jerked his head to a sudden strong beat in the music and burst into song for the melody. "Well, I guess I'm picking the doing, but damn do I love the teasing you part, too. Building you up until you are begging for my cock."

She couldn't disagree one bit. "Well, I could have your cock right now, if I really wanted it." She flicked her eyebrows up and down rapidly. "Road head."

He shook his head. "Nope."

She swung her head back with exaggeration. "What? Are you serious? You're refusing road head?" She glanced around wildly with a panicked look on her face. "What fleet of aliens stole my husband and replaced him with you?"

He burst into a boisterous laugh. "I'm saving the boner. You can't have it yet."

She feigned pouting as he continued to joyfully laugh.

"I think I've fallen into an alternate universe." She couldn't think of a single time in their fifteen years together that he'd said this.

"I have a new technique, but I'm not sharing anything about it yet." He nodded his head as he flicked on the windshield wipers to swipe the cleaner across the windshield. They were in bug country and the dead bugs on the window had speckled the window in droves.

"Oh!" Marlayna exclaimed, her lust mounting any sense of logic. "Do tell. Please."

He shook his head. "Not gonna happen, babe."

She shoved her hands under her C cups and squeezed her hands into fists. Then she softened her gaze and made her eyes demure. "Please? I'll give you lots of sexual favors in return."

He scoffed. "You already do that."

She guffawed in disgust. "You really want to tell me, don't you?" she cooed.

"No." He released a quick breath. "This is not something I've done to you before."

Her hormones jolted around her body like popcorn popping. Her nerves had zings of anticipation ramping up her adrenaline. Something new? She felt they'd done just about everything short of some more hardcore BDSM stuff that neither of them wanted to try. What could it possibly be? "One hint?" she begged.

He pursed his lips in silence for thirty seconds. "Mmmmm. It involves my mouth."

She threw her hands down to her thighs in a quick motion. "Well, that's the worst hint ever. That's like so many things."

"Yup," he agreed, clearly very happy with his level of seduction.

"Ooooh," she said in an irritated tone. "This sucks. I need more."

"You'll get lots more at the hotel. You'll be lost in orgasmic reverie."

She shuddered. "Well, I'm so very up for that!" They were adventurous sexually, but in recent years, they'd really started to experiment.

"You hungry? Need to stop for lunch?" He played with the radio because the station had gone to static. He settled on a country station, likely because that's all that they could get for radio way up north in the woods as they were.

"No," she said curtly.

He chuckled in amusement. "I've got you in a tizzy, don't I?"

She wasn't admitting squat. She shook her head as she tried to hide her grin.

"I see that," he said in a knowing tone.

"What?" she asked haughtily.

"That grin. I'm right," he said with absolution.

"Nope," she shot right back. This whole flirty exchange had her brain slipping back to the last time he brought her to the brink of sexual insanity, which happened to be the last time they'd graced the big oversized cabin in the woods three years ago, almost to the day. The wooded lot the mansion of a cabin occupied had heard her beastly overstimulated screams before. And with all this buildup her amazing man was throwing at her, this promised to blow the roof off the place. Her passion felt that ballooned, as if a bomb might rival the blast. He was such an incredible man to plan this once again for her that it set her love for him on overdrive, where her heart already was. It was just time for her brain to catch up.

"Can't fool me. I know you, babe." His arrogance might have been annoying if he weren't such a thorough lover and partner. He left no stone unturned for her needs and wants. He glorified in bringing her satisfaction so much that she beamed with excitement to return the favor. Needless to say, she wasn't just happy with her relationship, it was magnificently unmatchable.

She struggled for a smart comment to strike back at him with, to enter the tango of his tease, but all she could do was smile and stifle the full birth of it. "Are we almost there?" She already knew the answer; she was the damn navigator.

"You just proved it," he said smugly as he reached over to firmly squeeze her knee. "Get those vocal cords ready because I'm giving them a workout."

She could hardly contain her anticipation. Her pussy was hot, her mind was aroused, and her pulse was on stampede mode. "Fuck," she muttered under her breath.

"Yes," he said with extreme amusement.

She swatted his shoulder and tried to pout, but it was a lost cause as her smile beamed. "You fucker," she teased as she finally gave in and stroked his hand that still was atop of her knee.

"I know that look too," he teased. "If we weren't so close, I'd pull over and fuck you."

It was exactly the kind of thing to say that sealed the deal in her brain; he was her ideal man. "We aren't that close," she countered.

"Yes, we are," he said in a stern tone. "How's my pussy doing down there?"

"It's very hungry," she said in a bratty voice.

"Good, I'd like to starve it a bit more," he glanced at her, giving a quick snarl, "and rage it to max level." He crawled his fingers slowly over her fleshy upper pussy mound and pressed his full hand firmly to her womanhood.

Her hormones burst inside her and she stiffened. "Fuck," she spat as she squirmed away from his press. "Oh, I'm there!"

He snickered as he pressed his finger downward, trying to pry the cleft in her lips open. "What if I just press," he said, pausing as he pushed his fingers deeper, "here?"

Her body jolted in response to his press to her clit. "Shit, you devil," she whispered.

He wiggled his finger to stroke back and forth as she writhed in the seat. "Blasphemy, you love it," he teased, his voice thick with lust.

She wanted to smack his hand away, but it felt so damn fucking good. She knew he wouldn't bring her to climax in the car, not after all that talk, so this was just meant to be an excruciatingly arousing edging.

He played with her clit while driving one-handed, his gaze jumping from the road and back to her on repeat.

"You're going to get us in an accident," she said, her words forced through lapses in her panting.

He kept at it until he yanked his hand away.

She was startled and looked around quickly. "What was it? A deer?"

He laughed. "No, I just didn't want you to come yet."

She raised her arm and smacked his bicep. "You are a horrible tease," she retorted, then pressed her lips together as she shot him an accusing stare.

He put his hand back on the wheel and gripped it hard. "I want you so ravenous that you run to our room and strip, fall to the bed, and present your holes to me."

She already knew all that would happen, but she refused to let him see her face. He'd read her eyes and knew he was winning this teasing round, like a fucking champ.

"Marlayna, look at me," he scolded. "You know I'm in charge."

She knew it well, because she'd granted it to him. And he knew that she knew, but him saying it and doing his best to convey it to her always hit her yummy lewd buttons. She wanted it, craved his talk, and loved it even more when he did things to remind her. She laughed despite her attempts to corral her emotions to hide them from him.

"Your silence speaks," he said definitively.

She turned up the radio and proceeded to sing along, the mood of the song filling her. It was a great mask, and she loved staving off his win.

The rest of the ride went quickly as they passed through the thickening woods. When they pulled into the drive of the resort, a breathy calm stole her thoughts, and she was once again filled with awe.

"This is such a beautiful place," she cooed, leaning forward.

"It is, and it's ideal to spend a hot primal night of sex in."

"The woods?" she asked, grinning, knowing he hadn't meant that.

"Now there's an idea for tomorrow's hike," he said, tilting his head to the side.

He parked the car in front of the path they'd hiked every time they'd come. He gave her a charming smile and said, "Now, let's get you onto the hotel bed so I can make you scream that roof off."

She couldn't stop the gleam in her eyes from glowing, nor her smile from mirroring his lecherous one. "I'll race you," she said as she opened the door.

She dashed to the back of the car and pulled the trunk open. She had her suitcase out before he made it to the back of the car.

He snatched her wrist and pulled her to him, eliciting a squawk as he pressed her to his body. He bent down and slid his tongue into her open mouth. They fell into a passionate kiss as the birds tweeted in the nearby woods.

She rolled her body against his erection that was trapped between their torsos, a deep sigh escaping her lips. "Please, I want you. I need you." She reached down and firmly grabbed his hard shaft. "Want this in me asap," she demanded.

"Ah, there's that begging I so love," he released her and grabbed his own suitcase. "Let's go, babe."

She followed him along the smooth blacktop, the sounds of their suitcase wheels whining in unison.

Once they were inside the lobby, the rustic comfort décor soothed her once more, the memories of past visits flooding her. So many good sexy times they'd had in this place. It was astounding to her that such a small, out-of-the-way resort had become such a relaxing and sexual haven for them. They didn't need to go far, they just needed each other and a room to fuck in. A cozy room to pleasure each other in, to sleep a good night, and get fed unbelievably good food. This place fits the bill to perfection.

She watched as her hubby took the keys, his eyes brimming with desire as he searched and caught her in an eye lock. She wanted to tear off across the lobby for the elevators, but that might disrupt the older couple strolling towards the dining room, so she restrained her yearning. When Jason reached her, they both walked in parallel to the elevators.

"You seem a little...off," he accused with a twinkle in his eyes.

"I want you to fuck me into oblivion," she stated with mock annoyance.

"I already promised that," he said with a silly told-ya-so look.

The elevator walls were smooth and dark, rough-looking like tree bark as she imagined them going at it against them, biting her lip.

"You're thinking about elevator sex, aren't you?" he mused with a raise of his eyebrow.

She nodded, her breathing rate hiking up to a faster pace. "Yeah," she said breathlessly.

The elevator stopped on the third floor and they exited the elevator. She followed Jason down the hall, noting the artwork on the walls. They hadn't been on the third floor yet, and every floor had a different decorative nature theme, this one being deer. Just beyond the picture of the mom with two baby fawns was their room.

Jason slid the card into the reader and she leaned in, pressing her breasts to his back before reaching down for a butt grab.

He jumped as her fingertips pressed into his left butt cheek.

"I can't wait to return that," he responded.

"Please do," she quipped. She glanced around the room, noticing that the deer theme was carried into the hotel room as well. Nature wooded scenes of deer were placed in a few places along the wall, faux antlers made the lamp stands and the light fixture, and a rack hung above the fireplace.

"Fake, I hope," she said with a cringe.

"Yeah, looks fake to me." He rolled his suitcase in and spun around. "You, right here, I'm stripping you, then tossing you onto the bed." His eyes were feral with want as he grasped her shirt and tugged it off over her head. He reached around and unclasped her bra as their lips joined again.

Their grunts commingled as their tongues danced. He mauled her back, pressing her bare breasts to him.

She ran her hands up and down his back, massaging his biceps as they deepened their kiss.

He pulled back and tugged her pants down, revealing her freshly shaved landing strip pointing to the cleft in her lower lips.

"Nice surprise," he muttered as he fingered the strip of hair on her pubic mound.

She wrinkled her nose above her grin. "Just a little somethin' somethin'," she whispered.

"Oh, it's something alright," he agreed wholeheartedly.

He continued to rub it. Then he squatted down and scooped her up with one hand under her knees, the other at her back, and tossed her onto the bed.

She squealed as she sailed through the air, and landed with a plop, her breasts gyrating violently across her chest.

"Yes," he seethed through his teeth while slipping his shirt off and his pants down. "Scoot back and get ready," he instructed.

She situated herself on the bed, allowing her thighs to spread apart.

"Keep those legs bent," he said as he slid beneath her bent right leg, perpendicular to her body, so they were shaped like a T.

He wriggled himself under her leg so that her shin and heel rested on his back.

"Oh," she said with delight. "This is new."

He settled in so his face was parallel with her vaginal opening, his grin salacious and enticing. Prying her lips open, he exposed her clitoral head. "Wet lips," he said with relish. "This has an official name, but I'm calling it 'Around Her World,'" he said in a low voice filled with sexy, purposeful intent.

She nestled against the soft comforting blanket, smiling, as she said, "Oh, well, I can't wait for this." His seduction was working on her full force, and she felt on the brink of her orgasm rise already. "Good name. I want it. Whatever it is, I want it. I want you."

"I want you," he spoke into her pussy, his hot breath blasting her labia lips. He tickled the tip of his tongue along her lips, slit, then dabbed it at her bean.

She squirmed and pressed her fingers to his scalp. He had her so aroused she was ready to scream already. He flicked his tongue back and forth across her clit, which sent delicious pings through her sexual organ, thickening her clit and readying her for more. He kept going, varying his speed fast, then slow, then fast again while he used his nose and fingers to stimulate all the fleshy bits of her womanhood hole. She squirmed and his press of ownership where his hand held her pelvis served to ramp up her lust. It said to her that she was his, and that's right where she wanted to be.

"Oh, fuck, that feels amazing. Please, don't stop," she begged in a slurred tone, breathy and wanton.

He aggressively ate her out and she hollered as the pleasure mounted. He reached up to play with her right nipple, pinching it and tugging it. She unleashed her sounds of enjoyment, her moans and verbalizations wrecking the silence in the room. He snickered, then pulled back just as she was reaching her peak.

She gasped and panted as he rearranged his position to be in line with her body, which was his usual way of eating her out. He moved swiftly; he hiked her body up slightly and secured her thighs in place with his arms before latching on to her swollen lower lips. He ran his tongue up and down her slit, visiting her bean before attaching himself to the lower area of her opening and swirling his tongue about her perineum. He continued to pleasure her orally, much like his usual pattern. She twitched and gyrated, and he matched her motions, never letting his suction slip off.

She rose to another height, nearing her peak of orgasm again, her rise blisteringly unbearable to stop. She launched into near orgasm, only to have him move just when she was about to blast off.

"Fuck," she muttered, panting heavily. "I was so close." She didn't let her disappointment at not coming sink in because she knew he was doing this on purpose to edge her into a greater climax.

She played with his hair as he gently licked her privates. Then he moved again, mirroring the position he'd done on her right to service her from the left side. When his tongue touched down to flick her swollen head again, she rapidly soared to her peak, her hormones soaking her insides as she fell the first step into her climax, only to have him jerk back so as to ruin her orgasm again.

She guffawed with exasperation as he pulled himself away from her body again, his grin wicked. He was clearly enjoying driving her wild. He was on the move again, this time he aligned his body parallel to hers, but inverted.

"Sixty-nine," she exclaimed.

"Only for a minute," he dictated.

She readied to take him in her mouth, her desire peaking at getting her mouth on him as well. With him up on his hands and knees, she grasped his firm manhood and wasted no time getting him inside her. She sucked him as he sucked her clit. She couldn't lay still, the stimulation was too much for that shit.

She hummed with him in her mouth, her sounds turning into moans and grunts quickly. He hopped off her quickly, pulling his cock from her mouth.

"That was not a minute," she protested.

"You're too close, need to move," he stated. "I need another tour of your world first."

She fell limp with a laugh as he positioned himself on her left again. He took the tour, pleasing her to almost to the point of no return at every angle, until finally he was on her right side again. He pressed two fingers into her hole while moving his tongue rapidly back and forth in a side-to-side way across her clitoral head and she smashed into her peak.

She was elated he finally was allowing her climax.

"Come for me, baby," he whispered into her pussy before reattaching himself to her bean head.

She lurched forward with a loud cry, her torso curling towards his head, her body twitching and flopping as the contractions overtook her body and made her fall silent. She held her breath as the full wave collided with the rest of her body in a full-strength orgasm. She gasped and sputtered as she began to descend the peak, but he sucked harder and pumped her G-spot harder and she launched into a second orgasm.

"Oh, double, double, double," she chanted as the orgasm stole her control and ran its delicious course.

She lay panting as he pounced on the bed beside her.

"Hands and knees, my sweet slut, I'm going to ride you doggy," he said, his voice thick with dominant intent.

She was woozy from the big O's, but lumbered up into position on her hands and knees.

He wasted no time and lined his meaty head at her waiting entrance.

"Going to beat this meat into you until we both come," he stated.

She had zero doubts about that. His tone was gruff and she knew it meant he was going to fuck her roughly. She grinned as she placed her face on the bed.

"That's right, head down, ass up. Let's go," he cheered as he pressed himself to penetrate her from behind.

They both cried out as he entered, slowly moving himself into her inch by inch with each pump until he got his full length into her. Then he began to ram her, making her butt jiggle as their bodies slapped together. The skin-smacking sounds and their pleasure moans filled the hotel room.

She loved this position because it fulfilled her kink to have him be strong and dominate her, to take his pleasure was a turn-on.

"Get that clit," he instructed as he gripped her hips harder and pounded himself into her at a faster pace.

She followed his wishes and played with her clit as he massaged her internal clit with his pumping. She twitched first, and she quickly succumbed to the pressure. Her pussy walls clenched on his cock inside her and she was flung into her full orgasm.

He groaned. "Oh, fuck," he muttered as she noted his usual sounds of preeminent ejaculation. "Here it comes. Coming." His body served a few final ramming pounds into her before he slowed his thrusting.

She smiled as the increased wetness inside her became evident.

He stayed inside her and fell to the bed, pulling her along with him. They lay on the bed, both panting heavily, him the big spoon, her the little.

"Wow," she finally said between pants. "That was fucking incredible."

He rubbed her hip as he nuzzled his face into her hair. "It was. It was fucking incredible." He paused to kiss her head. "So, you liked the new technique?"

"Oh, hell yes! That was phenomenal! You had me on edge so many times, I thought I'd explode, then you pulled back."

"It made your orgasm big, didn't it?" he asked, sounding proud of himself.

"Yes, it really did." She shifted to her back so she could look into his eyes. "You're an amazing lover, you know that?"

"Only because you are," he parroted back.

"No, it's more than that. You really want me to come. You're as driven as I am about my climax, that's it. That makes it so hot to me."

"Oh, you know me. I want you coming first, babe. I'll come. There's no question about that. That's easy." His grin was sexy and satisfied.

"You can tour my world anytime," she said, smiling, biting her lip.

"Oh, that's a new staple move in my book. You were livid, and I loved it."

"I love you," she said as she snuggled into him.

"I love you," he mirrored back with love in his voice.

"This place is magic," she cooed, inhaling his ocean-breezy scent. It was likely the new deodorant she'd recently bought him.

"It is, and we have three whole days here, and I'm not missing a single day of making you come as much as I possibly can."

She laughed with glee. "Count me in."

He caressed her back as they laid in full skin-to-skin contact along their lengths. "A yummy breakfast in the café after morning sex, then a hike, maybe a nap, and more sex, or just orgasms for you, then dinner and whatever we want to do the in evening. Sound like a plan?"

"Yep, for sure," she said happily. She knew they'd fall asleep if they kept close like this, and she was fine with that. Dreamily reliving her climax and floating in her post-orgasm hormones was exactly where she wanted to be. There were no bad feelings that could touch this high, even if heaven on Earth wasn't ever credited as a legit thing, they might just be wrong about that. She had good faith stock in that belief. She drifted into her elevated state as sleep loomed. Bliss shifted to pure bliss as everything felt oh so right.

The End

Head Road Rage

"You ready to hit the road?" Paul asked as I snagged one last pretzel dipped in cheese.

"Yeah, I'm ready." Watching my boyfriend talk all night to friends had me starving for some alone time with him.

His mouth slipped into a suggestive smile. "I'm ready to go home and fuck. I don't know about you."

I returned his lusty leer with a raise of my eyebrow. "Well, I was already ready to go. Now I want you to speed home. And, hell yes, I'm so ready for that." I adored this man and how he was as obsessed with sex as me.

"Then let's get out of here asap." He grabbed my hand, and we said our goodbyes to our friends.

I had half of a mind to drag him to a bedroom and just fuck him before we hit the road, but I knew that would just be a quickie and I was more in the mood for a long sensual fuck than something quick and rushed. Plus, multiple orgasms were my jam, and I knew with a quickie that wasn't likely to happen.

Paul glanced back at me as he pulled me through the front door into the deep black night air. Our friends Melissa and Don lived in the wild of northern Minnesota, deep in the woods where glimpses of stars only happened on the roads or immediately above homes. Otherwise, the ceilings of tree tops prevailed. We lived about twenty minutes east of the lake in town, so we weren't so heavily wooded at our place.

"Think we'll make it home? Or have to pull off?" he asked as we dashed through the humid dark air, the trees surrounding us like giants with mystical arms reaching upward.

"I'm not sure if you'll make it with what I have planned," I snickered as ideas flooded my brain of how I could tease him as he drove us home. I had intentions of being relentless. I watched him, my mind ramping up in excitement with the burst of physical activity.

"Oh, is that so? I'm intrigued." He paused his jog to swipe a hand down his bulging groin. "Have I mentioned how much I love you and that dirty mind of yours?"

"Yes, and yes, and the same back at ya." I took off in a sprint towards his truck. "First one to the truck doesn't have to drive," I called. He'd already said he was driving, but I still wanted the tease of a race. I knew if I hadn't had a bit of a head start, though, I'd surely lose. With his strong long legs, I had no shot at winning any race against him, unless he let me win.

I reached the truck way ahead, which meant he didn't even try to win. But, I guessed most likely right that he more wanted to find out what I had planned for the drive over winning this little game. I watched his expression shift into excitement as he reached the vehicle, his brown curls flopping on top of his head as he jogged lightly. I thought back with fond memories of the last time we'd been at our friends' house, and how we had done a quickie in the bathroom. He'd wrangled me into doggy in a heartbeat, his hands gripping my hips as he'd fucked me rapaciously from behind against the bathroom sink, my face hovering above the bar of lavender soap at the mirror end of the counter, above the incessant drip of the faucet. The music had droned on quietly in the distance as he'd made me come so hard that I watched my own body twitch in the mirror like I'd been electrocuted. He'd come up my pussy with a yummy masculine grunt, and I'd loved wearing his cum down my thighs for the rest of the party.

I slid into the truck passenger seat, my pussy on my brain. Meditating on my pussy had become a practice of mine after I'd read a book that talked about how thinking about the lovely feminine sex organ, the clit, was proclaimed to improve libido and bring sexuality to the forefront of the brain, thereby leading to better sex. The author was right, it was working. Think the pussy, live the pussy. It was brilliant. I was already a very sexual person, but this practice had me dwelling more in the moment of it on a regular basis.

I glanced at Paul, and he looked as excited as I felt.

"Shayleigh, you just get me," he professed with a lecherous grin.

"Oh, I'm getting you alright," I shot back with an equally lewd expression. I was already breathing heavily, thinking about pulling his cock out while he drove.

He started the truck and backed up, readying to head up the winding driveway. The long driveway itself was a meandering wilderness tour with the thick forest and vegetation. His eyes shone with energized lust.

With our moods matching in a delicious way, I pulled my shirt over my head and whipped my bra off in a flash.

He gazed at me with happy eyes and said, "Yes!"

I was thankful I was wearing my loose pants so I could sneak my hand in them to stimulate myself as I crawled across the bench seat towards him.

I bent down to hover my top half over his lap, making my ass pop higher in the air as he released a yummy groan of anticipation. I grasped the top of his shorts, undid the button, and grappled at his zipper.

He drove one-handed as he groped at my tits with the other. His hands worked their magic on my hardening nips, further arousing me.

I pulled his zipper down one tiny notch at a time, rather painfully slow, but this was on purpose. I gave him a saucy look as I bit my lip.

He tugged on my left nipple, then rolled the peak of it between his fingers.

"Mmmm, that feels incredible," I confessed. I took his zipper down a few more centimeters as he squeezed my hardened flesh.

"I have a feeling you might make me crash this damn truck tonight," he spilled playfully.

"I promise not to," I lied.

"With you on my lap like this, I'm already in the danger zone."

"Wait until I get my mouth on you," I taunted while wiggling my ass.

"Hey, I think your toy is still in the glove compartment. Put that in you."

I sat up quickly, making my breasts swing and jiggle before they settled.

"Oh, please do that again," he begged.

I laughed as I scooted back across the seat.

"And that too," he begged.

I jiggled my body on purpose to make my breasts bounce. "I think you are right because I didn't bring it in the house either." I pulled the glove compartment open, and there lay my beloved little pink bulbous toy.

"Get that in you," he said with authority, his strong dominant streak thick in his sentence. "Let me spit on it."

I snatched it up and crawled back to him. I placed the toy on his lap, then tugged my shorts off, pulling my panties to my ankles too.

"Leave those around your ankles," he slurred in a suggestive voice.

"Yes," I mewled. I raised the toy up and he spat on it. I smoothed his saliva all over the bulb and spread my lower lips. It penetrated my slit with ease and popped right in place.

"You're wet." He stated the obvious.

It was a turn-on to have him say it. "Yes," I agreed with relish. I pressed the little button and the buzzing action of it whirred to life. I placed the little stem along my clit for maximum stimulation and settled myself to hover above his lap again.

I tugged the zipper down all the way. I admired his significant dick bulge, dragging my forefinger down it. "You want some road head, do you?" I asked in a teasing voice.

"Yes," he said emphatically. He stroked my head and pressed the back with his fingers, urging me to start.

I leaned down and kissed him through his underwear, then I licked the fabric.

He groaned impatiently. "Fuck."

I stroked his erection through the fabric on the side closest to my mouth and rubbed my fingers along his length on the opposite side.

He squirmed in the seat.

I smirked. He was trying to get more of my touch, but I wasn't giving it yet. I laid my head fully in his lap and curled up, so my eyes were in line with his boner.

He scoffed. "Like the show?" he asked, then laughed. "It could get a lot more exciting."

I giggled and poked my tongue at him.

"This isn't a long drive," he complained, but he still sounded good-natured.

Sensing his impatience was about to erupt, I continued to play with his clothed cock.

He writhed and petted my head as I continued to minimally stimulate him.

"You want more, do you?" The toy inside me was ramping up my arousal and I wiggled on the seat next to him, nuzzling my face to his fat cock.

"Yes," he said definitively. "I need more."

I chortled. "Need?" I sealed my mouth around the base of his cock and pressed my tongue firmly, then softly. I moved up his cock, alternating the pressures. My mouth was getting too dry sucking on fabric, so I changed my plan and yanked his underwear off.

His cock swung out and he sighed. It was a delicious sound, and I was ready for more of them, so I grabbed his shaft and took his swollen purplish head into my mouth. I ran my tongue up and down his frenulum, then sucked his head with strong suction.

He squirmed, then jerked, his pleasure sounds elevating and obliterating the song on the radio.

Then I popped off and laid back in his lap, smiling up at him as his face shifted from elation to calm.

"That's it?" he asked in desperation.

I nodded.

He pouted.

I waited enough time to get him annoyed, then took him into my mouth again. The move paired with the toy inside me pushed me up my orgasm hill and I almost reached the peak.

He leaned over, pushed his fingers between my thighs, and I was ready for some loving touches, but he tugged the toy out of my pussy.

I sat up abruptly as he chuckled.

"What? What did you do that for? I was so close!" I complained, my movements slightly restrained by my panties claiming my ankles.

"Two can play at edging," he said proudly.

I scoffed. "You're ruining my plan," I stated, unable to keep my annoyance out of my tone.

I moved to grab the toy from him, and he jerked it away, which made him shift the wheel.

"Careful," I exclaimed. "A police officer might pull you over doing that. Are you sure you are okay to drive?"

He nodded. "I haven't had a drink for hours now, plus I ate four pieces of the pizza. I feel completely sober." He dropped the toy in his lap and took the wheel in two hands. "But you're right, I don't need that problem."

I grabbed the toy off his lap. He tried to reach for it, but I was too fast. I slipped the humming beauty back inside me and smiled. "Now that's better." Being already half tanked up my climax, I began to give in to the pleasure again. I slipped my mouth over his bulb again and made enough carnal moans and slurping sounds to surely drive him to the edge of his orgasmic cliff, only to slide off as his sounds escalated.

He glanced at me with horny rage, then softened his gaze, laughing at himself. "Well, fuck, now I was about to come."

"I know," I said proudly. I pressed my thighs together so he couldn't sneak his fingers between them again. The increased pressure was luscious and made me moan with enjoyment. "Mmm, so fucking good."

I put my head in his lap again, my body fully along the seat. I poked at his cock. It looked so full and angry, his flesh taut as could be. I licked up his length and danced my tongue tip all over.

He twitched, which made his cock bob in front of my face. "A nice juicy cock, just for you," he said in a tone meant to tempt me. "All yours."

"Oh, I know, it's all mine alright." That was true, and I loved it. Our relationship was so good these days, it felt unreal. Gone were the troubles we'd had a few years back, and now it was always smooth sailing, and our newfound discussions about sex had been key to get to this point. We had been on the brink of breaking up before I had found a quiz online, which led me to find a sex coach. We had several sessions with her and found that we had both been holding back. Once she'd helped us work through the communication blocks, we found we both had a few hidden kinks in common. It had saved our relationship. "You look ready to burst."

"Oh, that's no lie. I'm ready to blow."

I snickered because I hadn't even had much of him in my mouth yet.

His hand left the wheel to caress my ass. I fidgeted on his lap, my clit quivering, ready to burst too.

"Pull up those panties," he instructed.

I pulled my mouth off of him and did as he wanted.

He secured the hem on the panties in his fingers and tugged upward, giving me a wedgie. "Suck me, babe."

My body lurched in reaction to his rough tugging of my panties and I took him inside my hot, wet mouth again. The dual pressure on my asshole and my clitoris launched me as I sucked him harder, his increasing moans reaching his usual pre-cuming peak. He was close.

I scooted away from him quickly, effectively forcing him to lose his grip on my panties and they snapped back to my skin. I had a little wedgie kink, but that was my limit. I took the panties down and tossed them to the floor.

"Aw, I was having fun doing that," he complained with humor.

"Me too, but now I'm done," I settled back down, accepting the rise to my own arousal in a delicious way. "I'm ready to come."

"Good, we're already at the hardware store. We'll be home soon."

I settled myself on my hands and knees, preparing to suck his cock aggressively. I collected my hair into a ponytail, and he took over that job, and driving one-handed again, he released a very appreciative sigh as I rode his cock fast and hard. My head bobbed and I savored the feel of control over his climax as I sped up my sucking, and slowed it down, ever alternating what I knew would make him climax with what I knew would only edge him.

He released my hair, and it spilled all over, covering my face and his thighs. With his new freed-up hand, he snuck his fingers between my lower lips and shoved the stem of the toy out of the way. He rubbed my thickened clit head with strong pressure, and I dropped over the edge, my body curling as I began to climax.

The truck swerved, faltering off course, and he parked it quickly along the curb.

My body jerked as I twitched along the wave of my climax, the toy inside me delivering continuous strong pulsing to the internal part of my clitoris. I took as much of him in my mouth as I could, gagging slightly as I began to descend the high of my big O, and he launched, groaned, his cock spurting his cum inside my mouth.

"Fuck," he gasped out.

I fell off him as my tolerance waned and began to stroke the rest of his cum out of his cock. It splattered across my face as I laughed.

"Wow, that's a big load," I said, wiping my face.

"Whew, that was hot! I couldn't stop it."

"Me neither," I said as I relaxed my body. I was limp as a rag doll. "I needed that. I feel awesome now," I cooed.

"Same. I've been so horny all night watching you."

"Me too. I had half a mind to pull you into the bathroom again."

He sighed as he ran a hand over his chin, swiping down his face stubble. "You should have. Remember, don't ever hesitate with your urges. I want to know. Just like Maria said in our last session."

"Yeah, you're right. I should have acted when I felt it, but I was having a good chat with Janice and Kitty."

"Yeah, I'll admit, when I was watching you three, I couldn't stop fantasizing about you three fucking each other in our bed."

I laughed with exuberance. "Shit! Really?" My face flushed, not from embarrassment but from being turned on. "I have a confession."

He peered at me with extreme eagerness in his eyes.

I released a sigh and reminded myself of all the good conversations we'd had recently about sharing sexual thoughts, desires, and wishes. I held my breath and glanced up at him, then away, then back into his eyes. "I had the same thoughts."

He clapped his hands and hooted. "Yes!"

I giggled as I curled up my body. "I did."

He stroked my hair off my face. "Would you? I mean, would you ever do it, and could I watch?"

Thoughts of fucking my two friends were definitely arousing, but I couldn't imagine asking them. I didn't want to ruin our friendship over such a thing. "I would, yes, and you could. That would be a turn-on." I paused as his face grew more excited. "I don't think I could ever ask them, though."

His face fell. "Well, maybe over drinks one night, casually bring it up," he suggested.

"How? I'd seriously be terrified." I shook my head, images of their shocked faces torturing me.

"I think," he said before pausing, "you could talk about how our relationship has changed and how we now talk so much more about sex." He shrugged. "Hey, blame it on me. I don't care. Say I suggested it and pretend like it was all my idea only and see how they react. I don't give a shit if they know I want to watch that."

"True, that would be a good way to do it." I stayed still as he stroked my hair and played with it. It felt so amazing and nice that I didn't want to ever move. Post-orgasmic hormones continued to relax my body, and then add in the loving touches from my man while we talked about other sexual fantasies, and this was the ultimate way to savor the post-climax afterglow.

"Oh, shit," he said, his body quaking beneath me. "Someone is coming up behind us." He peered into the mirror. "Fuck, it's a cop!"

He lifted his hips, yanked his pants up, and zipped them.

"Oh," I shrieked as I scrambled to find my shirt. In the dark, it was impossible to find my black shirt. I tapped the flashlight app on my phone to try to find it. I grabbed it and sat up, readying to slip it over my head.

I glanced up and gasped. I was too late.

The officer was standing at Paul's window, grinning.

Paul rolled down the window and released a friendly laugh. "Max!"

The officer was around our age, but his uniform and glinting metal were menacing. We could be in really big trouble, DUI, public nudity, swerving while driving. We were fresh bait for him to exercise his power. The only calming effect was his blue eyes didn't look angry, they looked amused.

"Hey, Paul, thought that was your truck." His grin was treacherously happy as he scanned my naked body. "Good thing you pulled over for the rest of your fun. You were swerving pretty heavily back there."

I relaxed, but was still on edge. Paul had drunk a fair amount of beer earlier in the day. I hoped that since they were apparently friends, he might let this slide.

I was thrilled that Paul didn't seem to care that his friend was seeing me naked.

"Max, this is my girlfriend, Shayley, the one I told you about at the bar the other night."

"Oh," I said realizing. "This is the Max you went to the bar with. Got it. Nice to meet you." I didn't bother to cover up at this point, figuring giving him an eyeful of my tits might make him amenable to not making Paul walk the line and do sobriety tests. It certainly had to help that they'd spent a fun evening together at the bar recently.

"Nice to meet you," he said, his eyes alit with mischief. "I'd kill to have my girlfriend do this with me. You lucky dog."

His jovial nature was a good sign.

"Just thought I'd do my duty and stop you." He took a step back. "Have fun. Wish it was me!" He took another step back and saluted. "Jake's this Thursday again? And bring Shayley, I'll bring Jenna. We could all hang."

"I'm guessing we're damn lucky it was you in that police car," Paul said appreciatively.

"Um, yeah, you'd be heading to the station if it were some of my colleagues. Consider yourselves very lucky." He cocked his head with a jerk. "That being said, I'd never want to discourage you from having such fun. More power to you!"

"Thanks, bro. I really appreciate it." Paul made eye contact with me, and I too felt the relief in them.

Paul waved and rolled up his window as Max left.

"Well, that was lucky, holy shit," I said when the window was all the way up.

"Yeah, very lucky. I should have pulled over when I was getting close rather than swerve." He scanned my nude body. "I think it's hot he saw your gorgeous body, too."

I smiled, loving that we both knew about the exhibitionistic kink in each other. "I'm so very happy you think so. Drinks will be more interesting now."

"Yup, now to even things out and I get to see Jenna," he said with a leer.

"Oh, I'm in for that." I was right with him on that. I'd really enjoyed opening up about my bi-curious thoughts with him too, and the resulting woman-on-woman porn we'd watched as a result before sex. It had made the sex after so hot. "I'm thinking Max might be kinky, after that."

"I think so too," he said, starting to pull away from the curb. "I like you naked when I'm driving at night. This might be a new kink too." He smiled at me.

I bit my lip. "I'm enjoying it too. Maybe I'll keep a blanket in the car for quick coverups, but I'm all for naked riding in the car again."

"Perfect," he said with a cheeky grin. "Let's go home."

He drove down Main street, with me naked by his side, but we didn't see a single car the rest of the way home.

Once we pulled into our driveway, I gathered my clothes and purse and slid out of the truck.

He grabbed my hand and smiled down at me. "I love you being naked. I wish you could always be naked."

I flashed him a big, brilliant smile. "I agree, I'd like that."

And as we walked into the house, I savored every second of striding along nude outside. New kink indeed. I'd always enjoyed walking around the house naked, and being outside was an electric turn-on.

As we entered the house, he turned to me, a sly smile on his face as he grabbed and shook his erection in his pants. "Wanna fuck?"

I squealed and said, "Yes!"

He scooped me up and our eyes locked in a gaze that showed our shared passion had flared again.

The End

The Licking Sip Coffee Shop

Lana peered around the corner from the back room, her leggings pooled at her ankles like cuffs. Many tables full of patrons already. Is he here yet?

The droning of machines filled the air as they spilled brown drink delights into cups. The freshly ground coffee aroma, rich and thick, plugged her nostrils full. Full enough to block out the shock wave of aftershave that usually hung in the coffee shop like a near-toxic fog. Her brain now associated the smell of coffee with her swollen erotic feelings, swelling enough to seek popping. She smiled a naughty smile. Gonna get fucked. Fuck, fuck, fuck, yeah. Pounded today. Her clitoral bits blissfully sent out a twitch.

The cool air brushed her now bare buttocks as she adjusted the waist of her skirt below her belly button. The saliva thickened in the back of her throat as she tried to swallow her lust down to her gut.

I need him here today.

"Order for Michael is ready," Celeste waved her arm towards the blue-green cup with a white plastic lid, a lone drink on the orders-up counter. She pulled her wench top-down, snugging the elastic below her C cups. "Hit me." She stretched her arms wide, pushing her peaked breasts out, her head back.

German wenches. Harley's pick for uniforms without a single hesitation for the coffee shop waitstaff. The owner gets what the owner wants. Right? A truer fantasy of her husband's never played out so well as when he had chosen the costumes: white top off the shoulders, a circle of fabric clung to the women's biceps, the elastic-edged fabric of the top needing just a quick tug down to bare breasts. Big ones. Small ones. Saggy ones. A cups. He didn't care. He loved them all. But most of all ... all the nipples.

He had insisted on the ruffled short skirts, so going commando meant the lower ass cheeks were visible below the ruffles even on the skinniest women. "Spank bait," Harley had said as he had bent her over the table to fuck her from behind in the crisp new German wench outfit, christening the first day of business at The Licking Sip a mere three years ago. His cum had clung in thick drip lines down the insides of her thighs as she had served the first customer a simple deep rich cup of straight-up boring black coffee. The lucky first patron's eyes had never left her breasts as she handed him the hot cup, his skin crinkling around the gleam of lust in his eyes. A warm feeling had bathed Lana. She liked to be used and this was gonna hit her sweet spot every day she worked. Her libido tweaked, she went about the first day of business to be sucked, fucked, and spanked like a good girl.

Lana's eyes fell to her friend, her coworker, her confidant. Lerise was in a precarious position, slightly bent over a table occupied by three men, all eyeing her up like centerfold meat. The man nearest to her had his hand raised above her ass. He delivered one spank before Lerise briskly shuffled off.

Nora nodded and finally pointed the whipped cream can downward, hovering above Celeste's erect giant pink nipple. She had the kind of nipples porn stars would die for. 'Can't plastic surgery your way into a good nipple', as Harley always says.

Lana stacked a loose pile of scratch paper in front of the register, her stomach growled. She had forgotten to eat real food after swallowing down Harley's cum this morning. She shrugged. "Aw, fuck it."

The scream of the pressed nozzle of the whipped cream can blended quickly into the eruption of cheering sounds in the shop, making it more like white noise than a promise to suck. The clapping slammed her ears as shouts rang out. Skin slaps rang out across the room. The whole shop buzzed with lusty growls and hoots.

Someone's getting fucked. Most likely Lerise.

Upon entering the shop Lana had seen Lerise near one of her regulars, who'd usually grab her and fuck her right up the ass like he was giving her a tip. While Lana cringed, the memory popped in her head of when Lerise had admitted one late night over tequila shots as they had cleaned the big coffee pots that really, she loved it more than she ever wanted to admit. Lana had bitten her lips together hard so the secret would never escape.

Lerise's top was missing, not that she appeared to give a fuck where it went as her body was gyrating from his hard thrusts, her wild hair danced. He had claimed her butt once more.

Lana shook her head as she caught Celeste's gleaming eyes. Her tits were now smothered in whipped cream, the peaks jutting out only to be smashed by Michael's mouth in an instant, his coffee ignored on the counter behind Celeste as he mouthed the cream off her right tit, a bulb of cream squeezing out the corner of his mouth as he worked her nipple over. Michael sucked her deep into his mouth as Celeste arched her back, her head almost knocking over Michael's coffee cup. She moaned.

Lana shifted in her shoes. These damn heels pinched her toes. Why hadn't she chosen the usual red ones? The tile floor proved a worthy opponent, forcing her to walk like she had a stick up her butt in these ones.

She glanced across the shop in time to see Lerise's orgasm face, her eyes drooping shut, her perky, pointed tits jogging across her chest as Fernando wildly fucked her ass from behind, her fingers pressing her clit near the surface of the table. Her dark skin glistened in drip lines from her breasts to her belly, a bit of white cream still smeared across the bulge of her right breast. She cried out and there were cheers as Fernando leaned back to give her ass a few more smacks. His body gyrated like a jackhammer against her butthole until his body shook with a massive groan.

Lana shook her head as she tied an apron around her waist, its frayed cut edge just barely an inch longer than her ruffled skirt on the front side. She was to start behind the counter making the coffee drinks and would rotate to the floor in an hour. Lerise had done her job and the cups with lids were lined up for the rush. Good girl, Lerise.

Lerise pulled a Ziploc baggy from the waistband of her skirt and held it open for Fernando to drop his condom in. She slid her fingers across the seal with a grin. Fernando gave her ass another smack as she stood there. He pushed a wad of money into her palm with a devilish grin. Sitting next to his friends, he looked like the pirate of the group amongst clean-shaven businessmen, men who probably fucked their secretaries bent over their big, dark wooden desks that housed pictures of their wives and kids. But Fernando, he fucked her every time he graced The Licking Sip with his brutish self. It was a tradition many patrons came to watch, if lucky enough to catch the show.

Lerise forced a tight smile as she flung her thick mass of curly dark hair behind one shoulder. The space beneath the table failed to provide her with her missing shirt, even on all fours, with hands grabbing at her ass as she searched didn't produce the flimsy white top. Fernando probably flung it like a slingshot across the shop, to be found by janitors behind a coffee bean display.

She stood and shrugged her shoulders. She and her bare top half joined me behind the counter. Her breasts round and bulging like she was walking with shiny dark hams on her chest.

"Nice orgasm?" I laid a towel over her bare shoulder, its hem landed near her right dark-pointed tit.

"Fuck, yes, I did. That man knows how to push me face first into the best orgasms." She winked. "He's a pro ass fucker."

Secrets. Yes, we all held them like sweet screams in our hearts. How is every man not a pro ass fucker? I wouldn't know. But seems a thrust is a thrust no matter the hole. "Good for you. Need a drink?"

"Earl Grey tea for Mr. Boring." She fluttered her long eyelashes as if she were sweeping fresh air into her eyes.

I laughed. "He might be boring, but he can't get enough of watching you get ass fucked by Fernando. I think they both have your schedule."

She raised her eyebrows at me three times. "Mr. Boring greases my backside. Shh! Don't tell a soul." Lerise's whispered words dropped Lana's jaw. Girl is a genius at double-dipping!

"He pays you? Or fucks you?" Lana widened her eyes.

She shook her head, eyes full of mischief.

"Lerise!"

She smacked her own right hip. "I ain't delving, bitch." Her smirk a slap across Lana's face.

"I'd never tell Harley, Lerise, and honestly, he wouldn't care. He'd probably call you an entrepreneur making extra money like that."

She walked away shaking her head, finger waving in the air.

"I'm serious." Lana's pussy flared as *he* walked in. Fuck, yes. He's here! Her heart pounded as he caught her stare and nodded, eyes afire like the devil himself.

He's come with his friend, Alex, the one who always looked like someone was pulling a turd out of his ass with a pair of cold metal tongs. Poor man, a face loved by a mama and grandmama only.

She bit her lip so her face wouldn't betray her internal chuckle. Darren knew her floor shift wasn't for an hour, she had texted him earlier this morning. Curious indeed why he's early. Her pussy flared as he raised an eyebrow from across the room. He grabbed his cock through his loose jeans and shook the bulge, a big fat naughty grin pillaging his face.

Well, fuck it now, Darren. Please.

Celeste slid up to Lana's side. "Harley coming today?" She grabbed a napkin and wiped Michael's saliva from her tits.

"Most likely not." I shrug.

She tosses the napkin and continues walking to the tit-washer, a Harley original invention, one some local illegal brothels paid Harley big bucks to make for their own establishments too. A patent will never grace its existence, but word of mouth and bought under the table is better anyway, as Harley always says. More money in his pocket.

He had said, "Ain't no government on this planet gonna let me patent a titty-washer." He laughed so hard he cried and wound up in a coughing fit, a lag of drool slipping out to wet his goatee.

Celeste leaned over the titty-washer and stuck her breasts in the holes of the machine. She pressed the button and the water sound whirred in the chamber as the brushes inside whirred their spin and cleaned her breasts. Harley had run a hose for a hot water line to the unit and attached a soap dispenser that leaked soap into the water when the button was pressed. It was like a foot soaker bath, but for boobs instead. Harley proved to be a genius because now it was really easy to wash our tits between customers sucks.

Celeste stood up, all nearby eyes on her wet breasts. Her massive hard nipples glistened even in the calming dim light of the shop. She never bothered to dry them, none of us did. The patrons loved seeing wet boobs and nips. Made our shirts wet from drips but we got slipped extra tips walking away from the machine, so not one of us ever complained about a wet shirt. Plus, the titty-washer felt erotic as fuck, so we all got off on it, while patrons looked at our asses bent over. It was a win-win all around.

We just got away with what we did, and no one ever complained, so our coffee shop kept its sucking, fucking, and licking quiet. We looked legit from the curb, asexual as worms.

Nora was straddling George, who was seated at the table near the bathrooms, his beard painted in cream as he mowed her creamy dark nipple into his mouth, his hands cupping her bare ass, fluffing her skirt up more as he squeezed. Her red hair shimmering like fiery rays of sun down her back.

"Nora is peddling today, huh?" I secured the lid on a cup and handed it to Celeste. "I need to suck those tits of yours today, Celeste."

"Get in line, babe." She smirked, grabbing both tits and aiming them at me, giving her head a backward jerk. "Yeah. Her shirt was down from the second she walked in, so yeah. She's giving suckles today."

"Beautiful. Happy customers make my Harley happy." Lana cocked her head at her friend. "And me as a trickle-down."

The doorbell jingled. Lana's loins spread as a young man in his late twenties walked in with biceps the size of pineapples, and a mop of chocolate hair that needed her fingers to mess it up.

She blinked to make sure he was real. Bring this girl your wood, Sir.

She kept the hold of their mutual gaze, constant for a full minute as he approached her at the ordering counter. New meat to grace the honey pot. Fuck to the fuck yes, please. Harley will like watching the video of him riding me from behind, no doubt. Let's provide the husband with live porn, youngster. Her lips sloshed together because she had just wet them. She leaned forward to take his order with a moist lip smack, though it's not even her register post for much longer, but she's taking him.

"What can I get you, Sir?"

His grin flexed Lana's pile of pubic hairs. Not really, but fuck, please grace me with that. Her pussy juiced herself upon her eye scan, taking all of him in. What a delicious man.

"What's your poison?" Her index finger feels up her tongue. She sucks it as she gives him fuck me eyes.

"I'll take a campfire mocha and creamed tits." His chest shook as he laughed, his cheeks rosy and taut above his grand smile. So jovial. Hot as fuck. "Do I actually order it like that?" He scoffed with a head jerk as his muscular hand fondled his jawline the way she wanted her thighs to. He glanced back at his friend with a wave of his hand.

"Yes, you actually do." Lana leaned forward further, making her tits graze the computer screen. "And you can pick the tits. Any waitress with her shirt pulled down is free game for a whipped cream titty suck. And more." She raises an eyebrow at him. "Potentially."

"Ah, gotcha. Shirts up mean sucky." He glanced around the room with a quick eye sweep.

Harley, though he's a dumbass, was really pretty smart. Easy down wench tops with elastic at the top proved as easy to pull down as they are to pull up. Police officers, unless known, politicians, unless outed, teachers, unless regulars, and all other known respectful folk, or kids, approaching the door was shirts up, otherwise, it's tits out, unless taking a break from being sucked. On the occasion that happened, but tips were always less, so most waitresses kept their shirts down.

Lana tugged her shirt lower as it had crept up her under-boobs and had started crawling its own way up her breasts. Naughty mode was always really easy with a simple shirt yank. Fuck yeah. Her grin seeped naughtier.

"Nice to meet you. I'm River. You are behind that counter, though. Do I come back there to suckle your beauties then?" He raised an eyebrow at her as he licked his lower lip. "Yours look just my style."

"DD." Lana gave him a deep smile. "Lana."

He nodded with a lecherous grin. "Yes."

Her clit twitched from the lusty look in his eyes. Her pussy gaped and she resisted the urge to touch her wetness. "Anywhere you want me." Her voice barely a whisper as his friends behind him dropped their jaws. "It's our way here."

"For real?" the man with shaggy red hair asks, his flannel shirt a step away from wear holes over his elbows.

"I told you, man. This place is a titty suck place, legit. Don't you and those big ears of yours ever listen?" This sexy man, River, who wanted her tits shook his head at his friend, then said, "Fuck. It's like you cotton-eared, fucker." He returned his gaze back to Lana.

Lana leaned back to peek at her tits. "Want those lips of yours to grace these nipples, little boy?"

He rubs the giant rod pressing out his jeans. "Yeah, that's what I'm talking about. You sneak in a few strokes too, beautiful?" He chuckled with a nod as he rubbed the giant mound at his crotch. "Fuck, this place kicks ass. I heard about it, so nice it's bald, ya know? Just as I heard it was. No coverup." He glanced over at Celeste being spanked, bent over the table by a man twice her size, his gray beard gracing his chest, wiggling like Jell-O as he slapped her butt. "Fuck me! Spanking too?"

Lana swiveled and twerked her butt up at him. "If you want. I'd like it."

"So, do I pay extra to suck and spank?" His eyes flared wide.

Lana shook her head. "It's tip-based, love. We aren't a brothel."

He nodded. "Got it. Honor system. Well, I'd never stiff you. Not that way, anyhow." All three men laughed.

Lana tried not to naughty smile, but it slid out as she took his card to ring up his order.

"Fuck yes," he muttered. "Love this place!"

Lana giggled inside. There might be drool slipping out of his mouth.

From across the room, Darren's eyes were on her as she batted her eyelashes at the husky young man. "Where do you want me, love?"

"Back there would be hot if I'm allowed."

His large hands made her pussy drool. Those wide and strong hooks smacking her ass, those wide meaty fingers up her pussy. Fuck yes!

"As you wish." Lana motioned him back with her hand. She locked eyes with Darren as a little grin spread his lips open into a leer.

Lana raised her arms as Celeste readied the whipped cream can. She coated Lana's nipples and breasts with the cream as Lerise made the man's coffee drink. His friends' faces were glued to Lana as she lowered her arms. Celeste moved out of the way as the big, sexy man squatted down a bit and pulled Lana's chest closer to his face. He licked the cream and then attacked her nipple with a wide-open mouth, cream squishing out the sides of his mouth and dropping to the floor. He moaned like he hadn't had tit in way too long.

Lana's hands tangled in his thick dark waves, tugging at his hair in chunks as he grunted before sucking her nipple deep into his mouth, deep throating it. Lana moaned, squeezing his scalp firmly with her fingers. She suddenly yearned to nurture this lusty, hungry man.

"Aw, fuck yeah," the red-haired man slurred from the other side of the counter. "I want that. Fuck. Need me an oral fix too. I want that dark-skinned goddess." He licked his lips and left his mouth open slightly after showing the slight space between his front teeth.

"No shit. Wonder if they suck cock?" the other friend asked as he ran his hand down his thin frame to cup his crotch.

Nora came up behind him and whispered in his ear. He nodded with a grin. "Okay. That's it. This is our new hangout. I can't believe this place isn't more packed."

She dropped her eyes to the man's bobbing head at her chest. The movement of his mouth on her nipple was ramping her lust up pretty damn high. His hands, his amazing big strong hands pressed her back before traveling to cup and squeeze her ass cheeks. He dragged his tongue across her cleavage, driving his tongue through the mountain of whipped cream, slurping it into his mouth as he licked. He devoured her left nipple as if it were his air and groaned out his pleasure as he sucked.

Lana sighed, his deep throat sucking sending her gut into tumbling lurches as his hands snuck under her ruffled skirt where he firmly pressed his fingers into her skin. The strength of his grip made her gasp. He finished off the cream with a tongue swirl, then a nibble on her nipple. He leaned back slightly, Lana let her eyes fall closed as he manhandled her hips. She felt floppy like a rag doll as he squeezed and fondled her entire torso, then up, caressing her neck and face. He threaded his fingers through her hair. She moaned and fell against his solid chest.

He spun her around and pushed her onto the back counter against the wall. Her bare tits slammed into the cold steel as he pressed her down flush. Bending over flared her skirt up and she felt the wind of his movements behind her flutter across her skin, then smack!

"Oh, fuck yeah," he muttered. He laid three more spanks on her cheeks as she jumped with each slap. "Making my cock harder. Fuck!"

A whimper escaped her lips on the next spank, the vibrations of the slap spread to her clit in a twitch. She moaned. "Oh, fuck, yes," she muttered as she laid her cheek against the cold metal, tipping her ass up as much as possible. "Spank my ass, Daddy."

He chuckled. "Yeah, you bad, naughty little girl." Smack, smack, smack.

Her ass skin felt on fire reddened to peak color as he leaned against her, his hard cock pressing her ass like a metal rod, his chest flush with her back.

He whispered in her ear, "How far do I get to go?"

Lana felt her pussy flare. She wanted Darren to fuck her, but this man too. Fuck! He was making her so crazy horny. Want him in.

He reached under her and she raised up slightly so he could fondle her breasts. "You gonna cum for me if I fuck you right here in front of everyone? I want you to cum for me, sweetheart."

Lana melted. She loved a man who cared if she came. For that, he might get her full pussy. She let her breathing ramp up faster as his breath flooded her ear.

He licked her ear and then sucked the top curve of it into his mouth. His tongue traveled the hard bend and snuck along the nook of it down to her earlobe, wetting it before closing his lips around it. She squirmed.

His breath hot on her ear. "Can I eat your pussy first? Make you cum into my mouth, baby. Want to taste you. Mmmmmm."

The hum of his voice sent jolts through her clitoris that further shot out to her body like the blasts of wild wind. She imagined at least one person was watching and it sent her lust into a rage.

His cock a thick wedge between her buttocks as she instinctively did a Kegel squeezing with her vaginal walls.

She cooed. "I bet that cock feels amazing in a pussy."

River pinched her nipples with both hands as he hugged her from behind with the length of his body. "Women love my cock, sweetheart. It's big and thick like me. I'll make you cum. Make you feel so good."

Sex is just sex, but even with just sex, some men had a way of intimate passion about them that made all the difference in the world. He's such that kind of a man. She nodded.

Lana's pussy spread without her effort as fresh wetness oozed out her lower lips. She snuck her fingers into her pussy and dipped them in. "You've made me so wet."

"I'll do a lot more than that if you let me. I have mad tongue skills, sweetheart. I'm a pro pussy eater."

She glanced back as Celeste zoomed by with two coffee cups in her hands, a slight look of frenzy on her face as she attempted a weak smile at Lana.

Tingling all over, Lana glanced out the drive-thru window they never used and saw a man walk by. He stared in at her and the huge man glued to her back, a smirk flitting across his face. Lana recognized him in an instant. The man who often came with Darren. He'd spanked her and sucked her tits but never fucked her as Darren had, but he had often watched Darren pile drive his dick into her though. It tickled her in so many delicious places to be watched while fucked, wanted, desired. Her pussy was a wanton brat.

She let out a slow breath, dragging her fingers out of her pussy. She held it up for him. "Taste me."

His mouth closed around her fingers, his tongue dancing along her skin. "Mmmmm, you taste amazing. I must have more. May I?" He cleared his throat and said in a louder, exquisitely commanding voice, like the Dom one Harley often used on her, "Out of your pussy?"

Butterflies danced in her clit. A flutter exquisite all on its very own.

The titty-washer whirred in the background as she nodded. "Yes. You can." Her voice sounded foreign to her, like it was meant to answer a different question. Strangely, she thought about the load of laundry she forgot to toss into the dryer in the back. Who the fuck needs towels?

"Thank you, baby." He lifted himself off of her and her breaths came and went easier without the weight of him pressing her down. Her legs felt weak as he knelt down behind her. He nudged his face between her thighs; his breath on her pussy sent shivers up her body.

Savoring her anticipation of his warm sucking mouth, she hummed. She obeyed the twitch of his head against her leg and spread them further apart.

Lana might melt into a puddle.

His nose pressed between her ass cheeks as he dove his tongue to caress her pussy. Pure lust radiated from her as he mouthed his way around her delicate, fleshy lips.

She reached back and gripped her hips as a moan spilled from her mouth. "Oh, fuck!"

His tongue darted into her pussy and went further in than she thought possible while his lips quivered against her labia lips, then he mashed them into her hard, a loud slurp filled her ears. A move she had not felt before. It sent shock waves that only intensified once he traveled his way, sucking to the point of what felt like hickeys along her lips towards her clit.

As his mouth met her clit, she let out a loud gasp, then a sigh followed by a whimper, one much louder than she had intended but she couldn't stop the sounds coming out, they just piled out as if the air itself owned them.

He sucked her relentlessly, took her clit fully into his mouth. His suction was unmatched. Like, did he do mouth push-ups? Fuck! Man has some mouth muscles! He flicked her clit while alternating sucking it hard and gentle, then full-on hard. She lost it and screamed. Her hands caressed the metal, flailing about in search of something to squeeze.

He held her so tight to his face she was trapped, and her pleasure verged on agony as she rode that climax to the top. Her hands finally found her hips in vise grips. The orgasm took her in a mountainous crash and her body jerked against the cold metal counter, her thighs squeezed his head. The convulsions began at the edge of her pussy and spread out, one after another, so many contractions she couldn't even count them. Twelve? Thirteen? It was almost too intense.

Choked with clitoral sensitivity, she shivered, yet he didn't stop sucking and she fought him as he slurped more from her pussy.

Her arms felt drained, her desperate pushes on the counter to raise her body worthless. "Oh, fuck. Oh, shit. Oh, Gawd," she chanted as he continued to mouth her sensitive clit. Her whole body throbbed, even down her legs, reaching her toes. The cold metal kept her from passing out.

He wrapped his arms around her legs and lifted her up, sliding her body further onto the counter.

He guided her all the way to the little window, her body arched up and her tits pressed against the cool glass, flattening them against it. Her senses fought as her skin suffered the cold metal bite while her lust raged a fire inside her. His mouth never left her pussy in all of that, and he continued to suck her.

How can he even breathe? Even his nose was mashed up against her skin.

She panted and whimpered as she was forced into another orgasm, her body was under his control, not hers. She could barely move other than to slightly writhe against his face. His arms wrapped around her hips securely, keeping his face smooshed against her pussy as she tried to wiggle but failed. His tongue and lips rode her pussy, in and out, along the flaps of her clit.

He introduced two fingers into her pussy, and she yelled out. There were shouts coming from somewhere, but they were muffled like she was inside a closet listening to the sounds of the outside room. Hoots and hollers and claps. She was so entranced it was as if she were in a bubble.

A faceless, nameless man from somewhere behind her yelled, "Yeah. Make her come again."

She dove into the chaos of orgasm, its victim, it rode her high up that hill and shoved her down it relentlessly, aggressively, her clit owned her, and he owned her clit. Her body curled, every part that could curl, her fingers, her toes, her feet, her lips, her neck, her legs, and her arms. She shook as her clit sent the spasms out to her body. Her quaking didn't slow his suck one bit. He was a master.

He moaned and made slurping sounds.

How do those sound so loud and others like plastic bubble wrap is surrounding them? Did he slip me some drugs? she wondered sheepishly, knowing this was impossible.

He rose off her pussy and laid across her back once more, hovering his hot breath above her ear. "Can I put my cock in your pussy? Do I have your permission?"

Lana was still. Her heart thudded in her ears. She nodded with a twitch of her right hand that she immediately closed into a fist. Again, she gave him a nod.

He grasped her hips and pulled her to the edge of the counter, so it was as if he had just bent her over it. The tip of his cock pressed at her pussy lips, the throbbing of her last orgasm still ringing there. Her gasp struggling to make it out of her mouth.

Fucked into the inability, or desire, to move, she simply let her hands rest on the cool metal countertop, her right cheek heavy against the coldness. Harley flitted to her brain. How he will love watching this and want to reproduce it. If nothing else, her husband loved to give her sexual pleasure.

He had a particular craving to see her get royally fucked by another man, then taking her because she was his. She grinned, imagining him watching it live right now, cock in hand hard as concrete, precum packed ready to go, and in the comfort of bed no doubt.

River pressed his cock in and they both groaned. The luscious penetration a few hundred licks better than any sexual dream. He slid in easily after her rounds of coming, it was almost too wet, but she knew he'd rub that out quick and the friction would become exquisitely insurmountable.

He pumped slowly at first, her lips accepting and hugging him as he rode. As he picked up speed, her body bounced off his thrusts, his big hands gripping her hips. He leaned back and gave her ass a smack.

She could feel his eyes burning her flesh, looking at her asshole.

She cooed and arched her head, the vibrations of his body smack slamming her clit with their strong wave.

He pounded and she moaned and he man-growled and grunted. The sound of their skin slapping together alone was enough to drive her closer to an orgasm.

His hands drifted to her thighs and held them so her legs were out straight.

Lana felt spacey, like she couldn't tell if she was lost in fantasy or if it was real until he shouted, "Oh, fuck yes!"

He growled again and rammed himself into her pussy so hard, her ass cheeks shaking from each body slap as he pounded her.

She was a meat hole. The thought made her pussy contract.

He dropped her legs and pounded her faster than she recalled ever being pounded ever before.

She scrambled to join her body to his, raised her ass up using her tippy toes. He grabbed her thighs and lifted her so her feet could no longer touch the floor and he pounded into her so hard and fast she slammed into the rise of another orgasm.

He grunted and rage fucked her, sliding in and out so fast she felt dizzy.

Then the flood of his wetness grew inside her as he grunted.

He stopped thrusting but gyrated his hips slightly against her ass, cradling her body with his.

She squeezed her pussy to milk his cock to the max.

An epic fuck.

Her clit twitched as if it were trying to come all by itself.

Possibly the raunchiest, most mind-blowing doggy fuck of her entire life. And both Harley and Darren had gotten to see it.

Plus, a whole room full of people?

Her hand flew to her mouth as she curled her body to lie on her side. Her eyes fell wide. It seemed everyone in the whole coffee shop was standing at the counter. A wall of men littered with her topless coworkers. Their faces all set in phases of sheer lust, delight, joy, and want.

It was beautiful.

The only thing that would have made it more beautiful was if somewhere her outer skin was also glistening with cum.

Speechless, she curled further into the fetal position on the counter. His juices oozed out of her as she moved like rolling an almost empty tube of toothpaste. He turned and leaned against the counter, slightly swaying as he steadied his large form against the thin metal counter's edge.

"Fuck." He panted. "Just ... fuck."

Lana blinked. Celeste appeared in her sight and touched her thigh. Instead of jumping, she leaned into Celeste's palm.

"You okay, love?" Celeste smoothed Lana's hair behind her ear, her eyes full of concern.

Lana moved her lips, but nothing came out. She nodded.

The man who had just fucked the very blood out of her brain stroked her shin. "I didn't hurt you, did I?"

Should she cry?

Lana tried to focus her gaze upon his face. His eyes were tender and a bit shockingly sweet after that wild fuck. "I'm okay. And. Wow. Holy fuck of all fucks." She tried to sit up but couldn't. Both Celeste and the man helped her sit. The metal was cold yet comforting on her hot puffy pussy lips. Fluid ran out of her pussy onto the counter as she sat erect and all she could think about was needing to remember to sanitize it at some point.

She almost laughed at that being her thought after such a wild sexual display.

"Holy fuck, that was amazing." She shook her head as she allowed her eyes to meet all the eyes in the crowd. Her hands cradled her temples as she scanned familiar eyes and new ones until her eyes met Darren's. He held his mouth in a deeply satisfied grin and his eyes were filled with joy.

I could think only one thing. "I'll make you another coffee, sir. I'm sure that one has gone cold."

This man at her side laughed. "I couldn't care less. That was probably one of the best fucks of my entire life. You brought that out in me, sweetheart." He rubbed her leg.

She couldn't help but crave the idea of River coming back and doing that to her again and again, like forever.

She smiled a little smile that quickly grew giant. "Likewise. One of the best. Ever." She slid off the counter and stood, wavering slightly as she gripped the counter. "Wow." Their combined juices ran down her thighs.

How on earth did that just happen?

Lana tried to take a step but faltered, grabbing for the counter again to steady herself. Her whole pelvis felt deliciously swollen.

"Go easy, love," Celeste muttered, a mama look in her eyes. "You need to move very slow right now."

Well, it's not like she had gotten shot! She wanted to laugh but couldn't seem to.

Lana swayed as she got her footing and began to walk out from behind the counter. The titty-washer caught her eye as she hobbled. Gratefully she leaned over it to brace her shaking body. She shoved her breasts into the machine's holes and scrambled to find the machine's button, but her fingers kept just sliding not finding the machine's little indented circle to press.

A male voice from behind her whispered, "Let me help you, baby."

Was it him who fucked her or someone else?

"I got you, babe," he said.

Someone screamed from across the room. Was that Lerise?

"Here, sweet baby." His hand gently caressed her bare back.

That voice. The voice held something familiar.

Oh. It's Darren. Thank Gawd it's Darren. She yearned for his arms around her.

He stroked her hair as the brushes caressed her boobs inside the machine's chamber, lathering up her skin before the rush of warm water. He helped her stand and she turned to face the shop. The water dripped off her breasts falling to the ground, raining also onto the bare skin of the tops of her feet.

When had she taken her shoes off? She cocked her head. "I have no shoes?"

Darren led her to a nearby chair and helped her sit. She winced as her skin touched the cool wood.

"Ow, laugh out loud," she muttered with a sheepish grin. "He really got my ass good."

"Tell me about it," Darren said with a laugh. "That was seriously one of the sexiest things I've ever seen in my entire life." He cupped her cheek. "I'll go find your shoes. You sit tight."

The man who fucked her, Mr. River last-name-unknown, coffee cup in hand strode over to her. The pounding of her body that he had caused still raged her heart inside her chest. Slow down, heart.

He kissed her on the forehead and rubbed her cheek with his thumb. "Until next time, sweetheart."

How does softness manage to live in the eyes of one with so much power?

River turned and joined his friends. Instead of getting a table, they walked out the front door.

Lana stared long after the door shut, her eyes wandering the patrons sipping coffee, one man feeling up Nora's ass as she leaned over his lap, hovering like she was waiting for him to push her down to his thighs, her face to hit booth cushion.

Darren returned with her shoes. He slipped them on as she watched Celeste's right tit get slobbered on by a man probably thirty years her senior. She dropped her pretty head back and her petite hands went to hold the sides of his head. She moaned and massaged his temples as he sucked. They looked simple, like a voiceless porno. Or more accurately like some masterpiece ancient sculpture created by a genius artist from old Europe, where naked was celebrated with hours of chisel carving at a block of marble.

Breathing in the aroma of lust, Lana hugged her breasts and let her eyes hold Darren's. He raised her chin and gave her a peck on the lips.

Savored, Lana let her arms down and her breasts settled, still chilled from her wet skin, a smile spread across her face.

What a good day for the wildest fuck to land in the most ordinary of moments.

The End

Hooking Up, A Quickie at the Gym

She knew she wasn't supposed to have sex with him, but that hadn't stopped any of her fantasies of him smacking his cock into her wanton fuck hole. Why couldn't she just pick someone else to lust over? She shook her head as she unlocked the front door of the gym. She was the opener for the day and she knew it would be packed again, as it always was the first of the year. Everyone got bitten by the get-in-shape bug to start off every new year. She couldn't blame them. Sometimes a fresh start was just the kick in the pants she needed too.

She was horny. She had woken with a clit boner and wanted to rub one out, but she had forgotten to change her alarm clock to an earlier time. No matter. She'd make herself come in a torrent of orgasms that evening. She'd seriously considered bringing in a sex toy to work and swelling her clit to explosion in the bathroom. But it was just too gross. She'd wait.

She snickered to herself. Who was she kidding? Several of her fantasies were of him grabbing her and fucking her up her wet, sopping cunt in the locker room. In many of the scenarios, the locker room had been filled with naked wet men with raging cocks.

She pushed the thoughts out of her head, but it was too late. She was panting.

She switched on all the lights and made her way to the coffee pot. A task was just what she needed to get her mind off getting fucked. She lamented. Why shouldn't she bring that sex toy? It's not like it took up much room in her purse.

She slopped the coffee grounds into the filter and grabbed the pot to fill it. The fridge made its usual shriek and hum as the front door dinged.

Someone was coming in already. She set the coffee to brewing and made her way to the entrance quickly so she could do her job welcoming whoever it was.

It must have been the stars aligning because it was Alex. She gasped as he smiled at her, the smile sending jolts of electricity through her pelvis. Those lips on her lower lips were exactly where her mind went.

She stuffed her desire for him into her throat so it would get out of her brain. Then she'd be able to think and not sound like an imbecile.

"Hi, Alex," she managed to say as his smile deepened. Did he do that on purpose? He must know how goddam fucking sexy that grin was covering his handsome face.

"Hi, Melissa. Happy New Year." He removed his shirt and his muscles announced themselves. He was always a friendly guy, too.

She sighed. Her fingers belonged on those bulges. Her eyes drifted down to his cock. The other day, he'd come in with a raging boner. She'd been mush all morning after that. She fantasized about sucking his cock as he lifted weights. What the fuck anyway? That wouldn't work, for fuck's sake. He'd probably drop the weights on her head and she'd die while giving head. That would be just her luck.

"Happy New Year," she said meekly. She knew her eyes said 'fuck me' because she couldn't stop them. "You are here early." She didn't know his age, but she did think she was a bit older than him, which was only a turn-on anyhow.

"Yeah, wanted to beat the rush. It's always insane here. Being a regular doesn't help when everyone suddenly wants to work out." He lapsed into an amused but annoyed expression. "As usual this time of year." He stopped and gazed into her eyes. A slow grin grew across his face and a lecherous zest sparked in his eyes. "If I can get a quickie in before the rush, I should."

She knew he meant a quickie workout, but there was something in his eyes that told her he might mean more than that. She knew it was wishful thinking. Stupid thinking. But it was what she'd most certainly use to dream of him the rest of the day. She should have thanked him for saying it.

"Yeah," she said, as if she knew no other words. Her heart fluttered into a rage as he turned and walked towards the machines. He had the best ass on the planet. She imagined running her hands over its firm roundness as he sucked her bare tits.

"Damit," she muttered, frustrated with herself. These thoughts were not helping her calm down. She needed to focus and set the mindset of acceptance of a full day of work before she'd get satiated.

He stopped and turned back. "What's that?"

The way he had said 'quickie' seemed like he wanted to fuck. She rolled her eyes. That's ridiculous. He's here to work out and work out only.

But what if she asked him to fuck? No. That could get her fired if he's a vanilla person and he reported her. She didn't need to get fired again. But then would he be flattered and want to fuck her from behind in the shower stall with her face pressed to the tile? If they did it now, no one would be here yet to catch them.

Fuck.

She drew in a breath. "I just forgot something, nothing to worry about, though," she lied.

The front door swung open and three people piled in. Too late. Now it was going to be the rush of patrons. She'd missed her opportunity again. But then, maybe he didn't want to fuck her. Maybe he had a girlfriend and all her wishing was in vain. He'd not fuck her, anyway. Her brain flitted about with possibilities.

She busied herself with getting stuff set for the day as more and more people piled into the gym. She kept her eyes on Alex as he lifted, his thick muscles so deliciously toned she wanted to drag her tongue along them and not stop. His dick would be her destination, but she really wanted to taste his entire body with her mouth.

Wait. What if she just asked him? But what if he said no? Her body filled with dread. It would be so awkward to see him every day going forward if she asked and he turned her down. She'd never heard him speak of a girlfriend, but maybe it wasn't something he'd tell her, being she just works at the gym. It wasn't like they were friends chatting over a beer. She was the worker bee. He was the gym user.

Her over-inflated sense of self kept her at the front desk, greeting people for the next twenty minutes. She had a job to do, and she was going to do it. But her eyes did their usual scan of Alex about every other minute without fail. He'd catch her gaze with his own, and she'd quickly avert her eyes to something else. Did he know she was watching him? Or did he think she was just doing her job monitoring the whole gym? She was obsessing and she needed to stop.

Melissa sighed as her libido nagged at her incessantly to ask him to fuck. But she couldn't leave the front desk. If another coworker walked in and she had left the front desk, she'd get tattled on and fired. She was trapped. The minutes dragged and she knew Alex would soon leave and she'd have missed her chance to hook up.

She guffawed.

Who was she kidding anyhow? This fuck was not going to happen. She was a fool.

The next time she searched out Alex, he was already looking her way. Her heart leaped as she imagined that might mean something. He was getting close to the end of his workout, she could tell. She knew his usual routine and he was moving into the final phases. She'd need to do something quick.

Could she be this forward and just ask him for sex? Would he think she needed to date him? I mean, it wasn't like she wasn't attractive, and what she lacked, she figured she made up for with her enthusiastic approach to sex. So, she'd make a good fuck buddy. What if she asked him, and then every time he came to the gym she could get fucked by him? That was a fantasy she could buy into and enjoy on the regular.

She puffed up her chest with the gumption to ask. Maybe she could snag his interest by rubbing her tits against him while she pretended to be spotting for him? Or she could do it as she was checking the equipment, but which she never really did. That wasn't her job. Plus, that would make her leave the front desk and then she'd again be at risk of getting canned. She needed this job, so she needed to keep her libido in check and behave.

She checked the work schedule. Maybe when Josh came in, she would sneak in a break and entice Alex to rail her in the break room. No one would likely be in there yet. It would be perfect. She blew a breath upward and her brown curls lifted, then fell.

Alex started to pack up and her heart sank. He'd leave now and her chance would be gone again. A panic rose in her, which was odd. He'd left the gym literally hundreds of times before and she'd not felt this dread. She was feeling a loss of something great.

He drank water and rested for a moment, his eyes searching the room and settling on her.

She held his gaze, willing him to understand with her eyes that she just wanted him to fuck her. She also knew she was being very passive, and that she should be aggressive. She should ask for what she wants. Maybe he'd like a hookup too? Maybe he liked assertive women. It didn't have to turn into anything else, but if she was honest with herself, she would be happy if it did. Whether that was a usual fucking when he came to the gym, or it turned into dates, she'd truly love either path.

Josh entered and she nodded at him. He was sexy too, but there was just something extra special about Alex. She felt a kismet connection with him. Perhaps she was dreaming it up, or perhaps it was legit and their primal sexual energies were speaking silently to each other. Either way, she was way too turned on to just sit. She stood up off the stool and shifted her weight back and forth.

"Mind if I take a break once you get settled?" she asked Josh hopefully.

He nodded, running a large hand through his dark hair. "Sure, not a problem. I'll be right back."

He disappeared into the back, and she searched the floor for Alex. He was gone. He'd likely gone into the locker room, and she'd now missed her chance at seducing him. She realized that was dumb. She wasn't really seducing him, she was just stalking him with her eyes. But eye contact was something.

Josh returned and she skedaddled towards the men's locker room. She imagined herself slipping in and catching Alex in the shower. She'd strip quickly, not caring if any of the other men saw her, and pull the curtain back to see his wet naked body. Then she'd say, "Want some company?" Surely, he'd think that was an invitation to fuck. He was a smart guy.

Her heart raced in her chest as she slunk into the locker room. She didn't look back to see if anyone saw her, she just slipped right in. This was not about them or their opinion of her.

She wildly searched the locker room. Two showers were running. One just had to be Alex. Without any rational thought, she strode towards the showers, driven only by her raging libido. It wasn't like she didn't know Alex. She'd talked with him on a daily basis for more than almost eighteen months.

With a boldness she had no clue where she had harnessed it from, she removed her clothes. Her breath came fast and hot. Her pussy hole flared. She was so horny, she'd fuck a stick. But she wanted Alex's cock.

She paused. What if it wasn't Alex in the shower, but someone else? Would she turn and run? Being naked, she'd have to take time to dress before she fled.

Her heart was beating so hard in her chest that her flight reflex was starting to rear its head. She could dress quickly and leave without anyone knowing she was about to come on to Alex. He was such a nice guy. Well, he seemed so anyway, he'd likely not pick on her for coming on to him so strongly. Maybe he'd let her down gently, like a gentleman.

She wrung her hands, suddenly terrified. And naked. Her lust for Alex had her doing something out of her comfort zone. Her desire had her in a trance and she was waking up. Panic flooded her.

What the hell was she doing? She couldn't do this! She'd get fired for sure. He might laugh at her and reject her.

But ... what if he said yes?

The shower curtain moved, and she jumped back, making her breasts flop. She gasped too loudly as the curtain was flung open.

It was indeed Alex. Relief and terror flooded her brain.

"Well, you going to come in? You need a special invitation? Join me?" He was smiling. That was a very good sign.

Her heart exploded into so many pieces, it bounced off her skin and sent fireworks throughout her body. She grinned bigger than she had in a year, no five.

"Yes." She knew she needed to say more, but she didn't want to fuck this up.

"I enjoyed you watching me," he admitted as he made room for her in the stall.

She felt as if she were in one of her fantasies with Alex and not really standing naked with him under a stream of water. It was too surreal to even breathe.

"Yes, I always love watching you," she confessed sheepishly.

His dick was at full erection mast, and it looked delicious.

"You have a gorgeous cock." She gave him her full passion in her gaze.

He snickered, then smiled. "Thank you."

"I've wanted it for a long time." She was shocking herself with what she was saying, but it was the honest truth.

"I know." He reached up for her cheek. "May I touch you?"

She nodded. His accepting her calmed her panic to a still. "Yes."

"I have to be honest. I came here early, hoping you'd be the one working." He caressed her cheek and cupped her face with both hands. "Want to go on a date with me? We could get a pizza or burgers or whatever you want."

This was way more than she expected. She just wanted his cock up her cunt and here he was asking her on a date.

She was at a loss for words as he leaned in to place a peck on her lips.

"Yes," she stammered the word into his open mouth.

They kissed and their bodies collided. He felt so fucking amazing. Her skin on his was so devilishly scrumptious that her passion raged to a primal level. She was giddy. She was going to get fucked after all.

It was more than a dream. This was fucking real.

He kissed down her neck. He murmured against her flesh. "Your eyes told me you wanted to fuck, and then when I saw you strip next to my shower, I knew."

"Yes," she murmured as he took her right nipple into his mouth. She was not very creative with her words; her brain was too focused on getting fucked.

"You have gorgeous nipples," he said before devouring her tit again.

Her head fell back and a moan escaped her lips. "Thank you," she whispered as he moved on to her other nip.

"I hoped it was me you were seeking." His voice was smooth as chocolate and his dick hard as a beautiful rod against her tummy.

"Yes, I almost left when I wondered if it wasn't you."

"I'm so happy you didn't." He caressed her upper lip with the two of his and slipped his tongue inside her mouth.

They kissed for several minutes, their bodies writhing against each other in the warm stream of water. The steam rose along their comingled bodies as the locker room door creaked open on repeat.

They smiled at each other as their hands continued to grope. She traveled her fingers along the body that she'd lusted over all these months. She kissed his tummy, making her way down, the water full on blasting the makeup off her face. She didn't care. The quickie sex would be worth it going without any for the rest of the day.

She grasped his cock and caressed his balls as she opened her mouth wide. She took his cockhead in her mouth, and she sucked and stroked his thickened cock.

His groans thrilled her as she pleasured him. She figured any men in the locker room knew what was happening because neither of them was being quiet about their enjoyment.

He pulled her to stand and kissed her again, reaching for her mound. He pressed his fingers along her bush.

"I like the hair. It's refreshing to see a woman who is natural." He wiggled his fingers inside the cleft of her lips. He stroked her clit, pressing and mashing it.

"Oh, fuck yes," she muttered. "Please. Fuck me, Alex. Will you?"

He inserted his fingers into her pussy and rode her slit gently, but quickly picked up the pace as her moans increased.

"Doggy?" he asked with a sly grin.

She nodded and waited for him to spin her around. She wanted him to take charge and position her. She bit her lip and said, "Yes. I'd love to."

He grasped her shoulders firmly and spun her around, then bent her over.

"Yes," she cooed. "Yes, just like that."

He played his cock along her bottom and spanked her ass cheeks lightly.

Without any condom, he plunged into her cunt. There were no rational thoughts as he began to ride her from behind.

"I'm on the pill," she said between pants.

"I'm clean, but I can come on your ass instead."

"Okay," she said with a nod. "I like to be fucked hard," she instructed.

He exclaimed, "Oh, hell yeah." He began to rail her from behind, smacking his wet, strong naked body into her butt.

"Yeah, like you are spanking me with your pelvis," she said with desperation.

He reached around and rode her clit with his fingers. "This strong enough?"

She melted to the wall as he played with her clit, while still sliding his cock in and out.

"Yes, keep going. Don't stop." She panted and grunted as she felt an orgasm approaching. She was so hot she knew she'd come in seconds. "Yeah, like that." She writhed as he finger fucked her, ensuring his thumb was taking care of her clit. "Oh, fuck." She raged into an orgasm and cried out. "I'm coming."

He kept the pressure and the stroking up as her body twitched its way through her climax. Then he grasped her hips and pounded himself into her like an animal.

Her tits swung wildly, and her satiation fed itself. She was going to get hers and climax a second time.

She grunted and reached for her clit and blasted into another orgasm as he jack hammered her pussy.

"Oh, fuck yes, I'm going to come again."

"Get your clit. Get after it," he instructed with a growl. He picked up the pace and fucked her hard. He pulled his cock out and groaned. "Oh, fuck!" His cum splatted across her skin, but the water whisked it right off as she twisted in the water.

"Holy fucking shit, that was insanely good." She stood up and swiveled to face him. She pressed her breasts to his torso and smiled up at him. "Okay. I'll admit. That's basically been my masturbation fodder for months. That was even hotter, though."

He kissed her wet lips and said, "I've noticed you eyeing me up, but figured you were too sexy to want me." He sighed. "And I'm thrilled the real me is better."

"No contest at all." She took a step back, aghast. "And. Seriously? No."

He nodded. "I'm relieved you made the first move."

She guffawed. "Well, this is more than a move. It's more like a launch."

"True. But I like it." He chuckled as he pulled her back into an embrace. They held each other in the water stream for several minutes. "I really want to take you on a date, but honestly, I figured that part would come before this part." He leaned back, smiling down at her. "Oh, but I'm not complaining."

"I like sex. I'm kind of obsessed."

He snickered. "I think we are going to be very compatible."

She smiled back, then pressed her face to his chest. "Yes. I'm thinking so too. When can we do that date?"

"You free tonight?"

"Yes. I am. I'd love to."

"I have a shower at my place, too." His look was excited.

"I'm not surprised. Feed me a lot and fuck me a lot and I'll be one happy girl."

"Oh, now I know for sure we will really get along." He stroked her arm lightly with his fingers.

"I guess I'd better get back. Josh is probably wondering what the fuck I'm doing."

"Not who the fuck you are doing?" he teased.

"Oh, I don't ever do this. In fact, I still can't believe I did."

"Me too."

She stepped out of the shower. Two men were changing. They just smiled at her.

"Hi Melissa," one of them said.

"Hi," she said sheepishly, but without any guilt.

"The towels are behind you," the other man said. "But you probably know that, being you stock them," he said knowingly.

"Yep," she said as she grabbed one.

Alex connected with her gaze. "How about six?"

"Perfect." She dressed and left the locker room with a huge, happy grin and an orgasm-soaked body. It was a good day at work, the best ever, and it was promising to be an even better night.

The End

Gas Station Hookup,

When Stopping for Candy Brings Way More than Just Satisfying a Sweet Tooth

Deciding on a candy shouldn't be this hard, but after the week she'd had, it was proving damn near impossible. Chocolate, sugary sweet, or sour? The thoughts of them all swirled in her head. She glanced back at the guy at the cash register. He'd been checking her out the whole time. Well, the time was getting long. He probably was thinking 'pick something, ya weak ass!' It's not like it mattered, for fuck's sake. It was a candy she'd consume in less than ten minutes, but making this decision just wasn't clicking.

All she could think about was Michael dumping her, losing her job, then getting the notice that her apartment lease wouldn't be renewed because she missed the deadline by one damn day. She just had this one decision and had her car. She could always sleep in it, or go to a friend's house for the night, but that wouldn't work for long. She could go home, but that seemed like a failure, and she'd avoid that like the plague. Maybe her sister would let her crash at her place until she found an apartment. And a job. And, oh damn, her life was now a mess.

She toyed with the zipper on her sweatshirt as she glanced back at the man behind the counter. He was flat-out staring at her and didn't avert his eyes when she caught his stare. A slow grin spread across his face, but he continued to stare. He looked maybe ten years older than her, but that was never a turn-off to her, more it was a turn-on, in fact. He had a goatee, scraggly dirty blond hair that looked like he'd styled it to stick up in sections, and full red lips to die for.

"Hi, can I help you find something?" he asked in a kind voice.

She jumped when he spoke, as if she hadn't expected him to actually talk to her. "Um," she said as she looked at her phone, realizing she'd stared at the candy aisle for damn near twenty minutes now.

"Lots to choose from. It's a hard choice," he offered with a twinkle in his eyes.

That twinkle could get a girl in trouble.

She smiled a weak smile. "Just having a hard time picking. A lot on my mind, I guess."

"Want help?" He looked a bit like an acquaintance of her dad, but he was too young to be him.

"Oh, I don't know," she said as she fought off tears.

He came around the counter and joined her. "Hey," he said. "It's okay. A good candy will always help. It's kind of like a drink, but you can drive after it." He smiled deeply at her with his head tilted, a soft concern emanating from his eyes.

She sighed and bit back the flood of tears. "It's hard to decide anything when your life has fallen apart." A micro tear slipped out and she quickly swiped it away.

"I'm like the bartender. You can tell me anything," he said with a giant grin that made him even cuter when combined with that statement. "People stop by on a whim or when they just need somewhere to go, or just another human to exchange a few words with."

She shifted her feet and wrung her hands as a bubble of a sob escaped her lips. "He dumped me. I lost my job. I lost my apartment." Her chest heaved as she gasped back, trying her hardest not to full-on burst into tears.

"Ah, I'm so sorry. That blows." He dipped his head lower to try to look into her eyes. "I know you don't know me, and I'm not some freak, but do you need a hug?" His eyes grew even softer. "Sometimes we just need a hug."

Tears poured down her face and she released a small cry she failed to hold inside. She nodded slowly. Accepting a hug from a perfect stranger seemed safe in a gas station filled with video cameras.

He reached for her, his chest looking like the best thing she could imagine at the moment, and she melted into his body. He smelled like mint and aftershave.

He cradled her in his arms and then pet her head. She released a series of sobs as he continued to stroke her head.

"It's okay. Oh dang, honey, it's gonna be alright."

His words comforted her even though she didn't know him from Fred. The tender way he was holding her was a shock to her system after all the hardships of the past twenty-four hours.

"Let it all out. It's just you and me here. Cry it all out, it's okay."

She followed his lead and cried loudly at first, then as it began to slow, she noticed a long hardness along her belly. She gasped as she realized he was hard.

He'd been rocking their bodies as one as he'd caressed her hair.

"I'm sorry. I didn't mean to turn this sexual, but I couldn't help getting turned on. You are so sexy and feeling your body on mine ... well, I had little control over being able to stop it." He sounded genuinely apologetic and sincere.

"Oh, wow," she said, not sure what the fuck to say to that.

"I'm not a jerk. And I'm not coming on to you," he stated in his defense. "I just can't hold a beautiful woman like you and not get turned on."

Instead of being creeped out, it made her smile. "Well, I can't fault you for that, I guess." She couldn't deny herself that him comforting her and then being aroused by her wasn't a turn-on. "You have a nice way about you."

He chuckled as he went back to swaying them. "That's what my girlfriend used to say."

'Used to say', rolled around in her head. She allowed him to keep holding her despite his raging hard-on. It might be risky of her, he might be a predator for all she knew, but she hadn't seen any of that in his eyes. Her intuition also told her he was a nice, decent guy, and she was usually right.

They swayed in silence for two minutes.

"Will you get fired when your boss sees the video cameras?" she asked, concerned he'd lose his job over this.

"Nah, mostly no one looks at them unless there's a problem. And what will they do? Fire me for giving a hug?" he said with a scoff. "People are assholes, but I don't think my boss is."

She sighed a breath of relief. "That's good."

His arms felt nice, his chest was a warm cave to hide from the world in, and his dick, well, his dick was darn tempting.

She'd always been one who was driven to sex after being held. This man couldn't have known she was a sucker for being wrapped up and made to feel good, but she felt her arousal beginning to swell. Maybe it was all the emotions colliding, maybe it was how generous he was being with her, even though she was a complete stranger, or maybe it was just his thick cock she wanted. It would certainly be even more comforting to climax. But could she climax with a complete stranger? Sure, they were connecting on a more intimate level, but she'd never fucked a complete stranger before, so could she? Should she?

"I'm a good listener if you want to talk. Or I can throw in a fresh pizza and we can sit at the table and chat while we eat it. Are you hungry?"

She nodded. "That sounds good."

He released her and she instantly wanted him wrapped back around her. "You are very kind," she said meekly.

She followed him like a puppy dog as he made the pizza, watching every move he made. He was most certainly a sexy man. Her mind wandered as she pondered what he did. Was this his lifetime job, or was he working towards something else?

When he pulled out the pizza and set it on the table, she joined him at it.

"How long have you been working here?" she asked, because every other sentence she had seemed stuck in her.

"About a year. I'm in grad school, so this is just a little job I'm doing on the side. I got a scholarship to Stone U, thank goodness, but I need a little spending money, too."

Oh, wow. He was doing big things. Bigger than she was. "Wow, that's incredible." She mused he must be smart or something to get a scholarship like that. She admitted her interest was piqued even further. She didn't want to talk about her career, or lack of a job, so she didn't offer up a thing.

"Yeah, I'm lucky. I'm not some genius or anything, just lucky."

They ate the pizza while talking about the weather, movies, and what they liked to eat.

"You still want a candy? My treat. And we can split it." He grinned at her as he stood, grabbing the garbage to toss.

"Yes. Your choice. Surprise me." She was warm and cozy, full of pizza, which was a good thing because she hadn't eaten in at least fifteen hours, which was also why she hadn't been able to decide on a candy. Her brain just didn't work right when she was hungry.

He came back with a bag of Reese's peanut butter cups.

She smiled hugely, and said, "One of my favorites!"

"Mine too!" he said with delight.

They enjoyed several pieces together in silence, but made eyes at each other. She expected him to ask her out or something. She'd say 'yes' in a heartbeat. Her mind drifted to his erection and she wondered if he still was sporting one.

Her thoughts spun as she got up the courage to ask for another hug. "I'm feeling amazing. You really are quite wonderful for doing all this. But could I have another hug? It would really make me feel fully better. You are such a good hugger."

His face spread into a happy look. "Of course, I'd love to."

He stood up and approached her with wide open arms. She allowed him to curl her up. She pressed her full front to his and, within seconds, she felt his erection refill.

She looked up at him, which she knew was often taken as an invitation to kiss. She smiled at him and let her lust sizzle in her eyes.

He returned her gaze with a blaze growing in his own.

"You have any places in here where there aren't video cameras?"

His body jolted in a jerk. "Why?" he asked quickly.

"Just ... fuck. I can't believe I'm about to say this. But an orgasm always makes me feel better."

His eyes grew wide and filled with shock. "Oh, I can understand that. Me too."

The look that took over his face was utter excitement at the prospect of possibly getting laid.

She released a curt laugh. "I've never ever in my life instigated a hookup. You are my first." She didn't care if he didn't believe her. That just didn't matter. She just wanted to feel his cock inside her, rubbing her clit and G-spot until she was gifted the release of dopamine in her brain from climaxing that she needed so badly.

"I've only done that a few times, but I'm game if that's what you want. I'd never turn down sex with someone as gorgeous and amazing seeming as you."

She laughed. "Seeming? Oh, you sweet talker, you," she said in a teasing voice.

"It's only in the bathroom, though." He cringed slightly.

"Oh, shit. I suppose that makes sense." She shuddered, even though she was in his warm arms. "Well, we'll have to make do."

His eyes flew open wider. "Serious?"

She nodded.

He stepped back from her and grabbed her hand, leading her to the condoms. He snatched one and pulled her towards the back of the gas station where the restrooms were located. He opened the family bathroom door and led her inside.

"Not very romantic," he said as he pointed to the little stool in the corner.

"I'm not going for romance," she said with glee. "I just want to come."

He chuckled and said, "Oh, I understand, completely."

He dropped her hand and pulled several paper towels from the dispenser, his deep blue eyes glinting with mischief. He laid the towels over the stool to fully cover it.

"Your throne," he said, motioning for her to sit.

She laughed with joy and promptly stripped for his appreciative eyes.

"Wow, I knew you were going to be sexy as fuck. My dick is like a brick right now." He dropped to his knees and pointed at the stool.

He pushed his pants down his thighs, pulling his underwear with it, and his cock sprung out. It was an average-sized cock with a nice curve to it. He slipped the condom on. "Gotta be ready."

"Perfect," she said happily.

She sat on the stool and spread her thighs for him. He nestled into her mound and dragged his tongue down her slit several times before teasing her clit with the tip. She gripped his scalp and pressed her fingers when he latched on to her clitoral head.

He sucked her hard and pressed two fingers inside her moistness, riding her hole with ever-increasing speed.

He was skilled at eating a woman out, of that she was convinced about a minute into it.

She threw her head in a loud moan as he hoovered her engorging clit into his suctioning mouth.

He had his arms wrapped around her hips so his face was crammed tight as it could go to her womanhood.

Her arousal slid right up the climax climb and she burst into a motherload of an orgasm at lightning speed. Her body jerked and twitched as it traversed the big O. He didn't stop, so she hit the peak again, and then a third time, her body jerking with the flood of hormones. She was floating in the feelings as he stood up.

At first, she couldn't speak or stand, but only smile. "Wow, that was incredible."

"I love eating pussy," he said with a wet grin.

"It shows," she said with a laugh. "Your turn. How do you want me?"

"Doggy, if you don't mind." His grin was wicked, but there was a sweetness to him still.

"Your wish is my command," she said as she rose and swiveled, giving him her backside. "Fuck me."

"With extreme pleasure," he said with obvious anticipation.

She cradled her face in her arms and stuck out her butt at him.

He caressed her slit with his hard cockhead and slowly penetrated her core.

His groan was delicious as he pushed himself into her to the hilt. She moaned too as his length filled her.

He began to thrust into her, going faster and faster, harder and harder, until he was panting heavily as was she. She reached back and caressed her clit. She didn't particularly care for condoms, but it was a necessity for this, so she massaged her external clit to bring herself near a climax.

"Fuck, you are so sexy. Oh my God, I can't believe this," he said through his labored breaths.

She felt the swell of everything that aroused her, the taboo act of doing this, his clear desire for her from that first hug, the connection they felt over the pizza, and she slammed into another delicious big O, even despite the condom masking her full pleasure.

Her contractions choked his cock, and his body curled and shuddered over her. He yelled out, signaling his own climax.

Afterward, he lay slightly on her back as his breath slowly returned to normal.

"Holy shit, that was incredible."

She nodded; her head still nestled in the crook of her overlapped forearms.

He stood up and helped her to stand.

"Um, thank you, I guess," he said with a curt guffaw. "Seems stupid to say, but I mean it."

"No, thank you. You didn't have to be so nice to me when I was taking up space staring at candy forever."

"You looked so sad. I couldn't help it." He pulled up his pants, and with a sexy grin, he said, "I'd better get back in case someone comes in. I can't believe we got away with that without a soul entering." He pointed at the ceiling. "It would have dinged if someone had walked in. So, I'm good."

"Ah, got it. Yup. We got away with it." She didn't feel a shred of guilt, only elation at being pleasured by a sexy man in a very unexpected place.

He opened the door, despite her still being naked. "No one's here," he said quickly. "But would you want to get a real pizza sometime? Like at a restaurant, not in this filthy place?"

She couldn't stop the smile from filling her face. "You know, I'd love to. Anytime."

"Great!" he said with obvious excitement. "How about tonight?"

She snorted. "Yeah, it's not like I have anything to do. I'm an open book."

"Good. Consider yourself booked."

He left and she dressed. Never had she ever thought she'd hook up with anyone, but he was different somehow, and she couldn't wait to find out exactly what that meant.

She dressed and left the bathroom. He was behind the counter as he had been when she first came into the gas station. Only now, he looked very relaxed.

She pulled out her phone. "What's your number? I'll text you my address."

He pulled his out and they made eyes at each other over their phones.

"Perfect."

"Seven work?" he asked as he slipped his phone back into his skinny jeans pocket.

"Yup. I'll be ready and hungry again." She bit her lip. "And not just for pizza."

His face spread into joy as he waved. "Can't wait."

"Me neither."

She left the gas station with a hopeful outlook, one she never imagined she'd get from a simple stop at a gas station for a bar of candy. Her sweet tooth had hooked her way more than appeasing a desire for something sweet. It had hooked her to him. She glanced at her phone. There was his contact information, and his last name. Jason Millow.

She hopped in her car and sped off with all the remnants of her orgasms still sending her body soaring.

The End

Next Door Temptations,

Finally Got my Neighbor's Cock

I drove past slowly. Cal looked up and waved at me. My loins stirred and began to thicken. He was so fucking sexy. His hair was dark, grayed at the temples, and his body was slender and toned. He always had a smile and a few nice words for me when we met at the store or out walking our dogs.

If I was being honest, his sex appeal wasn't just from his appearance or his kind, approachable demeanor, but the way he had taken care of his wife, too. He was a caretaker, a doer, and it shone in his eyes that he loved it. I could only surmise how amazing he likely was in the bedroom with a body like that and the interest in his eyes that I assumed an attentive lover would have. Likely he'd made her come so many times she was spent like an overcooked spaghetti noodle, hot, wet, and ready to be slurped up.

He took immaculate care of his yard, his house, and his family. All that was hot as fuck. I'd get with him in a heartbeat if he were single, but all I could do was smile at him.

When I drove back home after my store run, he was still outside. It had been a while since we had chatted socially, so I pulled my car to the curb and got out for a quick exchange of words. I didn't want to interrupt his yard work, but he was pulling weeds, so that seemed like a boring job that could use some conversation to help the time pass.

"Hi, Cal," I said as I slammed my car door shut. "Beautiful day."

He smiled up at me, his scrumptious frame bent over. "Hi, Melissa, indeed it is. What are you up to today?"

"Just out getting some groceries. My kids eat so much that I can't keep up." I smiled at him as pleasantly as I could. Even though I wanted to fuck his brains out, I could rein that back and have small talk. I was used to not getting what I wanted.

He nodded with a knowing glint in his eyes. "Don't I know it. Mine too. It's like I plan a meal and then go to get the ingredients, and they've been eaten, so I have to run out to the store for one thing, but then I buy twenty."

He clearly got it. And this told me he was the cook and shopper in his family, just as I had been. This made him even more appealing. "Oh, dang, do I know exactly how that goes. I've gone as far as to label or even flat-out hide things so I didn't have to find them missing when I went to make the dish."

"Oh, yeah. Done that too." He grasped the big weed in his fingers and gave it a yank.

All I could think about was wishing that was my hip he was grasping as he fucked me from behind, making my tits swing in circles as he pounded me.

I tried not to let the lust for him show in my eyes.

He gazed at me, then cocked his head as a giant smile spread across his face. He took in a deep breath, then released it. "I don't suppose you've heard."

Instantly intrigued, I asked, "About what?"

He had an air of masculinity about his movements and an easy way of creating a facial expression that seemed without any manipulation or ill intent. Maybe that was just my brain stalling on wishful thinking because my ex had always worn a pleasant face socially, but his vile monster would come out when he drank too much or when he was angry with me for not agreeing with him. One would think that would have taught me to not trust a happy face, but with Cal, there was just something different about him, even if I couldn't quite put my finger on it.

"She left me." He stood up and brushed his dirt-covered hands together, then raised them up. "Said she's in love with someone else." His tone was stoic.

The sentence hit me like a shock wave, and I steadied myself. I searched his face for any shred of sadness about this, but I saw none. "Seriously? Holy fuck." I didn't usually swear in front of Cal, but this was definitely 'holy fuck' worthy.

My eyes fell to the flowers he was weeding. They were rose bushes. It struck me at that moment that any man who could take care of rose bushes and make them flourish the way he did was most certainly a desirable man. He was willing to do what it took.

"Yup. Left me and the kids, though we've just barely started the proceedings. It will be shared custody." He tilted his head and then stared off into the distance as if searching for something. "Maybe he will please her better than I ever could."

I scoffed. "Well, that's doubtful." I knew exactly what kind of woman she was. The kind who said she wanted onions when she ordered, then changed her mind and told the waiter to take it back because she wanted zero onions in her omelet.

He laughed heartily as his eyes twinkled.

I had always sensed a major spark between us. Maybe I'd imagined it, but if put to a lie detector test, I think I'd have passed the question with flying colors.

I let my shoulders relax and tried to convey my empathy via my eyes. "Are you okay? That's quite a blow."

"Yeah, honestly, we've just been going through the motions for years. We'd really become transactional." He flicked at the caked dirt on his hands.

I nodded. "Yup, I get it. Mine had become that way too. Plus, we just grew apart and no longer meshed as a couple." I yearned to tell him it all, but that would likely be a huge turn-off, and an avalanche. My ex had been well-liked by the neighbors, including Cal. Some things needed to stay hidden for the sake of small talk. But then again, we'd surpassed small talk on a big-time level.

It was a slow realization that we were both now single. My smile threatened to beam. My heart fluttered as I imagined holding his hand as we walked into a restaurant for dinner on a legit date. He'd pay attention to what I said, and not in a way that just was to get me to suck his dick. But the thought of that, too, raged my lust further as I continued to search his face for any sort of clue that he might be interested in me. It was too soon, they'd all say. But ... knowing a relationship is over for years, saying too soon doesn't apply.

I gulped and made a decision to not pussy foot. "You don't seem that upset."

Relief flooded his face. "I'm that easy to read, huh?" He smirked and doubled over to aggressively grab a weed. "I'd been feeling it'd been over for years, but you know, the obligation of taking care of my family. But once I realized she didn't want me, it was like I was free." He succeeded in pulling the thick dandelion root stalk from the earth. He tossed it to the pile of weeds to his right. "I can't believe I let this garden get this bad."

That wasn't like him. I never saw a thing out of place, or even many weeds in his yard for that matter over the years. He never had a stray week where the grass was too long, or his driveway got ice-encrusted from a late plowing. He was on top of his shit, always.

"It happens," I said, dismissing his guilt for him.

"Yeah," he said with the first sprinkle of wistfulness in his voice.

His two girls burst into the garage in a barrage of giggling voices. A friend was with them, and their boisterous banter made me smile. I fondly remembered being just like that with my girlfriends as a teen.

"Dad, we're going shopping. We'll be back for your dinner." She turned to her friend. "My dad makes the best chili."

They piled into the car and sped off with a wave.

"They are cute." My smile remained as I connected my eyes to his. "How are the kids handling it?"

"It's rough, but they seem mostly okay. Caitlin was hard on them, so I don't know, at times they seem relieved." He shook his head in silence before continuing, "And, yeah, it's a sleepover, so I asked my girls pizza or chili. My son said chili first, but the girls chose it, too." He looked satisfied.

Dads like him were hot. I wanted to tell him that, but my cheeks flushed instead.

The sun was burning my skin, and a sheen of sweat birthed on my neck. I had to figure out dinner for my kids, too. Summer made working from home hard, but I wouldn't trade it. Soon they'd be gone, and I'd be alone in a big ol' house. Maybe then I'd get a condo or townhouse so I wouldn't have to mow or plow. They helped me with all that, but doing it all alone, I think I'd rather move. Besides, I wouldn't need four bedrooms at that point anymore.

"I think girls do sleepovers to a later age than boys."

"Yeah, that makes sense." He looked distracted.

"Well, if you need anything, I'm here. That's what neighbors are for." I smoothed my hands down my jean shorts and played with the frayed hem. "I suppose I should let you get your work done."

"Wait," he said in a voice that told me he didn't want me to go yet.

I turned to face him with a happy expression. I waited, but he didn't continue, his face in a slight grimace.

His son burst out the front door wearing a small backpack. "Dad, I'm going to Logan's. I might stay for dinner." He snagged his longboard from the garage and laid it on the driveway.

"Okay, Trevor. Have fun. There will be chili leftover. I made a big pot."

He said, "Okay, Dad. Bye."

"Bye," Cal repeated.

"Bye, Trevor," I said with a wave.

He saluted and rolled off down the sidewalk.

Once Trevor was down the road, Cal asked, "Would you like to come in for a glass of iced tea?" He took a step towards me. "I could use a break and the company of a friend."

My heart jumped and my hopes followed. "Yes, I'd love to. Thank you."

I followed him into his house. I'd been in their house years ago, and it was impeccable then, as impeccable as it was now. Not a thing out of place, which was very unlike my house, where I had projects and pages of half-finished recipes for my next cookbook strewn about my counter, coupons and a spattering of pens I couldn't seem to keep in the pen holder for the life of me. Post-it notes with grocery lists and reminders to refill subscriptions and make the kids' appointments were scattered across my countertops at all times. I was a hot mess, whereas he was a neat connoisseur.

He motioned for me to sit at the island on a bar stool, then he washed his hands. The kitchen was white and black with red apples on the counter. It looked like a decorating magazine image, making my kitchen seem almost comical. I made a mental note to not invite him over, at least not to my kitchen. Now, the bedroom... I stifled my wicked grin.

The cool air of the house was refreshing after standing in the blazing sunshine. I watched him move; his movements were hypnotic. When he turned, he caught my stare and smiled.

"Would you like lemon or honey in your tea?"

"Yes, please," I said as I continued to watch him with blazing eyes like a sex-hungry MILF. I almost chuckled because that wasn't really wrong.

He connected with my gaze, and something shifted in his eyes that I liked a lot. He nodded, then went about setting up two tall cups with brightly colored sailboats on them, filling them both with ice, then tea.

My heart continued to race faster as I let my excitement build. They said foreplay starts outside the bedroom; I was now convinced it started with pouring a tall glass of iced tea on a hot day.

He pulled lemon slices from the fridge, and I was impressed he had some already cut. "This air conditioning feels amazing." It was something I should have said when we walked in, so it felt like old news. And massively lame.

"Yes. I was sweating out there, even at this hour. It's going to be a really hot day."

I was hot inside, despite the cool air in the house. I was roasting, well, maybe on the verge of panting was a better way to describe it. I couldn't stop the little smile from staying on my face. "Thank you," I said as he handed me the glass.

He sat next to me, then rose. "I think the couch might be a nicer place to sit. Let's move there."

I nodded and followed him to the living room.

He sighed as he sat down, comfort filling his face. "Ah, that feels better. I've been working outside for hours. I wanted to get as much done as I could before the afternoon heat hit."

"Yeah, it's heating up something fierce out there." I was confused as to why I kept talking about the weather when what I really wanted to say kept swelling on my lips, threatening to grace his world with words I wouldn't be able to take back.

"Can I be honest with you?" he asked with a raise of his left eyebrow.

"Of course you can." I waited with bated breath, hoping he felt the burning flame of lust I shared for him.

"I know my separation is new, but I," he paused, "I've always found you extremely attractive."

My heart leaped off its ledge and soared. "Oh my God," I said, unable to hide my shock.

"Fuck. I'm sorry, I can't believe I just said that." He rose off the couch and started to walk away.

I sat up straight and raised my hand. "No. That's not a bad 'oh my God.'"

He swiveled and hope flooded his eyes. "It's not?"

"Nope. Not even a little bit." I patted the couch where he had been sitting. "I've always found you extremely attractive, too." My heart was thudding so hard in my chest that I wondered if he could hear it.

"Wow, serious?" He quickly moved back to the couch and gazed into my eyes. "Okay, so I'm not crazy."

"No, you aren't. You read me right." I bit my lip and fluttered my eyelids. I clenched my teeth, then told myself to be brave. I took a deep breath and then blurted, "I've always wanted to fuck your brains out."

The room felt more silent after my confession, which seemed odd because the only sound we heard was the light blow of the air conditioning. I wanted to run away and ravage him at the same time. I was swollen with the urge to push him back and ride his cock like a jockey hungry for the win, then hop off and swivel, giving him my ass to doggy fuck me into our mutual bliss.

I didn't hold back. I let all that raunchy want show in my eyes so he'd see my full lust for him.

"Holy fuck me." He looked aghast, which didn't register as making sense to me. But his eyes were loaded with desire.

Our eyes locked, and in an explosion, he rushed me as I opened my arms. He fell to the couch beside me, immediately grabbing for me. He pulled and I followed his lead to sit on his lap. Our eyes lit like firecrackers as our open mouths collided.

I released any shred of control and hungrily tasted him, as he did me.

He fondled my ass and I ground my pelvis against his hard-on as we deeply French kissed. Our mutual groans told me he'd pined for me as much as I had for him. The buildup to this had been years of neighborly pleasantry, chatting at the grocery store, talking at parties over bonfires, and sharing food at neighborhood potlucks. Not to mention the umpteen times I'd driven by his house and we'd both waved. This wasn't a last-minute attraction; it was one that had simmered and boiled behind the closed doors of the facades of our marriages but clearly had burned brighter than they ever had.

"I want you. I've wanted you for years," I confessed as he kissed down my neck.

"God, I've wanted you more than I can say," he muttered as he kissed down my breasts, sneaking his tongue to lick the tops of my breasts at the rim of my tank top. "You are the sexiest woman I've ever had the pleasure to lay eyes on. And your breasts, holy fuck, your breasts," he said as he nuzzled my boobs with his face, his hands firmly pressing my back.

I pulled my tank top off for him and he groaned.

"Oh, fuck yes, you are gorgeous."

He'd seen me in a bikini several times, so this wasn't new for him to see me in a bra, but I loved his reaction. My lust for him swelled greater and I reached for my bra clasp faster than he could say the next word.

I ripped my bra off and my breasts swung up then settled in their full D cup splendor.

His lust exploded and he devoured my right breast with his mouth, consuming my whole areola, the nub of my tit to the back of his throat as his fingers played with my other nipple.

I squirmed into his tit sucking and whimpered when he lightly bit my nipple. My body jolted as he pinched and twisted my other nipple with his fingers. Then he repeated his sucking routine on my other nipple as I moaned.

"Oh, fuck yes. I knew you were a boob man," I cooed as he continued to eat my tits.

"I can't tell you how many times I've wanted to see them. Fuck, they are stunning."

I'd always received compliments on my breasts, but none hit home to flare my desire more than him saying this to me.

He kissed all along my neck before kissing me deep again, our tongues twining. I pressed my pussy mound to his engorged cock as a new confidence welled in me. I massaged his big erection with my lower body as he pawed me, and I threaded my hands in his lush hair to press his scalp.

I scooted back and helped him remove his shirt. I suckled down his chest, visiting his nipples for a quick suck, then continued my way down to his meat. He was packing what looked like a damn good sized hard-on beneath his shorts.

I unzipped him as I held his gaze. I smirked and slipped the waistband of his underwear down off his cock head. It glistened with a small cherry of precum at the tip. I leaned down and licked it.

His body jolted in response, and he released a moan of delight.

I unsheathed the rest of his boner and settled between his legs, my knees both secure on the floor. I took his meaty head into my mouth and began to ride his cock. His hands meandered into my hair as I bounced on him. I wanted to make him come as I tasted his salty arousal flooding my tongue. He certainly wasn't too dehydrated from the outside work as his precum continued to leak across my mouth.

He grunted then forcefully pulled my mouth from his cock. He slipped my shorts down and grinned wickedly as he saw I was commando. The delicious look in his eyes as he gripped my hips and pulled me upwards made me gasp. He lifted me up so I was above him, then he slid down to slouch so he could maneuver his face beneath my pussy, like a mechanic beneath a car.

I quivered, struggling to remain in the position, until I leaned forward and placed my hands on the back of the couch. His firm grip on my thighs supported me from beneath, and it was a good thing because once he touched his lips to my labia lips, I grew weak. I scrambled to secure myself as he made his way to my clit with his tongue.

"Oh, fuck," I whispered. When I opened my eyes, I could see kids playing in the neighboring yards, and a bit of reality of what we were doing hit me. But his mouth won as I got lost in the pleasure as he continued to eat me out.

My eyelids fluttered and I moaned and sighed so he'd know right when he sucked me the right way. I faltered, almost falling back, but he pulled me in closer, wrapping his hands around the tops of my buttocks, while his arms secured my lower buns in place. He latched on my clit and sucked harder and longer than my ex ever had. I hadn't even known this was possible as I neared the height of my climax.

"Oh, fuck," I whispered between pants. "I'm going to come. You are ..." I couldn't finish because the orgasm came for me. It wasn't tiptoeing, it was a tidal wave as my pussy sent out the signals of pleasure in contraction after contraction. My body rolled in response, leading to the deep arching back of my head. My tits were on display if anyone looked at the window because my nipples grazed the smooth glass.

He didn't stop sucking me but sucked harder with each second and I launched into a second orgasm peak with a loud roar. He gripped my rump harder as the full climax traveled my body once more.

I struggled to grip the back of the couch as I panted, my body loose as overstretched rubber bands.

I shivered and whimpered as he lowered me to sit on his lap. When our eyes met, his fire for me still burned there as brilliantly as before.

"I've never …" I started but the next stage erupted before I could finish.

He raised me up off his body. I followed his lead and stood so I could slide my wet hole down his length. I was so ready to choke his engorged shaft.

Years of desire piled out of me as I began to ride his cock. We held our eyes together as I rode him, secretly acknowledging our indiscretion, my big tits flopping like Ziplocs of wet sand.

He groaned then growled, gripping my hips in a death grip which I figured would show as bruises in the am. But this only raged my desire for more with him.

He thrust his fattened cock up into me like a piston on steroids. I had been right. His fit body was a fucking machine. He shoved himself up into me and I felt slack with ecstasy.

He grabbed my legs, then pulled my body to him as he stood. Carrying me, he turned and then laid me on the couch, the plush cushions a welcoming place to land for my already orgasm-stroked body.

He fucked me with a passion I'd only read about or seen in porn. He pressed my clit as he slowed his pumping for a few moments, and he didn't let up until the crest of my next orgasm peaked, then waned.

Then he took a step back, which made his cock fall from my cum-soaked pussy. He grinned a wicked grin and jerked his head upwards.

"Doggy," he said with relish.

I smiled back and quickly flipped over, presenting my ass pertly to his impending mount.

He entered me and began to thrust as his hands sought my breasts. He fondled and fucked me as delicious man growls spurted from his lungs.

"Oh, fuck yes, Cal, fuck me. Fuck me good." I paused to catch up with my panting. "Yes, just like that."

I sought out my clit and rubbed it as he relentlessly took his pleasure from my body. I was about to climax again, but he pulled his dick out and his hot seed landed in streaks across my ass and back, one stream hitting the top of my back.

I breathed heavily as I lamented the loss of the orgasm, but my excitement rose as he dropped to his knees behind me and pressed his fingers into my wanton cunt. He began to finger fuck me so fast my body gyrated from the force. He smacked into my clit, giving me pussy spankings as he rode my G-spot with his fingers, ensuring my whole clit, both internal and external were getting stimulated. He sped up his hand pumping and I soared into another climax.

I yelled out as I arched my back and, making my big O face, I submitted to his guidance and relinquished control as I came like an open floodgate. My body quaked and quivered as he rode my swollen feminine bits until the aftershocks of my climax slowed, and my body stilled.

He collapsed on the couch beside me and cuddled me to him.

"Wow, well that was unexpected." He didn't sound a bit disappointed. On the contrary, he sounded like a very satisfied man.

And that felt good.

I laughed curtly. "I'll say." I wiggled against him to get as close to his warm flesh as I could. "But very, very, very good."

"Good," he said, and I could hear the smile in his tone.

"I must confess, I've fantasized about such things with you many times."

"Same," he said with gratification.

"That was risky. The kids could have come."

"Yes, but I didn't think they'd be back yet." He squeezed me to him. "Anyone seem to see you through the window? That was pretty hot. Thinking of someone seeing you in my window as I ate you out was very arousing."

I snickered. "It was very hot. I did see some people, but they were too far away to have made me out."

"Oh, damn, I hadn't thought of that."

"We're good," I said, relishing the fact that he liked the idea we might have been seen. I had been used to the jealousy and the prudishness viewpoint, not this exhibitionistic one, a kink that actually matched mine.

"Whew!" he said as he ran a hand through his hair. "This old man needed that. I hadn't gotten laid in quite some time."

"Same," I confessed. "I really, really needed that. I love my toys, but there's nothing like a cock attached to a man."

He laughed heartily. "Well, that's very good to hear." He kissed the top of my head, and it surprised me, which was odd to me that it would after he'd just fucked me like a ravenous beast.

"I suppose we should go on a date now," he said with laughter laced throughout his sentence.

I laughed too. "Yeah, we are kind of doing this backward, aren't we?"

"Are we?" he asked with amusement. He grabbed my chin and his face turned serious. "Is what we did okay? I didn't overstep, did I?" His eyes were solid with concern.

"Oh, hell no. I would have stopped you if I hadn't wanted it. But I wanted it as much as you. Maybe more."

"Oh, I don't think that's possible." He reached for our tea glasses and handed me mine. "I'm parched."

I took a sip of the sweet honey and lemon-laced tea. "Ah, that feels good. Especially after such a good fuck."

He smiled down at me. "I love that you say 'fuck.'"

"Oh, I say lots of things."

"Excellent. As I'd love to hear you," he said, seeming to relish that idea. "How about a lunch date, since I have the chili with the kids for dinner? You in?"

I nodded. "I am. And I'd love to. Let me text my kids." I gasped and a hand flew to my mouth. "Oh shit! I forgot all about my groceries! I bet they are ruined in this heat. Fuck! I had frozen stuff too." I laughed so hard I was grateful I didn't snort. "Damn, you mesmerized me, and I completely forgot all about them."

"I have special powers. Have to say I find that very sexy, and endearing."

I hopped up and began to dress. "I'd better go see what I can salvage."

"I'll pick you up in a half hour?" he asked with hope.

"Yes, I'll text you if I need that to change."

He motioned for me to come back and pulled me onto his lap again. We kissed briefly and he gave my ass a generous squeeze. I rose and waved, then sailed out his front door as if cloud nine were my very feet.

The End

Hooking Up with the Horny Gamer Next Door

Alexis slopped the rest of the mac and cheese onto her plate. Another microwaved meal. She sighed. Somehow, the microwave could even screw up simple mac and cheese and make it not as good as that made in a pot. But she never ate a whole box by herself, so it was a waste to make, because mac and cheese really wasn't that great leftover. So, the single-serve microwave meal was her usual plan. She missed having a roommate, but she understood why he had wanted to move in with his girlfriend. She lamented him finding her; it had been an end to their roommate friends-with-benefits situation. So not only was she lonelier now, but she also wasn't getting any action at all either.

Work was work. Going out with her girlfriends had been the only fun she'd had these days, outside of reading or listening to erotic stories and getting herself off with toys, alone. She needed to start searching for someone to date. She was getting desperate for cock on a level she'd never sunk to. She'd always had roommates or friends to fuck, but now being out in the work world instead of college, it was coming to be increasingly difficult to find fuck buddies.

Maybe she'd advertise for a new roommate and hope to find a single or swinging male. She just wanted a bit of cock here and there, nothing had to be regular, just something attached to a body now and then and being shoved up her wanton cunt 'til she gushed.

She settled on the couch, letting her pink glitter slippers fall to the floor as she tucked her feet under her. She scanned the living room, realizing she'd become a slob now that she lived alone. Her yoga workout mat had become a permanent piece of furniture in front of the TV. She never bothered to put her weights or yoga foam pieces back in the basket, because why bother? She'd just be taking them out in twenty-four hours, anyway. She was proud of herself for keeping up on the dishes, though. She didn't need to encourage bugs or roaches to take up residence in her apartment.

With only one minute into watching her favorite show, a knock rang at her door. Odd. She didn't expect anyone. No friends had texted they were stopping over, but that reminded her, she needed to connect with her bestie Corrine again. It had been too long.

She slid off the chair and ambled towards the door, mac and cheese cup in her hands. She rose on her tiptoes a tiny bit to get a good look in the peephole. It was a bit too high, on the abnormally high side for a peephole. She hadn't noticed that until she'd moved in. When Max had lived there, she hadn't worried so much about checking who was at the door, but being alone, now she was hypervigilant about checking.

It was Aaron, her neighbor. She smiled as she saw his disheveled hair, like he'd just woken with a mop of sandy blond bedhead. He had on an open red and black checked flannel over a gray t-shirt and he wore sweatpants. He looked the sight of a dude of leisure.

She opened the door with a smile on her face. It was nice to actually talk to another human being.

"Aaron, hi! What's up?" she asked as her eyes scanned down his body. He was sexy in a comfy teddy bear sort of way, and she couldn't stop the deepening of her grin when she saw he had a bit of a mound pushing out the crotch of his sweatpants.

"Alexis, it's an emergency! Do you have any batteries? I'm fresh out, and I'm in the middle of an … important … game." He was panting, and looked like he'd just run on a treadmill or something, but she'd been in his apartment and had never seen a treadmill. He sure as fuck wasn't the type to run in place.

"Oh, let me check. Come on in." She waved and he strode in.

He looked like a junky looking for a fix, with the same crazed look in his eyes she'd expect. "I'm … fuck, I can't focus worth shit."

Was he strung out? It seemed like possibly he was, but she couldn't be sure because he was a bit scatterbrained at a baseline.

"You okay, Aaron? You seem a little unwell," she stated with concern in her voice.

He shook his head. "I'm fine. I'm just ... a little worked up. I need to finish this game."

It seemed very important to him, so she shrugged her shoulders and dug in her junk drawer. She found an empty container of AA's.

"Oops. Looks like I used them and forgot to add them to my shopping list." Her heart sank a bit that she couldn't calm his agitation. "So sorry, Aaron."

"Damn." He paced in her kitchen, which was funny to watch because there really wasn't room to pace, so he'd take a few steps and then turn and quickly bounce back the other way.

"It's an important game?" she asked, softening her eyes. This was a silly conversation, but it was all she had, so why not lean into it?

"Yeah, very." He ran his hand through his hair, making it stand up higher.

She noticed his hand swipe through his bangs had left a white glob of something. She snickered, wondering if it was cum or lotion, because that's exactly what it looked like. She couldn't stop staring at it. She really wanted to ask, and her face flushed slightly.

He grinned at her. "I'm sorry. I must look like a crazy person."

She relaxed her shoulders and tried to maintain eye contact, rather than having her eyes drift to the white blob in his hair or his erection.

He sighed very deeply and slunk his arms. "I took a pill."

Her eyes widened. "Oh?" Drugs? He didn't seem like the type, though he definitely seemed erratic.

He laughed at himself. "Okay, you are going to think I'm crazy."

She folded her arms under her large breasts and smirked. "I like crazy."

"I took a ... blue pill." He cracked up. "I was playing a porn game and my remote died before I could finish."

Her face reddened and her arousal peaked. "Oh, I see." She glanced down at his cock, which now looked even larger with the way he was standing.

"My friend did this, and I wanted to try it too. But now I've had this," he said as he cupped his crotch, "and I can't get rid of it. I thought if I came, it might go down."

She folded over as hysterical laughter sang out of her mouth. "You fucked yourself over."

"Yeah. I kinda did." His expression was very sheepish, but also quite amused.

"Well, you could go to the emergency room. I've heard that whole urban legend story. Maybe they can help deflate your cock." She wondered why the fuck he didn't just jerk off like a normal guy.

"I can't deal with it. I've come twice and it's still hard," he admitted. "So, I thought maybe if I got really turned on, I could come hard, and it would settle the fuck down."

Her lust was barking at her as she eyed up this poor man. Her first instinct was to offer to fuck him, but she didn't even know if he was into her, and she wanted to be desired, not just be a hole. She guffawed. Well, maybe it didn't matter with how dry her sex life had been. She squashed her doubts and let her eyes twinkle at Aaron.

"I'm so sorry. I should stop bothering you." His eyes looked lost as he turned towards the door.

It was time to be bold. She bit her lip, fighting with all her might to flatten her fear of rejection.

He turned the knob and started to pull the door open.

"Wait!" she blurted. "I'll help."

He froze in place, then spun around faster than she had expected he could move. He connected with her gaze as a tiny smile sparked at the corners of his mouth. "You will?" He sounded aghast, but quite pleased.

"Yes. Don't go." She took a few steps towards him as her arousal raged further. "Please stay."

He shut the door behind him and glanced around her apartment for the first time since he'd come in. "Are you alone?"

"Yes, Max moved out. Haven't you noticed him not being around?" she asked with surprise.

"Well, now that you mention it, I haven't seen Max in a while." He and Max had occasionally gamed together. Not being a gamer herself, she'd at times gone over to Aaron's too, but with a drink in one hand and her phone in the other. She'd read and drink while they gamed.

"Bummer for you. He told me how you guys used to be." The sassy grin on his face told her Max had shared their sexual escapades with him.

"Umm, yep," she said as she blushed a deep red. "We fucked all the time."

"Pity he's gone." Aaron snorted. "Shouldn't we, like, go out to dinner first or something? I don't know how this works."

She gave him a skeptical look and held up her half-eaten mac and cheese. "You really want to go to McDonald's right now with a permanent brick in your pants?"

He laughed, and it made him look even cuter as the laughter reached his eyes. "Well, true. That would be awkward."

Besides, she just wanted his cock, not his company over a burger and fries. "I think we just fuck."

His body jolted at her words. "Serious?"

She nodded. "Yes."

"Fuck. Oh my God. I never thought I'd ever hear that." He looked happy, like a man who knew he was about to get sex.

She liked it. She wanted more of it. She wanted to feel his balls smack her flesh. Images of what his cock and balls might look like invaded her brain. She always imagined what men looked like naked, and how they would fuck. She couldn't help herself. Her brain just went right to sex, even when she was just at the grocery store. She saw sex everywhere she went.

"I'm really super horny. Haven't had dick in way too long. And you have a dick that needs to get used. Seems like a perfect match up to me." Her direct gaze sent a shiver through his body.

"Well, fuck yes, then. I'm in." He started to strip, removing his sweatpants first.

She chuckled. He was certainly an eager beaver.

"I haven't fucked anyone in a long time either." He took off his flannel and t-shirt, then slipped his underwear down. His cock swung out all angry and red.

"Wow," she said as she watched it bob as he moved. He looked about seven or eight inches, with a nice hook of a G-spot curve at the tip. "That blue pill does good work."

"Oh, I don't need the pill. I just did it to enhance the game. I don't usually do that." He clearly wanted her to know he had no trouble getting it up.

She strolled towards him with seduction filling her face. "Certainly good to know that, Aaron." Her inner Goddess flared as she approached him. She liked that she was still dressed, and he was the naked one. Once she reached him, she touched his cheek, then ran her finger down his jaw, neck, and onto his chest. She dragged her fingertip along his peck until she reached his nipple. She circled it with her finger then leaned in to suck it.

He recoiled at her hard suck and she grabbed his cock firmly. She began to stroke him as she suckled his nipple. She meandered her wet tongue across his chest hair and vigorously sucked his other nipple.

He was making a nice amount of precum so she spread it out along his taut flesh. "You must be quite hydrated," she said salaciously. "I hope that applies to your cum, too. I'm thirsty."

He cackled like a kid and reached to touch her, but she yanked him by the cock, which disrupted his grab. She pulled him the short distance towards her living room, squeezing his cock in her hands as she strode along.

She glanced back at him. "That's good boy," she said with a smile. She'd role-played both the dominant and the sub with Max so many times that all the moves and words came to her so naturally. "I want your cum, Aaron."

His dick looked even bigger, which she hadn't thought would be possible when she first saw it.

"My boy is quite aroused, isn't he?" She pushed him to fall back on the easy chair and he landed with a plop.

She began to strip for his hungry eyes, eating up all the appreciation his gaze granted her. She loved that he seemed to want her. "Ever jerk off to me?" She raised an eyebrow in warning as her eyes turned stern. "Be honest, or I'll know."

"All the time," he admitted quickly. "Just this morning, in fact. I saw you come home with groceries last night and imagined you coming to make me dinner while I sucked your tits."

She sensed the wicked truth in his words was spot on, and her arousal thickened. She was ripe to pluck this fattened pig and ride him home to her own climax. She doubted coming would deflate his cock, but she wasn't about to raise any doubts before she got off. She needed this too badly.

"I've fantasized about you fucking me too, Aaron. Doggy style in the shower. A titty fuck while you game. I used to fantasize about titty fucking both of you to the spilling of your jizz while you gamed."

His expression grew aghast. "What? Why the fuck didn't you?" He looked like he felt cheated.

"I used to for Max, but here in our apartment." She danced in front of him as she seductively removed her thong. "How do you want to fuck me, Aaron? Because I very much want you to fuck me."

He screwed his face into a few expressions from joy to contemplation to lecherous lust.

"You are taking too long." She sat on him, ensuring her wet folds landed right on his shaft.

"Oiy, damn. Fuck," he muttered in appreciation. "You are so hot, Alexis. I've dreamt of this."

"Same." She attacked his open mouth with hers and kissed him.

His hands grabbed at her ass and he mauled her hips and butt cheeks as they kissed. She writhed on his lap, pressing her breasts down to his warm body.

She moaned as she squirmed on his lap. His hands found her breasts and he squeezed them and fondled her erect tits. She intended to let her cunt slurp up his spunk. "You clean?" she asked. "Was hoping for a cream pie."

"Yes, I am," he said with confidence. "I haven't fucked anyone in several years."

She felt bad for him, but she knew his luck was about to change, as was hers.

"Good." She hopped off his lap and bent herself over, placing her cheek on a foam yoga square, and her right knee on another. "Fuck me crooked, in doggy," she demanded. She pressed her clit as she impatiently waited for him to rise and mount her.

He quickly lined up behind her and pressed his cock at her slit. "Fuck, this is so fucking hot."

"Fuck me," she moaned. "And I like dirty talk and clit action. Nips too. Tug me like I'm the reins of your horse ride."

"Oh, you got it." He pressed his cockhead slightly into her lower lips and groaned. "Your cunt smells nice and juicy. Love your musky pussy scent."

"Yes," she seethed. "Tell me more. Tell me how you want to fuck me. Tell me what I am to you," she begged as she ran her fingers in circles around her clit. She was so aroused she was almost ready to come. She panted as she rubbed and when he penetrated her, she groaned out loudly. "Oh, fuck yes, fuck me good. Ride me."

He dug his fingers into her hips with a groan of appreciation and began to pump his cock into her. The skin smacks of their bodies slapping as they fucked filled the room and Alexis couldn't focus on the sounds from the tv anymore. She was lost in the bliss of being savagely fucked in doggy. He rocked her body and she fell off the yoga blocks.

He pressed her head down into the yoga mat and declared, "Head down, ass up, whore."

She melted at his dirty talk and claiming of his use of her. "Yes," she slurred as he pounded relentlessly against her ass, making it jiggle. "Oh, fuck yes," she cooed through her panting.

He was breathing hard too as he fucked her harder. "Take my cock," he instructed.

She squealed when he grabbed both her nips and yanked up.

"Neigh for me, horsey," he said with humor laced in his words.

He pulled on her nips like he'd yank on the reins of a horse.

"Fucking horsey," he mocked as he fucked her from behind and aggressively tugged her nips. "Neigh for me."

She couldn't believe they were going there, but it turned her on so she muttered, "Neigh, neigh, neigh."

She felt a laugh building in her gut, but the pressure he was gifting her G-spot, the press of her own fingers to her clit, and the strong nipple stimulation he was giving her launched her into her climax, and the laugh dwindled to the power of her big O.

"Oh, shit, fuck. I'm going to," she yelled. Her body curled towards the ground and she tilted her head to the side. Her eyelids fluttered as her toes began to curl. The contractions began to spasm out her juicy walls and she clamped down on his cock over and over again as she came.

He grunted, growled, and then groaned as her womanhood clenched around his thick shaft inside her.

Her pussy felt wetter, and the sloshing sounds of him going in and out of her wet cunt told her he had come as well. He continued to pump into her, his dick still as hard of fuck rod as when they had started.

She was floppy as a ragdoll as she collapsed to the yoga mat. "You can keep fucking me. You are still hard. I'll come again."

He didn't hesitate to slide his cock back into her juicy hole and begin to ride her prone doggy. She grasped at the foam bricks and dug her fingernails in as he fucked her so hard she worried she might get a rub mark on her cheeks from gyrating across the bumps on the mat.

She'd not say a peep of complaint, though, because his rapid fucking of her was sending her flying high again. She slid her hand down to her clit and mashed and spanked it as he pounded her G-spot.

"Gonna," she muttered as her body sputtered into another full-body orgasm.

Her hot pussy cave closed in on his cock again and squeezed it, gifting her a double orgasm to his one.

He collapsed on the mat beside her, panting heavily. "Fuck, it's not going down."

She giggled. "Well, it sure works, doesn't it?" She snuggled up to him, admiring his still blood-packed cock. "It looks mad," she snickered.

"I think it is." He ran a hand over her cheek. "That was really hot. Thank you for trying."

"The plague of an endless boner. Whatever shall we do?" she poked at his hard cock. "Better than the porn game?"

"Oh, fuck yes it was," he said clearing his throat. "It was hot as fuck." He scooted down so his face was even with her tits. "I didn't get much chance to love on your luscious nipples."

"Boob man?" she asked with affection for him growing in her gut. She never expected all of this out of Aaron, but she was very happy at the turning of things.

"Yes," he said with desire in his eyes. "And I've been lusting over yours for quite some time. Especially when you wear those tank tops in the summertime."

"Ah, yes, I miss summer."

He attacked her left tit like a mongoose and began to suckle, quickly sucking her nipple to the back of his throat. He suckled her nipples as she played with his hair for a half hour.

He thrust his still-hard dick against her side as he suckled her nipples. She reached for a sex toy she hadn't bothered to put away from last night, and pressed the hole of the clit sucker to her bean. She writhed as he sucked and thrusted against her body. She came first, and he spurted a small splat of cum on her flesh.

"Ah, that was so good." He sighed as he cuddled her to him.

"Yes, it was." She glanced down to assess his cock. "It looks smaller, Aaron. Is it shrinking?"

He nodded with relief on his face. "Yes, it finally is deflating." He belly laughed. "It only took coming six times."

"Wow, I can't even believe you could that many times." She hadn't been with a man who could climax that much before.

"Yeah, I've always been able to come a lot in a short amount of time."

"You don't need a silly blue pill, you goof," she teased.

"No, you're right. I'm not sure I'll go there again."

"Thank you, Aaron. You don't know how much I needed that."

"Same." He squeezed her tight to him. "Hey, want to go to McDonald's and get that burger now?"

She laughed. "I hate McDonald's. How about a pizza?"

"Done. I'm in."

They dressed, both taking sneaky glimpses of each other.

"Can this be a thing?" he asked in an unsure voice.

"Definitely. I'd have been sad if it didn't."

She smiled at him and grabbed his hand, and they scooted out the door.

The End

About the Author

Ruan Willow is a spicy romance author, blogger at https://ruanwillowauthor.com/ , sexuality and erotica fiction podcaster at the Oh F*ck Yeah with Ruan Willow Podcast, and an audiobook narrator/voiceover actress. She is also published on Medium, Frolic Me, and Literotica, and coming soon on Theo Reads. She loves spending time with family and friends, interacting with fans, cooking, sharing/chatting with and educating people about sex, reading, travel, being outdoors, swimming, learning about sex, podcasting, and more sex. Did you catch all the sex? She's giggling right now thinking about you reading all about sex. She values openness and talking about the natural act of sex. And. Yup, she loves to laugh!

Other pen names for Ruan Willow:

RuAnn Willhoe (taboo erotica on Smashwords)

R.U. Ann (Open Door Romantasy, dark romance, paranormal coming soon)

Ruin Willow (hotwife)

Thank you!

Thank you to all my family and friends who support me. I wouldn't be where I am without you. You are all the magic and the light in my life, the love that grows in my love. I am honestly thrilled and humbled by the supportive people in my life. Love you!

To Fans:

Thank you for purchasing and/or reviewing this book!

I peddle fantasies for the purposes of your enjoyment, entertainment, and expanding your sexuality and openness. Always remember that no fantasies are bad, they take place in your head only, so indulge in your heart's desire to the fullest! You should enjoy your sexuality and your fantasy life as much and as often as you can. Sexual pleasure is your birthright!

Thank you for reading my book! I write for myself and for my fans. My fans are my main focus though, but of course, I want to like what I write too, and I thoroughly enjoyed writing these stories. I love to write about empowered women exploring their sexuality with supportive partners. I love open door because I want the FULL story of the relationship, not a partial view that is chopped off.

In writing erotica/erotic romance, I'm always excited for the erotic journey! I'm on a path of sexual empowerment, enlightenment, and enjoyment. Thank you for reading this and I'm honored to be a part of your journey as well. I don't know about you, but I love open door to get the FULL story rather than be shut out of intimacy between characters, I find a lot can be found out about characters when they are at their most vulnerable, raw, genuine states during sexual relations.

I am where I am because fans have responded to me and my content, so I owe everything to you! Thank you! Thank you! Thank you! You are a blessing in my life, and you give me more joy than you will ever know. I love interacting with all of you and I will never give that up.

My stories are erotica, so they have a generous amount of sex in them, as I believe our relationships should have as well. I hope you enjoyed this novel for what it is, literature that is in the erotica genre. It is very different from the sweet romance genre, and there are different levels of heat in the erotica genre as well. Explore them all!

If you'd like more of my work, please see below for my list of published works on the following pages, visit my sexuality and erotica podcast, find my audiobooks, visit my website, my Patreon, visit my profile on Medium, and my linktree with all my links at https://linktr.ee/RuanWillow

Thank you for purchasing this book, I'd love to hear your thoughts in an honest review on the site where you purchased the book from. I'd absolutely love it if you shared my book with others. It warms my heart profusely when I see someone who has taken the time to review/share my book. Love you all very much!

All my best, yours truly, with overflowing love from a full heart,
Ruan Willow
Erotica author, sexuality/erotica podcaster, and erotic book narrator

Oh F*ck Yeah with
Ruan Willow Podcast

It's free on podcast apps! Also airing on the internet radio station Full Swap Radio website and app Tuesdays and 6 pm CST, and Wednesdays 8 am (subject to change, check for the current schedule online) AND the PodNation TV Network/Roku TV station/Fire TV/powered by Podnation Pods anytime VOD on the app, and Sundays and Mondays After Dark Hours around 11 pm Eastern Time Zone (subject to change).

Oh F*ck Yeah with Ruan Willow Podcast on Buzzsprout[1]

---

1.   https://ohfckyeahwithruanwillow.buzzsprout.com/

Ruan's other books and novellas:

Series:

Ruan's Getaway Series: Heterosexual, MILF Age Gap

Ruan's Cabin Getaway (ebook, paperback, audiobook)

Ruan's Beach Getaway (ebook, paperback, audiobook)

Ruan's Lake Getaway (coming soon!)

The Sex Challenge Series: Heterosexual, Middle Aged 2nd Chance I Dare You

Servicing the Work Men (hotwife with dominant alpha male wife sharing) (8 books)

The Stars Aligned Series: Heterosexual, Twenty-Something's

Skinny Dipping at the Pond on a Hot Summer Day, Book 1 (ebook & audiobook)

The Rush (ebook)

Spring Break (college aged multiple partner fantasy books)

Spring Break & Stranded with Her Best Friend's Brothers, Books 1, 2, and 3.

GET THE SPICIER VERSION by RuAnn Willhoe Spring Break & Stranded with Her Best Friend's Brothers Plus 6 Men, on Smashwords.

Next Door Temptations *(middle aged couple, second chance at love and sex, friends to lovers)*

Next Door Temptations, Book 1 (in ebook, audiobook)

The Secret's Out book 2 (in ebook)

Seducing Her Ex's Best Friend *(a story of revenge, angst, deception, and romance, HEA)*

Seducing Her Ex's Best Friend, Book 1 (in ebook and audiobook)

Wingless Hunger *(HEA Romantasy, book 1)*

Standalone's:

Decadent Erotica, An Anthology: 10 Tales of Extreme Sensuality, Indulgence, Dominance, and Submission (in ebook, paperback &

audiobook

She Dominated Him Out of a Speeding Ticket (Female Domination story) (ebook and audiobook):

Never Say, Never Swing (a first-time swinging story) (in ebook & paperback coming in audiobook)

Magic In Her Kisses (woman loving woman Domme/sub BDSM) (in ebook, paperback, & audiobook)

The Mardi Gras Unmasking (reverse harem) (in ebook & paperback)

The Licking Sip Coffee Shop (a steamy explicit coffee shop)

Santa Gives the 12 Orgasms of Christmas

Neighborhood Secrets (also Neighborhood Sex Secrets) (ebook and paperback)

The Sugar Daddies (in ebook, paperback, and audiobook)

FRIENDS WITH BENEFITS: A Spicy Four Short Story Adventure (in ebook, paperback, and audiobook)

Spicy & Wicked Tales (in ebook and audiobook)

Hookups & More? (in ebook and audiobook)

Weekend Hotwife Surprise (in ebook, coming in audiobook)

Tantalizing Tales (ebook, audiobook)

Group Fun at Work: Spicy Unions of Three (ebook, paperback, audiobook)

SFW Fantasy audiobook novel narrated by Ruan:

Heroes of the Caroylngian Age written by author Joseph Samaniego:

The following books have SFW covers in paperback: Neighborhood Secrets, Servicng the Work Men, Magic In Her Kisses, and I Dare You. Check online sellers and books stores for these books with discreet SFW covers. Don't see them in your local bookstore? Ask the bookstore staff to order them.

Audiobooks:

Check out Ruan's books available on online audiobook sellers: Sharing the Itty Bitty Vixen Series, written by Lacey Cross, multiple books written by Amber Collins, books by Luc Lopez, and also Casey Donatello, Benson E Wolf, Joseph S Samaniego, plus her own books as well. Coming soon also in taboo erotica of All These Roadworks.

Anthologies and Award Nominations

Ruan has stories in the following anthologies:
He Will Obey (which was AWARDED THE 2020 SILVER PIGTAIL IN BEST ANTHOLOGY CATEGORY
The Femdom Coven (nominee for 2021 Golden Pigtail Smut Awards)
Inside of Ruan Willow (also available in an audiobook)
(this audiobook was a nominee for the 2021 Golden Pigtail Smut Awards)

Decadent Erotica An Anthology **3rd Place Winner in the 2022 Golden Pigtails Smut Awards for Dark/Taboo Category**
Nominations for the 2023 Golden Pigtail Awards include:
Servicing the Trash Man, My Filthy Hotwife Adventure
Dressing Room Domme
Anthology Ruan has a short story in the nominated anthology titled Hearts and Flowers, Whips and Chains

R*uan is in the following anthologies:*
Femdom:

He Will Obey (stories of female domination)
The Femdom Coven (erotic horror and fantasy)
Hearts and Flowers, Whips and Chains (stories of kinks & power exchanges)
Halloween Anthology:
Trick or Tease II (ebook)

Other:

Ruan's website with free erotic stories Ruan Willow Author[1] Ruan Willow on Goodreads Ruan Willow Goodreads Author page[2]

Ruan Willow on BookBub https://www.bookbub.com/profile/ruan-willow

Sign up for Ruan's newsletter: https://subscribepage.io/ruanwillow

ARC copies are usually on BookSirens and StoryOrigin App. Check those sites for FREE ARC of books and audiobooks.

---

1. https://ruanwillowauthor.com/

2.   https://www.goodreads.com/author/show/21312130.Ruan_Willow

Did you love *Zesty Entanglements*? Then you should read *Servicing the Work Men, Her Filthy Hotwife Adventures*[3] by Ruan Willow and Ruin Willow!

Book Bundle Books 1 to 5...When Laney plays, John stays. Laney lost her job. Even though she'd always been a strong, hard-working, career-minded and independent woman, both she and her husband John agreed they liked her as a housewife better for several reasons. Staying home, Laney enjoyed learning to gourmet cook, working out like a gym rat, and making love to her husband on a daily basis. They had even ventured into the alternative lifestyle of a hotwife way of life and had found they loved it. Whether John arranged the dates, or Laney found her own conquests, they both were satiated by the secret taboo wife sharing acts, and especially the reclaiming of Laney by John after the steamy sex-filled dates. Laney lusted after all the work men that came to the house and John loved to see her happy and satiated, so he encouraged her playing with them, but only if he was nearby as director and overseer of the event. They enjoyed their life and the work men got to

---

3. https://books2read.com/u/mgDNwz

4. https://books2read.com/u/mgDNwz

live it with them for a short hot stint of pleasure that none of them would ever forget.But Laney was insatiable, as was John so their journey was just beginning.